Kat… …lish at London University. She worked in publishing and then moved to TV advertising, where she met her husband.

In 2000, Kate decided to write her moth… …nary story …g up in Russia, China and India, and this became *The Russian Concubine*, which was a *New York Times* bestseller. All her books since then have had an exotic setting and Kate has travelled widely for her research. She now has two sons and lives with her husband by the sea in Devon.

Visit Kate's website at www.katefurnivall.com

Praise for Kate Furnivall:

'Fabulous' Lesley Pearse

'Wonderful . . . hugely ambitious and atmospheric' Kate Mosse

'The definition of a terrifically well-written page-turner' Dinah Jeffries

'A thrilling plot . . . Fast-paced with a sinister edge' *The Times*

'Gripping . . . poignant, beautifully written . . . will capture the reader to the last' *Sun*

'Truly captivating' *Elle*

'Perfect escapist reading' *Marie Claire*

'An achingly beautiful epic' *New Woman*

'A rollicking good read' *Telegraph*

Also by Kate Furnivall

The Russian Concubine
Under a Blood Red Sky
The Concubine's Secret
The Jewel of St Petersburg
The White Pearl
Shadows on the Nile
The Far Side of the Sun
The Italian Wife
The Liberation

The BETRAYAL

Kate Furnivall

SIMON & SCHUSTER

London · New York · Sydney · Toronto · New Delhi

A CBS COMPANY

First published in Great Britain by Simon & Schuster UK Ltd, 2017
A CBS COMPANY

3 5 7 9 10 8 6 4 2

Simon & Schuster UK Ltd
1st Floor
222 Gray's Inn Road
London WC1X 8HB

www.simonandschuster.co.uk
www.simonandschuster.com.au
www.simonandschuster.co.in

Simon & Schuster Australia, Sydney
Simon & Schuster India, New Delhi

A CIP catalogue record for this book
is available from the British Library

Paperback ISBN: 978-1-4711-5558-1
Trade Paperback ISBN: 978-1-4711-5559-8
eBook ISBN: 978-1-4711-5560-4
eAudio ISBN: 978-1-4711-6624-2

Typeset in Bembo by M Rules
Printed and bound by CPI Group (UK) Ltd, Croydon, CR0 4YY

MIX
Paper from
responsible sources
FSC
www.fsc.org
FSC® C020471

Simon & Schuster UK Ltd are committed to sourcing paper
that is made from wood grown in sustainable forests and support the Forest
Stewardship Council, the leading international forest certification organisation.
Our books displaying the FSC logo are printed on FSC certified paper.

To Carole,
my twin sister,
with love

CHAPTER ONE

PARIS, 1930

There is blood on my hands.

I am not speaking figuratively, you understand. Literally. Under my nails. Embedded in the soft valleys between my fingers. Strings of scarlet, glossier than paint, are dripping from me on to the Persian rug, ruining it. I stare at them, bewildered. My mind jams.

Where has it come from?

I lift my head and instantly hear a loud thumping sound deep inside my ears, like a drum beaten in an empty room.

Lift my head?

Why am I lying on the floor? I sit up, heart racing, and wait for the room to stop performing handstands around me, while I struggle to remember what happened. But a black hole lies where my memory should be. I shake my head to drive it away, but pain tramples through my mind and when I look again the black hole is still there. Bigger this time. Darker. An inky pool with a sheen skimming its surface and I feel panic uncoil inside me.

I rise jerkily to my knees and find myself facing walls lined with books. My heart gives a lurch of joy. I am at home. In my father's study. I know those books intimately, I love those leather-bound volumes of Victor Hugo, Zola, Maupassant and my favourite, Alexandre Dumas. Their covers bear the sweat imprint of my fingers and their pages have witnessed my tears. I am safe at home here in Paris, even though I am for some unknown reason lying tucked up against my father's big oak desk.

I start to convince myself that I am asleep. This is a nightmare. I close my eyes, waiting to wake up, and the thumping in my ears grows duller, fainter, but I am aware of a pain down the left side of my head. I touch it. My hair is wet. My eyes shoot open to examine my fingertips, but I know what I will find. More blood. I am not asleep.

I drag myself to my feet and leave crimson handprints on the wax-polished surface of Papa's desk as I cling to it. He will not like that. Panic starts to bubble its way up through me and I open my mouth to scream. That's when I see the shoes. They are my father's shoes. Stylish black brogues, their leather so soft it looks as though it came from an unborn lamb.

My scream dies in my mouth.

There are feet in the shoes. Sprawled on the floor. I can

see a strip of black sock above each shoe before the ankles disappear behind the corner of the desk.

'Papa,' I whisper.

There is no answer. I scramble to the edge of the desk and look down on my father's body flat on its back on the floor, his pale grey eyes staring and sightless. My heart stops. The noise in my ears becomes a roaring and my eyes feel as if they have been skinned. A paperknife is sticking straight up out of his throat and his white shirt is the colour of my hands.

I am afraid. Afraid of myself. Afraid of what is inside me. I am alone in a closed room with my dead father and I know I have murdered him.

In his lifeless hand lies a paperweight in the form of a brass pyramid that he brought back from Egypt years ago and one of its sides is streaked with blood. My blood. I know it, though I can't tell you how I know it. I touch my hair again, feel its curls sticky with blood. I touch the raw edges of my scalp, split like the skin of a peach.

I fall to my knees beside Papa. His fingers curl around the brass weight even in death, as though still trying to defend himself from me. I pump his shirt front to force air into his lungs, even though I know it is futile. What good is air in your lungs when you have a great hole in your windpipe?

I can't breathe. It feels like bands of steel tightening around my lungs as I lay my cheek on his broad chest to listen for his heartbeat. The wet shirt is warm on my skin. I quickly raise my head to search once more for a flicker of life in his face. A face without life is not a face. It is a mask.

I am staring at Papa's mask. The same wide forehead and strong oppressive brow that used to scare me; the heavy jowls and broken veins of a bon viveur. They are still there. All the unmistakable features of the ruler of this household. Tears cloud my vision but I can see that the man whose word was law is no longer part of the body that lies broken on the parquet floor, which he insisted must be polished every day, except on a Sunday. Yet I bend forward and press my cheek to his.

Behind me I hear the click of the study door but I do not turn. Soft footsteps enter. The door closes. I know who it is even without lifting my head, in the same way that my right hand knows exactly what my left hand is doing. It is my sister. Her violent intake of breath sucks the air from the room and I am conscious of her standing over me.

'What have you done?' She doesn't shout. Her low-pitched tone is worse, far worse, than a shout. 'Oh God, Romy, what have you done?'

'I've killed Papa,' I whisper.

My words break something inside me. Suddenly I am frozen by grief. I cannot move. I cannot speak. I cannot think.

So my sister does my thinking.

'Why did you kill him?'

I shake my head.

'You are seventeen,' she says. 'You will go to prison and

then you will be executed by guillotine. In public. Outside St Pierre prison.'

Her words are slow, picked out separately to make sure I understand.

In the terrible silence that follows, I can sense her heart-beat is as rapid as my own, and her fingers grip my shoulder, digging in hard. Carefully avoiding the pool of blood that is seeping into the oak floor, she forces me to my feet. Then she does what I cannot bring myself to do – she stares at the paperknife embedded in our father's throat. She glances down at my hands and I do not ask what images are rearing to life inside her head. She slips out of her blue cardigan, her favourite cashmere one, and uses it to wipe the silver handle of the paperknife. Over and over, she rubs it hard and I see the scarlet lips of the wound widen. I want to beg her to stop but I don't.

Finally she backs away from Papa's body, her limbs stiff, her face rigid, but when I take a step towards her she turns away and starts to rub the surface of the desk. Removing all trace of me. Brisk and thorough. Then she switches her attention to my hands and cleans them as best she can. The blue cardigan has turned purple and I murmur her name, I want her to look me in the face but she won't. She frowns and stares at the paperweight cradled in Papa's hand.

I move. For the first time since she forced me away from his side, I jerk into life. I copy her. I pull my lilac jumper over my head and I snatch the pyramid from his limp fin-gers. I scrub it hard with the unstained back of my jumper, but the blood from my head wound has seeped into its brass indentations and won't come out. I hurry over to the ebony cabinet that stands by the window with a decanter of Papa's finest cognac on top of it. I long to drink it, to drown in it, but instead I tip the amber liquid all over the paperweight to swill out the last pockets of blood, and I rub it furiously with my jumper.

Satisfied, I replace the pyramid on the desk. Where it belongs. The relief I feel is strong. To be doing something. Anything. To see my hands functioning. To know I am not dead. Yet.

I do not ask myself if what I am doing is wrong.

My sister opens the door a crack, peers out into the black and white tiled hall, seizes my arm and drags me out of the study, pushing the door shut with her foot. To me it has the hollow sound of a lid closing on a tomb, condemning Papa to eternal blackness. I cannot bring myself to abandon him, but she wrenches me forward and up the stairs at a run.

She is strong, my sister Florence.

My twin.

'We won't get away with it,' I state.

'Hush, Romy. Of course we will.'

I am standing in the bathtub and Florence is washing me down like a muddy dog. Nakedness has never worried us. Maybe because we spent nine months entwined naked in the womb together. When I step out of the tub she pats me dry, her hands gentle, but she is worried about the gash and the swelling on my head, though I tell her it is nothing. She has bathed the blood from my hair and stands over me for ten minutes with a cold flannel pressed hard against the wound to stem the bleeding. I make no sound. The pain is deserved.

I see her hand trembling when she reaches into my wardrobe for a fresh outfit for me. I go to her. For a brief moment we embrace, our limbs entwined once more. It is a rare occurrence. Strangely, though we constantly touch each other, brush shoulders, nudge ribs and bump elbows, we rarely embrace. We do not hug or kiss cheeks or show overt affection. It would feel all wrong. Like hugging or kissing oneself. But the love is there between us, binding us to each other like an umbilical cord and we accept it as naturally as we accept that we both have curly blonde hair.

She sits me on my bed. I tuck my feet under myself as if I can tuck away what lies unheeded downstairs. Florence perches next to me, wraps the quilt around my shoulders and it is through her fingertips that I feel her nervousness. It does not show on her face.

'Now,' she says matter-of-factly, 'tell me what happened. Tell me quickly.'

She fixes her gaze on me. I look back at her intently. Our faces are alike, but we are not identical twins. She has large round blue eyes that know how to melt your heart, eyes that are warm and capable, eyes that you don't want to look away from. My eyes are a muddy amber. Long and narrow. Cat's eyes, Florence calls them. I have claws to match. Her face is narrower than mine, more delicate, something I always envied, but we have the same straight nose and angular jawline. And identical mouths that are too wide for our faces. Hers is pulled tight now. She was born only twenty-five minutes before me, but sometimes it feels more. Much more.

I try to speak in a calm manner. But I fail. I hear my words quivering and want to snatch them out of the air and replace them with sturdier ones.

'I don't remember what happened,' I say. 'I don't remember anything.'

'You must.'

'I don't.'

'*Merde*!'

Florence never swears, and despite the fact that I have just murdered my father, I am shocked. She pushes her face forward, closer to mine, and seizes a handful of my curls. Not harshly. But firmly. She draws me even closer and I see the tiny black flecks of anger embedded in the soft blue of her irises.

'Don't lie,' she says.

A white-hot flame of sorrow flickers at the base of my chest. We never lie to each other. To our parents, yes; to our teachers, *bien sûr*; to the priest at the Jesuit Église Saint-Paul-Saint-Louis, of course. Even to God himself. But never to each other.

'I swear I remember nothing. I woke on the rug in Papa's study and found him . . . like that. Blood on my hands. So I must have . . .' I can't say it. Cannot. Cannot.

Florence says it for me. 'Stabbed him.'

I nod.

'The paperweight?' she asks.

'Papa hit me with it.'

'Why?'

'I don't know. I can't remember.'

'That will not save you.' So soft. So painful. My sister's voice aches for me. 'The police will take you.'

'Help me,' I whisper.

She rests her forehead against mine. I can smell the scent of fresh-cut grass on her hair and it triggers a flash of memory. Of standing in the hall, sunlight streaming in through the open front door, carrying with it the scent of freshly mown lawns. Maman's voice calling out from the kitchen, asking for someone to fetch roses from the garden. And the shadow of a man in the doorway.

It is gone in a flash. The wound on my head is throbbing.

It is as if Florence can see inside my head because she says, 'Roland was here. He and I went into the garden to pick roses for Maman. Remember?'

I sit back. 'Yes.'

'Anything else?'

'No, nothing after that. It's . . .' I blink hard, 'gone.'

I stare around at my room. It is plain. Much plainer than Florence's, which is a shrine to the Paris Opéra and Ballet and the power of pink tulle. Mine is stark. Pale modern furniture, much to Maman's disgust, a simple wooden hairbrush on the dressing table and one framed picture on the wall. It is a photograph of the first woman in the world to pilot an aeroplane, Raymonde de Laroche at the wheel of her spindly Voisin aircraft in 1909 in Paris. I look hard at each item in the room, soaking up every colour and curve, the sheen on the satin quilt, the way the brass door handle catches the light. I may never see them again.

Florence takes my hand and wraps it between hers, holding it tight on the lap of her elegant cream skirt. I hear her breathing hard the way she does when she is about to do one of her dives into a swimming pool. Sharp little snorts of air.

'Romy.' Her eyes are quick, darting over me. 'I know what to do. We will say you were with Roland and me in the garden. The three of us. Picking the flowers.'

I am transfixed. By the lie. The blatant deception that falls from her lips, and I feel it entwine its tendrils around the coils of my brain, soft and tempting tendrils that paralyse me so that I cannot move, not even an eyelid.

'Well?' She gives me a smile, but it is all crooked.

I snap the tendrils and take her delicate face between my hands.

'You would do that for me?'

'Of course.'

'If we are caught, you will be put in prison as an accessory.'

'We won't be caught.'

'What about Roland?'

She rolls her beautiful blue eyes. 'Roland will do whatever I ask.'

My heart is thundering. I open my mouth to shout yes,

yes, yes. Lie for me. Save my life. But instead different words come out of my mouth. 'What about the gardener?'

'Pardon?'

'The gardener. Karim. Did he see you?'

Her tongue flashes across her lips and I know she is thinking of lying, but she doesn't. Not to me.

'Yes. I spoke to him. He was cutting the beech hedge.'

'That's it then. He knows I wasn't there. My head will roll.'

I touch my neck, a white slender column that the angled blade of the guillotine will slice through like celery. The tips of my fingers are frozen, but I draw a line with them across my throat.

'Poor Papa,' I whisper. 'Poor Maman. I am sorry.' The words drain something from me.

Florence slaps my face. Not hard. But hard enough. 'Listen to me, Romy. Together we cut the roses for Maman and I handed them to her through the kitchen window. You were with me every minute. Then the three of us . . .'

She pauses, her brow creased, thinking up an alibi.

'. . . Lay on the lawn in the shade of the willow tree,' I venture.

'And we talked about . . .?'

'Josephine Baker.'

Florence smiles a tight smile. 'Yes, of course. That's good. About her sultry dance in *Siren of the Tropics*.' Two dark flares have risen on her cheeks and her eyes glitter. 'You hear me?' she demands fiercely. 'You hear what I'm saying? You were with us all the time, then Roland left and you and I came up here to wash off the grass stains.'

'But what about Karim? Where was he?'

'Don't worry about him.'

'He will tell the police I wasn't there.'

'No one will believe him.' She slips off the bed. 'Come on, we must bury your bloodstained clothes before the police arrive.'

I seize her arm and drag her back. 'No, Florence. Roland may lie for you, but Karim won't.'

A scream pierces the silence of the house and hurtles up the stairs. The hairs rise on my arm, the skin prickles on my neck, and I know it has begun.

'Karim will not lie to the police to save me,' I murmur. 'He will tell them I was not there.'

'But his testimony will be irrelevant. Because I will swear he wasn't anywhere near enough to see you.'

'But you just said you saw him by the hedge.'

'Did I? I was mistaken.'

'What?'

'I didn't see him. I remember now, Karim wasn't in the garden.'

I frown uneasily. With growing caution I ask, 'Where was he?'

'In the study with Papa.'

I stare. For a long moment I don't understand. Or is it that I don't want to understand? Florence has fixed her gaze on me and she shakes my shoulder hard.

'Understand, Romy?'

I grip her wrist and feel my twin sister's pulse racing as fast as my own. A pool of my father's blood seems to open up at my feet and without hesitation I step over it. An image of Karim's face swims inside it, a long dark-skinned face with sad eyes and a polite mouth, but I look away from it.

'Yes,' I whisper. My words are only for my sister's ears. 'I understand. I was in the garden. With you. And Roland. I remember now. Karim went into the house.'

We both know we will go to hell.

CHAPTER TWO

Eight years later

PARIS, JULY 1938

'Come on. Lift. Lift, you bastard.'

Romaine Duchamps yelled the words at her flimsy Gipsy Moth as it plunged nose-first towards earth like a screaming bucking banshee.

'Don't give up on me now. Just pop your nose up a fraction. A centimetre? That's all I ask of you, my little one.'

She had been racing before the storm, fleeing the black wall of raging clouds that was tight on her tail. But it reached out, caught her, and knocked her right out of the sky. One moment she was flying her tiny aircraft straight and steady through sparkling blue heavens above the silky green heartland of France, and the next she was hurled around the sky the way a hound flings a rat back and forth to snap its neck.

Tossed up a hundred metres, smacked on to one wing, tipped on end, then dropped like a stone.

Fear gripped her. Not of death itself – she knew for certain that it was heading her way in the next few seconds – but of leaving her life. Unfinished. Undefined. And in such a wretched mess. Rain sheeted down into the open cockpit, soaking her, flooding her goggles, blinding her. Battering the fragile plane as ferocious winds wrenched it out of her control. Every muscle in her body was rigid, taut with effort as she fought back, hauling on the control stick. Aware that the unseen ground below was hurtling towards her.

Fear does strange things to you. It strips you. To bare bones. Everything bleeds away from you. She couldn't breathe. Couldn't think. Couldn't see. Yet her hands were strong and knew exactly what they were doing, even while she could feel the plane trying to tear itself apart as it dived, shaking and shuddering. Within the semi-darkness of the storm cloud, the luminous instruments glowed an eerie green from the dashboard and she struggled to read the altimeter. It was hidden within the blur of water.

How high? Five hundred metres?

One hundred?

Less?

She braced herself against the safety harness. Muscles twitching. Bones ready for impact. But still her hands would not give up. They were as stubborn as her mind and pulled relentlessly on the stick, praying that the control rods to the elevators would not snap. And just when she could almost smell the summer grass growing beneath her, she felt movement. A change of angle. Faint at first, but growing. Centimetre by centimetre the nose of the Gipsy Moth clawed its way up into the air. The de Havilland engine roared in triumph and Romy let rip with a roar of her own.

She breathed again. Felt her grip on life tighten once more. Heart pounding, skin sweating, mind soaring, she gave the engine full throttle, circled to gain height and pushed on through the rain northwards up the Rhône valley. To Paris.

The lights of Paris gleamed through a grey veil that obscured the features of the late afternoon. The rain came down on the wings of Romy's biplane like a million silver bullets, the visibility so bad that even in the cockpit the wing tips were shrouded from view. To her, it felt like having her fingertips cut off. The city spread itself beneath her, the pulsing heart of France that never missed a beat or a wild dance step, however severe the summer storms that raged overhead.

It was with a rush of relief that Romy spotted the string of landing lights as she dropped altitude and held the biplane steady in the teeth of the buffeting north-westerly. Easy now, don't panic. The small private DeFosse airfield was tucked away on the eastern edge of Paris and emerged reluctantly through the gloom. From above she caught a glimpse of the windsock and of two figures running towards the centre of the landing area, hunched over against the rain. They stood there in yellow oilskins, waiting to catch hold of the wing tips of the aircraft the moment she landed.

'Martel,' Romy muttered through chilled lips, 'one of these days I'll take your bloody head off if you're not careful.'

She eased back on the throttle, reducing her approach speed to fifty-eight knots and fighting the wind all the way. She felt the wheels touch down and strong arms seize the wings to hold the plane firmly on the ground, defying the wind's attempts to flip it over. The men ran alongside and, as she taxied over the grass to the hangar, muddy sprays of water rose like a bow wave on each side of her.

Landing a plane did something bad to her. It was always the same, in rain or in sunshine. Each time she felt the wheels clutch at the grass strip, she experienced a profound sense of failure, a fierce twist in her gut. She wasn't meant to be down here. She belonged up there, high above the clouds, all alone. Yes, of course she faced dangers when flying. Yes, sometimes she teetered on the edge, chest tight with fear. But it was always *her* hand on the control stick, no one else's. Down here, caged within the mean streets of Paris, she felt battered by storms far worse than those in the sky.

She throttled back to 900 rpm, keeping the throttle fully open until the airscrew ceased its rotating. She checked that the ignition, electrics and fuel cock were all turned off, then with reluctance climbed stiffly out of the cockpit on to the wing, flexing her knees, and jumped down to the concrete floor inside the hangar. Immediately, the larger of the two oilskins hurried towards her and the weight of a heavy hand landed on the sodden shoulder of her leather flying jacket.

'What the devil do you think you're doing, you bloody fool? Flying in a storm like this.'

Romy shook her shoulder free. She tried to undo the strap of her leather helmet, but even inside fur-lined gloves her hands were numb with cold.

'What are you grumbling about, Martel?' She had to shout over the drumming of the rain on the corrugated roof. 'You've got what you wanted.' She shifted the package that was tucked under her arm and dumped it into the big man's hands. 'Here, take it.'

But she could feel his anger still there in the damp air that she breathed, clinging to her skin, dragging her back into this grimy world on the ground. His voice buzzed in her ears, like a wireless not quite correctly tuned. She always had to reaccustom herself to the sound of people instead of the warm steady throb of a four-cylinder de Havilland engine.

'Any message from Mendez?' he asked.

'Yes. He said to tell you the package is complete.'

'Good.'

Something resembling a nod of satisfaction escaped him. He pushed the square brown-paper package under his dripping oilskin without a thank you.

'You could have got yourself killed. *Merde!* Will you never learn?'

But she wasn't fooled. 'You're only worried about who would fly your precious planes if I weren't around,' she responded.

The lights of the hangar flickered on and off in the storm,

sending strange-shaped shadows crawling up and down the walls. Beneath her flying boots the concrete grew dark as water ran off every part of her, while at the far end of the hangar a mechanic broke off from working on the sleek blue Caudron C.460 racing plane that she coveted. He raised his head from the cowling and watched them with interest. Only then did Romy realise how loudly she was shouting.

Léo Martel was not a man to waste words. He uttered a long sigh as though a pocket of air had stuck in his windpipe. 'Don't kid yourself, Romaine. There are plenty of other tadpoles in the river. Eager pilots out there, queuing up to get your flying job or any other job around here that means messing around with planes.' He started to turn away but stopped himself and gave her a hard, exasperated stare. Raindrops still glistened like diamonds in his thick black eyebrows, ruining the effect of his stare. 'And they are men,' he added. 'Who have more sense than to risk destroying my plane.'

She gave him a tight smile. 'But they are nowhere near as good as I am and you damn well know it.'

She stepped aside to fetch the chocks to tuck under the Moth's wheels, but when she turned, Martel was already hurrying off without a backward glance, broad shoulders hunched against the summer storm.

'You bastard,' she called after him.

'Don't mind him.'

It was Jules Roget, the other yellow oilskin. A tiny wisp of a man who barely came up to her chin. In his early fifties, he had a permanent grey stubble on his chin and possessed clever hands that were far too big for him. A mechanic's hands. They had the patience of Job and could cajole and beguile the most stubborn of engines to succumb to their persuasive touch. Romy smiled at him.

'*Merci*, Jules. Thanks for coming out in the rain.'

'How was the flight?'

'Bumpy. Cold. Wet.'

'So you had a good time then.'

She laughed. 'Yes, you're right. I had a good time. The Gipsy ran sweet as a bird.'

She took down a chamois cloth from a hook on the hangar wall and started to wipe down the sleek blue fabric flanks of the plane with long sweeping strokes that caressed its skin. She wasn't ready to abandon her Moth. Not yet.

'He worries,' Jules said to the back of her flying helmet.

'Of course he does. He worries about his plane and his package.'

Jules' voice, when it came again, was sharper. 'No, *ma chérie*, he worries about his pilot.'

The DeFosse airfield was small and cramped, with a bad habit of throwing up clumps of turf under your wheels on take-off. But its bar was long and inviting and abundantly stocked with an array of the finest wines that could rinse the grit off your tongue and the aches from your bones. The place was a favourite with the pilots and Romy was sorely tempted when she heard the contented hum within it now, but with reluctance she turned her back on the bar and headed down the corridor. To a green door with a plaque that declared *Martel Enterprises.*

Romy entered without bothering to knock. She steered clear of the hard chair in front of the desk and slumped on to the sofa against the wall, despite its horsehair innards oozing out like a disease. She threw her satchel on the floor, stretched the cramps out of her back muscles and pulled off her wet flying helmet. She mussed a hand through her short dirty-blonde curls, but immediately she regretted losing the firm grip of the leather on her head. In an odd way it stopped her thoughts from spilling out.

Martel's office was ramshackle. Heaps of files sprawled on every surface. He was seated behind his desk with the brown-paper package open in front of him and was reading intently from a sheet of paper that looked like a list of some sort, though Romy couldn't read it from where she was sitting.

He was a big man, wide-shouldered and too muscular for a suit. Like a lot of big men, he looked older than he was. Romy guessed he must be somewhere around thirty-five but he could easily pass for more. There was something about his grey eyes. A sense of too many things seen and done, and much of the time his eyelids hovered at half-mast, as though he was only half engaged with the world around him. It was not the case, but some were fooled into the mistake of believing it was. He flicked a glance in Romy's direction.

'Is everything there?' she asked.

He nodded. 'Yes. It's all here.' He placed the sheet of paper face down on the desk. 'Any problems your end?'

She could have told him about the hailstones that tried to punch holes in the fabric of her wings just north of Limoges, or about the mist over the Pyrenees mountains, so dense it was like flying through milk. Always expecting a jagged chunk of Spanish cliff to smack her in the face. Or she could have mentioned the welcoming committee of three Fiat CR.32 fighters belonging to the Spanish Nationalist Air Force that meant she had to drop like a stone into a deep valley where the shadows hid her Moth from sight.

But she said none of these things. She shrugged and said, 'No problems.'

'Did Colonel Garcia Mendez take delivery of the crate himself?'

'He did. He and his Republican troops were waiting on the airstrip and unloaded it fast from the Moth to a truck. He gave me that package for you.'

'Nothing else?'

'No.'

She lied well. She knew she did. So why did he blink like that, damn him? As if he could smell the lie. He rose from his chair, poured a shot of his favourite pastis into two glasses and walked over to her. He handed her one glass without comment. She drank it down in one slug, faster than she meant to. She didn't want him to think she was desperate for it. But he took no notice and did the same with his own, then squatted down on his heels in front of her. Still big, even when making himself small.

'*Alors*, Romaine. What happened?'

She could lie again. He needn't know. Sure as hell Garcia Mendez wouldn't tell him. The Spanish colonel knew exactly what Martel thought about stepping over the line.

'Cigarette?' she asked. Buying time.

Impatiently he pulled out one of his black Turkish smokes, handed it over and lit it for her. His eyes watched her like a hawk.

'There was a man,' she said. 'He needed a ride. The front cockpit was empty.'

'*Merde*!'

Romy inhaled hard on her cigarette, silencing herself.

'His name?' he demanded.

'I didn't ask.'

'Where did you drop him?'

'Outside Béziers.'

Martel's breath came at her, a blast in her face. 'Romaine, for Christ's sake, you know my orders. You fly to Spain to do the job I ask and fly back here. Nothing more. The risks are high enough as it is.'

'The man was wounded, Martel, and Franco's troops were after him. He had to get out of Spain. He needed help. That's what we're committed to doing, isn't it? Helping the Republicans to win the civil war in Spain and defeat Fascism, that's what we're working for, you know that.' She turned her face from him. 'I couldn't leave the poor bastard there to die.'

'Yes, you could. And yes, you should.' Martel rose to his feet, towering over her. 'One man, Romaine. Is one man worth putting our whole network at risk for? Use your brains, girl.'

Romy was wet. Cold. Hungry. She stood up.

'Go to hell,' she muttered and edged around his bulk, heading for the door. The heat of the alcohol in her empty stomach made her crave more.

He let her get as far as one hand on the door handle before he spoke.

'Aren't you forgetting something?'

She glanced back. He was standing in front of his desk holding her satchel in one hand and a Manila envelope in the other. His gaze was skimming over her from head to toe, the way he would assess an aircraft to see if it was sound. Romy cursed under her breath and retraced her steps. As she took the envelope from him she slipped him a smile of sorts.

'I don't mean to get you riled up, boss.' She shrugged. 'It's just a natural talent I have.'

His face didn't change expression but his broad chest in its faded denim shirt heaved for a moment, as though suppressing a ripple of laughter. She reached quickly for the satchel. He held on to it.

'What the hell have you got in here?' he demanded. 'It weighs—'

'An engine part picked up in Spain for Jules.' She removed the strap from his grip.

'Lying around on the airstrip, was it?'

'Something like that.'

She slung the strap over her shoulder and strode to the door again.

'Where are you off to in such an almighty hurry?' he asked.

She tossed him a grin now that she was safely out of reach. 'I'm going to a party.'

CHAPTER THREE

Romy rode the Paris Métro, taking Line 2 from Place de Clichy, and walked the rest of the way down Avenue Kléber. Named after one of Napoleon's generals who threw his weight around in Egypt at the end of the eighteenth century, it was one of the twelve grand boulevards that spread like the points of a star from Place de l'Étoile with the imposing Arc de Triomphe at its centre. This part of the city unsettled her. Like walking on glass.

This was where her sister lived.

The rain had eased back to no more than a drizzle. It painted a silvery gloss on the elegant avenue and drew forth the whisper of the leaves on the plane trees and the scent of the earth in the millions of window boxes that adorned the City of Light. Paris had always had a special smell in the wet, a perfume all its own that Romy inhaled with relief. There had been moments during that last storm when she had not expected to enjoy the scent of Paris again. Except in a wooden box under the rich black soil of the Père Lachaise cemetery.

Avenue Kléber ran directly through the 16th arrondissement to the Place du Trocadéro and Romy approached with her usual caution. As if it might bite. The road was lined with grandiose seven-storey buildings, embassies and the palatial government offices that had once been the Hotel Majestic. They all boasted intricate stonework and sculpted classical figures. Paired columns flanked doorways. To live here you had to be rich. Or powerful. Preferably both. It was always the same, the urge that seized her to run to the house with the stone lions guarding the massive doors and hammer like a mad creature to be let in.

And yet. At the same time she had to shut down the urge to turn. To flee. Her breath came hot and fast, scalding her throat. She hurried up the wide front steps, hitched the satchel on her shoulder and jabbed at the brass doorbell.

Don't mess it up. Not this time. Smile, be nice, don't rattle her. How hard can it be? Oh Christ, flowers. I should have bought flowers for her. She glanced to the end of the street where a bedraggled *vendeuse* under an umbrella was selling blooms from a barrow and took a hasty step in her direction. But too late. The door swung open.

Her sister's apartment took up the whole of the sixth *étage* and the door to it was open by the time Romy stepped out of the lift. A maid in a black dress and white lace cap stood on the threshold, wielding a polite smile that didn't quite hide the unease in her eyes.

'Good afternoon, Mademoiselle Romaine. Madame was expecting you earlier. She's busy now with—'

'The party. Yes, I know, Yvette. I'm late.'

She entered the handsome hall that greeted her with the fragrance of roses. Six lavish arrangements of white roses adorned the semicircular reception area, overwhelming Romy with their scent. She longed to light up a cigarette to banish it. She didn't care for roses. Not any more. Their sickly-sweet perfume carried too many tainted memories.

The maid hurried away to inform her mistress of the new arrival and Romy was left to stand under the watchful gaze of two vast portraits. They stared down at her from heavy gilt frames that, until Florence's marriage, used to hang in her parents' house. They were the formal paintings of her two formidable grandfathers, resplendent in full military regalia and intimidating moustaches. Romy could not bear to look at them. Instead she set off in the maid's wake across the expanse of black and white Italian tiles to the drawing room.

It was one of those lavish *fin-de-siècle* Parisian salons with high ceilings, moulded cornices and silk wall hangings that cried out to be filled with music and champagne and formal dancing. But today three rows of children in party dresses were perched on chairs watching a puppet show of woodland animals. The children were wide-eyed and giggling. Behind them a line of well-groomed mothers sat with wine glasses in their hands, but at the side of the room the maid was speaking to a tall young woman in a chic silver-grey dress. It looked far too stylish for a child's party. The woman was Florence.

A triple strand of pearls accentuated her long creamy throat. There was no mark on it. No bone or tendon severed by the flash of a guillotine blade. A pain, short and sharp in Romy's own neck, made her lick her lips. In need of a drink. Yet even now she admired her twin sister's cool elegance. The sweep of her long blonde hair, like a swirl of sunlight, in a knot at the back of her head that looked so casual but had probably taken hours to perfect. And the way she carried her chin just a little higher than most people, daring the world to cross her.

Florence's huge blue eyes narrowed in an unconscious sign of displeasure as she listened to the maid and her gaze shot to the drawing-room door. At the sight of Romy standing there, she froze. No more than half a heartbeat. But Romy saw it. Then Florence hurried over with a wide-open smile and an outstretched arm.

'Romaine, I'm so pleased you're here at last.' She brushed her sister's cheeks with her own. She smelled expensive. 'Come,' Florence said, lowering her voice. 'Let's not disturb the children's show.'

She started to steer Romy from the room but a small head with golden ringlets whipped round and an excited young voice cried, 'Tante Romy!'

Feet scampered across the room and suddenly two small arms fixed around Romy. Instantly she scooped up her niece and whisked her out into the hall, away from watching eyes, where she kissed the rosy, flawless cheek. She felt the usual ache in her throat, as familiar and as destructive as the scent of roses in this apartment.

'*Bon anniversaire*, little one. Are you having a happy birthday?'

'Yes. Maman gave me a doll. It's a princess in a shiny gown with gold . . .'

Romy let the eager words wrap around her. The excitement of the six-year-old in her arms was infectious. Cornflower-blue eyes bright with laughter, breath as sweet as clover.

'We expected you earlier, Romaine,' Florence said.

'I'm sorry. Bad weather messed up my flight.' She eased the child to the floor. 'But I've brought you something, Chloé.' From her satchel she drew a rectangular box wrapped in a swathe of white silk that she had salvaged from a damaged parachute. The agent who'd dangled from the other end of it had broken his neck. Before his final flight Romy had shared a beer with him. Had spent the night with him. He had been her friend. After cutting around the machine-gun bullet holes in the silk last night, she had dreamed of him.

'Thank you, Tante Romy.'

'I warn you, it's not a doll.'

'May I open it now?'

'Of course.'

The small hands scrabbled with the white material and

carefully unwound it. Both pairs of blue eyes, mother's and daughter's, grew as round as coins.

'It's an aeroplane,' Florence exclaimed. Romy detected no pleasure in it.

'It's an aeroplane,' Chloé echoed, her voice brimming with delight.

'It's a flying model,' Romy explained. 'It has to be assembled – that's easy – and then it will fly. It is called a FROG Interceptor. Look.' She lifted the lid. 'Power-driven by a rubber band with a duralumin fuselage and doped paper wings.' Her own fingers itched to take it out.

Chloé's smile set the hall alight. 'Can I fly it now?'

Before she could reply, a door opened. Romy felt a shift of air, sensed a tightening of the skin on her cheek as if it knew who was coming. She looked up at the library door, solid as a drawbridge. It swung wide and two men in summer suits, both in their thirties, emerged and crossed the hall. One was blond, tall and unknown to her. The other was a muscular figure with hair as black as an oil slick, and he strode chest first through the hall as if he owned it. Which he did. He was Roland Roussel. Florence's husband.

Romy could hear the snick of irritation in each step as he approached, but there was no hint of it in the tone of his voice.

'Well now, what is all the noise going on here?' He turned towards his sister-in-law. He greeted her with a smile that was polished to perfection like the blade of a knife. You could cut yourself on it, if you weren't careful. 'Good afternoon, Romaine.'

'Good afternoon, Roland.'

She matched his smile, tooth for tooth.

'Tante Romy is here for my birthday party,' Chloé announced.

'Is she indeed?' The words slid out smooth as glass. 'In which case I'd have expected her to change into a party frock before she arrived.'

'Oh no, Papa.' The small hand touched the damp leather of Romy's flying jacket, the way believers touch the stole of a priest. 'I like it.'

'Which is the reason I wore it.' Romy grinned at the child and kept her eyes off her brother-in-law.

The blond stranger stepped closer, tall and soft-spoken. He extended a hand to Romy. 'At last,' he said. 'I've been looking forward to seeing you, Romaine.'

'This is my sister, Romaine Duchamps,' Florence said with a sharp warning look in his direction. 'She is an aviatrix.' It was a term that Romy had never heard her sister use before. It bestowed a glamour on the act of flying that didn't exist in reality. 'Romaine, let me introduce Horst Baumeister from Berlin. He's here to work with – ' her glance skipped to her husband ' – with a government delegation from Germany.'

His handshake was firm and brief, but he regarded Romy with interest. Not the kind of interest that made her skin crawl, no, not like that. His pale blue eyes tightened as his gaze took in her face and her curly hair, cropped short as a boy's. He took note of her flying jacket with its scuffs and mends. Her shoes, brown and practical. He observed her the way a scientist in a laboratory might observe a species of moth. That kind of interest. Studying her closely. She did not object. Did not feel the slither of scorn that often uncoiled inside her when men looked at her. Because there was something in his gaze that pleased her. It was respect.

'You actually fly?' he asked.

'I do.'

'Roland, *mein Freund*, where have you been hiding this *Fliegerin*?'

To Romy's surprise, her sister laughed. 'Don't go encouraging her, Horst. We are trying to civilise her.'

Civilise?

Is that what the silk chemises and kid-leather gloves that arrived outside her door with monotonous regularity were for? To civilise her? As if she were some kind of illiterate barbarian. She looked at her sister and wanted to ask her which was more civilised. A person who knew how to wind her hair into an elaborate chignon and set a room on fire with a syncopated foxtrot? Or some grubby flier who could coax an aircraft over mountains to Spanish people in desperate need of arms and equipment in their fight to defend a nation against the stranglehold of Fascism. Which one, Florence? Which would you say does more for civilisation?

'So, Fräulein Duchamps,' the German continued, 'where have you been flying today in this filthy weather?'

'To Lyon.' The lie came easily. 'Delivering a business client to a meeting. I flew low beneath the cloud base and followed the railway line.'

Well, part of it was true. Railway lines were an invaluable aid to navigation.

'Do you fly?' Romy asked.

'No. But I love aircraft.'

His eyes dwelled on the model plane in the box and he nodded approval, but it was Roland who drew the conversation to an abrupt end. 'Chloé, I think you should go back inside the salon now and rejoin your friends at the party.'

'And Tante Romy too. Please, Papa?'

'No. Your aunt is leaving.'

'Why?' There was something fearless in the clear blue eyes that the child turned on her father. 'Just because she is not wearing a party frock?'

'Because she is busy.'

But Romy did not let him get away with that one. 'I am never too busy for you, *ma petite*,' she assured Chloé.

Though she was looking at the child, she caught the uneasy flicker of her sister's eyelashes, the quick nip of her lip by perfect white teeth. It was always the same. That awareness. That consciousness of her sister's every movement even when her gaze was directed elsewhere, as if it were a continuation of her own movement. A shadowing. A ripple that flowed from herself to her sister, but one she couldn't control.

'But I want her to stay, Papa. To fly my aeroplane with me after my party.'

Romy bent down, her face on a level with her niece's. 'Tomorrow,' she said. 'It's too late now. I'll come back tomorrow and we will fly it then.' She touched a wave of the long silky hair, soft as a spider's web. 'Bright and early.'

A small finger curled around one of hers. 'Before breakfast.'

Romy laughed. 'No. But straight after, I promise.'

She kissed the birthday girl's forehead, said speedy good-byes, shook hands with the German again, and without looking back she found herself descending once more to the ground floor in the lift with its beautiful Lalique pyramid electric lamps. Each one probably cost more than she earned in six months. There was a gilded mirror too, but she kept her back turned to it. She couldn't stand to see her face.

Somewhere deep in a cold place inside her chest there was the usual pain when she left this house, as though a propeller blade had nudged up against her ribs.

CHAPTER FOUR

It was dark by the time Romy turned into rue Lamarck beyond the cemetery, eager to get her business over and done with quickly. She had other plans for the evening. She headed straight for the shop on the corner. The pinkish light from its window spilled into the street, turning a grey cat purple and painting the bumper of a parked Citroën the colour of candyfloss.

She was back in the narrow streets of Montmartre where she rented a room in one of the dingy alleyways of the 18th arrondissement. She felt safer here. Though that was probably not the right word. Montmartre was anything but safe. It crawled with penniless artists and writers, pickpockets and addicts who would happily stick a knife to your throat in exchange for a handful of grubby centimes to buy their next glass of illegal absinthe.

The wind had driven the clouds from the night sky and stars fought a losing battle with the sulphurous glow from the city. Millions of street lamps cast shadows over the worst of the grime and softened the city's sharp edges. In Montmartre it was the dirt that seemed to hold the buildings together and it was best not to think about what lay underfoot on the cobbles.

A bell rang above her head when she pushed open the shop door and entered its rosy interior. Strings of soft pink fairy lights garlanded every surface.

'Mademoiselle Romy!' exclaimed the man behind the counter. He blew her a kiss. 'You brighten my dreary evening. I haven't seen you for weeks and I've missed my favourite customer.'

Romy laughed. 'You say that to all the girls, I'm certain. And the boys.'

'Ah *non*, *chérie*. Only to you.'

He grinned, pulled out a bottle and two glasses from under the counter and proceeded to fill them with a heavy viscous red wine that was the product of his family's vine-yard. He was a slight, willowy figure with eyes that didn't take life seriously. He was wearing a white shirt, a scarlet bow tie, a black velvet skirt to his ankles and poppy-red nail varnish. His name was Louis Capel and his shop bought and sold second-hand clothes. His weakness was for fur coats. Among other things.

Romy placed her heavy satchel on the wooden counter in front of him. 'How's business?'

'Slow. I live on bread and water.'

'And wine,' she added as she took a mouthful from her glass and felt the alcohol light a small fire inside her.

'You have something for me?' He prodded a finger at her satchel. 'Another pair of kid-gloves?' He rolled his eyes in mock exasperation.

'No, Louis. I've brought you these.'

Out of the satchel she tipped three guns. They clattered on to the counter. Then silence. It settled in the shop as softly as feathers and Romy gave a chuckle at the back of her throat to dispel it.

'Interested?'

Louis' immaculately groomed eyebrows rose. 'Spanish,' he announced and picked one up. 'A Star Bonifacio, but an early one. About 1919. 6.35 mm. The left grip is cracked.'

'Interested?' she asked again.

'I won't ask where they came from.'

'I wouldn't tell you if you did.'

She glanced pointedly around the shop at the rows of shimmering gowns, velvet capes, flounces and feathers and glossy fur coats. She had no doubt that most of them fell out the back end of a burglar's sack with no questions asked. Louis was good at keeping his mouth shut.

She finished off her wine, licked her lips, leaned her elbows on the counter and watched him flutter his long black eyelashes at her.

'How much?' he asked.

Romy knelt beside her bed.

The air in the attic room was sticky. It felt as though it had been breathed by too many city people already and had found its way into her room to die in the corners. The electricity didn't reach this high up in the house, so she burned cheap candles. She possessed an ancient oil lamp that she kept on a shelf, but kerosene cost good money, so she only lit it when she had to. Tonight she didn't have to, so she put a match to the stub of a candle and her fingers worked efficiently in the gloom.

They unlocked the bootstrap that tied up the split in the underside of the mattress, though it was more a gathering of lumps and bumps than a mattress. She thrust her hand deep into the stuffing of tangled horsehair and felt her heart perform its familiar skip of relief when her fingers closed on the small scrap of canvas tucked inside. It was still there. Her fear was that one day it would be gone. And she knew if that day ever came, she would not be able to stop herself rampaging through the rooms of the other tenants in the house with a carving knife in hand until she found it.

She shivered. Hid that thought away. She'd done enough damage for one lifetime with a paperknife.

Like most Paris streets, the house consisted of six storeys plus attic rooms that became a furnace in the summer and an icebox in winter. It was a crumbling, rumbling, shabby building with water pipes that shook the plaster off the walls, rats that camped out in the cellar and a roof that leaked. Romy kept a bucket in the middle of her floor for the drips, but on days like today it became a torrent that overflowed to the floors below. Other tenants came and went with regularity, except for Madame Gosselin on the ground floor who was a fixture. She was the black-clad concierge and kept an eye on everyone's movements with a dedication that made Romy's heart sink.

If ever the mattress was empty, she would know where to go looking first. But today it wasn't empty. She tugged on the canvas and out popped a small drawstring bag which she opened and carefully checked its contents. It contained a wad of neatly folded banknotes. She counted them twice and added to them the new roll of francs she'd earned today from flying down to Spain and from the sale of the three Spanish guns. Her mind flipped back to the Spaniard, the one with the bullet wound in his wheezy chest and the fear in his dark eyes as he climbed into her plane.

'Take them,' he'd said when she'd landed in the rutted meadow outside Béziers and he kissed her hand in gratitude. 'Take the guns.' He had thrust them into her hands, three old Spanish pistols. 'I will be arrested if they are found on me.' And now they were on Louis' back shelf, wrapped in a length of oilcloth, waiting to be passed down into the hands of the criminal underworld of Paris. That was another thing Romy chose not to think about.

She tightened the drawstring on the pouch of money, pushed it deep into the mattress and rethreaded the bootlace stitching, but not before she had removed two hundred francs and slipped it into her pocket. She was tempted to take more. To risk it. She had a feeling in her gut that the cards would dance in her favour tonight.

That thought made her smile. A wary smile. She had once

lost half her savings on a pair of aces. Never again. Two hundred francs. Not much. Inflation had destroyed the value of French currency. But that was all she allowed herself. First she had a meeting to go to and Martel would be there.

She was still on her knees beside the bed, ready to rise to her feet and have a wash before heading out into the dark, when a sudden wave of tiredness hit her. It caught her off guard. The day had been long. Her emotions were wound tight. Without thought she rested her forehead on the mattress and immediately started to slide into that nameless, formless place that is the frontier of sleep, where all defences melt like walls of ice in the sun. *Don't risk it.*

But it was too late. She was tumbling on the very edge of sleep. The place where danger lay. Warm and defenceless.

Mademoiselle Romaine, why you tell those untruths to the judge? The voice in her ear was soft-spoken and insistent. *Why? You know I never went into the house that day.*

Romy's eyes shot open. She was breathing hard. Staring wildly around the room. It was empty. Just the black window and the dusty naked floorboards. Nobody whispering. No body. No ghost. She jumped to her feet and thrust her hands into her trouser pockets to stop them shaking. Her heart felt as if it had split open and was trickling blood – or was it tears? – into her chest cavity. She spat on the floor, expecting to see scarlet, but it was only spittle that ejected painfully from her mouth.

A long narrow face. Swarthy skin. Gentle eyes. Hair black as coal dust. They started to take shape inside her head.

Emerging from the confusion of anger and fear. She clearly saw his full heavy lips open to speak again, but she wasn't having that.

'I need a drink,' she mumbled and dropped to her knees again.

Her hand reached blindly under the bed for the whisky bottle. She ripped off the cap and poured the amber liquid down her throat straight from the bottle. It burned. Burned her so raw inside that there was no room for blood or tears or soft soulful eyes that reached from hell. The whisky scoured her clean.

A knock sounded at the door, startling her. She took another quick swig from the bottle, spilling some, but the knock came again.

'Go away,' she shouted.

The person knocking didn't listen. Rapped once more. A voice called out, 'Romaine, open up. It's me.'

CHAPTER FIVE

FLORENCE

Dear God. She's drunk.

The realisation hits me the moment my sister opens the door. Romaine stinks of drink. Her eyes are muddy and out of focus. She is swaying slightly, as though she's been punched. I walk into the shabby little room, closing the door firmly to shut out the smell of bad drains that spirals up through the heart of the house. I put down the bag I am carrying, reach for my sister and wrap my arms around her.

It isn't an embrace. No, nothing like that. It is a holding of Romaine together, my arms acting as girders to prevent the broken pieces of my sister falling apart. I hold her tight to my chest. Breathing for her. Aware of the intense heat within the slight figure, a furnace burning inside her. We stand there on the bare boards with no sound. No sobs. No murmurs.

Minutes pass. The noise of a car driving too fast filters up from the street. Somewhere in the house a child is crying. The minutes stretch. The last time I held Romaine like this was when Chloé was born and I'd agreed that my sister would be godmother, despite Roland's disapproval.

'She'll make trouble,' he'd stated. 'Romaine always makes trouble. Always has to fight against the rules.'

'But no one on earth,' I'd argued, 'will love our child as much as Romaine will.'

So he gave in. That time.

Why did Romaine turn up at the party today looking the way she did? She must have known all the children's mothers would be there. Why did she do it? Except to provoke. Was it Roland she was trying to provoke? I gently rub my head against the short damp curls. One day she will push him too far.

I cannot protect her forever.

It is as though my twin is tuned into the thoughts inside my head because a sudden shudder runs through her. She regains control and steps back, away from the circle of my arms. She retreats to the open window and stares out at the empty black sky and the spill of silvery moonlight over the rooftops.

'I'm sorry,' she says.

There is a stillness to her now. It makes me even more uneasy than her earlier collapse.

'What happened?' I ask. 'You were happy enough at Chloé's party.'

Slowly Romaine turns to face me. 'Happy enough? Is that what I was?'

I am so tempted to walk over and shake her. 'What happened?'

'I had a flashback.' She shrugs. As if it is nothing. 'I saw Karim.'

Dear God. We both know it isn't *nothing.*

'We agreed never to mention his name again,' I remind her sharply.

'I know.'

'Why do you do this?'

'I'm sorry.'

We face each other across the stiflingly hot little room and neither of us speaks. I am aware of the single candle flickering on the wicker table. Of the shadows slinking up the walls. Of the black mould that has colonised the corners of the ceiling. Of the zinc bucket in the centre of the room. How in God's name can my sister live like this?

How much longer is she going to keep punishing herself?

I am the first to look away. I bend down to my large leather bag on the floor and lift out its contents. 'Look, Romaine. Look what I've brought you. Isn't it exquisite?'

I hold up an evening gown. It is a simple column of finest midnight-blue silk with a weighted hem, a low-cut back that is all the rage, and slender beaded sleeves of chiffon that shout Coco Chanel. It cost the earth in the Chanel salon on rue Cambon, a quick dash across the street from the Hotel Ritz, but I know its understated glamour will appeal to her. In my other hand dangles a pair of navy satin evening shoes.

I am rewarded with a smile from Romaine. 'You expect me to fly the model aeroplane with Chloé tomorrow wearing that?'

I laugh. Keep it light-hearted. I spin the gown around full circle as though it is dancing. A scent drifts through the dismal room, the fragrance of gardenias, and I recall that I was wearing a corsage of white gardenias the only time I've worn the dress. At the Bal Tabarin nightclub in rue Victor-Massé. A giddy night of champagne cocktails and a tango with Scott Fitzgerald before his American wife, Zelda, came and laid claim to him with her blood-red talons and a glare capable of skinning any Frenchwoman at twenty paces.

'Don't be absurd, Romaine. It's for you to wear tonight.'

The smile freezes. Somewhere outside a cat is yowling.

'Darling,' I murmur, 'don't look so horrified. I've come to invite you to Monico's Club this evening. You'll love it. Horst Baumeister has insisted that I invite you.' I frown uneasily. 'He has taken quite a shine to you, it seems.'

'No, thank you.'

'Don't be difficult, darling.'

Romaine comes closer, too close for comfort. The smell of whisky grows stronger. Her amber eyes stretch long and narrow and she studies me from under her thick golden lashes.

'It's Roland, isn't it?' Romaine says.

'What do you mean?'

'He made you invite me.'

'No, of course not. Horst requested it. These Germans like to have their way.'

'I have a meeting to attend tonight.'

'Tomorrow evening then.'

'Tell Roland the answer is no. He may want to climb into bed with a Nazi bastard but I don't.'

'That's not what—'

'Florence, don't you realise what is happening in Germany?' Her voice is low and intense. 'Haven't you heard what that murdering bastard Hitler is doing? Not just in Germany, but in supporting General Franco's Nationalist Fascists in Spain too. He has unleashed the full force of the Luftwaffe's Junker and Heinkel aeroplanes to bomb the hell out of Spain's Republican troops. And they've formed the Condor Legion to—'

'Stop it, Romaine.'

Romaine raises her hands, as though to ward me off. 'Don't you care that they terror-bombed Guernica? You know they did. The Condor Legion, they call them. It was market day. Nearly two thousand people killed on the orders of Von Richthofen. So don't tell me to stop it.'

I sigh, struggling with the desire to walk out. 'It was a legitimate military target and the number of deaths has been grossly exaggerated for propaganda purposes.'

'You are blind, Florence. Their panzer tanks will be rolling into France next.'

'That is why, my *chère* sister, Roland is working with the Third Reich's envoys – like Horst Baumeister – to hammer out a peace agreement between our two countries.'

'You can't trust the Germans. Hitler breaks every treaty he signs.'

I attempt a smile. 'We have to try.'

'No.' Romaine shakes her head vehemently, sending her curls in all directions. 'Tell Roland I will take no part in his Nazi arse-licking. I have no wish to dance with Horst Baumeister.'

I make no sound, but I feel a flicker of anger in my throat. That is all. Something shutting tight. I walk over to the bed and lay the dress on the counterpane, a dusky pink brocade one that I gave her last Christmas. With care I spread out the chiffon sleeves and the light from the candle shimmers on the blue silk like moonlight skimming the sea at night. Very precisely I place the shoes beside it, then I turn and face her.

'Do it, Romaine. Do it for me.'

Neither of us breathes. Romaine remains mute. Just a faint shake of her head, but her gaze flicks to the dress. Time seems to stumble to a halt in the silence.

'I have forgotten how to dance,' she murmurs at last. 'It has been so long since . . .'

I step forward. I slip an arm around my sister's slender waist, drawing her close. I lean my head against hers and take hold of her hand. We stand there, cheek to cheek.

'Dance with me,' I whisper.

Slowly we begin to dance.

CHAPTER SIX

The meeting room was situated above one of the busy pavement cafés in the Place d'Estienne d'Orves, where Parisians gathered to nurse their wine, burn through their Gauloises and berate their new prime minister, Édouard Daladier, leader of the Popular Front coalition. They had no patience for his timidity. He had shown no backbone when dealing with the industrial strikes that were sweeping the country or in facing down the threat to European peace presented by the rearmament of Nazi Germany. Everyone was jumpy.

'Meeting room' was rather too grand a description for the place. It was, in reality, a storeroom stacked with tea chests and dusty cardboard boxes on which a white Persian cat liked to laze and listen. The evening was warm, the air sluggish. But the window was kept firmly shut, locking in the heat and the cigarette smoke, to avoid any secrets leaking out into the street below. Because that's why they were here, five men and two women. To exchange information and prepare for their cell's next move. They made an odd, disparate group – a union foreman, a shop owner, an engineer, a barber and someone calling himself a finance official. Though as far as Romy knew, finance officials didn't usually go around with a gun tucked under their armpit. Plus herself, of course, a pilot.

Then there was Léo Martel. Romy was never quite sure how her boss at the airfield came to fit in here. He was an intensely private individual, not given to pouring out his soul, but it was he who had recruited the six of them, he who coordinated with other secret cells hidden within the city. It was after she had worked for him a while that he had taken to talking to her about the Spanish Civil War, about the morals and principles involved. He described to her the terrible time that the partisan army was having against Franco's Fascists who were backed by the Germans and the Italians. She loathed the dominance of dictators and was excited to be recruited to fly planes down south to the Republican forces.

Romy asked no questions about the others. Each was known only by their first name. They trusted Léo Martel. As soon as everyone had taken their usual place in the circle of chairs, he leaned forward, his strong hands on his knees, and regarded each face in turn.

'It has begun,' he announced.

There was an intake of breath.

'I have just heard the latest news from Spain,' he continued. 'The Republican Army of Spain has crossed the Ebro River on the bend between Fayón and Benifallet. They are up against the powerful Fiftieth Division of the Nationalist Fascist army, but they caught them completely by surprise.'

Manu, the barber in the chair next to Romy, whipped the beret off his shiny bald head and tossed it in the air with delight. *'Allez-y, mes braves! Mes petits.'*

They all knew who the *petits* were. Twelve new divisions of the Republican army had been formed in Spain. These included the Quinta del Biberón, the ones that Manu feared for. The baby-bottle call-up, that's what they were dubbed, because conscription was widened to include those as young as sixteen years old. Romy tried not to think of it. Fresh-faced Spanish youths, the pride of the country, getting their limbs blown off by Nazi planes.

'Allez-y, mes petits,' François, a trade unionist, echoed under his breath.

The civil war in Spain had taken a punishing toll on its people over the last two years, and now Franco's Fascist army under General Dávila was seizing more and more swathes of Spanish territory, as it tried to force its way eastward through Republican bastions to reach Valencia on the Mediterranean Sea. This battle of the Ebro River would be crucial. Everyone in the room understood its importance. It would stem the tide of Nationalist victories and prevent a wedge being driven through Republican-held regions, cutting them in two. But it all hung on a knife-edge, on whether Lieutenant Colonel Modesto could hold his fragile Republican army together.

'How did Modesto's troops cross the river?'

It was Grégory, the engineer, who spoke. His hands flew through the air, sketching angles and junctions, as though building bridges.

'The commandos of Fourteenth Corps slipped across the river at night and silenced the enemy guards. They fastened lines,' Martel informed them, unable to keep the excitement at the Republican advance from his voice, 'for the assault boats to follow.'

'How many?'

'Ninety boats. Ten men in each. Nine hundred men as a spearhead. They have pushed forward twenty-five miles as far as Gandesa, using pontoon bridges for supplies and reinforcements.'

Was this the breakthrough that would turn the tide of the war? Romy thought about the rifles she had delivered to Spain yesterday, and prayed to a God she had long since lost faith in that they would save the life of some raw-boned sixteen-year-old on the banks of the Ebro River today.

Diane, the dark-eyed woman seated opposite Romy, rose slowly to her feet. She started to hum *El Himno de Riego*, the Spanish national anthem, in a powerful contralto voice. It matched the strong mannish features of her face but was at odds with the stylish, flimsy twists of tulle and satin that she wore as a hat on her sleek dark hair. She was a milliner. More to the point, she was milliner to the wives of two government ministers who loved to talk. It had taken Romy many months to discover that she was an expert code maker, as well as a hat maker.

The financier, Jerome, a strange, thin, oily man, grinned up at her, showing long wolfish teeth, and said, 'Sit down, Diane. You embarrass us.'

But the woman continued to the end of the anthem and only then did she resume her seat and ask Martel, 'Do we have more planes to send to them?'

'Yes, we do.'

She turned to Romy. 'You ready for this, girl?'

'Of course. I'll fly as many as we can get hold of.'

Everyone's eyes sought out Jerome. Except Martel's. His gaze remained on Romy. She could feel it heavy on her skin and she wondered what he was seeing. It was Jerome who secretly raised the funds needed to buy aircraft to supply the Republicans. No one asked how. Diane always joked that she didn't want to know where the bodies were buried each time Jerome handed over a cheque. He would laugh his weird laugh and assure them that there were people throughout Europe who understood the need to fight Fascism. If it wasn't stopped, it would rampage across the whole of Europe. And what then?

'Well, *ma petite*,' the financier stroked the waxed ends of his moustache with sensual pleasure, 'button up your flying helmet.' He slapped a hessian bag down on the tea chest in front of them, yanked open the drawstring neck and tipped out thick bundles of franc notes into a pile with all the flourish of a magician producing a flock of doves from his hat.

Martel whistled through his teeth. 'What did you do, Jerome? Rob a bank?'

Again the weird strangled laugh. 'Something like that. We all know that this war in Spain is providing combat experience for the latest technology by the German military, despite the fact they signed the French-British embargo on any munitions or soldiers going into Spain. The Nazi Condor Legion is going to be bombing the shit out of those poor bastards on the Ebro River. They are going to need every aircraft we can get to them.'

Romy nodded. 'I heard when I was down there that the Condor have just poured in more Stuka bombers to reinforce the Fascists.'

'And the International Brigade? Are they there too?'

It was Grégory who asked.

'Yes,' Martel said at once. 'They are there.'

'Which division?'

'The Forty-fifth. Under Lieutenant Colonel Hans Kahle. The Fourteenth Marseillaise Brigade is there too.'

For a split second no one breathed. Grégory's younger brother was in the International Brigade, which was made up of thousands of volunteers from all over the world, fighting on the Republican side.

'And the Garibaldi Brigade?' Grégory whispered.

'Yes. The Garibaldi is pinned down at Ebro. I'm sorry, *mon ami*.'

There was a long silence. Romy wanted to go over to Grégory and take his strong hand in hers, but she didn't. Instead she leaned forward and gave him a half-smile of encouragement, the kind of smile that was no help at all.

'With luck your brother will come out of it unscathed,' she stated. 'You heard what Martel said. The Fascist troops are on the run. Your brother will soon come home to you.'

Gregory pushed back his chair, its feet scraping across the wooden floor with a squeal that set nerves further on edge, and he hurried to the door.

'Grégory.' Martel's voice was suddenly sharp. 'A warning. Before you leave.'

Grégory paused, one hand on the doorknob, but he didn't turn. Did not face their pity.

'There has been a killing,' Martel said.

'Where?' Romy asked.

'Here in Paris. Over in Montparnasse. Two members of another group within our network. They were leaving a restaurant together. A bullet in the head. Silent and efficient.'

'A professional killer?'

'It bears the marks of it.'

Grégory spun around, his face contorted by grief. 'I would take a killing like that for myself if it would bring my young brother home from Spain in one piece.'

He opened the door jerkily and slammed it behind him, making the dust motes dance in the air.

A bullet in the brain. An assassin stalking the streets of Paris.

It concentrated the mind.

CHAPTER SEVEN

'Let me walk you home.'

Martel fell into step beside Romy, slowing his stride to hers. The street was dark and almost empty. To her surprise he threaded her arm through his and held it there.

'I'm not heading home yet,' Romy pointed out.

'Then I'll walk you to wherever you are heading.'

'There's no need, boss.'

'You should go home. Get some sleep.'

She shook her head. 'Sleep is for when you have nothing better to do.'

'It's been a long day, Romy.'

They had stopped at a kerb, waiting for a horse and cart to trundle past, piled high with sweet-smelling hay. She glanced up at Martel and found him looking at her, his large features softened by the yellow blur of a street lamp.

'You have something better to do?' he asked.

'Yes.'

He didn't ask what. He didn't need to. For a while they walked on in silence. She could feel how tense the long muscles of his arm were.

'Is there a chance that the Ebro army will succeed in driving back General Dávila's Nationalist forces?' she asked.

'Every chance.'

'Honestly?'

His pause was so slight, most others would have missed it. 'Honestly.'

'Poor Grégory. He loves his brother so much and worries himself sick over him. I would be the same,' she declared, 'if my sister went to war.'

Martel gave a snort of laughter that startled a rat out of the gutter. They turned a corner into a narrow street where the street lamps were not all working and the air felt as soft and black as velvet on her cheek. She didn't mind. It was easier to say what she had to say in the darkness.

'Is there someone watching us?' she asked. 'Watching me?'

She heard him inhale. 'Why do you ask?'

'Because I noticed a black Citroën parked within spitting distance of a shop that I was in this evening. Then it appeared at the corner of the block where we had our meeting, just up from the café. When we left, it had moved to the opposite corner.'

'You are imagining things, Romy. There are thousands of black Citroëns in Paris. They are like crows. You can't tell them apart. Don't worry about it.'

'*Merde*! Don't treat me like a fool.'

'I've never thought you a fool.'

'You know how when you're flying, you have to be aware of everything around you. I mean *everything.* At all times. The weather, the clouds, the wind direction, your speed, your instruments, your fuel, the pitch of your engine, other aircraft in the sky or on the ground, railway lines, rivers, fields where you can crash-land if necessary, church spires as markers, the condition of a landing strip, where the trees are, the state of your—'

'I know, Romy.'

Of course he knew.

'What I'm saying is that I notice everything. That's one of the reasons I'm a good pilot.'

He turned his head to her. In the darkness she couldn't see his face. 'I know,' he said quietly.

'I'm telling you that it was the same black car each time. That's all.'

Martel said nothing. The only sound was their footsteps echoing over the cobbles and somewhere the faint plaintive wail of a violin. The people of Paris loved their music. He wrapped his arm around her shoulders, drawing her closer.

'So where,' he said in a voice that rumbled up from deep inside his broad chest, 'is the bar you're heading for tonight?'

He watched her drink. He didn't have one himself, so she ordered a glass of wine and made herself take it slow. What she wanted was a whisky. The bar was tired-looking, nondescript, but as familiar as an old shoe. The *patron* and several customers greeted her by name. They were seated in a corner at a small wooden table with wonky legs.

'So?' she asked. 'The black Citroën.'

'I wish I were the one flying aircraft to Spain instead of you.'

Romy experienced a ripple of shock, which she kept off her face. Martel had made it clear long ago that the subject of his own piloting experiences was strictly off-limits. She had come to work for him four years ago and at that time he walked heavily with a stick and his face was tight with pain. He'd looked much older than his thirty years. Martel himself never referred to his stick or to his limp, but his devoted shadow, Jules Roget, had told her. About the crash.

Léo Martel had been a stunt pilot. One of the best. Even flew a Curtiss P-01 Hawk in the dogfights in *Wings*, the 1927 Hollywood Gary Cooper film, and competed in pylon races and flew circus wing-walks. He lived and breathed flying. Jules swore he had aviation fuel running through his veins. Just after dawn on his twenty-first birthday in 1925 he had been crazy enough to risk his neck in a wild stunt – flying a Blériot biplane right through the archway of the Arc de Triomphe. Just the thought of it made Romy's heart hammer fast as a piston engine. He'd got away with that one.

But five years ago his luck ran out. On a cold breezy morning. Landing at Le Bourget in a Caudron Luciole, a nippy little two-seater firefly of a plane with a seven-cylinder radial engine. Not even Jules would talk about it. But Romy caught the bare bones. It seems Martel was about to touch down when an ancient Caproni dropped out of the sky on top of him like a dead cat. The Luciole flipped. Tail over nose. Smashed his legs to pieces. Each year since then he took the medical for his pilot's licence and each year he failed.

Romy couldn't imagine what it did to him. Not flying. She leaned her elbows on the table and pushed her glass of Bordeaux towards him.

'Here,' she said and shrugged.

His slate-grey eyes stared at it for a long moment before he curled his fingers around the glass and knocked the wine straight back in one swallow. Almost immediately the rigidity of his large jaw slackened and his deep-set gaze lifted to Romy's face. She wanted to say, *Order another. You'll feel better, I promise*, but she wasn't in the habit of telling Léo Martel what to do.

'The Citroën?' she prompted.

His eyebrows were thick, almost black, and always expressive. They swooped down now in disapproval.

'Forget it,' he said.

'Forget it? It could be a threat to—'

'It's one of ours.'

'What do you mean?'

'It's there to watch our backs. After the murder of those two in the other group, we need to be more careful.'

She blinked. The last thing she wanted was some hard-eyed stranger hounding her footsteps, making notes on the dark paths she chose to tread.

'Who are they?'

But before he could reply, a door at the far end of the bar flew open and a young woman carrying a tray of empty glasses on one hand flounced out of the back room. She was wearing a dreary black waitress dress, but she had cinched it tight at the waist to show off her abundant curves. Her hair was a startling fox-red that made Romy smile. She knew it could be creamy-blonde or raven-black tomorrow. Éloise was easily bored. She managed the tray and the swing of her hips with equal skill as she wove her way over to Romy's table where she put down the tray and embraced Romy warmly.

'Where have you been, *mon ange*? They have been expecting you?'

Romy's glance flicked towards the back room. Someone had already shut the door, but she felt her heartbeat quicken. Something stirred in her, the first knife-edge of excitement. She could taste the adrenaline, as tantalising as the first hit of whisky.

'I said I'd be here,' Romy murmured.

But already Éloise's easy smile had slid to Léo Martel and her hand took the liberty of ruffling the short dark hairs at the back of his head.

'My darling Romy, who is your handsome friend?'

Romy grinned at Martel's discomfort. 'He's my boss.'

'Well, boss, what can I get you to drink?' Éloise's smile was like honey. She knew how to make it look as if she'd been saving it up all night just for you.

Martel removed her hand from his shoulder and rose to his feet. He was too big for a tiny bar like this. 'Romy, may

I remind you that you are flying tomorrow. You need a good night's sleep.'

She nodded. 'I know. I'll just stay for a chat with Éloise and then I'll head off.'

The lie slipped off her tongue so smoothly, she almost believed it herself. But even above the rumble of voices from the other drinkers she heard Martel's sigh, saw disappointment cloud his face.

'Goodnight, mademoiselle,' he said to Éloise.

He walked out of the bar with no goodnight for Romy. She should have minded. She should have listened. She should have picked up her jacket and left at his heels. She knew all that. But it was not enough.

'How many are in tonight?' she asked Éloise.

'Four of them.' The waitress leaned closer. 'One is a newcomer. He's just your type.'

'I don't have a type.'

It was true, she didn't. All shapes and sizes, colours and creeds. She liked whichever showed courage. And nerve. Yes, they were the best, the ones who knew how to ratchet up the excitement. She walked towards the back-room door. Kept it nonchalant. As though she were in no hurry at all.

Romy had studied her own face in the mirror with indecent frequency. She had peered closely at its curves and kinks, knew intimately each sweep of bone and blemish of skin. She was only too familiar with its faults. The muddy colour of her eyes and the angular chin that had a habit of jutting forward when she was angry and forgot to restrain it. But she knew her face's good points too, one of which was the calmness of her facial muscles, smooth and silky. They fooled people. Their stillness was a mask. Most people didn't see beyond it, and that was the reason she examined her face so minutely. To look for cracks.

Tonight she put on her poker face.

The cards came and went through her fingers, the stakes rose and fell, and the small pile of chips stacked in front of her rose and fell with them. She started slowly. To get the feel of the game. To test out this stranger. But the more she won, the more she risked and the pile grew steadily.

A pair of kings.

Ace high.

A low flush.

Nothing spectacular. Just enough to keep her in the game. Her face never changed, her expression a stone wall, her focus pin-sharp. Observing. Listening for the smallest quickening of breath. Between hands, she smoked cigarettes, eyes narrowed against the fog of Gitanes as she watched the other four players set out their own poker faces.

A straight flush. Better.

The other three players she knew well. Old adversaries, accustomed to duelling to the death. She knew how to read them and their plays. But Anton? The new one.

Who was he?

He was thin, with long manipulative fingers that fidgeted with his chips like a beginner, and a high-angled forehead that made her wary. Too much room for clever thoughts in there. Good-looking, if you like your man overconfident and snappily dressed. He sat on Romy's right, talking too loud and losing badly. He made it too easy. But she wasn't stupid, she knew his brashness could be a false tell.

Romy bluffed one hand and scooped the pot. The whisky glass in front of her filled, emptied and refilled without her noticing.

She folded the next.

Poker is a game of skill. Of tactics. Of deceit. That's why she was good at it. She had an instinct for it. She told herself she only cared about the money, but she knew that wasn't strictly true. There was more than that to these nights spent in smoke-filled back rooms. Much more. When the adrenaline hit like a train, ripping the breath from her lungs. When she knew she held a winning hand. When she had out-thought her opponents. It brought out the best in her. And the absolute worst. She knew that. Some days when she hit a downswing and saw her hard-earned cash slide into another's greedy pocket, she vowed on her sister's life never to play again.

Play. As if it were a game.

But when the cards were flying and the winnings were piling up in front of her, when the cards danced in her hands, well, then it was different. All-consuming. She could think of nothing else. *No one else.* That's what she craved. She saw only the sad and implacable faces and crowned heads of the red and black kings, bloodless and bearded between her fingers.

'Romy.'

It was Anton. The newcomer. He was staring at her. His eyes darted from her face to the chips stacked in front of her and back again.

'You play well,' he murmured. 'You're allowed to smile now.'

She pasted a smile on her face for him, a teasing one, and circled her chips protectively with her hands. She cast a glance at the paltry few left in front of him. 'You should quit now,' she told him with a small show of teeth, 'before I win the shirt off your back.'

The flicker of irritation in his dark eyes was gone in a flash, but she'd registered it. Maybe now the loudmouth would cease his chatter. Opposite her, Georges, the beer-bellied owner of the bar, had risen from his chair, taking a break from the table, and was hunched in a corner, inhaling white powder with a swift sharp sniff. After a moment he returned, brushed specks of cocaine dust from his moustache with no embarrassment, and declared, '*En avant, mes amis.*'

Romy heard Anton echo under his breath, '*En avant.* Forward.'

From that moment, he started winning. With a speed that sent a chill through the swill of whisky in her stomach, he turned the game around. She started losing. She tried tightening up her game, taking fewer chances, but even then Anton always seemed to have the upper hand. Somehow his straights always went a little bit higher, his sets were just a little stronger.

The darkness outside slid into the room like oil, stifling the air, and as he dealt, Georges muttered something she didn't catch, because all she heard now was the whisper of the cards. The soft snick as they brushed against the table. The loose grunt of satisfaction when the others leaned forward to draw the pot towards them. Because the others *were* winning. All of them – Georges, Xavier, Didier and Anton. Especially Anton. Only *she* was losing. Hand after hand.

She tightened her grip on her dwindling pile of chips. When Anton dealt, she fixed her eyes on his quick clever fingers. Could spot nothing. She drew three cards. He drew one. Which meant he most probably had two pairs. She had a pair of tens. Nothing else. Reluctantly she decided to give up on the hand. The way things were going, he probably had her dead in the water before even drawing that last card. She tossed her cards on the table. Anton grinned, turning over his cards. King high.

Putain.

She swore. He laughed.

'Enough?' he asked.

'My deal,' she said and shuffled the cards.

When she checked, another hour had passed. Bit by bit, he stripped her bare. Left her nothing. Not even a shred of pride. Anton was cheating, she was positive, but she couldn't spot the hell how. She knew she should have quit when the chips were dancing her way. It was gone midnight now. She pushed her chair away from the table. 'I'm done,' she announced and resisted the urge to snatch a handful of the wretched chips that gathered like a swarm of black flies in front of Anton. She finished off her whisky.

'*Bonsoir, chérie*,' Georges chuckled. 'Better luck next time.'

She left. Concentrating on walking straight. Outside the bar, she leaned against the wall in the dingy street, lit a cigarette and dragged in the smoke to suffocate her foul mood. She waited. No black Citroën saloons in sight. She exhaled heavily into the damp night air, the taste of disgust sour in her mouth.

He made her wait nearly an hour. When the tall figure with the sloping forehead and the felt fedora finally emerged from the doorway, she fell into step beside him in the darkness and slid her arm through his.

'Now, Monsieur Anton, let me walk you home.'

CHAPTER EIGHT

The sex was fierce and brief. With a stranger she liked it that way, wild and abandoned. With a stranger she had nothing to lose.

The moment they stumbled into his apartment opposite Galeries Lafayette on Boulevard Haussmann their hands were on each other. Tearing at clothes, seeking out bare flesh. His lips hard on her mouth, his fingers encircling her throat, tight, painful. He cursed her trousers when they thwarted his desire for her, but she would not let him rip them and she stepped out of them with ease, her limbs naked.

Instantly the same long-fingered hands that had played his cards so cunningly began to play her body with equal skill. Where they touched, stroked, teased, her skin burned. His mouth closed on her breast, sending heat coursing through her, and he tangled those long fingers in her hair. Pinning her there. His tongue circled her nipple and swept up the curve of her breast to the hollow of her neck. He sank his teeth into her collarbone and she heard herself cry out, but whether from pain or from hunger for him, she couldn't tell.

She abandoned the bed, threw his pillows on the floor and pulled him down on to them where she straddled him. Blood was pounding in her ears, deafening the voices that had whispered and scuttled through her day. With no inhibitions, she and Anton kissed, clawed and devoured each other, welded together by sweat and need, as though trying to tear each other's skin off.

When finally it was over, their bodies shuddering and heaving for breath, the heat still throbbing deep inside her, her hand reached up and gently stroked his cheek. She could feel the rasp of his stubble against her palm and smell the black tobacco on his breath. He was a person. Not just a card sharp. Not just a drug she craved to take her out of this world for even a few frenzied minutes. She climbed into his bed and he followed. To her surprise he wrapped his long arms around her waist and tucked his knees up tight against her.

'You're a rotten poker player,' he whispered with a chuckle, as he kissed her ear and instantly fell asleep.

She listened to the easy rhythm of his sleep and smiled in the darkness. She was grateful. As her heartbeat slowed and her skin felt warm and soft, she told herself the words that she'd told herself a thousand times before.

Surely tonight she would sleep. Surely tonight the dreams would not come.

*

The dream came at her, violent as a mountain storm. It battered her. Shook her. Left her nowhere to hide. The books stared out at her, they always watched her, mute and musty witnesses to her crime. Her father's study was smaller, stuffier, so cramped it seemed to squeeze her. Her bones ached and she heard them crack and creak with each movement, as though ice lay where the marrow should be.

The rug was there, exactly the same.

The pool of blood was there, exactly the same.

But she was naked and shivering. On her knees. Seven uniformed figures leaned over her, blocking out air, blocking out light, and their accusations hammered at her until she knew her eardrums would split and the guilt hiding inside her head would spill out like grey ash on to the rug for all to see. Already there were telltale flakes of ash on her arms and her thighs. On her lips. She tried to brush them off.

'You killed him.'

'No!'

'You whore.'

'No!'

'You butcher.'

'You slut.'

'*Putain*.'

She was shaking her head fiercely from side to side, slamming her thoughts against the walls of her skull.

No. No. No.

The darkness deepened around her. The uniforms were sucking the last scrap of light from the room. She could hear sobs. But when she looked down to hide her guilt from the uniforms, she saw her own naked skin glistening in the gloom with strings of scarlet. And one of her hands was rising and falling. Rising. Falling.

In front of her lay the body of her father, the sockets of his eyes black and empty, and she was stabbing him in the chest with a bayonet. Over and over. She couldn't make it stop.

Romy dragged herself out of sleep, gasping and trembling. Her heart was trying to kick its way out of her chest and for one sickening moment she had no idea where she was. No idea who lay beside her. Her mind was in turmoil. Moonlight had seeped through the slats of the shutters and lay across the tangled bed sheets like a row of silver ingots spread out for her to steal.

She jerked upright and wrapped her arms around her shins in the darkness, her chin jammed on to her knees to prevent her teeth chattering. She was angry. Angry with herself. With the hated dream. Even angry with the man at her side for not being enough to keep the nightmare at bay.

She slid out of bed and padded on bare feet to where her clothes lay in a black bundle on the floor by the window. She scooped them up and, by the ice-cold light of one of the slats of moonlight, she saw the small leather pouch that Anton wore under his shirt. Her naked skin was slick with sweat but her mouth turned dry at the sight of the pouch. She glanced back at the bed. No movement.

With a quick flip of her hand she opened the pouch,

removed her two hundred francs, no more, no less, from the pile of banknotes inside it and tucking her clothes under her arm she hurried from the apartment. On the landing, the air nipped at her skin, with only a dull glow rising from a light bulb on the floor below, and a faint rustle that was hard to place. As though the walls themselves were whispering. She had no idea what time it was. She pulled on her trousers, shirt and shoes, raking a hand through her hair, and only then did she notice the man leaning over the balustrade of the landing on the storey above. He was in the dark but she could make out the pale oval of his face turned in her direction. He had been watching her naked body slide into her clothes.

Softly he called out, 'I can pay. I have money.'

A banknote fluttered down the well of the stairs like a bird shot from the sky.

'Go to hell,' she muttered.

She hurried down the three flights of dimly lit stairs and out into the chill night air. Somewhere, a church clock struck three. She set off at a rapid pace along the cobbled street as if she could outrun the voices in her head.

The police officer sits me down on the velvet chair in Maman's music room as tenderly as if I am made of fragile porcelain. He perches on the piano stool, hands on his knees, and his voice is kind. Does he have a daughter of his own, I wonder? I do not look at the other stern-faced gendarme with beetles for eyebrows, who stands by the window taking notes.

'Mademoiselle Romaine Duchamps,' the officer starts with a soft tone, 'you have stated that you didn't see Karim Abed in the garden this morning. Is that correct?'

I nod.

'You were with your sister and Monsieur Roussel, I believe?'

I nod.

'Did you see Karim Abed enter the house?'

I find my tongue. It feels too big for my mouth. 'No.'

He pauses, so I offer more.

'I did not see Karim enter the house.'

'Your sister says she did see him go through the side door when she went to the orchard to pick an apple.'

Oh, she is bold, my sister.

'I saw the wheelbarrow,' I say. 'Full of hedge cuttings. But no gardener.'

I sit on my hands to stop their tremors. But immediately I pull them back out. I don't want to look as though I am hiding something. How would an innocent daughter act, what would she do? Cry.

I cannot cry.

'I know this is deeply upsetting for you, mademoiselle, but I have to urge you to think hard. Did you see anything at all unusual this morning?'

'Yes.'

He leans forward, alert as a gundog. 'And what was that?'

'I walked past the window of Papa's study. I was taking dead-headed rose blooms to the compost heap.'

It is as if I have lit a fire under the investigating officer. He jumps to his feet. Stands right in front of me.

'What did you see?'

I stare straight into his intent eyes. I do not blink. 'I saw Karim's face at the window. Inside Papa's study.'

There. The lie is told. My cheeks burn but I do not look away. If Florence can do it, so can I. I do not want a cold blade to sever my neck. I let my distress show on my face and he presses a pristine white handkerchief into my hands. With relief I bury my face in it and pretend to cry.

Moonlight streamed into Romy's attic room, daubing silver on the walls, so bright that she felt no need to light a candle. She filled an enamel bowl with cold water downstairs and carted it back up the five flights to her room, where she stripped, washed and pulled on a clean skirt and blouse. They were her smartest. She didn't want to embarrass Florence again, nor did she want to come to Chloé stinking of whisky, cigarettes and sex. Especially not sex.

She knelt once more beside her mattress and again unlaced the strap holding the split together. Her hand fought its way through the horsehair lumps until it closed on the canvas bag and dragged it out. But this time instead of placing the two hundred francs she'd retrieved from Anton back in, she removed another three hundred. Five hundred altogether. The moonlight's touch turned them into lace between her fingers, with winged Mercury gazing up at her.

She took an envelope from a box under her bed, a plain

manila one, and tucked the money inside. In pencil she wrote on the front a single name: Aya.

It was the first day of the month.

The dawn had nudged the darkness of the night hours westward in the direction of Versailles. In its place a pinkish veil spread over Paris and transformed the graceful dome of the Sacré-Coeur basilica into a sumptuous vast *glace à la fraise.* The dirty and dilapidated streets of the Goutte d'Or district of the 18th arrondissement were turned into the rose-tinted haven that its north-African inhabitants yearned for. A brief whisper of the wind from the deserts of their homeland.

Romy liked it here. The smell of spices and unfamiliar oils and herbs hung in the air. Strange garbs and languages from other corners of the world filled the narrow streets. Even at this hour of the morning the colourful Barbès market was buzzing with life, as dark-skinned fingers prodded the silvery scales of fish for freshness and scooped handfuls of fiery-hot chillis into hand-woven bags. The area rang with shouts and arguments in unknown guttural tongues and reverberated with the rumble of the Métro overhead.

This was the world from which Romy had wrenched Karim Abed. A soft-spoken gardener, a family man. A man who had placed ripe strawberries in front of her each summer and chopped wood for her bedroom fire each winter. She stood now in the musky shadow of an alleyway and observed the door of the house in rue d'Oran where Karim used to live. She ignored the odd looks she received, a white female face that didn't belong in the Arab quarter, and kept her eyes fixed on the door. It was red. With long threads of peeling paint, like strips of skin flayed off a slave's back.

She did not have to wait long. The door opened and a woman slid silently into the flow of humanity in the cobbled street. She looked about forty, small and self-contained in her black robe and black headscarf. Her tiny feet scurried along at speed, eager to get wherever she was going, but she kept her eyes downcast, unwilling to engage with the busy world around her. Romy knew exactly where she was heading. To one of the big hotels near the Opéra. She worked long hours for a pittance as a kitchen skivvy. Her name was Aya. Aya Abed. Romy said the name aloud, not once, but twice, as if doing so would empty it out of her head.

She returned her attention to the door, but it was another half-hour before it opened again. This time a boy emerged, caught in that gangly state between childhood and manhood. Romy knew his age – thirteen. She knew his name – Samir. Samir Abed. She knew where he went to school. So it came as a surprise to see him wearing dirty overalls and turning in the opposite direction away from the school.

What was the boy up to?

She felt a twist of disquiet and quickly fell into step some way behind him. Samir was taller than his father had been so his dark head was easy to spot in the crowd, but he had inherited his sloping shoulders from his father and the intent way of holding himself, as though aware that each step was an important part of his journey through life. At the foul-smelling tallow factory he hurried through the tall gates, but just as he was disappearing from view, he glanced over his shoulder. Straight past the other workers crammed around the gates. Straight at her.

Karim's eyes. Dark and accusing.

She turned and fled.

The lock clicked. The red door opened. Romy extracted the hook-pick and slipped it unobtrusively back into her bag. She had won the set of picks in a poker game years earlier from a professional burglar and quickly learned to use them effectively. She knew the stubborn temperament of this lock, its tendency to dig its heels in if she applied too much pressure. Gently, gently. She tickled it open in less than ten seconds and stepped inside the building.

It smelled of too many bodies and not enough running water. A labyrinth of dim corridors ran back through the tenement, twisting and turning around a dingy courtyard where sunlight rarely found a foothold. Romy walked fast, sure of where to go. No one challenged her. In places like this, it was better not to ask questions.

Answers could be dangerous.

Romy stood in the centre of the small airless room, eyes darting around, seeking changes. There was one. One big one. The schoolbooks were usually stacked neatly on the table with a sharpened pencil laid out beside them, but now were pushed into a corner on the floor with a small pile of folded shirts on top of them. As if they had no more value than a stool.

Surely not.

Not that. A rejection of the only pathway out of this stinking rathole. She recalled Samir in the overalls. The gates to the tallow factory. The leaden footsteps of the men streaming through them. And it made her want to reach out and haul him out of there before the damage was done.

Why Samir?

Why now? For six years she had been coming here with her hook-pick and her envelope on the first day of every month, and for six years she had kept him in school instead of working the markets or weaving threads in the carpet sheds the way many of the children from Algeria were forced to in the backstreets of Paris.

What has happened, Samir?

She studied the room more carefully. Never had she touched anything. Not opened any drawers or rummaged through any cupboards. Never that. Once, only once, she had brought a pot of paint and the next month the walls were a pristine white and a dish of fresh dates had been sitting on the table when she arrived. Were they for her? She ate one. It was the only time a thin wire of contact had connected them. She could still taste that date, sweet and scented. A dark, savage part of her mind had suspected it would be poisoned, but still she swallowed it, and it wasn't poisoned.

The room was tidy, always clean and tidy. But bare. A pile of large threadbare cushions on the floor, a small table, two hard chairs. Screened from the room behind a faded curtain that must once have been a vivid magenta stood a narrow bed and in one corner lay a thin rolled-up mattress, with a few clothes precisely folded. All as usual. Yet something was missing. It took her a moment. It was the vase. The brass one. With hand-chased elephants on it and handles designed as cobras. It was gone. It was only when she stepped behind the curtain that she saw the medicine bottle by the bed and realised where the money was going. Aya Abed was sick.

It was too much.

She quickly placed the envelope on the table and hurried to the door, eager to be gone. That was her mistake, her haste. She forgot. She forgot to keep her eyes averted from the photograph that hung in a bamboo frame next to the door. It was Karim's long gentle face and his dark eyes were staring straight at her, just as he had done when he stood in the dock in court. She heard again the jangle of his handcuffs when he raised them in the air, showing them to her, and caught again the soft sobbing of his wife, the rustle of the papers that held the damning accusations. She could smell fear in the courtroom and knew it was her own.

She tore her eyes from the photograph and left the room, but as she entered the corridor a figure loomed out of the dim shadows. Her heart leaped into her throat and for one terrifying moment she thought it was Karim. But no. It was a woman.

'What the hell you doing in there? You got no right.'

The woman was large, with an abundance of very dark

rolls of flesh and large flashy beads that rattled as she waved an arm in the direction of Aya Abed's room.

'Who are you?' Romy countered.

'I'm Leilah. More to the point, who the fuck are you? A thief, that's what you are, you—'

'No. I'm not. I'm a friend of Samir's.'

The woman's large muscular hands, the scrubbed hands of a washerwoman, seized Romy's shoulders and almost lifted her off the floor as they slammed her against the wall, so hard that the back of her head hitting the already cracked plaster made a sound like a gunshot. For a moment her mind went blank.

'You ain't no friend of Samir's,' the woman yelled, her face a hand's width from Romy's, her nostrils wide black tunnels. 'I'm going to beat the shit out of you until I get the truth out of . . .'

But Romy knew how to fight. You don't hang around bars late at night without learning a thing or two about combat. The point of her shoe raked forward into a well-padded shin and her elbow twisted and shot up at an unguarded chin. She heard the crack of a tooth and the round eyes rolled in Leilah's head like marbles ricocheting off a windowpane. Her hands grew slack.

Romy ran. Today had not started well.

CHAPTER NINE

FLORENCE

Sunlight flashes off the aircraft's wing, painting it a shimmering buttercup yellow as it flies smoothly above the row of trees. But the wind has picked up, the warm dusty breath from the Sahara, and a gust of it snatches at the tail fin, spinning the fragile plane, sending it into a steep nosedive.

I hold my breath. My hands clench. From behind my sunglasses I watch it tumble to earth and a part of me is glad.

But I hear the cry of alarm. Witness the moment the aircraft hits the ground. See its wings torn off on impact as easily as an insect's, as it flips tail over nose. I long to run to it, but make myself remain seated on the rug. Face immobile. I am good at that. My teeth clamp down on my tongue to stop me shouting out.

I let her deal with it. It is what she wants.

*

'Maman, look! Tante Romy mended it.'

Chloé's voice is so full of admiration, her words so exuberant in their love for her aunt. I smile with delight and hide the shiver that runs through me.

'Isn't she clever?' I say. 'What would we do without her?'

My tongue is dipped in bile.

My daughter holds up the model aircraft for me to view its perfection, now that my sister has slotted its wings back on after its accident. Even I have to admit that it is an impressive toy. It flies above tree-height after no more than a metre take-off run and wings its way straight along the Grande Allée of the Tuileries Gardens, easing itself up over the long rows of trimmed chestnut trees as though hell-bent on reaching the Louvre. The museum's steep grey roof seems to watch us from afar, as if storing up more knowledge to cram into its bowels.

I like the Tuileries Garden. I like its geometric layout, its neatness. A formal garden that was based on perfect symmetry by its designer, Le Nôtre, who understood, all the way back in the seventeenth century, the need to teach people about structure. Discipline. Self-control. Calmness. I know that if I had met M. André Le Nôtre, I would have liked the man, we would have spoken the same language. All the way from the Place de la Concorde to the Louvre Museum he created a symphony of *allées*, terraces, horseshoe ramps, all graced with carefully positioned statues, lawns and flowers. And a pond sixty metres across. Not just an ordinary pond but an octagonal one. The geometric beauty of it soothes my soul. I like to walk around it, counting my paces.

Romaine sits down on the rug beside me, but her eyes are still on my daughter whose beaming smile is like a splash of sunlight in the shade.

'Did you have a good time, Chloé?' I ask.

She nods vigorously, setting her long curls dancing. It strikes me that if my sister had not cut her own hair short, how similar the colour and texture of their hair would be. Not like mine, which has no sense of natural decorum. I have to wrestle it into submission each day.

'Tante Romy says it has a flying speed of two hundred metres per minute,' Chloé announces. She stands in front of us on the grass, holding the plane up in the air, admiring the RAF roundels on its silver fuselage and wings. She is wearing a white broderie anglaise dress. She looks like an angel.

'I am impressed,' I smile.

'It arrives in its box in flying trim, Tante Romy says. I like winding the rubber band.'

'You do it well, *chérie*.'

'It has a phenomenal climb angle, a flat glide and a safe landing speed,' my daughter informs me.

I blink.

Chloé adds, 'That's what Tante Romy says.'

Romaine laughs and I realise I can't remember the last time I heard her laugh.

'Tante Romy,' I state, 'seems to say a lot of things.'

My sister has the grace to blush. Because no six-year-old girl should be conversant with climb angles and glides and landing speeds. It is not quite decent.

Chloé takes to running around us, plane in hand, swooping it up and down through the air, but instead of looking at her, I observe Romaine. She looks a mess, though I suspect she has made an effort in my honour. She is wearing a cap-sleeved white blouse and a sand-coloured skirt, but both are old and in need of an iron. She rolls on to her stomach, propped up on her elbows, chin in her hands. Her movements are always smooth and effortless, as if she's made of air.

'You'll come to Monico's Club tonight, I hope,' I say softly. 'A car will pick you up at eight. Horst would like you to come. It's a long time since we spent an evening together and I'm looking forward to it.'

Her amber eyes slide sideways to inspect me, the sunlight catching her golden lashes that are so much longer than mine.

'Why?' she asks.

'It will be fun. Sisters together.'

She says nothing. Her gaze is on my face.

'You will enjoy it,' I smile.

She looks away, back to Chloé who is now sitting on the grass, the model plane on her lap like a pet.

'Who is Horst Baumeister?'

'I told you, Romaine. He is an important emissary from Germany who is here to negotiate a defence agreement with France. Roland is a minister in the Ministry of Defence – just like Papa was – and he has plans to ensure peace between our two countries. That's what we all want, isn't it?'

'Not on Hitler's terms, no. Not on Mussolini's terms in

Italy. Nor on General Franco's in Spain. No, not on their terms. They are Fascist monsters, they are dictators, they are tyrants who rip the hearts out of their people.'

She is so fierce. So convinced. I should leave it there, but I don't. I can't bear my sister to be so blinkered and a twitch of anger gets the better of me. Sometimes I think she takes the high moral stance just to prove she has a mind that is independent of Papa.

'Romaine, are you blind? Do you really want Communism to sweep across our countries and turn us into the Union of Soviet Socialist Europe? Do you? Because that's exactly what will happen if we don't have men like Hitler, Mussolini and Franco to stem the tide.' I lower my voice to a murmur. I don't want Chloé to hear. 'Look at Russia, Romaine. Look at the way Stalin is crippling his country and forcing Russians to live in terror. Is that what you want for us?'

My sister's mouth softens into the hint of a smile. 'I like it,' she tells me, 'when you care about something other than hats and evening gowns. Even if you are wrong.'

I leave it there. I need her to come tonight.

The gardens are beginning to fill up with Parisians strolling along the *allées* before the sun grows too hot, promenading arm in arm to show off the latest Chanel navy costume or a new *chanteuse* mistress. I summon Chloé to me and fold up the rug while Romaine de-wings the FROG aircraft – she tells Chloé it is British-made and its name stands for Flies Right Off the Ground. As she is packing it away in its box, I say what I have come here to say.

'Maman wishes to see you.'

Romaine freezes. Her eyes narrow. 'Why?'

'I don't know. She didn't say. Just asked me to pass on the message.'

'I am busy at the moment. Flying every day.'

'You must go to her, Romaine.'

'Why must I?'

I don't reply. She knows why she must go.

I walk into the Avenue Kléber apartment, toss my hat and lace gloves on to the marble hall table with a brusque gesture of annoyance, and head straight for the telephone. It isn't a call I want to make. But even as I pick up the receiver the delicate fragrance of the white roses around the hall drifts to me and I inhale it with a shiver of relief. It is always the same. The way their scent calms me. Soothes the turmoil of my meeting with my sister. The nursemaid, Amélie, wisely sweeps Chloé away to be washed and fed, full of chatter about flying her precious aeroplane with Tante Romy.

What about the doll I gave you, Chloé? The one with the genuine silky blonde hair and the flawless porcelain skin to match your own. What about her? You and I both know she still sits in her box.

I dial a number for Chantilly.

'Maman?'

'Florence, I've been waiting to hear from you.' My mother's voice is as smooth and controlled as always, but I pick out the ripple of some emotion that I can't quite place, an undercurrent that tugs at me despite the coolness of the tone. 'Did you see her?'

'Yes, Maman. I told you I was taking Chloé to the park with her.'

'Is that wise?'

I laugh softly. 'Trust me, Maman.'

'Is she any different? Has she . . .' A long, pointed pause. '. . . improved?'

'No.'

A harsh rush of air makes the receiver vibrate in my hand.

'Be patient, Maman.'

'Are you patient with her?'

'She is my twin. I love her, so of course I am patient.'

'Did you do as I asked?'

'Yes, I told her you want to see her.' I put my face into a smile to soften the edges of my words. 'She didn't look too happy about it but I let her know it was an official summons to Chantilly.'

I recall the tight mouth when I announced the summons, the amber eyes, as hostile and as focused as those of a lioness at bay.

'Will she come?' my mother demands.

'She'll come.'

'What makes you so sure?'

'Because I told her to.'

'When?'

'Be patient, Maman.'

'Will she telephone? It would be courteous to telephone to make an appointment.'

'She is your daughter, not your hairdresser.'

'Then tell her to act like one.'

Her words came out angry. With claws. They take me by surprise, but I give not a hint of it.

'She is attending one of Roland's functions as a favour to him tonight. Horst Baumeister will be there.'

I hear her intake of breath. 'Why?' she asks.

'He wants to see her.'

'Is that wise?'

'He's not giving me any choice.' I switch the subject. 'I will remind her to telephone you. But Maman . . .' My throat grows suddenly tight and nothing more comes out of my mouth except the whisper of a sigh.

'What is it, Florence?'

'Don't be too hard on her.'

'Why not? She deserves it.'

'I need her, Maman. Remember that.'

As soon as I replace the receiver, the telephone rings, sharp and insistent. I know it will be my mother again. I eye the black Bakelite instrument with disfavour and am tempted to leave it to ring, but with a shrug I pick it up.

'Did she say yes?' It is Roland.

'Yes.'

'Good. Well done.'

'I told her you would send a car for her at eight.'

'I'll arrange that.'

I can detect my husband's impatience to have the coming evening over and done with. 'Roland,' I say into the mouthpiece with caution, 'she wasn't happy about it.'

'Now why does that not surprise me?'

'She might back out.'

'Make certain she doesn't.'

There is a pause. Both of us breathing too hard.

'We went to the park,' I tell him.

He sighs. 'Did she ask you for money again?'

'Yes.'

'Did you give her any?'

'No.'

'Liar,' he says and hangs up.

CHAPTER TEN

FLORENCE

Roland lies next to me, naked on the bed. We are breathing hard as though we have been running and have just collapsed in a tangle of sheets. A sheen of sweat cocoons his pale skin and glistens on the silky hairs on his chest, catching the light from the bedside lamp.

I can smell him. I can smell our sated hunger still clinging to his muscular limbs, heavy and moist in the dense curls at his groin. And the scent of him, that musk of something feral, it stirs my body's need for him again even before my sweat has dried. I stretch out a hand and trail it lightly over his chest, aware of the muscles twitching like a cat's tail at the touch of my fingers.

I turn on my side to face him. Before I can stop it, my tongue slips out and licks the damp skin of his shoulder. He tastes deliciously salty. I restrain myself from sinking my teeth into his flesh.

'It's nearly seven o'clock,' I murmur lazily. 'We should be dressing for dinner. We'll be late at Monico's.'

He takes my hand from his chest, lifts it to his lips and kisses each finger. He would never bite me.

'Horst Baumeister has been talking with General Ludwig Beck in Berlin,' he tells my fingertips.

I lift my head, interested. 'Chief of the German military?'

'That's him.'

I tread with care. 'What did General Beck have to say?'

'Horst confirms what we suspected. Beck is firmly opposed to the increasing totalitarianism of the Nazi regime and Hitler's aggressive foreign policy.'

'Towards Sudetenland?'

'Exactly.' His hazel-brown eyes flick to mine with approval and then to my breasts, his pupils still huge with desire. 'Beck is all for Germany taking back Sudetenland from Czechoslovakia – the same way they took Austria with the Anschluss last March, but . . .' He pauses and I think for a second that it flits through his mind that he tells me too much, but I can see the thought is gone as soon as it came.

I bend my head and kiss his throat. I feel his pulse against my lips. I picture his heart, strong and vital, pumping blood to the exact spot where my lips touch.

'But what?' I prompt.

'But where Beck crosses swords with Hitler is that he does not believe the Third Reich is yet ready for war. He is certain that France and Britain will not stand idly by, not this time. He calls it a "premature war". He bemoans the fact that

Keitel is giving Hitler poor military advice, or so he believes. Steering the Führer up a blind path.'

'Is he?'

'No. The drive to war is coming from Hitler himself.' He twists a lock of my hair between his finger and thumb like a thread of spun sugar. 'General Beck believes our new prime minister here in France, Édouard Daladier, will sneak up and seize the Rhineland in the west while the Wehrmacht is off in the east chasing after Jews in Czechoslovakia. But war is heading for France, believe me.'

I kiss his mouth, full and hard. 'We have to be . . .'

'Careful?' he suggests.

'No,' I whisper in his ear. 'We have to be on the winning side. For Chloé's sake.'

He laughs, a full-throated bellow of amusement that rattles my ribs. 'You and Chloé will be safe, I promise. General Beck is a cunning one. That man knows the value of keeping one step ahead.'

'But Hitler's spies are everywhere.'

Roland wraps his hand around mine on his chest, pinning it there. 'You know that Beck has created his own intelligence attachés to collect and leak information in all the capitals of Europe.'

'Men like Horst Baumeister?'

Roland smiles. He is handsome when he smiles. He touches my breast and heat races through my veins and makes me want to spend my whole life in bed with my husband. I swing one leg over him and straddle him.

'Florence, I have to shower. No time for more of this now.'

I lower myself down on him, skin to skin, my breasts pressed so tight against his ribs that they hurt, my mouth so close to his, I breathe his breath.

'This evening is work,' I remind him and take his bottom lip between my teeth. 'It will not be fun.' I bite into his lip till it bleeds.

I watch my twin sister like a hawk. I watch the way she turns her head with the unconscious grace of a skylark in the air. I watch the way she laughs up into Horst Baumeister's face. The four of us are seated at a table, and I see her slide her tawny eyes at me. And at Roland. As though to say, 'See. I do as you ask. I do more than you ask. I dangle your German like a ripe cherry from my little finger.'

I am shocked. Pleased, but shocked. I can tell by the way Roland smokes his cigar with long satisfied gusts of smoke that he is pleased with Romaine too. And each time his tongue seeks out the scab on his lip, he looks at me. We smile.

I smile a lot in Monico's nightclub. It always buzzes with a feverish energy that makes the hair rise on the back of my neck and the blood fizz through my veins like champagne. But it's not just that. I love it here because I meet people. At various times I have been swept across the dance floor in the arms of England's Duke of Windsor himself, shared a bowl of Provençal olives with the delicious Cole Porter and slipped oysters down the greedy throat of Ernest Hemingway. Only last week I laughed with one of our loveliest French film stars, Ginette Leclerc, when she whispered tales of her attempts to seduce Marcel Pagnol, the director of her latest film, *La Femme du Boulanger*.

Here you don't have to be normal. Here in Monico's on Place Pigalle you can be anyone you choose to be. This is where the chic society of Paris gather in their jewels and their furs and their glossy evening wear to see and be seen, as gaudy as butterflies as the music plays with syncopated rhythm and we each weave our own secret fantasy. I watch my sister and I wonder what fantasy she is weaving as she nods her head solemnly at Horst Baumeister and sketches something on the pristine white tablecloth for him with her knife.

'She looks nice,' Roland comments under his breath.

He's not right. My twin sister looks more than nice, she looks striking. Slender in the elegant navy gown, she looks like a different creature. It makes her move differently, no tomboy foolery, but with a smooth stride, and when she entered the club at my side, heads turned. The usual well-heeled clientele scented new blood in their midst and they liked what they saw. But she held herself aloof and indifferent to them. That's what nettled them. That she didn't care for their opinion. It showed. It galled them.

I am wearing the most exquisite Schiaparelli evening gown in the room, biscuit-coloured and flaring into a beaded skirt that flows and glitters around me like sparkling water as I walk. My shoulders are bare, my skin buffed and smooth as silk. Diamonds at my throat. Yet they look at her. Not at me.

I know why. She is not one of them and they sense it, they can smell her scorn. She makes them nervous.

'Not as nice as you,' my husband smiles.

I shrug a bare shoulder. As if I don't care. But he knows me well.

'What is she playing at?' Roland asks with suspicion. He is seated next to me and drops his voice below the throb of the music, glamorous in his white bow tie and jet-black evening jacket. I am tempted to slide a hand the length of his arm but I quell the moment of desire.

'She is doing what I asked,' I say. 'Being nice to Horst. That's what you wanted, isn't it?'

'Since when has she ever done what we ask?'

It isn't true. But I let it pass.

Roland takes out his silver cigarette case that gleams under the chandelier and offers a Sobranie. He carries them just for me. I accept one, slot it into my ivory holder, and Roland and I lean our heads closer as he lights it for me, so close I can smell the musk of his aftershave.

'What does Horst want from her?' I murmur. 'Why did he insist on her being here tonight?'

'I wish I knew.' Roland's eyes harden as he flicks a glance at them across the table, engrossed in the knife drawing. 'He says he finds her intriguing.'

'I worry.'

'We have reason to.'

'How long is he staying in Paris?'

'As long as he likes.'

I feel my skin spasm, as though spiders are crawling up my arms, and I exhale a skein of smoke to cover my unease. The German is questioning my sister minutely about something, some detail of the drawing. I squint at it.

'An engine,' Roland mutters in my ear, irritated.

Horst Baumeister is a good-looking man, in a German kind of way. Thick short blond hair swept straight back, strong regular features and a square jaw. Good skin. Intense blue eyes. Exactly the kind of man I'd expect Hitler to recruit to do his bidding. Just at that moment, Horst stands, smiles engagingly at my sister, then at us, and steers Romaine on to the crowded dance floor. A jazz number is playing, something achingly sad. The band of Negro musicians is swaying with the tempo and I observe my twin sister's feet. She acquits herself well. Horst's arms encircle her loosely, not trying to own her, and they talk while they dance. What about? What is it that they find to say to each other?

'*Bonsoir, mes amis.*'

I look up to find the flamboyant owner of Monico's nightclub beaming down at me. Bricktop is her name because of her red hair. Brick for short. She is an ebullient black-skinned American woman in her mid-forties who possesses a voice as rich as dark chocolate and a smile that warms the soul.

Brick started out as a cabaret jazz singer in Harlem, New York, but brought her unique style to Paris and we all fell under her spell. Her nightclub is all the rage and we flock here to listen to the finest jazz musicians in the world. Louis Armstrong and Duke Ellington love to perform here for her when in town, and Cole Porter wrote her signature tune for her, the irrepressible *Miss Otis Regrets.* Later she will be performing it for us, but right now Brick shimmies around the tables in her silver dress, stopping to kiss a cheek, rub a bald pate or tell a joke. She is smoking a cigar.

My husband rises to kiss her and she pats his cheek mischievously. 'It's good to see you here again, Roland. Because I hear you were slumming it at Mimi's measly place the other night.'

'Brick, you have the ears of a bat, my dear.'

They laugh and she asks, 'Who you brought for me tonight?' She likes to know who is in.

'A German colleague of mine.'

I spot the fleeting lift of her full lip, the closest she would permit herself to a snarl. I am confident my husband will have missed it.

'And my sister-in-law,' he adds.

As he speaks, the dancing couple detach from each other and make their way back across the crowded floor to rejoin us. Brick does not disguise her interest.

'Well now, Flo . . .' I hate her calling me Flo, 'that's a pretty little sister you got there.'

I ignore the inference that Romaine is younger than I am. I introduce them and we are all engrossed in pleasantries when a man approaches our table. Roland greets him warmly.

'Herr Müller, I'm delighted you could join us.'

Join us? Roland told me nothing of this.

The German has presence. He draws glances, both male and female. He is a large man with arrogant eyes that smile at us, but they are made of fine grey steel. Hair greying gracefully at the temples, and the most beautifully cut evening suit that frames his wide shoulders to perfection. A military man if ever I saw one, though he does not use his military rank tonight.

But something happens. I don't see it. Roland is talking with Brick and I am laughing at something she says, when I feel a sudden sense of shock. I know at once it is my sister, though I am not even looking at her. I turn to her, seated opposite me. Her face is as white as the tablecloth, her lips a sickly grey colour. No one else seems to notice. The two Germans are busy talking to each other and the tables around us buzz with champagne-fuelled laughter as the lilting music of *Embraceable You* swirls around us.

'Romaine,' I say urgently.

She does not hear. Her eyes have the glazed look of someone who has been slapped. Slapped hard. Her hand reaches forward, ignores her own champagne but grips Roland's whisky glass and she drinks it straight down. She pushes herself awkwardly to her feet, deaf to all comments, and moves immediately to my side. She seizes my wrist, her fingers strong.

'Come,' she orders.

I am angry. I don't know why, but I am consumed by an anger that burns the inside of my cheek as I try to bite back the words that threaten to burst out. What the hell is she doing?

I want to shake her.

But I look at the state of her and I can't. She has dragged me into a powder room, flicked on the light and shut the door firmly behind us, leaning her back against it to prevent anyone else entering. The powder room is typical of Monico's, an extravaganza of black and gold geometric design. Romaine's face is still paper-white but two red flares have lodged high on her cheeks, and her amber eyes are the dull, lifeless colour of mud. Her hand does not release my wrist.

'What on earth is the matter with you, Romaine? You must have scared the hell out of Horst.'

Her tongue flicks over her dry lips. 'I was there.' Her grip tightens till my bones ache. 'I *remember* being there.'

I do not ask where *there* is. For both of us there is only one *there*.

My father's study.

I stroke the back of her hand to calm her. Not that she is frantic or shouting. Nothing violent. Rather, she has turned inward, staring wide-eyed at whatever terrible sight has awoken inside her head.

'Tell me,' I say. 'What happened just now?'

'It was the Germans.'

'What?'

'Horst and Herr Müller. Hearing them talk.'

I frown, not understanding.

'They were speaking German to each other,' she explains, impatient with me. 'The sound of it triggered a memory.'

'What kind of memory, Romaine?'

But she does not respond. Her skin is cold. A corpse kind of cold, as though the warm blood has drained out of her. I can't have her like this. It's too dangerous. Not right under the Nazi noses. She is here to do the job of entertaining Horst, whether she wants to or not.

'You must not let Roland down,' I say quietly.

I break free from her hold on me and take her face between my hands, but it is like holding glass. I fear she will break.

'Look at me,' I order.

Slowly, painfully slowly, her unfocused gaze shifts and I see something slot back into place within her. She looks at me. Properly looks at me.

'Florence, I heard someone speaking German to Papa that day. It came to me just now. I was curled up in his reading chair in his study and I must have fallen asleep because . . .' She rubs a hand across her forehead, trying to drag the memory out by force. 'Because I remember being woken by a voice . . .' She pauses.

'Whose voice?'

'A German one.'

Papa's reading chair was a black leather wing-backed chair on a swivel base. Romaine had been in the habit of sneaking in sometimes, snaffling a book and spinning herself in the chair, so that it faced the corner, hiding its occupant. It was hot that day, I recall, the bees droning in the honeysuckle, and it would be easy to nod off to sleep over a book. I can picture it. Her blonde head lolling against the wing of the chair, her book sliding to her lap, Papa entering, unaware of her presence in his study.

'A German voice?' I echo. 'Why would there be a German voice in Papa's study? He was alone. The police established that.'

'I know. That's what doesn't make sense. Someone was speaking to him in German.'

I release her face and say softly, 'It is not possible, Romaine. He was alone. You must have been dreaming and thought you heard someone else in the room but the conversation was inside your head. Part of a dream. Nothing more.'

'It seemed real.'

It is her stubborn voice.

'I'm sure it did, but the police report stated there was no one else in the house. Roland and I were in the garden, Maman and the maid in the kitchen so—'

'Why would someone speak to Papa in German?'

'Romaine, listen to me. It didn't happen. Now let's get back out there, the men will be waiting for us.'

There is a pause. It slots into the gulf between us and I wait for her to break it. Finally she moves away to the row of handbasins, turns on a gold tap and washes her hands in cold water. It goes on so long I think she is never going to stop scrubbing at stains that only she can see.

'Enough,' I say.

She stops. Dries her hands.

'Roland will be worried. We'll say you felt unwell.'

She joins me at the door.

'Smile,' I say.

She smiles. There is an awful stillness to her face. I open the door.

'It was a dream,' I assure her. 'Just a dream'

CHAPTER ELEVEN

Romy returned to Roland's table. She didn't want to sit down. She wanted to flee. But she had promised her sister, so she resumed her seat and did not risk looking in Roland's direction.

She excused her sudden departure from the table earlier with some vague words about feeling briefly unwell, and brushed aside Horst's expression of concern. He stared at her pale face and she could feel that he was about to say more, but his intelligent blue eyes softened and he gave a brief Germanic nod. Instead he murmured, 'Let me pour you a drink,' and lifted the champagne bottle from its ice bucket.

She declined the offer, though it was like declining air. A small fragile flame of memory had been lit. She had no intention of dousing it with alcohol. Not this time.

Had she really heard German spoken in her father's study? Or was Florence right? Was it a figment of a dream that had floated up into her consciousness?

She drank a mouthful of water to dissipate the acid taste in her mouth and almost spat it out, it was so insipid. She felt confusion cloud her mind and then, hard on its heels, fear. It crept up on her, its breath cold on the back of her neck. Who was this person who seemed to be invisible inside her father's house eight years ago, unknown to the police investigators or even to her mother in the kitchen? In her head she could still just catch the echo of the foreign cadences, faint and elusive, and she turned quickly to Horst.

'Speak German to me.'

He looked surprised and she could see that he has misunderstood her.

'You didn't tell me you understand German,' he said. '*Du sagtest mir gar nicht, dass du Deutsch sprechen kannst. Möchtest du mit mir tanzen, Romaine*?'

She concentrated, waiting for the sound of the words to settle in her mind, but it triggered nothing more. She closed her eyes but no image of her father's study flared inside her head. Horst's hand gently touched her arm and her eyes flicked open.

'What is it, Romaine?'

'Nothing.'

'Would you like me to take you home?' he offered in a voice too low for others to hear. 'If you are feeling unwell, you shouldn't stay here with all this noise and—'

'Romaine, may I have a private word?'

It was Roland.

'Whatever you have to say, Roland, I'm sure you can say it in front of your friend Horst.'

The smoothness of her brother-in-law's smile didn't falter but he ran the palm of his hand along the side of his glossy black hair, an unconscious gesture when he was annoyed. Romy had seen it over the years, too often for comfort.

But Roland sidestepped her. 'Horst, *mon ami*, you don't mind, do you, if I steal your companion from you for a few minutes?'

Horst Baumeister's ice-cool blue eyes studied Roland for longer than was strictly polite and then switched to Romy.

'On the contrary, Roland, I do mind. I have just asked Romaine to dance with me and she has kindly agreed.'

He rose to his feet, took Romy's hand and led her quietly away from Roland towards the dance floor.

'*Merci*,' Romy said.

Romy could smell Horst's cologne as they danced. He was holding her close. But not too close. Just enough for them to talk without having to shout over the music and the laughter of the other dancers. The whole ritual of dancing was odd to Romy, the whole idea that it was socially acceptable to be in an intimate position with a near stranger. Hip to hip, hands entwined. That was why Romy didn't like to dance. If she was going to indulge in intimacy with a stranger, hell, she'd rather do it in a bedroom than a ballroom.

Horst was an excellent dancer. Light, skilled, attentive. He effortlessly avoided her missteps, but all the time as the band crooned out *Dream a Little Dream of Me*, she was acutely aware of his hand on her back. On her naked back, skin against skin. Was that why her sister had dolled her up like a mannequin with the back half of her dress missing? To tempt this German.

What was the purpose? Why did they need to tout her around for Horst Baumeister's entertainment? Weren't there enough *putains* in Paris already?

'You don't like your brother-in-law,' Horst smiled.

'Is it that obvious?'

'You cover it well, I assure you.'

'Obviously not well enough.'

He laughed, soft and easy, making her laugh too.

'So if you don't like your brother-in-law, why spend the evening with him?'

She liked that about him. That he talked straight. No hiding behind neat words.

'What made you come here tonight, Romaine?'

'You. It was Florence who invited me, not Roland. She said you would be here and I thought it would be an interesting evening. I was right.'

It was the truth. She hadn't expected to find someone among the sparkling socialites at Monico's nightclub who could talk Pratt & Whitney engines, as they had earlier. He was the reason she was here.

'I'm glad you came,' he said.

There it was again, that straightness.

He spun her expertly out of the path of a couple of dancers who were weaving unsteadily across the floor with an empty champagne glass still dangling in one hand.

'You are the first female pilot I have ever met.' He smiled broadly. 'Certainly the first aviatrix I have danced with, so this evening is a special one. Tell me, Romaine, how you go it alone up there in a flimsy crate. It is beyond me. I admire your courage. And the way you are pushing the boundaries for women, opening up new horizons.'

'I don't think of it like that.'

'How do you think of it then?'

'I am opening up my own horizons. That's enough for me.'

'We will need people like you when war comes.'

Suddenly his German accent was heavier, his consonants more pronounced. Until now he'd spoken French with very little accent, but now Germany loomed larger in his mind. 'Women are going to have to step up to the plate and do jobs that . . .'

When war comes? A shudder ran through Romy at the ease with which the words slipped from his tongue. She looked up at him intently. He was half a head taller than she was. 'You really think it will happen?'

He danced her through a full ten bars of music before he replied, 'No, I don't.'

'You are a poor liar, Horst Baumeister.'

He could have been annoyed at that. But he wasn't. He laughed, a low rumble of a laugh, and tightened his hold on her as though fearing she might make a run for it. It was impossible not to warm to him. His eyes would be labelled blue, but it would be inaccurate because they ranged from a deep greyish-navy to almost ice-white at times, depending on the thoughts treading behind them. A perfect Aryan face. The face of Germany in Paris.

'I am not lying, Romaine. I had dinner a couple of weeks ago with Generalmajor Hugo Sperrle who has Hitler's ear. I assure you he was confident that there will be no war between France and Germany.'

'Isn't he the one who commanded the Condor Legion in Spain and bombed the hell out of Guernica? That Generalmajor Sperrle?'

The edges of his mouth tightened a fraction. 'You are extremely well informed.'

'I read the newspapers.'

But she had said too much.

He fixed his gaze on her face, sharp as a bayonet, and said softly, 'The Führer does not want a war.'

She stared straight back at him. 'Anyone who believes that is a fool.'

Romy didn't know why she said it. So bluntly. So carelessly.

Anyone who believes that is a fool.

She regretted them now. When a saxophone riffed to the end of its solo, she and Horst had returned to their seats, her beaded hem swaying like a chill wave around her ankles, and Roland made no move to corner her again. Horst continued to be polite and attentive, but there was no more talk of courage or engines. She had forfeited that, it seemed. In his mind she had clipped her wings. Crashed and burned.

The rest of the evening flitted past in fits and starts, slightly out of focus, but punctuated by sudden moments of pinpoint clarity. Like when Roland kissed her cheek and murmured in her ear, 'You are cleverer than I thought, Romaine.' Or when their flamboyant hostess, Bricktop, delivered a sultry rendition of Cole Porter's *Begin the Beguine*, caressing the microphone as if it were her lover's lips. Then, crystal clear, came the sight of Florence frowning at her across the table, the muscles taut in her beautiful long neck, though Romy had no idea why.

The music shifted from the smooth and mellow tones of Sweet Jazz to the faster brasher sound of Hot Jazz. Around them the revellers in the nightclub laughed and drank and foxtrotted with a wildness, kicking up their heels as if the dance floor were made of hot coals. As if to stop would be to die. An air of desperation hung in the room, a sense of seizing the good times while they were here and wringing every last drop out of them. Dark shadows were stretching across Europe and no one knew what was hiding in them.

Herr Müller slid smoothly into the seat beside Romy, startling her. For a big man he moved well. She was boxed in between the two Germans and could not help feeling suddenly uneasy.

'So where do you fly off to in this aircraft of yours?' Müller asked with no more than what appeared to be polite interest. His accent was strong, but so was his grasp of French.

'To different parts of France mainly. Delivering packages or people.'

'You fly abroad?'

'Sometimes. Mainly to England. To Croydon airport. I was there last week, transporting a factory owner to a meeting in London.'

She looked closely at the military-looking man with his arrogant grey eyes that were too interested in her. Far too interested – she wanted to know why. He spoke French with a clipped delivery, as if his words came tightly packaged. She could imagine him laying down the law in meetings with his French counterparts, even with Deputy Premier Chautemps and Prime Minister Édouard Daladier, she could picture him placing his Nazi jackboot on their feeble and flaccid necks.

France was deluding itself. She was aware of that. Earlier this month Daladier's government had flaunted its military power in Germany's face, a slap of a Gallic glove across their Teutonic neighbour's cheek. On Bastille Day, 14 July, the greatest display of France's martial might for thirty years paraded down the Champs Élysées. A rippling sea of thirty thousand men had marched in strict formation from the Arc de Triomphe to the Place de la Concorde. They presented a rigid salute to the President of the Republic, Albert Lebrun, to Daladier himself and to César Campinchi and Guy La Chambre, ministers for the Navy and the Air Force.

Romy had been there. Stunned by the pride beaming from the faces of the young men in uniform, she had wanted to cry. Didn't they realise what they were marching towards? The shouts and cheers from the crowd watching the parade had deafened her for the two hours of the march-past.

The Guards, the Marines, the Chasseurs, the Cavalry, the Hussars, the Dragoons, the Cuirassiers and then the deep rumble of the heavy motorised divisions that made the air in her chest vibrate and heat up so she couldn't breathe properly. Tanks rolled past her like tigers on fragile leads, row after row after row of them. A threat it was impossible for Germany to ignore.

Romy wondered now whether Herr Müller had been there on Bastille Day. Had he seen them? Did they make him nervous? She let her gaze linger on his straight, humourless mouth and the heavy bulk of his jaw. No, this was a man who didn't frighten easily.

'I like to shop in Regent Street,' she told him, 'so I always jump at making flights to London. Have you been there?'

If she kept talking about London, if she made him think she was a frivolous spendthrift like her sister, it might not occur to him to mention Spain.

'Many years ago I studied in London,' he said. 'But tell me, Fräulein, do you ever fly to Spain?'

Her eyes widened theatrically and she shuddered. 'Far too dangerous, Herr Müller.'

She needed a drink.

'Where are you flying this week, Romaine?' Horst Baumeister asked on her other side, his hand lying close to hers on the table. She couldn't tell whether it was meant to be protective or aggressive. She glanced across at Roland opposite. He was talking to Florence but his eyes could not stay away from the Germans.

Romy shrugged. 'I never know where I'll be flying until I get to the airfield.'

'Which airfield do you fly out of?' Herr Müller pressed her.

'Why do you ask?'

'I am interested in you. You are a rarity, an exotic aviatrix. We don't have many in Germany.' He smiled and something about it scared Romy, his teeth too white and flawless to be his own. He raised his silver-tipped eyebrows and waited for the name of the airfield.

She had no intention of laying a trail to Léo Martel.

'I've never flown to Germany either. Where would you recommend for a first visit if ever I do, Herr Müller?'

'Berlin.' He took the bait with enthusiasm. 'You must come to Berlin. The Führer, with his architect Albert Speer, is transforming it into Europe's finest city.' He stretched his lips across his gleaming white teeth in what Romy assumed was a smile. 'You would be my special guest.'

It felt like a threat, but she must be imagining it. He could know nothing. To her surprise it was her sister who came to her rescue. Florence leaned forward across the table, offering the merest flash of creamy cleavage. 'Do tell us, Herr Müller, what Herr Hitler's plans are.' She added with an artless tilt of her head. 'For Berlin I mean, of course. What are his plans for Berlin?'

'To expand.'

'To expand where?'

'The people of Germany need more *Lebensraum*.'

Lebensraum. Space to live.

No one mentioned Sudetenland. No one mentioned Czechoslovakia. Or the fact that if Hitler ordered his army into that part of Czechoslovakia, France was treaty-bound to go to war to defend it. Instead Müller lifted Romy's hand to his lips and repeated, 'You must come to Berlin. I insist.'

Horst Baumeister balanced her hand on his. Only lightly. But even so, his strong fingers looped around hers and she could feel the pressure of them. She was on the dance floor with him again. Better than being seated next to Müller, who had all the charm of a crocodile. She had not yet worked out what that man's interest in her was.

As Horst spun her across the dance floor, it occurred to Romy that if neither Daladier nor the British Prime Minister Chamberlain could keep German troops out of Sudetenland, Horst Baumeister would have to don a grey uniform and pick up a rifle. She looked up at his lean handsome face and tried to imagine it. She couldn't. He was too sane, too interested in the inner workings of a Gipsy Moth engine. Only mad men went to war.

She wondered if he'd ever seen a dead body.

'Seeing a ghost?' he murmured.

She looked away and withdrew her hands. She'd had enough of tonight. She walked off the dance floor straight to the exit door.

'I'm sorry,' Horst said behind her. 'I didn't mean to cause you upset.'

'You didn't. I'm not used to this kind of evening and it . . .' she gave a small grimace, 'defeats me.'

He laughed outright. 'This from the woman who flies in an open cockpit, a bundle of glue and matchsticks and flimsy fabric through a storm. Don't let a nightclub chase you away.'

The noise of the club rushed at Romy. She looked back at the table where her sister was seated with Roland and Müller, deep in conversation, heads together.

'What exactly does Herr Müller do?' she asked.

Horst's tone was suddenly more formal. 'He is leading a mission to negotiate with the French government over plans that will ensure the continuation of peace between our two nations.'

'And you? What do you do?'

'I am part of that mission.'

'I hope you succeed.'

The prospect of failure was too terrible to contemplate. It thinned the air around them.

'Goodnight, Horst.' Romy held out her hand. 'It has been interesting.'

He shook her hand but did not release it. He drew her fractionally closer, leaning his head nearer hers. He smelled fresh and clean, as if the fog of cigarette smoke could find no hold on him.

'Have dinner with me tomorrow night?' he asked.

She didn't blink. Didn't spit in the face of the person who was part of the Nazi regime bombing the hell out of Spain.

'Why?' she asked.

'Because I want to know more about you.'

'I'm busy tomorrow,' she said softly.

'The weekend then?'

'I always take my niece to the park on a Sunday.'

'So Saturday?'

Her head flicked a brief nod. 'Saturday.'

He smiled at her. 'I'll pick you up at seven at your—'

'No. I'll meet you. At Le Chat Noir restaurant in rue des Dames. Saturday evening.'

She reclaimed her hand. The blue of his eyes had darkened but she didn't know him well enough to tell whether it was pleasure or annoyance.

'Let me take you safely home,' he offered.

'Thank you, but no. Go back to the table and give my sister my apologies. She will be annoyed.'

She opened the door and walked out. When she glanced back through the glass panel, he was still watching her.

Paris breathed on her. Its night scents a mix of tobacco, bad sewers and the city's loneliness. Romy inhaled a lungful of it to rid her of the stink of German complacency that was clogging her nostrils and turned sharply into a cobbled alleyway that was wreathed in darkness. At the far end of it a bar spilled a triangle of light on to the cobbles even at this late hour.

She could hear voices within. A Parisian will seek out his glass of wine day or night, as surely as the earth keeps turning. In her hand lay her coat that she had scooped up from the kiosk just inside the nightclub's entrance, and for a moment she paused, aware of the thinness of the material between her fingers.

Alone in the blackness, squeezed between the sleeping houses, she sloughed off her fancy couture gown and dropped it to the ground, a navy skin that crushed her too tight. She stepped out of her dainty navy shoes and slid her bare arms into her coat. She wrapped it around her and buttoned it for decency. She walked away from the navy blue reminder of her sister and into the bar.

There was always a twenty-franc note tucked into her underwear. For emergencies. She knew herself too well.

CHAPTER TWELVE

A note came for Romy before dawn. Delivered by the lame kid who hung around the DeFosse airfield, doing odd jobs and washing down the Gipsy's wheels whenever he got the chance.

The note was brief. Three words in Martel's strong disciplined hand. *No flights today.*

That was it. No explanation. No details. Romy's first instinct was to head out to the airfield anyway to see what had gone wrong, but she thought better of it. The note meant Martel didn't want her there. Otherwise he wouldn't have bothered sending the boy over with it. So what was going on?

What had gone wrong?

It could be trouble with the aircraft, an engine requiring a replacement part. Or a bad weather report down south. Or some kind of problem with the airfield itself. An accident? That happened sometimes, and when it did, the runway needed attention. Romy's mind was racing through the possible causes of the delay and each one added more fuel to the fire of her concern.

As soon as it was light she stripped off her flying gear, pulled on her blue dungarees and a cardigan and slunk downstairs to the bar on the corner of her street, which was just blinking into life. She sat at one of the pavement tables still in deep shadow, sipped scalding black coffee and thought about the two Germans last night.

'Maman, did Papa speak German?'

'Of course not.'

'Are you sure? Didn't he work with them?'

'Of course I'm sure. You think I didn't know him?' One elegant eyebrow lifted quizzically. 'Why do you ask, Romaine?'

'I remember hearing German spoken in his study one day, but can't recall whether it was Papa or someone else.'

'It must have been someone else,' her mother said dismissively. Matter closed.

They were strolling through her mother's garden, a place as rigid and carefully designed as a patchwork quilt. It was all miniature box hedges, cropped lavender ridges and amber paths that inserted grit into Romy's sandals as though testing her spartan spirit. The sun beat down, turning bare skin pink, but her mother revelled in it, as boneless as a cat in its heat.

Each time Romy entered her mother's house, a small, vital part of her died. It was the overflow of guilt; it dripped like acid inside her every time she looked at her mother. Every time she heard her voice. Every time she could not withdraw her gaze from the deepening of the soft wrinkles that had stolen on to her face in the eight years since the violence in the study.

Adelle Duchamps still wore black. Her dresses were all black as death, black as the grave, black as the sin that was committed. Beautifully cut, stylishly designed. But black. After the trial of Karim Abed she had moved to this oak-shaded villa in Chantilly, far too large for her, but it was as if she had something to say, a statement to make by choosing this house for herself. *I may have lost my powerful husband from my side but I am still someone to be reckoned with. Do not write me off.*

Romy didn't write her off. That's why she steered clear of her. She did not put it past her mother one day to work out exactly what had happened. The thought sent cold shivers down her spine.

'How are you, Romaine?'

'I'm well.'

Her mother's cool blue-eyed glance, identical to her other daughter's, slid over Romy. 'You don't look well. You look . . .' she paused and swallowed awkwardly, as though pushing aside a harsh word that lay on the tip of her tongue. 'You look tired. Do you ever sleep?'

Romy laughed, making light of it. 'Not if I can help it.'

'Are you still risking your neck in those . . .' she drifted a hand skywards, 'machines?'

'Yes, I'm still flying. But not today. I've come here to see you instead, Maman.' As she spoke, she slid her hand through her mother's arm and the sudden physical closeness made her mother's step falter for a brief moment, but she recovered quickly. She patted Romy's hand with her own, stiffly, uncomfortably. Romy could feel her mother's desire to bridge the yawning chasm between them but also could sense her bewilderment as to how to go about it.

For a full minute they walked in silence, attached to each other by the slender thread of Romy's arm as they watched a flock of starlings take flight from one of the oak trees, their wings glittering like shattered glass against the fierce blue of the sky.

'Romaine, I realise that your father's death hit you hard. I understand why you have gone crazy . . .'

Romy's cheeks flamed.

'Why have you asked me here today, Maman?'

'Because I have something to give you.'

'There's no need to give me anything.'

She had rejected outright the inheritance from her father. She could take nothing from the man she'd killed. Or from the mother she'd robbed of her husband.

Adelle Duchamps steered them both down a gravel pathway that had been freshly raked and jerked her head in the direction of the French windows that stood open into the salon.

'Come,' she said.

*

'It is time to pull yourself together, Romaine. Time to stop thinking only of yourself.'

Only of yourself.

Romy thought of young Samir Abed with his school-books on his shoulder. Of the manila envelope propped up in Aya Abed's living room each month. She imagined the pilots strapped into the planes that she had flown south to Spain.

Only of yourself.

'Yes, Maman.'

Only then did she look more closely at her mother's face, putting her own nerves and irritations aside. She saw the way the skin was taut over her cheekbones, something knotted tight beneath it. Her mother wore her tinted fair hair in a tapered shingle, so shapely that it made her look younger and more carefree than her fifty-four years. But her eyes were not carefree. Her eyes were frightened.

'What is it, Maman?' Romy asked gently.

They were seated at a low marquetry table in the salon where coffee and lemon madeleines had been laid out by the maid. Romy had no appetite for sponge cakes.

'What is the matter, Maman?'

'I want you to have this.'

From a delicate Louis Quatorze bureau with gilded legs her mother removed a small casket. No larger than a cigar box. It was made of vivid emerald malachite that seemed to glow from within. She placed it on Romy's lap. Romy didn't touch it.

'Do you recognise the box, Romaine?'

She nodded. How could she not?

'It used to sit on the windowsill in your Papa's study.'

'I know.'

'I want you to have it.'

'I don't want it.'

'I want you to have it,' she said again. 'I want you to understand that your father loved you.'

'And you, Maman? Can you still love me?'

Her mother sighed. 'Whatever happened that day is best left in the past, Romaine. You are my daughter and always will be.'

'I don't want the box.' Romy tucked her hands behind her back but she caught the sudden flash of sadness in her mother's eyes. So she reached for the box. Flipped open its lid. Inside lay her father's gold pocket watch, just the sight of it wrenched something loose inside her. It was an eighteen-carat gold full-hunter by Patek Philippe and its soft heartbeat tick stopped Romy's breath.

She closed the lid on it, put the box to one side of her seat and rose to her feet. She gripped her mother's arms, bird bones under the black tulle sleeves. When had she grown so thin?

'What is this about, Maman? What are you so worried about?'

Romy thought she would reply, *You. I am worried about you.* But that's not what her mother said.

'I am worried about your sister.'

'Florence?'

'Yes.'

'Why Florence?'

Her mother broke free, walked across the room and stood with her poker-straight back towards her daughter. She remained like that for a long moment, and when she finally did turn, her eyes were full of tears.

'She needs help,' she whispered.

'Florence needs help?'

'Yes.'

'Why?' Romy felt a sharp stab of panic. 'What's the matter with her?'

'Can't you see that something is wrong?'

'No, Maman, I was with her last night and she was her usual charming, glamorous self.'

'Then you weren't looking.'

You weren't looking.

It was true.

She wasn't looking. She'd only had eyes for the Germans.

Romy raced all the way back to Chantilly station, the pavement warm beneath her feet, the lime trees casting welcome pools of shade. On the train, as it rattled its way back to the centre of Paris, she closed her eyes and ran through every minute of the previous evening. She unpicked each single stitch of last night's tapestry of gaiety and music, with its gleaming diamonds and its laughter so sharp it could cut right through you. But this time she stripped Horst Baumeister and Herr Müller out of the picture.

She focused on Florence. On her sister's eyes. On the exact shade and shape of them. On her ever-ready smile. On the softness of her lips. On a tiny line of tension in one corner of them, almost nothing. On the graceful swanlike line of her neck and shoulders. There had been no drooping. No rigidity. Nothing. Nothing in her laughter and the languid gestures of her hands to suggest anything but complete enjoyment of the evening and the company.

There was nothing wrong. Her mother was imagining it.

Her mother had insisted that something was wrong because Florence had changed.

'In what way?' Romy had asked.

'Her manner is different. She has become secretive. Withdrawn. Cut off.'

Was that true? No. Romy couldn't see it. But then she had to ask herself how well she knew her twin sister these days and the answer came back quickly. Not well. Not now. Not for the last eight years.

'Madame is not at home, Mademoiselle Romaine.'

Romy stared at the pale young face of Yvette, her sister's maid, who relished exercising her small sliver of power over visitors. She started to close the door.

'When will my sister be back?' Romy pressed her.

'Madame didn't say.'

'Is Chloé home?'

'No. She is out for a walk with her nanny.'

That was it. The door continued to close.

'Yvette, I would like to make a telephone call.'

'Yes, Mademoiselle Romaine.'

'Don't worry, it will be brief.'

The maid looked uneasy about agreeing to it, as if she thought Romy might pocket the silver, but she had little choice but to allow her employer's sister into the apartment and to withdraw discreetly from the room. The moment the salon door clicked shut, Romy dialled the number of the DeFosse airfield. Léo Martel answered immediately, his voice tense.

'Are you all right?' she asked.

'Yes.' A pause. 'Though it's hot as hell here today. That's a Parisian summer for you, same as usual. No wind at all. But they say it will rain tonight, thank God.'

'Good. I'll take an umbrella if I go out.'

'You do that. I'm busy right now, so must get on.'

'Of course.'

She hung up.

Martel was all right. Relief hunched in a knot under her breastbone and she walked over to one of the tall windows to stare up at the sky, a sheet of intense blue stretched so tight over the city that it looked as though it might split. Beneath it, the ash-grey roofs rippled in the heat haze. She longed to be up there, flying away from all this.

Her few words with Martel had prepared her. He was

telling her that there would be a meeting tonight. Usual time, usual place.

But she must be alert for trouble.

Whatever was going on at the airfield did not sound good.

CHAPTER THIRTEEN

Romy waited another hour. Only then did a key turn in the lock, but it wasn't Florence. There was the sound of childish chatter and Chloé flew into the room and into her arms. It was as though a hand had reached out and dragged down the black curtains that were keeping the sunlight from her day. Romy breathed in the warm young scent of her niece and bestowed kisses on her sweet-tasting rosy cheeks. The Breton nanny, who stood quietly in the doorway with a shy smile, left them to play alone. They made aeroplanes out of sheets of paper and sent them swooping up to the ceiling with shouts of 'Contact' and 'Chocks away', while Chloé scampered over the chairs, stretching her arms to catch the planes. Romy loved watching her determination, her fearlessness of mind and body.

The game came to an abrupt halt when Chloé snatched one of the white darts out of the air and crumpled it into a ball. She stared at the destruction in her hand, her soft young fingers wrapped around it.

'Tante Romy, there is a boy in my class called Daniel. The other boys tease him. He is Jewish. They say all Jews in Germany are kept in cages.'

The laughter in Romy curled up and died.

'No, Chloé, that is not true, *ma chérie*. Of course they're not kept in cages. Jews in Germany are having a difficult time, but there are no cages. I promise you.'

Citizenship revoked, yes. Political rights denied, yes. Excluded from all professions and their businesses shut down, yes. Windows smashed. Family spat on. Beaten up. Imprisoned for any sexual relations with Aryans. Yes. Yes. Treated as lower than animals with tainted blood. But no cages. Not yet.

The child was upset. Bewildered by a glimpse of an adult world that showed no mercy. Her hand tightened around the paper plane. 'They say Jews are not allowed to fly aeroplanes in Germany. That is *merde*.'

Romy let the swear word slip past. Had Chloé picked it up from her? So she went over, knelt on the floor and drew Chloé gently on to her lap, looping her arms around the child.

'It is wrong for people to do things like that to another human being, Chloé.' She kissed the hot little head as it leaned against her collarbone. 'And each one of us has to stand up against bullies. So make sure you show Daniel that you are his friend, even when—'

A sound reached them. It was the front door of the apartment closing. Footsteps approached across the tiled hall, but they were not her sister's.

*

'Romaine! What the hell are you doing here?' It was Roland.

He looked hot. Irritated. His black hair gleaming. His white shirt clammy on him. To Romy he seemed out of place in this calm and elegant room, but probably no more than she did.

'I am waiting for Florence,' she said.

'Wasn't last night enough for you? Leave her alone.'

'I need to speak with her.'

Roland made a show of looking around the room as though his wife might be hiding somewhere. The implication made Romy's cheeks redden.

'No,' Roland stated flatly. 'She's not here.' His voice remained polite. 'Goodbye, Romaine. I'll tell her you called.' He held out a hand to his daughter. 'Come here, Chloé.'

She scampered across to him. As he bent to kiss her young cheek his gaze held Romy's. He had stolen the child from her and there was a flicker of triumph in his eyes. It was rare for Romy to be in Roland's company without Florence present. She couldn't remember the last time. It was something they both avoided. She stood up and stepped closer to him until only a couple of metres of richly polished parquet floor separated them.

'I need to ask you a question,' she said.

'Is it really necessary?'

'Yes.'

'Keep it brief.'

Chloé's curious eyes latched on to her father.

Romy kept her voice light and easy. 'Why is Horst Baumeister so interested in me?'

'How the hell should I know?' Roland gave a sharp snort of what was meant to be amusement. 'Maybe he has odd taste in women.'

Romy ignored the insult. 'Why are Müller and Horst here?'

'Don't be dense, Romaine. Florence told you. This is a critical time for our Prime Minister Daladier and his Socialist government. He is fighting to maintain peace and to curb Germany's inroads into Czechoslovakia, even though the Sudetenland is inhabited mainly by ethnic German speakers. For God's sake, it was part of Austria until the Versailles Treaty stole it from the Germans and gave it to Czechoslovakia. It rightly belongs to Germany.'

'As do the Rhineland and Austria?'

'Exactly. Which is why Hitler has annexed them. Baumeister and Müller are here as part of a delegation from Germany to—'

'To negotiate. Yes, so Florence said. But why are they really here?'

'Are you accusing me of lying?'

Chloé's round eyes leaped to Romy's face.

Romy smiled quickly at the child, smothering any sign of anger. 'Roland, do you speak German?'

His eyes narrowed, suddenly watchful. 'Yes, of course I do. And English. I studied Classics at both Cambridge University and Heidelberg University. What of it?'

'Did you ever speak German to my father?'

'Don't be absurd. Of course not. Why would I?'

He opened the door of the salon for her, still gripping his daughter's small hand.

'*Au revoir*, Romaine. I will inform Florence that you were here.'

She stood her ground. 'Did you see anybody, Roland? That day. In my father's study.'

A sound of impatience escaped him. 'I gave evidence on oath in court. You were there. So you know I saw no one. Enough of this nonsense.'

He turned away from her and she walked across the hall to the front door of the apartment but when she reached it she found Chloé at her heels.

'I'll see you on Sunday as usual, *chérie*,' she said as she embraced her and then disentangled herself from the child's arms.

Roland stood watching them in silence.

Once in the lift with the Lalique lamps and the muted whirr of the mechanics, Romy thought about her brother-in-law's stern face. They were bound to each other, Roland and herself, by a thin thread that neither could break.

CHAPTER FOURTEEN

FLORENCE

I enter the apartment. Kick off my shoes. At once I can sense her. Not in person. But in the air, something faint and distant, a wisp of her breath. I can smell her as surely as I can smell my own skin.

Romaine. What were you doing in my home?

My first thought is for Chloé. But I check her room and all is well. My daughter is safe in bed. It is always my fear. That one day my sister will take her.

Quietly I open the door to the salon and find my husband waiting with his back to me. He is in front of the fire screen, both hands gripping the edge of the high mantelpiece, so hard that his large knuckles stand out like white pebblestones. Tucked up beside the gilt curlicues of the clock sits a cut-glass whisky tumbler. It is half empty.

Or half full. Depending on your viewpoint.

To me it is half empty. I go to him. From behind, I wrap my arms around his broad chest. I cradle him, aware of the strong pounding of his heart under my hand. I press my breasts tight against his ribs. I kiss the back of his neck.

'What did she want?' I ask.

'You.'

Our eyes meet in the massive mirror fixed above the marble mantelshelf. He looks out at me from somewhere dark and labyrinthine and I grip him tighter.

'Why?' I ask.

He shakes his head. He doesn't know. I can imagine the scene, the tension as brittle as ice between them.

'She asked whether I spoke German to your father,' he adds.

A piece of me breaks loose. I stare back into the mirror. 'I will take her a bottle of whisky,' I say.

CHAPTER FIFTEEN

The black car was there again, the same one that had hung around the arrondissement last time they had a meeting. Romy spotted it the moment she entered Place d'Estienne d'Orves. The black Citroën. But this time it was tucked around the corner in a side street and she wondered what good it was doing down there. She moved through the dusk, the massive church of the Trinité with its ornate Renaissance façade and sixty-three-metre bell tower looming over the square, its stone figures keeping watch like spies.

It was a warm summer evening and the pavement cafés in the Place were brimming with Parisians enjoying a last glass of wine, and with lovers, hands entwined, delaying the moment of parting. The tips of cigarettes darted through the soft twilight like fireflies, and moths fluttered around the lamps, casting shadows. Romy had intended to head straight for the green door beside one of the cafés, the door that led up a steep flight of stairs to the meeting room, because she was eager to hear from Martel what was going on, what had upset his plans. But instead she veered to the left and ducked down the side street.

In the semi-darkness she could just make out a man in the driving seat of the Citroën and she felt a stab of annoyance when she saw he had fallen asleep on the job. According to Martel, he was supposed to be watching their backs. So what the hell was he doing here, the lazy bastard, with his chin on his chest and his felt hat pulled down over his eyes? She rapped her knuckles on the window, hard enough to startle him.

He didn't move.

A flicker of alarm made her uneasy. She tried the door. It opened.

Still he didn't move.

He was a big man, his beer gut jammed against the steering wheel and in the heat of the evening she could smell stale sweat on his skin. He was wearing a tight jacket and dark tie, his pale hands lying loose in his lap, crossed over each other like an old woman's. Under them lay something black. In the thick darkness of the alleyway it was hard to say for certain what it was, but it looked like a gun. It sent a chill through Romy.

'Monsieur?' she said urgently.

No response.

She jogged his arm. It felt stiff. She leaned inside the stuffy interior of the car and removed his hat. The man made no objection. He was bald and silent. Eyes closed. Mouth open.

A perfectly round bullet hole in the exact centre of his forehead stared right back at her.

Death.

It would not leave her alone.

Her hands panicked. They threw the hat back on to the freckled skin of his hairless pate to cover up the unblinking eye and slammed the car door shut. The bang of it reverberated through her, kick-starting thoughts that set her feet running before her mind had even had a chance to catch up. She clamped a hand over her mouth as she ran to stop it from screaming and tore around the corner back to the green door.

Someone was there. Before her. Opening it. Entering the building. In no hurry. Her breath came in gasps.

'Martel!'

He turned. A greeting started from his lips but froze at the sight of her.

'What? What's happened?' he demanded.

But she had no words. She pushed past him and raced up the stairs to the storeroom above the café. Maybe the others were late. Maybe they had not yet arrived.

This time. This one time. Let Grégory and François be late instead of always early. Please let them be . . .

They were there already, Grégory and François. The overhead bare bulb shone down on them, showing no mercy. The two friends were seated in their usual chairs, but instead of sitting upright they were slumped backwards, arms hanging loose at their sides as if their bones had been removed, heads tilted back. Grégory's Adam's apple looked huge and hairy in his scrawny neck. Romy had never noticed it before.

The third eye. It stared out from the centre of his forehead.

'Romy.'

Dimly she was aware of Martel's deep voice behind her, but her brain had disconnected and made no sense of the sound. She hurried to Grégory's side, brushed his freshly shaven cheek with her fingertips. It was still warm. She closed his blank eyes with a gentle touch, but she could not close the gaping one in his forehead.

She could smell it. Death. Smell its foul footsteps and its sour breath, as if it had risen from a sewer deep underground. She clutched Grégory's limp hand between her own, trying to force her own life into it, to trick its still-warm blood into flowing once more.

'Romy! Leave him.'

She turned her head. Shock made her movements feel as if she were fighting her way through mud. Martel stood beside her, breathing hard.

'They are dead, Romy. Both of them.' His voice was flat and harsh. 'We must leave now. Quickly. Come . . .' He seized her arm.

'No.' She shook off his grip. She made herself look at François as well as Grégory. His third eye didn't blink. 'Once before, I walked away from a dead man. Never again.' She scanned the room as though she might find the murderer hiding among the stacks of tins on the shelves. 'No, Martel, we have to call the police at once.'

'You want the rest of the members of our cell dead too?'

'What do you mean?'

'If we go to the police, the existence of our cell and the names of each one of us will come out in the open. Whoever did this will track down the rest.' He leaned closer, speaking fast, and she saw sorrow flare behind the dark anger in his eyes. 'You want to see Diane, Manu and Jerome with bullet holes in their heads? Do you want one yourself?'

For a long moment she stared at him in silence, feeling a thread unspool inside her until it finally snapped. She gave a brief nod and headed for the door.

Faces flitted past in the street. A flash of cheek, the turn of a shoulder, the scarlet lips of a *putain* in a doorway. An ebony cane in a gnarled hand and a dog pissing on a man's shoe. Romy's eyes saw these things as she hurried through the gloom, but her brain received nothing. Nothing except the eerie stillness of Grégory's face and the way François' nose was dissected from top to bottom by a thin trickle of scarlet.

They didn't run. They didn't draw attention to themselves, but they moved fast, Romy matching her stride to Martel's as they wove through backstreets. He spoke only once.

'I am taking you to a safe house.'

'A safe house?'

She hastened her pace and resisted the urge to snatch a glance behind her. The back of her neck felt naked, the perfect spot for a bullet. She wasn't breathing right.

'We must warn them,' she told him in a low urgent hiss.

'Diane, Manu and Jerome. They have to know that they are in danger if—'

Martel spun her into a doorway. There was the quick sound of a key and suddenly they were indoors in the dark. The key turned again, the door locked behind them. Only then did Romy feel her knees give up on her and she leaned against the wall behind her for support.

'Where are we?' she murmured.

'In the back of a small hotel called the Angélique.' His hand cradled her elbow, steady as a rock. 'Ready?'

'Yes.'

'The room is on the fifth floor. We're better off not using the lift. Are you all right to climb the stairs?'

'Of course.' The pale faces of Grégory and François seemed to float just out of focus in the dark corridor. 'Of course I'm all right. I'm still breathing.'

'Go. Go now,' Romy said.

Martel left her. He ordered her to bolt the door and open it to no one, and then he was gone to warn the others.

'Take care,' she had whispered and he had nodded.

She stood inside the door with her ear to it, listening for his departing footsteps, but she heard nothing. The silence put her on edge. If Martel could be so silent, who else might be out there, leaving no trace of themselves. After ten minutes of listening with her ear pressed to the door, she stepped back and inspected the room. Small and brown but with a high ceiling with elaborate belle époque cornices and a mirror, freckled as a bird's egg, that dominated the small space. A single iron bedstead, an ancient tiny wardrobe, a chair. That was it.

The shutters over the tall window were three-quarters closed and only a faint smear of light from a distant street lamp squeezed in. She didn't switch on the light in the room. Instead she paced the floor in darkness, nerves rumbling at the back of her eyes.

She would give him an hour.

No more.

She could not dismantle the image in her head of the killer stalking Martel through the streets of Paris, raising the barrel of a gun to his broad forehead. Pulling the trigger. It would be one of the hated Spanish Nationalists trying to put a stop to the supply of foreign planes to the Spanish Republicans. Or . . .

Her foot paused mid-step.

Or a German. A German supporting the Condor Legion.

Martel. Please. Please.

Hurry back.

Hurry.

She would give him *half* an hour. If he wasn't back by then, to hell with it, she would go looking for him.

CHAPTER SIXTEEN

FLORENCE

I am in the dark.

I feel my throat dry and my heart rate kick into a higher gear. It's not that I'm afraid of the dark, no, nothing like that. It is because the darkness slides between me and what I want. I have to widen my eyes to suck in any threads of light and I know that in the darkness mistakes can happen. I don't like mistakes.

I am in Roland's study.

Why shouldn't I be? This Avenue Kléber apartment is as much mine as his, in fact more so, because it was paid for out of my inheritance from my father. I have a right to enter every room in it, but the truth is that I rarely set foot inside my husband's study. It is his private domain. I do not intrude.

It is unspoken between us.

Roland is out this evening. I don't know exactly where,

he didn't say, just a vague wave of the hand in the direction of the Champs Élysées as if the venue of choice might be Le Fouquet's restaurant or the Lido with its jazz and its gaudy pink and blue marble swimming pool. His mood was sour. I was not certain whether it was because of my sister's visit or because of his meetings.

They did not go well.

I hate those meetings, the ones with Prime Minister Daladier. And with the Minister of Labour, De Monzie. These men put a rage inside Roland that I cannot bear to look at.

'They are both spineless,' Roland had shouted. 'Repellent and spineless. Daladier will let France blunder into a war with Germany when we should be negotiating a peace pact. Do you realise that Germany is producing twelve times as many aeroplanes as France? If we are stupid enough to go to war they will annihilate our air force in a matter of days. And our army is relying on the Maginot Line fortifications to protect our land border. Twelve years it took to build. Five hundred miles of tunnels, ramparts and gun emplacements manned by over a million troops. So what does the French Army do? It puts in an order for fifty thousand saddle horses. Not tanks. Horses! God preserve us.'

I saw his hand drag across his face, as though trying to tear off the mask. 'I cannot let it happen,' he insisted. 'We *must* negotiate with Hitler. We need him here to stop this country sliding into oblivion. De Monzie is never going to be able to stop the dock strikes that are about to hit us.'

Roland sank into his chair and I poured him another whisky. I touched his cheek as I placed it in his hand.

'Hitler must be laughing up his sleeve at Daladier's posturing,' I said.

He closed his eyes, frowning. Deep lines scoring his forehead, as if he could see things scrolling on the back of his eyelids that I could not begin to imagine.

'Thank God I have you,' he whispered.

I felt the words. The weight of them.

So tonight Roland is taking out one of Daladier's pawns and one of De Monzie's pimps to bend their ear and to enjoy the city's entertainments. I do not let myself think of what that will entail. I know what Paris is. There are places where women dance in nothing but chains, wielding whips and spurs to drag members of the clientele up on to platforms to do their bidding. In one club, couples perform the sex act naked as newts, in nets hung over the heads of their drunken customers. In another, animals are used. I do not ask which ones. How do I know these things? Because I am a Parisienne. I know Paris like I know the exact colour of my sister's eyes.

I am in the dark.

The reason for it is that my husband's study looks out on to Avenue Kléber, and if he happened to be passing and saw a light burning, he would demand to know why. But I do not need a light. My fingers find the key hidden under the third book on the middle shelf behind the door. Without hesitation I remove the portrait he commissioned to be painted of our daughter, the one that hangs above the empty fireplace, and with the key I open the safe. Even in the dark it is easy.

What is not easy are the thoughts in my head.

My fingers extract a small thin notebook. I take it into the well-lit kitchen and I copy its contents into a black book that I keep hidden at the bottom of my sewing box. As if I ever use a sewing box. When I have finished, I replace the thin notebook in the safe, lock it and leave the study.

I open a bottle of Dom Pérignon champagne and pour myself a glass, watching the bubbles rise to the surface like golden weightless lies. I take my glass and I sit on the balcony in the soft summer warmth of the evening, and as I gaze across the million lights of the city in the direction of Montmartre, I worry about my sister.

CHAPTER SEVENTEEN

Romy unlocked the door. Léo Martel stepped inside at once, bringing with him the scent of the streets on his jacket and a bottle of whisky in his hand. Her eyes scoured his face for damage, his shirt for blood, but she could find none and the relief of it made her reach for him. She wrapped his free hand between hers, pinning it there, and for a full minute they stood like that in the dark. She felt the blackness seeping into her head, a layer of it just beneath her skull, and it was crushing the sadness within her.

'Tell me,' she said.

'I found Diane and Manu, and warned them to get out of Paris. But not Jerome.'

'He might have gone into hiding.'

She wanted him to say yes. She wanted him to say, 'Of course Jerome has gone into hiding, the man is sharp at all times.' She wanted François and Grégory's foreheads to be wiped clean in that oppressive storeroom above the café.

'Romaine, a drink?'

His voice was gentle. She realised that he had been talking for some time and she'd heard not a word. She was horrified to feel tears streaming down her cheeks. Thank God it was too dark for him to see. She became aware that his hand between hers was cold despite the heat in the room.

'Sit down,' she told him.

He sat heavily on the solitary chair. The shadows blanked his face from her.

'Martel, who did this?'

'The enemies of the Spanish Republicans.'

'Nationalists?'

'Probably. They have spies everywhere.'

She heard him open the bottle and caught the glint of a glass that he drew from his pocket. Something inside her lurched with desire for the whisky bottle. She wanted to snatch it from him.

'I intended to inform the meeting tonight,' she told him, 'that I am in a position to do some spying for us. To dig out more information.'

She sensed his dark shadow become very still. He waited.

'I've met two Germans who are in a high-level delegation,' she explained. 'One invited me to dinner next weekend. I intend to try to discover from him what plans the Condor Legion might have to—'

'No.'

This time his voice was harsh.

'Stick to flying, Romaine. It's what you're good at. Don't

get involved in things where you will be out of your depth. You will be in danger, so you must say no to this German. I mean it, Romaine.'

There was the sound of liquid flowing into a glass.

'Here,' he muttered.

Her fingers found the glass. She drank it straight down and held it out for more. He refilled it and she heard him take a swig from the bottle.

'What about Grégory and François?' she whispered. 'Someone will have to be informed of their deaths.'

'I have made arrangements. They are being taken care of.'

'What exactly does that mean?'

'It means what I said. They are being taken care of.'

He rose to his feet and walked over to the window, his limp noticeably worse. He tucked himself behind the shutter, unseen from the road beneath, but a smudge of lamplight cut across his cheek. The muscles were tense.

'What is it that you arranged, Martel?' Romy moved over to him. 'For their poor bodies to be removed overnight? For them to be buried in some godforsaken unmarked hole in a forest, where only foxes will find them. Unknown to their families. Is that it?'

He turned. 'Yes, Romaine. *That is it.* Because this is not a game. It's not just about the thrill of piloting a plane for freedom fighters or throwing questions at a German spy whose only interest is to get you between the sheets. I tell you, this German of yours will have you locked up in some brutal hellhole before you can even say *dankeschön*, if he thinks for one moment that you know more than you should.'

'I know that. I'm not a fool.'

His pale face came close out of the darkness. 'But do you know this? We are at war, Romaine. A violent and vicious war even before a shot has been fired or hostilities have been declared. The enemy is organised. They have secret basements here in Paris where you would be interrogated. They are prepared. Rubber truncheons to beat you till your kidneys rupture, water baths to drown you until your lungs burst, electrodes to fry the most intimate places of your body, hammers to break bones and pincers to remove parts of you. Screwdrivers to stab into your eyeballs and—'

'Stop it!'

He stopped. She was shaking. His hand stroked her hair.

'Romaine, I want you to know. I want you to be terrified. It is the only way I can keep you safe.'

She stared at the black figure in front of her and wondered how many other dead bodies he'd seen with a bullet in their brains.

'Is that what you'd do to me too? If I died?' she asked. 'Throw me unseen under the cold earth for the worms to gorge on?'

'Yes.'

'Not even telling my twin sister?'

She heard a rumble in his broad chest. 'A twin? You have a twin? I didn't know that.'

'There's a lot you don't know about me, Martel.'

He said softly, 'I know you go once a month to the Arab quarter of Paris.'

A pulse ticked inside her ear. She turned quickly and felt her way back through the darkness to the whisky bottle. She put its neck to her lips.

'Don't, Romaine.'

She ignored him. She knocked back a large mouthful and felt it hit her gut with a punch.

'Don't get drunk, Romaine.' His tone was angry.

'You don't get to have a say over that, boss.' She tipped her head back. The whisky gilded her lips.

'I do if you're flying tomorrow.'

Slowly she eased the bottle away from her lips. 'Flying?'

'That's right. The bastard aviation officials who pulled the rug from under my company today have been persuaded to put it back where it belongs. You'll be flying the Gipsy Moth.'

'To Spain?'

'Yes.'

'What will I be carrying this time?'

'Me. You'll be carrying me.'

CHAPTER EIGHTEEN

Romy was nervous. Nervous as hell. As if she were on her first solo. Chest tight. Fingers clumsy. Her teeth nipping chunks out of the inside of her cheek. She was performing her pre-take-off checks.

Trim. A lever on the left side of the cockpit, to work the elevators, set into the middle position for take-off.

Throttle friction nut. Tight.

Fuel mixture. Rich.

Magnetos. Both working, up and on.

Fuel. On and sufficient.

Gauges. Set. Oil pressure 45 psi. Altimeter set.

Harness and hatches. Secured.

Controls. Full and free movement.

It was ridiculous to be nervous, she told herself. She could fly the little biplane with her eyes closed, but never before had she taken to the air with the figure of Léo Martel looming in the front passenger cockpit. He was not just a pilot, he was a top *stunt* pilot. One who could fly a plane *upside down* through the Arc de Triomphe. It made her feel vulnerable in a way she never did in an aircraft; vulnerable and absurdly insecure.

It had been a struggle for him to climb up on the wing and clamber into the front cockpit, but Romy had more sense than to offer a helping hand. It was almost dawn in Paris. The day was nothing more than a ribbon of gold on the horizon but the breeze already had the greasy smell of the tannery to the south of the airfield. Martel's grey eyes were as dark as the night sky in the west and, as she flicked the switches, she wondered what was going on in his head. This was his first flight since his accident.

Was he frightened?

More to the point, did he trust her?

Romy could not imagine Léo Martel frightened. But sitting again in the tight squeeze of a cockpit, his knees jammed against the additional petrol tanks, was it all coming back to him? In violent flashbacks?

The way Karim came to her. Her past was made up of mistakes. Of violence. Of lies. She could not outfly them, however hard she tried.

She started to taxi. On the ground, the pilot of a Gipsy Moth was blind, the forward-view was appalling. The Moth's long nose obscured whatever lay ahead, so she had to taxi in a zigzag fashion, looking along the length of the fuselage to ensure that the area ahead was clear. With the control column in her right hand, she used her left for the throttle. This was it. This was what she lived for.

She lined up into the wind, using a quick burst of power to help blow the tail around. Smoothly now, smooth as silk, she advanced the throttle. In that moment she forgot Martel's flying helmet in front of her, she forgot the bloody third eye in Grégory's pale forehead, she forgot the fear that she had forced into a dark corner at the back of her skull. All she could feel was the joy of this moment. Adrenaline was charging through her veins, more seductive than fifty open bottles of whisky, lined up and waiting for her.

The tachometer accelerated to 1800 rpm and automatically her feet did their job, keeping the aircraft on line with the rudder pedals. Careful now. Tiny adjustments to counteract swing or yaw. In her ears sounded the de Havilland engine's healthy roar as it claimed its territory. Romy smiled. It was impossible not to. Her whole body was in the grip of vibration when the engine and the airframe shook themselves like excited dogs as the wheels gathered pace over the grass, eager for her to ease the stick forward at 30 kph which would raise the tail.

The wind was in her face, buffeting against her cheeks, snatching at her helmet, but suddenly the world changed. The bumping of the airframe ceased. The Gipsy Moth took to the air, accelerating towards its climb speed of 90 kph. It struggled, weighted down by the full tanks and the weight of Martel up front, but once in the air Romy's mind seemed to turn itself inside out. Every thought in her brain spilled out on to the ground below, leaving it untrammelled by the past.

Briefly she looked in the cockpit and checked that the oil

pressure was still 45 psi and then she throttled back a fraction to save her engine cylinder heads from getting hot.

She was flying.

They refuelled at Limoges on the edge of the Massif Central. The heat was intense. The ground shimmered as though underwater while they filled the tank positioned between the Moth's upper wings. After five hours in the cockpit their limbs were cramped and jumpy, so they took a walk around the perimeter of the airfield to shake out the knots.

'Why do you need to go to Spain, Martel?'

'I told you. For a meeting.'

'It must be a very important meeting to drag you this far south.'

'It is.'

They had paused to rest his leg. They both pretended it was to light up a couple of her filthy black cheroots and watch a red kite swoop from the rich cobalt blue sky on to some poor unsuspecting prey. Martel leaned against a tree. Without his flying jacket on, Romy noticed he was wearing a grey suit. There was a serious elegance about it that spoke of good taste, something she had never associated with him before.

'Boss, I have a right to know why we're here.'

'The more you know, the more danger you are in.'

'If I'm going to get a bullet in the brain or a Spanish blade between my ribs, I want to know exactly who is pulling the trigger or gripping the knife. I don't want to be caught unprepared like Grégory and François.'

But he didn't listen. His mouth softened into a smile. 'You fly well,' he said.

'Of course I do. But that's not the point right now.'

'Tell me why you go to the Arab quarter at the beginning of every month.'

'That's none of your damn business.' She turned her face away from his scrutiny. 'How dare you follow me.'

'I didn't. I like cooking with Arab spices, so I go regularly to the market in the Barbès-Rochechouart quarter. I've seen you there.'

How could she have been so blind?

She ground her cheroot into the earth under her flying boot and continued on their circuit of the airfield perimeter. Martel fell into step beside her.

'Are you enjoying the flight?' she asked outright, because he had made no mention of it.

He took a long time to answer. 'Yes, I am, thank you. But it's a little dull.'

Dull?

How could flying *ever* be dull?

She had flown with meticulous care so that he would have nothing to criticise. Maybe too meticulous. Too careful. Taking no risks. This was his first flight since the accident and he was *disappointed*? She felt that she had let him down

She tucked her arm through his. 'You may regret that comment.'

*

The Gipsy Moth stooped from the sky. Fast as the red kite.

Engine screaming. Wings shaking. Struts threatening to rip from their sockets. The wind howled through the bracing wires and sought to tear the skin from Romy's cheeks. Adrenaline powered through her veins as the earth hurtled towards her and death opened its arms.

She whooped. Yelled with excitement. Fought for breath and kept her eyes on the glint of metal directly below, a double thread of molten silver that sliced through the honey-toned landscape.

Was this it? This time? Would she fly herself right into the waiting arms of death? A hundred times before, she had been tempted.

Just when the blackness reached out to her, at the last possible second she hauled back on the control stick. The weight of her whole body was still driving towards the ground and she heard the joints of the Gipsy Moth screech at her, when her fingers flicked switches, reset ailerons. Her feet wrestled with the rudder bar and her hands with the stick.

The nose lifted. Only metres from the silver railway lines the Gipsy got her way and slipped into straight and level flight with a sigh. The ground was so close Romy could almost run her fingers over the wooden sleepers like piano keys. A train lay ahead, its smoke belching out. With her heart thundering in her chest, Romy increased speed. The back end of the carriage drew closer as she easily overhauled it. She could have landed on its roof, she was so low. A touch on the rudder. Too little and she would slip into a turn, too much and she would feel the plane skidding outwards.

She sank lower still and the breath of the Gipsy's propeller ripped at the grass as she passed. She was racing alongside the train but the plane's speed was faster. Romy waved. She saw startled faces at open windows, mouths laughing, hands waving as she laid her life out in front of them. The plane leaped ahead to overtake the engine and scare the wits out of the red-faced engine driver.

Romy laughed, loud and joyful. In the passenger seat in front of her, the brown leather helmet turned sideways and she caught the edge of a broad grin on Martel's face.

'Not so dull now, boss.'

CHAPTER NINETEEN

Romy stubbed out her cigarette. Its glow made her an easy target in the dark. She paced back and forth in the central plaza of Santa Casilda, uneasy and watchful.

They said it was safe. They said no one had information they were here. But what did they know? What did anyone know in this brutal civil war? Secret information was a commodity, bought and sold as readily as guns. Information about a surprise attack could snatch victory from the jaws of defeat and betrayal was a currency passed from hand to hand.

Martel, take care.

She stared down into the valley below. Night had fallen, a dense black cloak concealing the raw granite crags and the treacherous hollows where snipers could hide. She was holed up high in the foothills of the Pyrenees over the Spanish border in Catalonia, where a unit of Republican troops had dug in. The Fascist Nationalist army continued to push forward in a spearhead movement to the coast and to Barcelona, in an attempt to split the Republican forces into two weaker halves.

Her hackles rose as a truck approached the village. Its headlights bored tunnels through the solid darkness as it snaked its way through the valley towards Santa Casilda. She could hear its engine now, grinding through the gears as it climbed. In the silence of the night, the sound of it reverberated off the face of the mountain cliffs.

One of ours, they said. From the fighting south of Berga.

How could they be sure?

She backed away from the road and flattened herself against the building where Martel had been closeted for the last three hours.

What were they discussing in there? Why so long?

The night air was cold in the mountains, the wind sheering off the cliffs. She pushed her hands in her pockets. She badly needed a drink to fight the chills. To stop her thoughts and drive away the spectre of death. At the corner of the plaza was a tiny cantina with a light still burning and she started towards it. One drink. That's all. One drink wouldn't . . .

Out of nowhere came the sound of boots pounding over the cobbles. A group of army uniforms rushed past her, shouting urgently to each other in Spanish, shouldering aside the darkness. What was going on?

Her heart hammered. She understood no Spanish. She glanced with concern to the far end of the village where her Gipsy Moth was parked, but she knew she'd never get Martel and herself out of here in the dark. It had taken all her skill to squeeze them into this narrow gorge in daylight without tearing off a wing.

Suddenly lights erupted into the plaza and the lorry from the valley lurched into the square where its rear tailgate was thrown open and hands reached in. Men stumbled out of its interior, men with faces twisted by pain, frozen in fear. Bandages were bloodied. The truck had come from the fighting south of Berga and she recognised the smell on it, knew it well. It seeped from the wounded like sour breath, in the fibres of their clothes, clinging to the hairs on their skin. It was the foul stench of death.

Her mind tried to run, but the stench caught at her and wrenched her back. She remembered a stretch of cobbles in the thin light of dawn. Karim Abed's face looked ravaged. It was a raw day, snow in the air. A wind that had teeth. Romy had arrived far too early outside the Saint-Pierre prison in Versailles and stood on the cobbles for hours in the pre-dawn darkness, the cold chiselling her features. It was a self-punishment. A self-laceration. To be scourged by cold while her guilt raged hot and sulphurous in her stomach. To force her eyes on to the dark monstrosity of the guillotine and to picture Karim's neck imprisoned in the wooden *lunette*. The blade hung there, suspended. Waiting to fall.

Dimly she was aware of a crowd jostling around her as dawn approached and of gendarmes holding them back. The space around the lethal contraption lay naked and empty, too dangerous to step inside. The National Razor of France, that's what they called it. Each machine was handcrafted lovingly, a tall thin upright wooden frame, a *bascule* bench for the prisoner, a *déclic* for the rope, leather straps for restraint. And the blade. All eyes returned again and again to the angled blade. Romy looked once. It was enough. More than enough.

Made of steel, it was attached to a heavy metal *mouton* to give it its speed. Weight: eighty kilos. Drop: four metres. Romy knew these facts, knew each detail. She had made herself become acquainted with its details, prepared for the way the delicate street lamp cast its shadow on the cobbles.

It happened quickly, too quickly. The massive door within the prison's arched entrance swung open and the executioner with his three assistants marched the prisoner towards Madame Guillotine.

'Karim!'

His name was shrieked out through the clamour of the crowd.

'Karim!'

Was it her own voice? Unrecognisable.

Off to one side an Arab woman at the front of the crowd was howling, howling like a wounded dog. Beating her breast. Gripping the hand of a small boy of about five years old, his eyes full of shock and terror.

Karim was shivering, shaking visibly. Fear or cold? He wore only a thin white shirt with its collar hacked off to leave his swarthy neck naked for the blade. His eyes found the Arab woman and the boy and for a moment his knees buckled, but a warder jerked him upright, and in that brief second of despair his gaze locked on Romy's. His dark eyes widened with surprise and then filled with immense sorrow.

Not hatred. Sorrow.

Hate me, Karim. Hate me.

It was over in seconds. The burly executioner – Romy even knew his name, Anatole Deibler and that he had despatched three hundred and ninety-five criminals in his career – moved with a smooth well-practised motion. Karim lay face down on the guillotine, the top half of the *lunette* was lowered on to his neck, the *déclic* was released and the blade sped down, separating head from body in a split second.

The voyeurs cheered.

Cheered.

Dear God, forgive me. Romy wanted to fall to her knees and weep. The body was tumbled into a large trunk and the head in a leather basket. Through her tears the basket swam out of focus and she could hear again in her head Karim's soft voice saying, 'Why you do this to me, Mademoiselle Romaine?'

Why? Why?

Because I do not want to die.

She was the last to leave. Sick and trembling and full of hate, she moved with no purpose, but ahead of her she spotted the Arab woman and the boy, the woman still wailing her grief. His wife and son. Romy quickened her step and followed them silently through the streets.

*

'Where have you been?'

'To the execution.'

'Karim's?'

Romy nodded. Her sister had been waiting for her in the hallway and dragged her into the dining room before their mother heard her return. Florence's cheeks were flushed and her blue eyes too bright.

'You shouldn't have gone,' she stated.

'I had to.'

Florence looked good in black. It suited her, the contrast with her creamy young skin and pale blonde hair, but she was not in mourning for Karim Abed. There was no chance of that. Roland's father had just died from apoplexy and she was showing respect.

'You look awful, Romy. Put a decent dress on, will you? You look like a rag.' Florence moved briskly over to the rosewood drinks cabinet in the corner and poured a double shot of brandy into a glass. 'Roland is coming over. He wants to speak to you.'

Romy felt the blood grow chill in her veins. Roland was the only one, other than her sister, who knew what she had done. She never wanted to speak to him again.

'Why, Florence? What has happened?'

Florence thrust the glass into her twin's hand. Romy did not like alcohol.

'Drink, sister.'

Romy drank it down in two mouthfuls. It burned her innards, as if she had swallowed flames. Florence studied her closely. She put a hand on either side of Romy's head as if she would crush the pain out of it.

'It's done, Romy. It's over. Now we get on with the rest of our lives. Forget Karim. He no longer exists. We will never mention him again.'

'How can you care so little?'

'If you mean would I prefer to have this pretty little head in the basket instead of his, the answer is no.'

There was a fierceness in Florence's eyes that frightened Romy. She pulled away. Refilled her glass and drank it down, feeling it burn the frayed edges of the pain.

'What has happened, Florence? What have you done?'

The flush on her sister's cheeks darkened. 'Roland has asked me to marry him and I said yes.'

A strange curtain, a kind of mist, came down behind Romy's eyes and she felt sick.

'Today? He asked you today? Of all days?'

'Yes.'

Romy drew close to her sister and wrapped her arms around her, cradling her gently. In a whisper, she begged, 'Please don't marry him, Florence. Please don't marry that man.'

CHAPTER TWENTY

Romy knelt in the church in Santa Casilda listening to a soldier's outpouring of grief in Spanish, not understanding a word of it, but murmuring quiet words of comfort. The wounded from the battle had been carried from the truck into the safety of the ancient house of God to bring healing to the soul, as well as to the body with medical attention. Twelve narrow metal cots lined the walls with military precision under the watchful eyes of saints, while make-shift beds were spread out on the flagstone floor, bundles of bedding, straw palliasses and even horse blankets called into service.

Romy had bathed wounds with antiseptic. She'd bandaged limbs, swabbed vomit and faeces from the floor and she'd held hands. More than anything, she held their hands.

'Don't leave me.'

'I won't leave you.'

This one was English. So very young. One of the

International Brigade, the thirty-thousand volunteers from all over the world who held such passionate belief in the Popular Front government of Spain and such hatred of Fascist oppression that they had come here to fight for freedom and risk everything for it. Romy wanted to hold this wounded young boy and his ideals in her arms and tell him to go home to his mother in the green shires of England.

'You're brave,' she told him. 'A hero. Spain is proud of you and grateful to you.'

He smiled. Such a small smile that it made Romy's eyes fill with tears. He was covered in sweat, his boyish tufty hair plastered to his head and his right leg was smashed to pieces. The doctor was low on morphine, so the men's moans rippled through the church to join the prayers trapped among the arched beams of the roof.

'I won't leave you,' Romy said again and bathed his burning skin. He closed his eyes, his breathing laboured, his soft mouth stretched in pain. For a long time he seemed to sleep, but opened his eyes abruptly and stared directly at her.

'I see an angel,' he whispered.

'What the hell are you doing in here, Romaine? I've been looking everywhere for you.' It was Martel's voice.

Romy did not lift her head.

'For God's sake, Romaine, you need to get some sleep.'

Romy did not reply.

A heavy hand rested on her shoulder, but its touch was warm.

'Come on, out of here.' A pause. '*Merde*, Romaine, that boy is dead.'

Of course he was dead. People died around her.

'Enough, girl. Do you realise what time it is?'

She didn't answer. She was thinking of the boy's mother in England, drinking her sherry, wearing her pearls. Waiting for her son.

'It's two o'clock in the morning,' Martel said with impatience. 'You have flying to do at dawn.'

Romy was lying on a bed of straw in a stable and over her was draped a military greatcoat to keep out the chill. Where Martel had stolen it from, she had no idea. She ached. Everything ached, inside and out. But she couldn't sleep. The sound of the darkness inside her head was too loud.

Two metres to her right Léo Martel was enclosed in his own nest of straw and though he lay unmoving she was convinced by his uneven breathing that he was not asleep either. Inside the stable, which held no horses – had the military seized them? – it was pitch black, too black to see anything but the thinnest slats of paler black that in places sneaked in between the planking of the walls. The mountain air smelled sweet but felt cold in her lungs. Everything inside her felt cold.

'Martel?'

The reply took some time to come. 'Go to sleep.'

'Why was the meeting so long? What is happening?'

'Don't ask, Romaine. I told you before, the less you know, the safer you are.'

Romy tossed aside the greatcoat. She was aware of the scurrying of mice somewhere close. Or were they rats? She shuffled over and squatted on her haunches beside Martel.

'This isn't what I want to hear.'

Unable to see him, she reached out in the darkness and tightened her fingers around his arm. The muscles were hard and tense.

'I have risked my life flying you and your planes here.' She kept her voice low, conscious of sound carrying at night in these mountains. 'At any time I could have been shot down by a Heinkel fighter or one of the Italian Fiat G.50s, we both know that.'

It was something that had been left unsaid between them till now.

'I bring you information. Packages from Spain. I've seen two men with bullets in their brains. Our secret cell is being decimated and there are others in hiding. Now two high-level Germans are showing more interest in me than is good for my health, for reasons that I can only guess at.' She gave his arm a shake. 'So don't tell me, Léo Martel, that I am not allowed to know what's going on. *For my own safety.* To hell with that.' She turned and spat her anger into the darkness. 'I have a right to answers. Who is doing this? What went on in that meeting of yours? Who should I be watching for? Tell me. What is going on?'

She finally stopped. Drew breath.

'Tell me. You owe me that much.'

Martel stood and walked over to the far end of the stable

where a skylight created a rectangle of blackness that was not quite so dense.

'Come here, Romaine.'

She went over to him and their faces were pale ovals. The smell of horse sweat was stronger here. Martel placed his hands on her shoulders, as though he feared she would run away.

'Romaine, I do understand your desire for more information, so I will tell you this much.' He spoke softly, his face drawing closer to hers, his breath tinged with nicotine. 'Colonel Mendez has learned that there is a tight organisation in Paris that is dedicated to removing all those who are helping the Spanish Republican cause.'

The image of a third bloodied eye flashed into Romy's head.

'Grégory and François,' she whispered.

'It would seem so. The assassin is code-named Cupid. He is efficient and lethal.' His hold on her shoulders tightened and she knew she was not going to like what was coming next.

'At dawn,' he said, 'we fly out of here back to Paris and that's the end of it for you. We cease all contact. You pack up that hellhole of a pit you call home and move to a new address. I will give you funds to keep you going until you find a new job that . . .'

She was shaking her head.

'Yes, Romaine. I will not accept any refusal on your part. It is finished for you. This is a seriously organised assassin, not just a rogue agent working as a loner.'

'No.'

'Yes. You must stay out of it.'

'No. I am a part of this operation.'

'It is too dangerous.'

'Just as dangerous as for you.'

'Romaine Duchamps, I don't want your death on my conscience.'

'Why now, Martel? Why banish me now? This is my cause, as much as yours. I am committed to the fight against Fascism.'

Abruptly he removed his hands. She reached out and attached herself to the edge of his leather flying jacket. It was old and familiar. It made up for the gap he was forcing between them.

'What is it? What is it that you are not telling me?'

'There's no need for you to know more.'

'Yes, there is.'

In the night-time gloom, she saw the swoop of his dark eyebrows as they plunged down, but he said nothing. To her surprise he wrapped an arm around her shoulders and drew her to his chest. He held her there, silent and reassuring, her cheek pressed against the ancient flying jacket; she could smell wide open places on it, endless horizons and air so clean it scoured your lungs.

'The assassin,' he said so quietly that his words barely reached her ears, 'with the code name Cupid. They think he is German.'

German?

There were lots of Germans in Paris. Hundreds of them. Yet she felt a chill creep down her spine. It was absurd to think Cupid might be one of the two Germans she happened to know. But Martel did not think it was absurd. That's why he wanted to bundle her out of their reach.

Cupid. The god of love. Of desire.

She remembered dancing in Horst Baumeister's arms.

Romy curled up on her side on her pile of straw, her knees drawn up to her chin. Martel pulled the greatcoat over her once more, patting it down around her shoulders, tucking it in. He then bundled more straw on top of it. The temperature was dropping fast. His hand stroked her head, plucking dog-ends of straw from her hair, his thumb feeling for the fierce pulse at her temple. Gently his thumb eased around it in a circle, as if he could draw the pain out of her head like a nail.

Outside, the wind had picked up. She thought about her plane. She thought about taking off in this narrow gorge and knew she would be threading her Gipsy Moth through the eye of a needle.

'Sleep,' Martel ordered. 'Sleep, damn you.'

He retreated back into his own straw nest and quickly settled into silence, but her skin still bore the imprint of his thumb, and in a way she didn't understand, it was a comfort. She had been touched by men all over her body, but never there. Never like that.

CHAPTER TWENTY-ONE

'A plane!'

Romy screamed the word.

'Wake up! Martel! Wake up!'

She hit him flat on the chest.

He reacted fast. On his feet, cursing, and over to the stable doors in the dark before she'd reached them herself. He swung them open. The drone of engine noise immediately grew louder. It had come at Romy out of nowhere, spiking into her disturbed sleep and jerking her awake. Her breath was still ragged from the grip of her dream, but she knew an aircraft engine when she heard it, even on the other side of the mountain.

She stepped outside. Into the greyness of that moment just pre-dawn when the day starts to elbow aside the night.

'Two of them,' she said.

Martel nodded agreement. 'A Messerschmitt 109 by the sound of it.'

A German fighter plane. The Condor Legion.

There were no planes for it to fight here. So why . . .? No planes. Except her own.

A sense of dread kicked at her heart. She didn't waste time on words, but started to run, hurtling through the grey mist, skidding on the cobbles. She heard Martel call her name but she didn't stop. She raced down the street of the small town while its inhabitants lay in their beds, asleep or fumbling their wives, unaware of what was bearing down on them.

'*Alto*!'

Ahead of her a soldier on patrol duty loomed out of the gloom, his rifle raised and pointing straight at her chest.

'Quick!' she shouted. '*Vite*! It's coming. Listen to the plane. Warn people to stay indoors or . . .'

The soldier shouted back at her in Spanish. Dear God, he didn't understand. She racked her brain for a Spanish word.

'*Rápido*.' She gestured skyward. 'Messerschmitt.'

He looked up. The whites of his eyes shining and startled as he scanned the night sky. But then he heard it. The growl of the Daimler-Benz engine that sounded like low thunder rumbling among the mountaintops. Immediately he fired off three rifle shots into the air to warn his comrades and all hell broke loose.

Romy laid a hand on her Gipsy's flank. The fabric skin felt ice-cold to the touch. She could almost believe it was fear. The biplane was tucked away in an open stretch of ground at the back end of town and Romy ran to the spot where a fence marked its boundary. On the other side of it, the black shapes of two cars lay hidden under tarpaulins. She had noticed them yesterday. No one in Spain had petrol for cars, not these days. It all went to the military.

Her fingers worked quickly. She untied the tarpaulins from the cars and dragged them over to the Gipsy Moth where she draped one over the tail fin and one over the propeller and engine cowling. There wasn't anything she could do about the high wings, but at least from the air and in this grey mist, the outline now looked much less like an aircraft.

The growl had become a roar as the enemy fighter sank into their valley. Suddenly the spit and crack of machine-gun fire ripped through the town and Romy heard screams. She raced back to one of the houses and flattened herself against its wall for cover. The thoughts in her head were buzzing with wild confusion. Odd ideas. Strange sensations. A firm conviction that the plane had come for *her*.

Tracking her down. Scenting her father's blood on her hands.

Because in the end you cannot run forever. So she stepped out into the open street where everything was grey and shadowy. Maybe this way the killing would stop. No one else need die.

She could see a plane at the far end of the street. The roar of its engine bombarded the air in her lungs as it flew low, coming directly for her, as though it had smelled the blood on her. Its guns were strafing the street, ripping into the soldiers' billets, shattering windows, kicking up chunks of rubble from the buildings.

She stood still in the road. Waiting for the bullets.

Around her she was aware of screams, shouts, gunfire from the ground, but the world receded into a dim backdrop and all her focus was on the Messerschmitt that grew huge and black above her, like the Hand of God. But something hit her like a truck from one side, sweeping her across the road and slamming her into a doorway. The force of it sent lights cartwheeling through her head so that for one split second she thought it was death that had come for her.

'What the hell are you doing? Are you crazy? Standing in the path of . . .'

It dawned on her that it was Martel. His voice blurred. She pulled back her hand and slapped him across the face, again and again. But he didn't release her. The plane roared overhead and passed on down the street, its guns finding fresh targets. Others would die instead of her. She slumped against the door behind her and would have slid to the ground but Martel held her on her feet, his grip on her unrelenting. She wanted to shout at him but had no words.

A new sound reached them. Far higher in the sky. They both recognised it instantly as the heavy grinding engines of a much larger aircraft. They couldn't pick out its silhouette in the greyness that billowed around the mountain ridges, but they knew what it was.

'A bomber.'

No sooner was the word out of Martel's mouth than the first bombs hit. Their impact shook the ground beneath Romy's feet and tore at her eardrums. The front wall of the house opposite her collapsed, exposing a man and woman sitting up in bed, naked except for a second skin of cement dust that turned them into statues.

More bombs hurtled down, explosions rocked the town and fires started to rage from one shop to another. The air shuddered and turned solid. Romy's lungs filled up with dust and smoke, but far worse was the fury inside her that made her want to claw the aeroplanes out of the sky and watch them crash and burn. Throughout it all, Martel held her there in the doorway. Not letting her run. Paying no heed to her screams of anger, not until the bombs stopped raining from the sky. Only then did he take his hands off her. She twisted away from him and ran to help the injured.

Side by side they worked, as they dug through masonry with bare fingers, lifted fractured beams from limbs and bathed blood from faces. The military swung into action with discipline and efficiency, soldiers extracting people from the ruins, dousing fires and shovelling aside the debris that blocked the roads.

At one point, just when the first finger of dawn slid like a spill of oil over the mountain and painted one end of the valley golden, Romy retreated back past the severed telegraph lines that writhed like black snakes on the ground. Back to the plot of land where her own plane was hidden away, but she knew what she would find.

Her Gipsy Moth lay in a thousand pieces. Its wood and metal carcass was ripped apart, its guts spread out like a sacrificial offering on the black earth, and a child was already stealing its magneto. Romy stooped blindly, picked up a chunk of its shiny wooden propeller and cradled it in her shaking arms, unable to let it go. She had no idea she was crying as she made her way back up the street to the church. They'd need her help. More than ever now in the makeshift hospital there.

But the church had taken a direct hit. Nothing of it or those inside it remained.

'What happened, Martel?'

'We were betrayed.'

'By whom?'

'We don't know for certain. But I told you, there are eyes and spies everywhere.'

'Surely you must have some idea who could have—'

'If we did, he would be strung up by his balls from the nearest tree with his throat slit wide open by now.' He said it quietly but cold rage was threaded through each syllable.

They were riding in the back of a dilapidated van that was wheezing its way through a mountain pass, its gears skidding into each other at random so that progress was slow. A Spanish partisan fighter huddled on a blanket on the far side of Martel, eyes cold and suspicious as he cracked his knuckles doggedly and dragged on a cigarette between his lips. He wore dark clothing and spoke no French. Across his knees was slung a rifle because he was their bodyguard.

But who wants a stranger as a bodyguard when you've

just seen a town slaughtered and trust is as slippery as a fish between your fingers?

The van shook and juddered. The road was rough. Though Martel said little, his face was grim and he kept one eye on the bodyguard at all times. They were heading for the train station in Marseille, but first they had to find a way over the Spanish border back into France. The sun was beating down on the small van, it was hot as hell in the back and the air was thick with cigarette smoke. But to Romy it felt cold. Cold and crowded. Because she had brought with her the spirit of her shattered little plane and the ghosts of all those slaughtered in Santa Casilda. They lay at her feet and their cold hands touched her skin.

Could she forgive him for saving her life?

The question stung inside Romy's head. And then there was the reverse side of it, like flipping a coin. Could Léo Martel forgive *her* for making him risk his life?

Having someone try to murder you is personal, really personal. Maybe that fighter pilot had checked her name off a list or maybe he hadn't, but still he had looked straight at her standing there in the middle of the road and moved his thumb to press his fire-button. If Martel hadn't barrelled into her, she would be dead. Her limp body would be one of those, beset by summer flies, piled up in the cemetery.

What about Florence? Her twin. Would she feel it? Would she know the moment that Romy's heart stopped beating?

'You're muttering.'

Romy's eyes shot open. Martel was leaning over her, his dusty hair silhouetted against an arc of silver-blue sky, and he was smiling, as if she had just made him laugh.

'I'm not muttering,' she insisted.

'Then who is Florence?'

She felt colour rise in her cheeks. Had she said that bit out loud? About her heart stopping.

She blinked herself fully alert. She was seated at the edge of a field of tufty wheat, her back propped against a gnarled old hazel tree, the air shimmering in the heat. Had she drifted into a doze? She stared up at Martel. What else had she muttered? He kept his eyes on her with an intensity that made her want to look away.

She held up her hand to him. 'Thank you, Léo Martel. *Merci.*'

'For what?'

He was surprised, as though a thank-you was the last thing he'd expected from her, but he folded his large clever hand around hers.

'For my life,' she said.

'Nonsense.'

She didn't argue. If he wanted it that way.

They were resting. The van was abandoned back up in the mountains and they had come down on foot into France using goat trails at first, their bodyguard acting as guide. He was still with them, sitting twenty metres away, chewing on a strip of dried pork, eyes like a hawk on every tree or fold in the terrain where an enemy could conceal himself.

Martel had walked, hour after hour, his limp growing more pronounced with each kilometre. Neither he nor Romy mentioned it.

She was the one who had called a halt in the wheat field. From her canvas bag she'd extracted a bottle of vile gut-stripper they called red wine and had proceeded to pour it down her throat. Martel did not comment, but neither did he share it. He was wearing a plain dark shirt and grey trousers but his suit jacket had gone missing. She looked around her. The wine bottle had gone missing too.

'Romaine, I have watched you trying to kill yourself for years, and today you almost succeeded. Tell me why. What are you running from?'

She fired a look of alarm at him. He still held on to her hand.

She shook her head, her short curls showering cement dust on her lap. 'No, Martel, you've got me wrong. I like taking risks, that's all, just as you did in your stunt days. That need for excitement, it's in our blood. That's all it is.'

She jumped to her feet and shouldered her bag, but he still didn't release her hand, so she was forced to look at him straight.

'What is it?' she asked and stepped closer.

So close she could see deep into his grey eyes. To the core of him. Could see the steel girders it was made of.

'I'm not wrong about you,' he said.

CHAPTER TWENTY-TWO

FLORENCE

I am uneasy.

My feet cling to the pavement as I walk in my tan heels, so that each step requires an effort. That is a bad sign.

She has gone. My sister. Gone missing. She came to see me but I wasn't there and she spoke with Roland. Now she is nowhere to be found. What did he say to her?

What? What?

No lies. Not this time.

I am walking down rue Bascome and as I pass Dominique's café, the aroma entices me. I could take coffee there, a brief refuge, the tables tempting in the shade. Or the Coq d'Or with its virginal white napery. The cocktails there are *magnifique.* My sister would sell her soul for one.

But no. No. I don't. I keep walking. Despite my feet.

It is a pretty street. But Paris has so many pretty streets, we are spoilt for choice. Like we're spoilt for whores. Such an abundance of tree-lined boulevards and handsome buildings, all a regulated height to emphasise the towering glory of our churches. I like that. I love to promenade in Paris in my latest Schiaparelli. It soothes me. To stroll among the lovers along the embankment by the River Seine and listen to the whisper of its waters lapping on the low *quais*. To be serenaded by accordion players. It is so seductive. So normal. It is what other people do.

Isn't it?

Yet I am uneasy today.

What is Romaine up to?

I have watched my sister. I know something is burning inside her, something that sends up shoots of scalding molten terror when I least expect it. Like at Monico's nightclub. In the powder room. I fear it will spill down us both and melt our flesh beyond recognition, fusing us to each other.

What then?

When she flies that plane of hers, she flees from whatever it is down here that terrifies her. Every second she is up there, she is in mortal danger. Yet she laughs at it, like a child playing with fire, though each flight changes the person she is. I see it. Each flight hones her. Like a blade on a whetstone. I watch the edges of her growing sharper and more dangerous.

She will cut herself.

Or she will cut me.

*

I walk into Hotel Farrelle. He is there. I knew he would be, just as I know he has no idea that I am here. I spot him through the glass doors that open into the salon. As I enter, the room stretches away from me in a sea of blue carpet and gilt mirrors and I head for a seat by one of the arched windows, as far away from the piano as I can get. The instrument is startlingly white, new-tooth white, but the keys are being coaxed into something barely resembling a tune by hands the colour of coffee beans. Jazz is all the rage now in this city. You can't go anywhere without tripping over it, though I have to say that Chopin is more to my taste.

I order coffee. My eyes drift to the man leaning one elbow on the piano. A sharp suit. Pinstriped and expensive. An oyster-grey silk tie and beautiful shoes. I approve of good shoes on a man. It shows integrity. He is tapping the flat of his hand against the piano's shiny white skin, relishing the syncopated rhythm. His blond hair is thick and full of energy but precisely parted on one side. A good-looking face, regular features, saved from being dull by the amusement that hangs around his mouth and by the intense blue of his eyes. The kind of blue I only see in Chloé's paintbox. His expression is open. No secrets, it says.

It lies. I know otherwise.

I turn my head away and wait for him to notice me but after several minutes he still has eyes only for the ivory keys, so when my coffee arrives, I jog the tray and it slithers to the floor with a crash of crockery. He looks straight at me then. He strides towards me, hand outstretched.

'Florence, what an unexpected pleasure. What are you doing here?'

I accept his hand and his small Germanic bow. 'I am supposed to be meeting a friend here but she cancelled.' I regain my hand. 'You may join me instead, if you like, Horst.'

It is Horst Baumeister, my husband's German associate. He slips into the chair beside me with a broad smile and summons fresh coffee, once the mess is cleared away. I am wearing my hair loose over my shoulders and my pale blue dress with razor pleats and a white collar. It makes me look innocent.

'Are you meeting someone?' I ask.

'No, I'm staying here at this hotel.'

'Really?' As if I don't know. 'What a coincidence.'

Then the conversation falls into one of those holes of silence that, when they open up, are hard to fill.

'You like the music?' I try.

'Yes. A wonderful Count Basie arrangement.'

I raise an eyebrow. 'I thought your Führer called jazz *primitive* and *depraved*. Goebbels regards it as degenerate music.' I smile sweetly. 'It is banned in Germany, I believe. Do you disagree with them, Horst?'

There is a moment, so brief it is almost not there, a moment when his lips whiten and his irises widen into black tunnels. And then it is gone.

'Ah, Florence, it is not jazz music itself we object to. It is very popular in Germany.' He leans forward and lowers his voice. 'It is the jazz musicians who concern us, the Negroes and the Jews who play it.'

His eyes fix on mine. Then the smile returns.

'Florence, you and I think alike. We may have different taste in music, but that is allowed.'

I laugh. I cannot resist.

'You are right, Horst. We both know that the only way forward for Europe is to tear up the ridiculous map that the Treaty of Versailles created. Hitler has a vision that will rebuild the economy of France as well as Germany, if we work together.'

Horst is pleased. I see it in his blue eyes. We sip our coffee and drift into applauding the stance of the British Prime Minister Neville Chamberlain. He is putting pressure on France to persuade Czechoslovakia to accept Hitler's demands for Sudetenland. To be amenable. Both of us like the word *amenable*. It is delightfully civilised.

Neither of us mentions that our troops rely mainly on horses for transport instead of mechanised vehicles. What antiquated idiocy. I am tempted to reveal to Horst that in one document I viewed in my husband's desk, it stated that the amount spent on petroleum in the French Army was less than one quarter of the amount spent on horse fodder.

How can that be true? It makes me laugh out loud it is so *incroyable*.

But now that La Chambre has replaced the treacherous Pierre Cot as Air Force Minister, and the Anschluss has given our politicians the kick up the arse they needed, France is about to commission five thousand new military aircraft. But Horst already knows this. Because my husband told him.

We order wine. I wait until the bottle is nearly empty and then I lean across the table and place my hand on top of his. My touch is light. But it pins him there. I feel a ripple of surprise shoot through him.

'Horst, tell me, *mein Freund*, what is your interest in my sister?'

To my astonishment, he blushes like a schoolboy.

'I like her,' he says. 'I like her very much.' His German accent grows stronger with his embarrassment. 'She is a very interesting young woman.'

'I don't deny that.'

'You don't object?'

'Of course not.'

But I do. I object. I object like hell. He doesn't deserve her.

He removes his hand from under mine and raises his glass. 'To twins,' he smiles.

'To twins,' I echo and down half my glass. 'As long as you have no other reason for being interested in Romaine.'

'What other reason?'

'Don't hurt her, Horst.' I look away towards the piano, so that he will not see what is in my eyes. 'Or I will make you regret it.'

CHAPTER TWENTY-THREE

The Gare de Saint-Charles is a railway station perched high on a hill to the east of Marseille city centre. Romy loitered in her new dress just outside the main building while Martel went inside to purchase train tickets.

It allowed her respite, as she looked out across the haphazard roofs of Marseille whose ridges were slick with gold from the evening sun. In the distance the church of Notre Dame de la Garde rose like a watchtower, but close at hand a magnificent flight of one hundred and four wide stone steps swept up to the station, dotted with evening travellers intent on their own business. A few men shot her a glance as they passed, but with nothing more than lust in their eyes. Lust she could live with. Suspicion she couldn't.

The wind off the harbour ruffled her skirt around her shins. The best that could be said for the garment was that it was dull. Not exactly a sack, but almost. It was Martel's choice – black, straight up and down, an old woman's dress he'd found in a street market. He claimed she would blend in on the train more effectively than in her flying dungarees. It seemed to her that the only thing she'd blend in with on the train would be the coal wagon, but she wasn't going to argue. He wanted her to be unnoticeable. They had got this far. Now there was just the night train to Paris.

Martel was suddenly at her side, brisk and businesslike.

'Here's your ticket.' He handed it to her.

'It's for a first-class couchette.'

'Yes.'

'Do you have one too?'

'No. Yours was the last of the couchettes. All the rest are taken. Don't look like that, Romaine. I am in the next carriage, in second class. Anyway, it's safer for us to travel apart.' His gaze scanned the one hundred and four steps and the Boulevard d'Athènes beyond. 'They will be looking for a man and woman travelling together.'

They? Who are they?

She leaned closer to him, her head near his, and seized the front of his shirt, a big fistful of the grubby black material twisted in her hand.

'Do you have a gun for me in that bag of yours?' she said in a low whisper.

The bag in question lay at his feet, khaki canvas with a fat brass lock on the front. She prodded it with her foot. It felt weighty. The silence that followed her words lasted so long, Romy thought he may not have heard above the noises of the city. She felt the heat of his chest under his shirt.

'No,' he said at last. Curt and crisp. 'I don't.' He picked up the bag as if it weighed nothing and started towards the station *quai*, his broad back blanking any further questions. 'Come on, Romaine, the train is . . .'

'Liar,' she hissed after him. 'Liar.'

'Lock the door. As soon as I leave, lock the door and don't open it for anyone. Understand?'

'Yes, Martel. I understand.'

'Promise me you'll do it.'

'Don't worry so much.'

'Promise me.'

'I promise.'

She didn't want him to leave. Didn't want him to go where she couldn't see him in second class. Where she couldn't watch his back.

'You could stay,' she said. 'Here.'

'Overnight? In your couchette?'

A smile softened his features and his gaze flicked to the bench seat that would soon be made up into a narrow bed for her. Martel was too big for this small confined space, like squashing a bull into a matchbox.

He shook his head.

'In the chair, I meant.' She gestured to the plush seat by the window. 'Why not? Are you frightened I might jump on you in the middle of the night?'

The moment she said the words she regretted them.

But he uttered a rich deep chuckle. 'No, I think I'd just

about manage to fight you off. But if I spend the night in your couchette, the conductor will know about it and that means that very soon the whole carriage will know about it. So what happens then to our intention of travelling unnoticed?'

But he was still laughing, little puffs of amusement escaping from him, and Romy could not stop her mind imagining what it would be like to jump on him in the middle of the night.

Don't, she told herself. Don't, Romaine, dammit. He is not a man who would want to touch soiled goods. She felt awkward and would have moved away but there was nowhere to go in the tiny compartment. He patted her cheek soothingly, as though she were a troublesome dog.

'Lock the door and you'll be safe,' he said and abruptly left.

The spinning of the train wheels became Romy's thoughts. Turning over and over relentlessly in her head, trapped on a track that did not let them go, would not let them escape. She sat on the bench in her tiny couchette, staring out at the black hole of night beyond the window, the lights of villages flashing past like reminders that there were other lives out there. Other chances.

You cannot go back. Only forward.

The Blue Train was the province of the rich. It smelled of money. And expensive perfume. The scents seeped from the lavishly wood-panelled and luxuriously appointed carriages. It was Martel's decision to take the night express train – called the Blue Train because of its blue-painted carriages – from Marseille to Paris Gare de Lyon, where it would arrive tomorrow morning. She had heard that famous people like Charlie Chaplin, Winston Churchill and even England's handsome Prince of Wales regularly bumped into each other in its glossy corridors or over a glass of fine claret in the dining car, cigar smoke drifting in their wake.

But who else was out there? Behind closed doors.

She worried about Martel. She wished more than ever that he had stayed here and cared less about attracting talk among fellow travellers. There was the noise of passengers coming and going in the corridor and at one point a high-pitched yelp that disconcerted her, but then silence.

A polite knock sounded on the couchette door. Romy made no sound but slid over and put her ear to it.

'Who is it?'

'The carriage attendant, mademoiselle. To set up the bed.'

It could be the attendant. Or it could be someone with a gun aimed at her head.

There were ten couchettes in each carriage. Romy counted the doors. She was standing in the corridor, swaying with the movement of the train, the lamps dim and all the doors tightly shut while she waited for the attendant to finish his job of converting her seat to a fully made-up bed. It looked comfortable enough, but his effort was a waste of time because she planned to sit in the chair in the dark facing the door. If anyone came for her he would be silhouetted against the corridor light, so she would see him before he saw her.

That was it. Not much of a plan, she was willing to admit, but the best she could come up with. And a spanner. She had taken it from the lorry's toolkit and secreted it in her shoulder bag. So yes, there would be a spanner in her hand.

'Haven't you finished yet, monsieur?' The voice came from a young woman standing in the open doorway next to Romy's. She was draped against the doorpost with a scarlet leather suitcase behind her. 'I'm dead on my feet with exhaustion.' She mopped her brow in a dramatic fashion. 'God only knows how much I need my bed.'

Romy smiled at her. It was impossible not to. She had the kind of face that was magnetic, the kind you couldn't turn away from, it exerted such a pull. Huge black eyes and a wide embracing smile that could swallow you whole. Skin as dark and glossy as polished ebony, its colour emphasised by the cream sleeveless frock that clung to her slender frame. Romy didn't blame the attendant for abandoning her own couchette and rushing to this startling young woman's instead.

'You okay, honey?' the woman asked Romy, coming to stand alongside her in the corridor. She spoke French with a strong American accent. 'You look kind of rough.'

So much for blending in.

'Just tired, thank you. Who is this little one?' She ruffled the ears of a honey-coloured puppy that was tucked under the woman's arm.

'This is Mimi, my Tibetan spaniel. Say hello, Mimi.'

The animal yapped obligingly. 'She is supposed to travel in a horrid cage in the luggage car but, hell and damnation, would you want to spend a night in a stinking cage? I sure wouldn't.' She laughed, long and loud. 'Our friend here,' she gestured to the uniformed attendant at work in her couchette, 'has kindly agreed to overlook it.'

Romy could imagine a lot of people overlooking things for this woman. She had recognised her at once – it was Josephine Baker, the famous American singer from the backstreets of St Louis. She had taken Paris by storm a decade ago, entrancing them with her wild uninhibited dancing in the Folies Bergère, outrageous in little more than a few bananas strung into a skimpy skirt. Yet here she was, seemingly travelling alone with her fluffy pet. The attendant departed but for several minutes they continued to stand in easy silence peering out into the blackness as the train rattled its way northward, seeing only their own blurred reflections in the glass.

'I don't suppose you've got a decent drink in that suitcase of yours,' Romy muttered.

Josephine Baker slid a look at her from under thick black lashes, inspecting her drab dress and the grazes on her face, and something in her eyes.

'Bourbon do you?' she offered.

'Perfect.'

'Marlene Dietrich strutted around like a German whore.' Josephine Baker laughed, a raucous sound as she rolled her eyes to imply antics too decadent to name. 'With her fat cigars and painted nipples and naked midnight swims.'

Romy liked her new drinking companion. They had talked far into the night in Josephine's compartment. Matched each other drink for drink, to the incessant rhythm of the wheels beneath them grinding away the hours. Together they eased their loneliness. Josephine loved to talk. Loved to relive moments of her life in vivid technicolour, her triumphs on stage, the time she danced naked, painted all over in gold, at a party in Neuilly, and her ever-growing list of husbands.

Romy waved her glass at Josephine, spilling some down her wrist. 'Are you travelling alone?'

'I am not alone,' the singer insisted brightly. 'My precious Mimi is with me.' She dropped a kiss on the dog's domed little head. 'My wretch of a husband abandoned me for an American slut, but I have a wonderful chocolate-factory millionaire waiting for me in Paris. You won't believe how he melts when I heat him up.' She laughed at that. 'What about you? All alone?'

'No. My friend is travelling in the next carriage.' She laughed at Josephine's raised eyebrow. 'No, not that kind of friend. He's my boss.'

'A boss who travels second class while his employee travels first class? *Mon dieu*, girl, tell me more about this rare animal. What kind of man is he?'

With no warning a rush of words to describe Martel poured into Romy's head, words that made her silence her tongue with a long swig of bourbon. She picked out one of them.

'He is loyal.'

'Tell me more.'

'Tall.'

'More.'

'Courageous.'

'More.'

'A pain in the arse.'

Josephine loved that. 'He's a man, so what do you expect?'

'And he saved my life.'

Five words. They slipped out. She downed the rest of her drink.

He saved my life.

'How? Don't stop there, girl. What did he do?'

But the train started to shudder and squeal as its brakes were applied and they both turned to look out the window. Lights were pricking holes in the darkness.

'We're coming into Lyon,' Romy commented.

'Forget Lyon. What the hell did this man of yours do to save your life?'

Romy shook her head, suddenly unable to speak. She felt again the impact of Martel slamming her out of the path of the Messerschmitt's bullets, the full weight of his body crushing her bones. She must have uttered a faint sound because Josephine's hand reached out and held hers.

An ill-lit station platform slid into view, wreathed in ghosts of engine smoke and restless shadows. A huddle of four men stood waiting on the platform. They were wearing police uniforms.

'Where did you embark on this train?'

'Marseille.'

'Where do you intend to disembark?'

'Paris.'

The gendarme held her ticket in his hand. He knew all this. He had led her back to her own couchette to question her.

'How long will you be staying in Paris?'

'I live there.'

'What was your business in Marseille?'

'I wanted to go to Nice. To see how the rich live in their yachts, maybe even get a job on one, but I ran out of money. So I slept on the beach and now I'm heading home.'

She shrugged and let her head sink on her shoulders as though dispirited. The gendarme, with the quick eyes and the wide flared nostrils that seemed to sniff out lies, glanced at her dreary dress and appeared to believe her. Perhaps Martel had been right to choose it.

'Yet you travel first class,' he pointed out.

'Yes.'

'How do you afford the ticket?'

'A gentleman friend bought it for me. I met him on the beach.'

He regarded her with distaste. Behind him stood a short rotund man who was not in uniform. He wore a smart black suit that belonged on an undertaker and a perpetual half-smile that frightened Romy far more than the other one's frown. Together they breathed all the air inside the tiny couchette, leaving none for her. She felt she was suffocating. She backed off until she was jammed against the window and opened the top slat to let in the night breeze.

'Why are you here?' she asked. 'What is it you want?'

'Have you been to Spain recently?' the gendarme asked, ignoring her questions.

'No.'

'Are you sure, mademoiselle?' the smiler added. 'We are looking for someone who has come to France from Spain.'

'Of course I'm sure. I told you, I travelled from Nice.'

'Indeed you did.'

'So it's not me. In which case, will you please leave?'

The smiler looked out of the dark window. The train was still stationary, the driver waiting for instructions. Romy could feel sweat gather between her shoulder blades and it took an effort not to take her spanner to the intruders.

As though reading her mind, the smiler announced, 'We wish to search your couchette.'

Without waiting for a response he reached for her bag. It was lying on the bed and she was too late to snatch it from his fingers. He pulled it open, rummaged roughly inside and extracted the heavy spanner. It looked threatening in his hand.

'What have we here?' His plasticine smile widened. 'Now why on earth would a young woman need to travel with a spanner, mademoiselle?'

She stared back at him through cold blank eyes. 'It gets dangerous on the beach at night. You should try it some time.'

The policeman moved towards her and she knew he was about to put handcuffs on her and remove her from the train.

'Well now, boys.' It was Josephine Baker's easy drawl. 'What's going on here?' She beamed at them from the doorway. 'Mademoiselle Duchamps and I have a poker date and you're holding us up.'

She raised a pack of cards in one hand and what was left of the bourbon bottle in the other. 'I know you brave boys have a job to do, but I'd really appreciate it if you could do it elsewhere.'

It was as simple as that. The celebrity singer seemed to reel the two men in on a string and then shooed them out into the corridor. She locked the door the moment they were gone.

'*Merci*,' Romy said quietly.

'Come on, girl,' Josephine grinned and started to shuffle the cards. 'I'm going to thrash your arse at poker.'

CHAPTER TWENTY-FOUR

It is a sin. To kill someone. To take a human life. It is a wicked mortal sin.

That certainty burned in Romy's brain as she dealt the cards with Josephine Baker. Again and again the ace of spades – the death card – turned up in her hand. It stalked her that night, so that when a faint tap sounded on the door of her couchette she was convinced that she would find the gaunt figure of Death on the other side of it. But instead it was a black-garbed figure she recognised.

'Martel,' she said and drew him quickly into the compartment.

The sight of Martel in front of her, solid and unhurt, tore something loose inside her. She crushed him tight against her to keep him from the greedy fingers of Death.

'Romaine, you're drunk.'

But his words weren't an accusation. They weren't angry or fierce. They were soft and quiet and cool as snow on her burning skin. His arms held her, kept her on her feet when the swaying of the train tried to topple her. She wanted to tell him she'd been sick with worry about him but the words were too slippery on her tongue, and so she just tucked her cheek against his neck. She felt his hand cradle the back of her head, as if he understood how heavy it was.

'Who are you?' she heard him ask Josephine. His tone was unfriendly and suspicious.

She's my friend. But the words remained locked inside Romy's head.

'I am Josephine. The lovely Romy and I have been passing the hours together. So you're her boss, are you?'

'I am.'

'Well, monsieur, let me tell you that she has been fretting herself silly over whether the gendarmes got to you too. She wanted to come and find you but was frightened that the police or the carriage attendant might still be watching her. She didn't want to lead them to you.' The singer released one of her infectious laughs. '*Mon dieu*, don't look like that. She has been tight-lipped as a clam. I know nothing about what the hell you two have been up to, though I admit I am mighty curious.'

'I saw the police climb off the train without you,' Martel told Romy. 'But I didn't risk coming here until now when the attendant left his seat in the corridor for a toilet break. Are you all right?'

Romy nodded. It didn't feel good. Her head had detached itself from her body. With his arm around her, Martel walked her gently to the bed. Josephine was sitting at one end with her dog, looking far fresher than she had any right to be, cards still in her hand, and at the other end of the bed was the spot where Romy had been seated. Beside it in an unruly pile lay a large number of franc banknotes. Josephine tucked Mimi under her arm and scooted off the bed, but as she squeezed past Martel to reach the door, she trailed her crimson fingernails along his arm.

'Dammit,' she purred, 'she can outplay me at poker even when she's drunk as a skunk. I do hope you are not a man to take advantage of a girl when she's not at her best.'

Martel eased Romy on to the bed as if she were made of glass.

'No, madame.' He was leaning over Romy and she could see his mouth pulled up on one side as if unable to suppress a smile. 'I am not the kind of man who would jump on a woman in the middle of the night.'

His smile spread, reminding Romy of her own words and she felt her cheeks flush scarlet. He laughed softly and kissed her forehead.

'Sleep well. We'll be in Paris in the morning.'

'Why not, Martel?' Romy mumbled, suddenly angry with him. 'Why wouldn't you want to jump on me? Am I too dirty for you?'

'Don't, Romaine.'

She felt his hand on her head, the warmth of it finding its way between her curls.

'Go away,' she snapped. 'Both of you, go away. Leave me alone.' She put a hand over her face.

'It's the drink talking,' Josephine said with an easy laugh. 'Ignore it. She'll be better in the morning.'

Romy heard Martel sigh. 'I don't think she knows how to get better.'

They left the couchette, switched off the light. She lay there in the dark, hating Martel and the bourbon. Hating the money that lay on the floor. Hating the dreams she knew would come.

Hating herself.

The sky was slate grey. Raindrops clung to the window and blurred the flat landscape outside as the train approached Paris. Romy sat in her crumpled black dress in her couchette nursing a blinding headache, a pot of black coffee brought by the steward and a fierce sense of rage. Rage at herself.

What had possessed her? How could she possibly have thought that diving into a bottle of bourbon last night was the answer to anything?

You're drunk. Martel's words. The look in his eyes when he said them wouldn't go away. It sat there between her and the rest of the world. It made her feel as if she'd put her skin on inside out this morning, the raw and tender side exposed. She sat very still. Because even the air hurt her skin.

Josephine Baker breezed in from enjoying breakfast in the dining car, looking stunning in a fitted jacket and harem trousers the colour of milk chocolate. Only a slight redness of her eyes betrayed any discomfort from the night before.

'Well, someone is not exactly a ray of sunshine this morning,' she laughed.

Her laugh was too loud. It dragged its nails across Romy's skin.

'Here, take this.' Romy held out her winnings from the card game. 'I apologise, Josephine. I shouldn't have fleeced you last night.'

'No, damn right you shouldn't, you thankless creature. But I guess all is fair in love and cards.' She grinned forgivingly, but nevertheless pocketed the money and breezed out again.

It was when Romy turned back to the window that she realised that the train was slowing down. There was no scheduled stop between here and Paris. She heard the brakes. It was stopping in the middle of nowhere.

'Come with us.'

Romy would rather go with a viper.

One uniformed gendarme filled the doorway of Romy's couchette and another stood inside with her, boxing her in. He smelled of rain and yesterday's body odour. His face was broad and self-satisfied, the face of a man who enjoyed his work.

'What for?' she asked.

'We need to ask you some questions.'

'About what?'

'Just pick up your belongings and come with us.'

'Where are you taking me?'

'To the police station.'

He gestured to the two police cars outside the train window, parked in the field of spiky wheat stubble that ran alongside the track.

Parked in a wheat field?

Couldn't they wait until she reached Paris? Something was wrong here. The police didn't park in fields. Did they? Yet the cars were real police cars and the uniforms were real uniforms and they had flashed a real badge at her.

Martel, are you all right? Have they come for you too? How do they know we are here? She wanted to barge past the policemen and run down the corridor to the next carriage to find him, but she didn't move a muscle. She wouldn't lead them to him.

The only reason for stopping the train between stations must be to remove her from the train in secret. Why would they need to do that? It didn't make sense. Her heart was a hard knot in her chest and her mouth was as dry and empty as the bourbon bottle on her bed. She made the policemen wait stiffly while she finished her coffee. When she put the cup down, it wasn't shaking. Her only shred of satisfaction.

If Josephine Baker heard the police in the next couchette, would she bother to warn Martel?

She picked up her bag. She was ready.

CHAPTER TWENTY-FIVE

FLORENCE

I don't like breakfast. It sets my teeth on edge. I would skip it if I had my way. For Chloé's sake I pick at my croissant. She likes me to be here at the table, even though she spends the whole meal with her nose in a book. Today it is *Patapoufs et Filifers*.

Roland sits in silence opposite me, though I barely see a trace of him behind his newspaper, *Le Figaro*. At intervals his hand becomes visible when it sneaks round for his coffee cup. I have often chided them both for this daily rudeness but I cannot break them of the habit.

I observe my daughter's face in repose and as always I am captivated. I could watch her forever. Even when reading, her features are mobile and alive, expressions of concern or amusement flit across her young face like sunlight on water, forever changing. She possesses my mother's beautiful cornflower-blue eyes and high forehead, but there is something of my father in the shape of her head, something of him in the set of her jawline. At times when she is soft and sleepy, I run my finger along it, lingering there, and imagine that I am reconnecting with my father. One day I will tell her. But not today.

'What are you doing today, Florence?' Roland asks.

He folds his newspaper with neat creases and regards me attentively. He asks me this every morning. Chloé looks up from her page, awaiting my answer. They keep tabs on me, these two.

'I have a manicure appointment this morning, then lunch with Marianne Rambert at L'Étoile. Afterwards we are off to a gathering in rue de Rivoli where Jean-Paul Sartre will be giving a speech.' I smile at them. 'Satisfied?'

They smile back, satisfied. They do not suspect the lie.

The rain has stopped. I walk past a woman washing her hair in a bucket on the pavement. I stare in shock. She smiles at me with no teeth and I throw her a coin because what else can I do?

How can my sister live in a street where people wash their hair in a bucket? On the pavement. How long is Romaine going to continue to punish herself this way? She has lovers but no love. She has jokes with her drinking companions but no joy. Her eyes light up for only two things – for her wretched aeroplanes and for Chloé. She loves them with a passion. Far more than she loves me. I can forgive her the idealistic left-wing claptrap that she spouts, but she can't forgive me my right-wing pro-Nazi stance. There is no middle ground where we can meet. Except Chloé. She is our no man's land. Our focus of love. In Chloé we see the best of each other.

The door to Romaine's building is thankfully open, but I find access to it blocked by a pair of broad female buttocks clad in a threadbare housecoat. The woman is on her knees scrubbing the doorstep and hallway. It strikes me as a valiant gesture amid all the dirt that surrounds her.

'Bonjour, madame,' I say.

The concierge hoists herself to her feet, hands on wide hips, damp cloth dangling. Her expression in repose is peevish, but at the sight of my couture pastel suit and delicately frivolous hat she beams goodwill at me.

'Good morning to you, madame, what can I help you with?'

'I'm here to see Mademoiselle Duchamps. I am her sister.'

She studies my face with interest. 'Of course you are. I can see the resemblance. But she's not here.'

I assume an expression of distress. 'Oh no, I need to speak to her urgently. Do you know where she is?'

Her eyes narrow. She is wary now. 'Out.'

I don't push it. Instead I extract two one-hundred-franc notes from my purse and slip them into the pocket of her faded housecoat. Neither of us mentions it.

'Do you think I could wait in her room for her to return?'

'It could be a long wait.'

I smile encouragingly. 'I'll risk it.'

'Wait here.'

She shuffles off to the inner recesses of the building and returns after only a couple of minutes with a bunch of keys.

'Upstairs,' she says and starts to climb, keys jangling.

I follow.

The room is no different from when I saw it the day we danced together. It is awful. Worse than awful. The zinc bucket in the middle of the room has ten centimetres of rainwater in it from last night's downpour and the smell in the air is damp and sour, but I ignore it all. I am not here for the room.

I am here for her secrets.

I look first at what clothes my sister has hanging up. It appals me how few and meagre they are. A couple of skirts, a dress, three blouses, a pair of black trousers. A sweater. A cardigan. That's it. She must be wearing her flying gear, as it's not here.

Where are the pieces I've given her? Silk blouses, chemises, a summer dress. Where? And the navy Schiaparelli gown she wore at Monico's.

All gone. What does she do with them? Give them away? Sell them? Anything, I suspect, rather than keep them here in her room where she will have to look at them. If she looks at them, she will have to think of me, and clearly that is something she cannot bear to do. The tick of a pulse starts up in my throat and I can't make it stop, but I know what it is. It is a pinpoint of pain. I am hurting.

'Romaine,' I whisper out loud.

Her name drifts through the room and memories come swirling with it. My father's voice, sharp and insistent. *Romaine, put down that knife.*

The pain in my throat is so fierce I cannot swallow. I turn my back on the sounds and their echoes and I inspect the room. I detach myself from the pain. From the voices. There is nowhere to hide anything, just a small box with a few bits and pieces in it, three packs of playing cards, a hairbrush, a penknife, and, surprisingly, a chess set carved out of a dark wood. I say *surprisingly* because I didn't know that my sister could play chess. I wonder who she plays with.

I look under the bed. I lie flat on my stomach and peer underneath. I should have known. Should have expected it, but even so it catches me by surprise and I feel stupid for being naive. There are whisky bottles hiding under the bed as if scared of the light. They are all empty, all twelve of them. My stomach turns with disgust.

So that's it, it would seem. The room has nothing more to show for itself. Nothing more to tell me. Except that I know my twin sister better than anyone else on earth and so I know exactly where to look. I flick back the dusky pink bedcover I gave her and untuck the sheet. It takes me no more than five seconds to find the slit in the side of the mattress that she has stitched together with a bootlace.

I undo it, push my hand inside and pull out a drawstring

bag. It brings pieces of black horsehair mattress stuffing with it but I brush them off and open the bag. I gasp. Romaine. I expected a secret stash of cash but not this much. I don't take it out, don't count it, but I can see it must add up to quite a decent hoard. So why ask me for money? Well, sister mine, I am impressed. No wonder you live like a pauper.

In an odd way, I am proud of her. She has a goal. I sit on my heels and try to work out what it is, until it dawns on me in a moment of absolute clarity. I know she has only two passions – Chloé and aeroplanes. Chloé has no need of Romaine's money. So it is obvious. My sister is saving for an aeroplane of her own.

I shiver. Part pride, part fear. But I laugh at myself for not having thought of it years ago, because I remember her as a child staring at the photograph of the aviatrix Elise Raymonde de Deroche hanging on her wall and swearing that she would own a plane herself one day. Her face tight with intent, her young voice booming out loudly in the room. Startling me.

Oh, Romaine, be careful. Those planes will be the death of you one of these days.

The thought chills my heart and I quickly close the drawstring, sealing the thought inside. Would you be happy, Romaine, if you had your plane? I sit here on my heels for a full minute waiting for an answer in the damp little room and then I open the drawstring bag once more. Into it I place all the banknotes I have in my own purse – ten thousand francs – and slide it back deep in the mattress. The horsehair is prickly but not unpleasant to touch. I rethread the bootlace that seals the split and pat it with satisfaction when it is done.

Now, Romaine. Now, will you be happy?

Will you forget that day in the study?

There is so much to forget. The whiteness of your skin, the redness of your hands. The rattle of your breathing, as if a can opener had got inside you. You were good when the police came. Oh, Romaine, you were so good that I almost believed you myself when you told them you were with me in the garden and begged them to track down Papa's killer. When you looked Karim Abed straight in the eyes and called him a liar. The police believed you. I could see it. They trusted you. More than they trusted me.

Papa is dead because of you, Romaine. How can either of us ever forget that? You changed our lives forever.

I shake myself. Literally. To strip the thoughts and images from my head, but their tentacles twine deep inside it. I jump to my feet. It is this room. It contains almost nothing, yet is so full of the past. I pace the bare floorboards and catch a glimpse of myself in a small square mirror that is the only object that adorns the walls. I look as though someone has slapped my cheeks. Red blurs on my pale skin.

The mirror reminds me of another of your hiding places as a child. I stride over to it, remove it from the wall and look at the back of it. I smile. You do not change, Romaine. On the back is stuck a photograph. I expect it to be one of your aeroplanes but it isn't. It is you and me. We are standing on a beach, barefoot, with our skirts tucked up above skinny pin-straight legs. No more than nine or ten years old, white-blonde hair to our shoulders, yours curlier than mine. We are holding hands and smiling. Not at the camera, at each other. Eyes fixed on each other as if nothing else in the world exists.

I start to cry.

There is more. Much more.

I stand there with the blurred image of us in front of me until the tears stop. I never cry. Never. But now I feel as though all my innards have been ripped out and shredded, and I remember the last time I felt this agony, the last time I cried. It was the night after Papa died.

I swore then – and I swear now – never to cry again.

I rehang the mirror. I dry my face. I stalk around the room once more, now that I know what I am looking for. I stop in front of the small bedside table made out of bamboo that has seen better days. I crouch down and look at its underside and yes, I am right. A brown envelope is pasted there. I examine it but it is sealed. I consider what might be in it.

I don't trust you.

I peel it away from the table, tear open the flap and take out a single sheet of paper. It is covered in my sister's bold black handwriting and a throb sets up behind my eyes because I know what is coming.

To the Police

My name is Romaine Céline Duchamps. On 18 July 1930 I was living with my parents, Antoine and Adelle Duchamps, at 14 rue Souchard, Paris, when my father was murdered.

I killed him. I cannot remember why I committed this terrible act but I know that I did. I became unconscious and when I woke up I was in my father's study. He was lying dead on the floor with a paperknife in his throat and I was covered in his blood.

I persuaded my sister Florence Valérie Duchamps, against her will, to lie for me, and her friend Roland Roussel. They are both innocent of any involvement in the murder of my father. I put the blame on our gardener, Karim Abed. I lied to the police and I lied in court. Karim was convicted and executed, for which I feel abject shame and sorrow. I apologise to his family and to my mother for the pain I have caused them.

This confession is because I want the truth to be known. I want Karim Abed's wife and son, Aya and Samir Abed, no longer to bear the stigma of being the wife and son of a murderer. He was innocent.

To my mother, Adelle Duchamps, and to Roland Roussel, I apologise from the bottom of my heart. I regret everything I did that day.

This confession is written and signed of my own free will and in sound mind.

Romaine Duchamps

I read the letter through five times. Then five times more. Then I tear it and its envelope into a thousand pieces and tip them into the bottom of my handbag, hidden under my scarf and keys. I leave the room. With every thump of my heart comes the same question.

Why didn't she apologise to me?

CHAPTER TWENTY-SIX

'Where have you travelled from?'

'From Nice.'

'Where are you going?'

'Paris. I live there.'

Romy was seated at a metal table. The room in the police station was small and airless, with that heavy smell of men in uniform. The single light bulb that hung from the ceiling was naked and too bright for comfort. It seemed to flicker and pulse in the corner of Romy's eye.

Turn it off.

But she stuck to her answers to the questions that the man seated opposite her kept throwing at her. Inspecteur Chardin. He was not in uniform but wore an exquisite grey linen jacket that looked too costly for a *sûreté* policeman. His expression was disarmingly gentle, his voice softly-spoken, only his eyes gave him away. Quick and observant.

'What were you doing in Nice?' he asked.

'I was looking for a job on a yacht. But failed to find one, so I'm going home.'

'How long were you in Nice?'

'Only two days.'

'Were you alone?'

'Yes.'

'Where did you stay?'

'Nowhere. I slept on the beach. I've told you this.'

'Were you in Spain?'

'No.'

'In the mountains?'

'No.'

'With a companion?'

'No.'

'I believe you are lying. Are you lying, mademoiselle?'

'No.'

The questions chased each other in circles. The same ones over and over again while the *inspecteur* waited for her concentration to slip and the truth to come tumbling out of her mouth. He paused to light himself a cigarette but did not offer her one. She badly wanted a glass of water – her mouth felt like the bottom of a dustbin – but she refused to ask for one in case he decided to play games and deny her it.

'Inspecteur Chardin, why am I here? I have a right to know. Why have you dragged me off a train and brought me here?'

'Because we received information that a woman would be

travelling on that train who has been involved in dealings with the Republican forces in Spain.'

'It is not illegal to support the Republicans,' she pointed out.

'True.' He smiled in his mild-mannered way as if she might have wrong-footed him. 'But it is illegal in France to supply them with aeroplanes. There is a law against it.'

She needed that water. Her mouth was bone dry.

'I was in Nice. Not Spain.' She stood up, her chair scraping on the tiles. 'I know nothing about Spain. May I leave now?'

He tipped his chair on to its back legs, easy and confident. 'I am informed you were travelling with a man.'

'You are mistaken, Inspecteur. I travel alone.'

He nodded. She had convinced him. He would let her go now and she could start looking for Martel. She was frightened for him. Had they hauled him off the train too? She took a step towards the door but immediately a uniformed officer in the corner moved in front of it.

'Mademoiselle.' The *inspecteur*'s soft voice pursued her. It had gained a sorrowful edge to it. 'You are lying. You know it and I know it. I need to hear more about the plans of those fighters up in the mountains, just across our border. There are people who need to know. It will be better for you to speak the truth to me than to be asked these questions by other interested parties. You understand me?'

Fear came. A quick sharp stab of it. Like a needle in her throat.

'I wish to leave now. You have no proof, so you cannot hold me here.'

'On the contrary, we have a friend of yours here too. I would like you to take time to think about why you are both here.'

Léo Martel. Her breathing stopped.

'Take her away.'

It wasn't Martel.

Relief pumped through Romy's veins when she was conducted into another small interview room – a room, not a cell – and found Josephine Baker in her harem suit sitting alone on the edge of the table, puffing on a hefty cigar and wearing an expression of extreme exasperation. At the sight of Romy she slid off the table and stalked across the room with the grace of a cheetah. A cheetah with its hackles raised.

'Girl! What kind of mess have you got me into? What the hell is going on?'

Romy went to the singer and for a brief moment hugged her tight, then released the tense angry figure. 'Got a cigarette?'

'You get nothing from me till you tell me why these *flics* are all over you.'

'I'm sorry you've been dragged into this. They seem to have mistaken me for someone else, I think, someone they are searching for.'

'Is that a fact?'

Romy nodded firmly. 'Have they questioned you?'

'You bet they have. A scrawny young officer still wet behind the ears.'

'What did you tell him?' Romy tried to look as if it didn't much matter. As if Léo Martel's life didn't depend on it.

Josephine pulled out a pack of Gitanes, offered one and lit it with a gold Dupont lighter. 'I told them we met on the train, that you were a bad influence on me.' She chuckled at that. 'And that we played cards and drank whisky for half the night. That's it.'

'Did you mention the gendarme on the train?'

'Oh yes, that too.'

Romy sat down at the table. Her legs were shaky. Josephine took the chair opposite and they looked at each other guardedly. Romy glanced at the door to make sure it was securely closed.

'Did you mention anyone else on the train?'

The singer dropped the stub of her cigar on the tiled floor and stubbed it out with her heel, then rolled her black eyes in Romy's direction. 'Anyone particular in mind?'

'No.'

'Good. Because I didn't mention nobody else.'

'*Merci*,' Romy whispered and exhaled a long string of smoke with relief. 'Have you called a lawyer to get you out of here?'

'You bet your sweet arse I have. And if he's not in his Voisin Aérosport right now driving like a bat out of hell to this stinking little *commissariat*, I will murder him with my own hands. Then the *inspecteur* will have a real case on his doorstep to investigate.'

A laugh rose in Romy like a shaft of sunlight within the

dark chill inside her. She liked this woman, she liked the way Josephine Baker seized life with both hands.

'Romaine, tell me what this mess is about?' Josephine's head cocked to one side appealingly. 'You must know what's going on.'

'I don't, honestly I don't. As far as I understand, they are searching for someone travelling from Spain.'

'Is this *someone* some kind of agent?'

Romy shrugged. 'It's possible. They are keeping everything secret. They took us off the train between stations so that no one will know where we are, but it's all a mistake. You must get out, Josephine. Quickly. Get that lawyer of yours to take you home to Le Vésinet. Don't get involved.'

'Too late for that, honey.' Josephine ran a hand over her sleek black hair, short as a lamb's fleece and oiled so that it gleamed like fresh paintwork. 'Hell, I need a shower to wash the stink of this place off me.'

The door opened. A blue uniform stood there.

'Romaine Duchamps, come with me.'

Romy kissed Josephine Baker's cheek. Was this the end?

Sometimes you can be looking in the wrong direction. Sometimes you can be walking down the road looking straight ahead, when a truck comes roaring out of a side street and smacks right into you. That's what happened when Romy stepped back into the interview room. She'd been looking in the wrong direction.

'*Bonjour*, Mademoiselle Duchamps. We meet again.'

'Herr Müller!'

Herr Müller? In a provincial police station? *Tell me, Fräulein, do you ever fly to Spain*? That's what he'd asked at Monico's, and now he was here to interrogate her again.

He approached her, a smile of greeting painted on his thin lips, hand outstretched. She shook it as if he were a friend, rather than someone she knew was here to hurt her. His firm grip held on to her hand for too long.

'Please sit down.'

Romy remained standing in the airless room. 'Herr Müller, why am I being detained here? I have done nothing wrong and yet I am being treated like a criminal. I insist on being released immediately.'

'Not like a criminal, I assure you, mademoiselle. We are just asking you some questions.' He released her hand and gestured towards a chair. 'Let us be civilised about this. Please do sit down.'

Civilised?

She could be civilised. She took a seat. She needed to find out how much he knew, especially about Martel. Oh Martel, are you being questioned too? Are they being *civilised* with you?

Herr Müller sat in the other chair. His pale suit matched the grey of his hair exactly and there was an air of authority that hung on him as visible as cigarette smoke.

'Horst Baumeister pointed out to me,' he said, 'that you are well informed about the Condor Legion in Spain.'

'I read the newspapers, that's all. That is not illegal. Not in France.'

'Mademoiselle Duchamps, there are people in Paris who are trying to hinder our attempts to—'

'You mean Germany's attempts.'

'Yes, that is correct. They are trying to hinder Germany's attempts to help Spain free itself from the Communist forces that have taken over its government. It is my belief that you are one of these people. You are involved with a group of radicals who are stealing Germany's military secrets and passing them on to our enemies in Spain.'

She laughed. As though the idea were absurd.

The German didn't laugh. He leaned across the table and slapped her hard across the cheek, a sudden stinging blow that rocked her head back and tore the breath from her. The shock of it changed everything.

Normal rules didn't apply. Not in here. Not anymore. Not with Herr Müller. She understood that now.

The slap had scared Romy even more than the gun she had glimpsed in a holster under his jacket when he'd leaned forward. Whatever was going on here, he was in charge and he intended her to be aware of it. All pretence of friendship had peeled away from his grey eyes and what lay behind them chilled her to the bone. But he didn't know her, didn't realise that she was not a person to lose her courage when a storm blew up.

'You left DeFosse airfield two days ago in a private aircraft,' he stated.

'No, you are mistaken.'

They hadn't logged the flight. He couldn't know. He was guessing. Surely he was guessing. She jumped to her feet, strode to the door and yanked it open. Outside, blocking her exit, stood a policeman.

'Close the door, mademoiselle,' Müller said behind her.

She closed the door.

'Now let's talk about who travelled with you in the aircraft. What is his name?'

'I travelled by train and I travelled alone.'

'I am not interested in your lies.'

'Herr Müller, this is France, not Germany. You have no jurisdiction here.'

He uncoiled from his seat and moved towards her fast. She readied herself for another slap but it didn't come.

'Don't for one moment think that is true, mademoiselle. If I choose, you will be on a plane tonight heading for Berlin. Keep that in mind. Now sit down, let us talk about your travelling companion, and while we do that, I will have Inspecteur Chardin bring us coffee.'

Romy sat down, her mind racing down wild paths. He ordered coffee, but it was obvious he was not going to release her. It was also obvious that he did not know who her travelling companion was. That was the only glimmer of light in this dark tunnel, as long as Josephine Baker said nothing, but even with her, Romy had been careful never to mention Martel's name.

'I will make a deal with you,' she announced.

'I don't do deals.' But he gave her a smile, a cold and lifeless smile. 'What do you have in mind?'

'The deal is this. You tell me how you knew I was in the south of France and on the Blue Train, and in exchange I will try to find everything I can for you about the people you are looking for in Paris.'

She thought of the gun in Herr Müller's holster and the bullet holes in the heads of François and Grégory.

'A double agent?'

'Yes,' she said.

'Why would you do that, mademoiselle?'

'Because I expect to be paid. And because I don't want to end up locked in a Berlin basement with someone like you.'

He didn't like that. A stream of German invective poured from him, harsh and angry, none of which made sense to her. Yet something snagged in her mind. One sentence. It climbed through the layers of her fear and got itself caught on something sharp and painful.

'*Ich möchte mich nicht streiten.*'

She'd heard it before. But where? It swept an overwhelming sense of sadness through her, though she didn't understand why. But the echo stayed. So strong, it silenced all else, reverberating inside her head. Just those few words. *Ich möchte mich nicht streiten.* They knocked her feet from under her.

'Mademoiselle Duchamps?'

Romy blinked. Müller's inquisitive eyes were staring at her, expecting a reply. She'd missed something.

'I'm sorry, Herr Müller?'

'I said how do I know I can trust you?'

'You don't. You have to take my word that . . .'

The door opened and Inspecteur Chardin entered with two cups of coffee. Müller nodded towards the table. It was quite obvious who was in charge here, but Romy couldn't work it out. How could a German be calling the shots in a French police station? But as she reached for the coffee, a female voice floated into the small room.

'Romaine, *ma chérie,* time to leave.'

Josephine Baker glided in with a small thin man with a worried face at her heels, presumably her lawyer, and stood with her hands on her slender hips, surveying the scene. Slowly a wide scarlet-lipped smile spread across her face.

'Well, well, look who we have here.'

Müller recognised the famous singer at once and leaped to his feet. He performed a courteous Germanic bow of his head. 'Madame Baker, I am Gustav Müller. What a pleasure to meet you, though unfortunate that it is in such dismal circumstances.'

Josephine extended her hand with all the grandeur of a queen and he bent over it with a brief click of his heels. 'I hope you've been entertaining my young friend, Romaine.' Without waiting for a reply, she switched her headlamp-beam smile to Inspecteur Chardin. 'And Xavier, honey, I didn't know you worked here. The last time I saw you, you didn't look quite so smart, did you? That party in Neuilly.' She rolled her black eyes and chuckled with a wicked whoop of amusement.

He remembered all right. Romy saw the French

policeman's face drain of blood, his lips turn grey. He looked sick.

Josephine beamed at him. 'How is Madame Chardin?'

'She is well, thank you.'

'Good. We want her to stay that way, don't we? We don't want to worry her with that little incident when you went swimming in the pool with two naked fifteen-year-old girls who proceeded to paint your balls gold.'

Romy uttered a snort of laughter. She left her chair and slipped her arm through Josephine's. 'Shall we go now?'

'No, Madame Baker,' Müller said sharply. 'I insist that Mademoiselle Duchamps remains here with me.'

Josephine let her eyes linger on Romy's cheek. 'What have you been doing to my friend, Gustav? I hope you didn't have an argument.' She smiled benignly at him. 'Argue with Xavier Chardin instead about whether Mademoiselle Duchamps stays or goes. In the meantime,' she blew him a kiss, '*au revoir.*'

Inspecteur Chardin flapped a panicked hand at her. 'Get out. Both of you. Get out of here. *Allez-vous-en.*'

CHAPTER TWENTY-SEVEN

FLORENCE

I find my sister. She is prowling back and forth, tense as a tigress among the foliage, hidden under the poplar trees at the boundary of the airfield. I come up behind her and she nearly jumps out of her skin. She is so focused on the handful of buildings and hangars huddled at the far end that she is unaware of what is right behind her.

'Florence! What are you doing here?'

'Looking for you.'

She looks a mess. A dress that resembles a shapeless black shroud and such dark circles under her eyes they twist my heart.

'Have you been in a brawl?' I indicate the purple bruise on her cheek.

'Yes.'

'For God's sake, Romaine, you have to cut back on the drinking.'

But she is not listening. She is elsewhere. Barely conscious of me. I follow her line of sight and find it concentrated on one brick building at least two hundred metres from us. People are coming and going in and out of it.

'What's in there?' I ask.

'Offices. A bar. Storage.'

'If it's so interesting, why don't you just wander in there?'

She says nothing and for a long moment all I hear is a jangling sound. It could be the wind stirring the silvery leaves above our heads and the flutter of flags along the top of the brick building. Or it could be her thoughts. Crashing into each other. A spindly old aeroplane takes off with a roar. It seems to bring Romaine back to me. She turns her head and frowns at me.

'What are you doing here?' she asks again.

'I told you. Looking for you.'

'How did you find me?'

'I am good at looking.'

I move close to her. I catch a faint hint of perfume on her, so faint it is barely there, but I recognise it because I use it myself. It is *Joy* by Jean Patou. It doesn't make sense. Who has she been with who wears such expensive perfume?

'Roland told me,' I say, 'that you came to our apartment looking for me the other day, but then you disappeared. I came to the airfield to find you because you weren't at your house.'

Her muddy eyes seek mine, and maybe it is because I have caught her unawares, but the barriers are down. Her eyes are naked and defenceless. And full of pain.

'What is it, Romaine? What has happened? Why are you out here among the trees, spying on what is going on at DeFosse airfield?'

'I'm searching for someone.'

'Who?'

I think she is not going to reply. She shudders and I wrap my hand tight around hers.

'Léo Martel,' she whispers. And then louder, 'Léo Martel.'

'Come then. Let's go and find him.'

I stride forward to cross the airfield, drawing my sister with me. Reluctantly she emerges from the shadows.

She leads me from building to building, from office to office. She knocks on doors, she asks questions.

'Have you seen Léo Martel today?'

'Have other people been asking after him?'

The answers are always the same. 'No, sorry, Romy. If I see him, I'll tell him you're chasing him.'

What I notice is the way these people – the pilots and mechanics and airfield officials – all seem so fond of Romy. Their eyes brighten around her. I don't think of her that way. With me she is always morose and silent, or sometimes just acutely sad, unless Chloé is with us. With Chloé she smiles.

I follow her through another door and it leads into a long, impressively stocked bar with glossy mahogany shelves and bevelled mirrors that reflect rows of bottles. Romaine goes through the questions with the barman and lingers a while, but she refrains from buying a drink. I am relieved. When

I see her glance at the bottles and lick her lips, I say quickly, 'Where next, Romaine?'

She leaves the bar without complaint. We go over to the hangars, which I find to be odd heartless spaces with various planes, tyres and overalls set out in rows. My sister seeks out a tiny weasel of a man whom she introduces as Jules Roget. It seems he is Léo Martel's mechanic but hasn't seen him for days. We are about to walk out of the hangar when I spot a young dark-haired boy of about thirteen or so in denim overalls too big for him. He is wielding a broom.

'You,' I call out to him. 'Come here.'

I only intend to enquire if he has seen this Léo Martel, but he turns his back on me. I cannot tolerate rudeness. It always flips a switch in me. I march over to him and tap his shoulder smartly.

'Boy! Answer me.'

He turns. But he does not look at me. He looks over my shoulder at my sister who is several steps behind me.

'Have you seen someone called Léo Mart—?'

'Florence!'

My name comes out as a stifled scream from my sister's mouth. I am bewildered. She hurries to my side and stares at the boy as if he is a ghost.

'What?' I demand. 'What?'

She touches my hand with her fingers and curls them around mine.

'It is Samir,' she says softly. 'Samir Abed.'

*

Samir Abed?

For a moment the name means nothing to me. And then it dawns. Karim's son. Of course he is. He has his father's long narrow face, his swarthy skin, his soft polite mouth, but not his father's docile eyes. This boy's dark eyes burn in his head.

'What are you doing here, Samir?' Romaine asks without releasing my fingers.

His eyes flit from my sister's face to mine to his broom. They remain on the broom, hiding from us.

'Why here, Samir? Of all places. You must have followed me.'

She speaks in a reasonable tone, but I can sense through her fingers that she is feeling anything but reasonable. I start to fear for her. For us.

'You should be at school,' she tells him.

'I need money. I have to work.'

'I know your mother is sick.'

What? What? How does my sister know that?

'She needs an operation,' the boy says. 'It costs many thousands of francs.'

'You *must* go to school, Samir. I will get the money for you.'

'How?' His eyes rise from the broom and they are angry. 'How will you get the money? You who drink and gamble your money away, you live in a slum and dress like a *vagabonde*. How will you get it? By whoring your way across Paris?'

She takes it. She just stands there and takes it.

But I don't. My hand darts out and strikes him. It catches him a stinging blow on the ear, so full of rage that it must have made his head ring. Romaine ignores my outburst.

'I will get the money for you, Samir, whatever it takes,' she says. 'I will not let you throw away your chance of an education and a future that would have made your father proud of you.'

At the mention of his father something changes in the boy. The edges blur. 'At least give him the respect of a name,' he whispers.

'Karim Abed.'

He nods. They look at each other and I realise that they know things about each other. Alarm bells start jangling in my head. She cannot hide the truth from this gardener's son. I see that now. She is in danger. My sister, with her wild unpredictable habits and her inability to lie to Samir, she will get us executed.

I drive Romaine back into the centre of Paris in my Delage D6-70 roadster. Even in her obvious distress I see her admire the car as she slides in – it is two-tone blue and cream with an elegant Chapron body and a six-cylinder engine. I let her settle. I don't rush her. There are things I need to know, but I leave her in silence until I can feel her untangle some of the knots that make her screw her hands into the limp black cotton of her dress. She drops her canvas shoulder bag at her feet and we motor along tree-lined boulevards in silence, the wind tousling stray strands of our hair.

'What do you know about the boy?' I ask eventually. I don't want to say his name.

She looks at me, dragging her thoughts together. Wherever they were, they weren't on the boy.

'For the last eight years I have watched him grow up. Once a month I go to the Arab quarter where they live and I put money in an envelope for them. But it seems Samir has retaliated and followed me around Paris.' She shakes her head, bemused. 'How could I not have noticed? This is the first time I have ever spoken to him.'

I am glad I am driving, otherwise I might have seized her shoulders and shaken my twin.

'Fool,' I shout. Because I am angry. 'You stupid fool. You must stay away from him.'

'Lend me the money for the operation, Florence.'

'No.'

'Please, Florence.'

'No.'

She places a hand on my thigh. I almost crash into the van in front.

'I will pay you back, I promise.'

'It is not the money, Romaine. It is too dangerous for you to be in touch with Karim's family.'

'What if I promise to stay away from them in future? Will you lend me the money then?' Her fingers squeeze my thigh.

'I'll think about it. I will have to discuss it with Roland.' It's not true but it buys me time.

She slumps back in her seat and withdraws her hand. She

knows what my husband will say as well as I do. I take a bend so sharply that it throws her against the door. Her amber eyes are dark and dull as she looks at me quizzically.

'What, Florence? What has got you so worked up?'

'Have you ever thought about this possibility, Romaine, during all your guilt-ridden breast-beating? That perhaps Karim, our Algerian gardener, did actually kill Papa?'

'Don't be absurd. He was in the garden.'

'How do we know he didn't at some point enter the house and have an argument over pay? Karim was wanting a raise, we know that. Who's to say you didn't walk in on them and get caught up in it and Karim hit you with the brass pyramid in a fit of temper? Knowing he would go to jail for it, he stuck the paperknife in Papa's throat and rushed back to his work in the garden with his innocent face on.'

She stares at me, open-mouthed.

'It's possible,' I say. 'He was the only other one there that day.'

I manoeuvre the Delage into a spot between two trucks outside the fine clock tower of the Gare de Lyon, which is where she asked to be dropped. It is mid-afternoon and the sun is hot on our shoulders in the open car, but not hot enough to explain why my sister's cheeks are suddenly a fierce scarlet.

'Don't pretend to me, Florence.'

'I'm not pretending.' I say it gently. It upsets me to see her upset and I feel my own cheeks burn in sympathy. 'I am pointing out that maybe justice was done. Maybe Karim did murder our father. So no need to wear sackcloth and ashes for the rest of your days.'

I pull on the handbrake and swivel in my seat to face her. To my horror I see her eyes fill with tears. I haven't seen Romaine cry since our cat died when she was seven. I reach for her and am surprised when she rests her forehead on my shoulder. I realise she is exhausted.

'Calm down, Romaine, and forget about the boy. You don't need to be responsible for him or his sick mother.'

But the moment is brief. She withdraws abruptly and I feel the loss of her.

'Go to hell,' she says but mildly. 'You just want an excuse not to lend the money.'

I shake my head, but she turns to climb out of the car. I hold her arm. 'Wait, please. Tell me who this Léo Martel is, the man you're searching for.

Her arm starts to shake. 'I told you, he is my boss.'

'I get the feeling he's much more than your boss.'

'No. Nothing like that.'

Liar. But I keep the word locked up.

CHAPTER TWENTY-EIGHT

Romy entered Gare de Lyon at a run. It was a long shot to come to the station. A very long shot. But it was all she had left. Plumes of smoke from the massive steam trains hung in the air, turning it grey and leaving smuts of soot on the skin like speckles on a bird's egg. The station *quais* were crowded with travellers and suitcases that knocked against shins, porters shouting and women adjusting their summer hats. There was a sense of purpose in the station that matched Romy's own, but she was blind to it all.

Her eyes raked the huddles of travellers, every broad back or black shirt or tall dark head. None of them matched the one she searched for. A long shot. That came to nothing. A train belched a cloud of smoke that seemed to settle inside her head, smudging the edges of her thoughts.

Martel? Have you forgotten me?

Did you leave the Blue Train here in Paris and disappear into the city's backstreets without a backward glance?

Or are you in an interrogation room somewhere? Is Müller battering you with questions? Or with something worse?

'Martel.'

She murmured his name aloud as if it could conjure him up, but it didn't rid her of the ache in her heart. She hurried over to the point in the station where Le Train Bleu restaurant was situated on an upper floor above the hustle and bustle below. It was the peak of dining luxury for wealthy travellers, approached by an elegant staircase with an elaborate curve of wrought-iron balustrading.

But it was not the restaurant itself or its glitzy chandeliers that caught her eye. It was a black figure. In a shadowy corner beneath the staircase.

She started to run.

He saw her coming. He threw down his cigarette and opened his long arms and she flew into them. Not with any grace or decorum but at breakneck speed. She launched herself at Martel's broad chest with a cry of joy and the force of her leap almost knocked him off his heels.

She found herself lifted off her feet and crushed against his ribs until she thought her own would break. Her arms fixed in a death grip around his neck and she could only breathe in disjointed gasps.

'You were gone. I couldn't find you. I don't know where you live, so I went to the airfield. I checked for police first. You weren't there.' She pressed her hot cheek tight to his. 'So I came here.'

'I've been waiting. And waiting. Meeting every shit-bucket train from the south.' He rubbed his face against hers, his stubble rough and reassuring. 'Waiting and cursing.'

'I thought you were dead,' she breathed against his skin.

They were in a basement. Martel had brought her to another safe house. It was a basement apartment near the banks of the Seine and smelled of the river, as if the grey water swirled just beneath their feet. He was seated in an armchair and didn't take his eyes off her as she prowled the room.

'Don't go anywhere near Horst Baumeister,' he said.

'But Horst can be useful to us. It might save lives.'

'Please, Romaine.' Martel was insistent. 'Stay away from him. Do you want to get your face slapped by another German?'

'Horst is not like Müller.'

'He is still a danger. I am frightened for you if you get too friendly with him.'

Too friendly. They both knew what that meant.

'Horst has access to all kinds of secret information,' she pointed out.

'It might save the lives of others, but what good is that to me if it takes yours?'

His words stopped her mid-stride. They left her stranded in the middle of the room, unable to move, listening to them pulse in her ears.

'Don't, Martel,' she said softly. 'Don't say that.'

'It's true.'

'Don't. You don't really know me.'

'Of course I know you.' He leaned forward, elbows on his knees, his grey eyes intent on hers. 'I know you are a pain in the arse, hell-bent on destroying yourself. The best damn flier I know, with enough courage for a whole squadron of fliers. With a generous heart and a frantic determination to drown yourself in a bottle. I don't know what the hell happened to you in the past, Romaine, or what makes you push people away to stop anyone getting close. But I do know it's time you let go of it. Anyway,' he threw back his head with a deep-chested laugh, 'Romaine, I'm not swapping you for some top-secret documents, thank you.'

It was the laugh that broke her. It came crashing through her defences. She heard them shatter, felt their sharp edges slice through her. He had brought her here and she had told him about the interrogation by Müller, but neither had mentioned that naked moment at the station. When they had been fused together.

She could not talk of documents and German secrets. Not now. She walked over to his chair and sat on the arm of it. She took his startled face between her hands and studied it intimately, her gaze lingering on the sweep of his thick eyelashes, the broad solid bones of his cheeks, the strong wedge of his chin. And the way his nose arched, too fine for his face, with the scar on the side like the coil of a seashell. They were all so familiar but she had never touched them before, or let her thumb caress his cheek as it did now. But it was his mouth that did the damage to any shred of defence she had left. Full, warm, sculpted. She bent her head forward and kissed it.

His lips tasted of honey and summer wine and strong Turkish cigarettes. Desire tore through her like a hot wire and her hand slid down to the taut tendons of his throat but . . . His lips did not respond. Under hers they were lifeless and indifferent.

She jerked back her head. Confused.

'Don't you want this?'

'No, Romaine, I don't.'

She shot off the arm of the chair like a scalded cat.

'I apologise,' Romy said. 'I got it wrong.'

'Yes, you did.'

Even her ears were burning. She was standing with her back to him, staring up at the window set high in the wall of the basement room. All she could see outside were feet hurrying past, because the outside world didn't stop, however much her inside one had juddered to a halt. She felt hurt and ashamed.

And yet. In the station, Léo Martel had crushed her to his chest as though he would weld her to his heart. She remembered the pressure of his lips on her hair. Romy knew men, knew more men than she cared to remember, and she knew beyond doubt that at that raw moment in the Gare de Lyon, this man had wanted to eat her alive.

She spun around. To her surprise he was standing right behind her, tall and watchful.

'I didn't get it wrong, did I?' she asked.

'No, Romaine, you were not wrong. You are rarely wrong about me.'

'Martel,' she whispered, 'what is it? What's wrong?'

'Look at you, Romaine. You are an amazing young woman, as courageous and as capable as you are beautiful. Now look at me. I am ten years older than you, I have a leg so messed up that it takes me ten minutes to climb into the cockpit of a plane and, in the war that's coming – make no mistake, it *is* coming – I will most likely die, because even though they won't pass me fit for service in the air force, I'll be fighting with the Resistance when the Germans invade. So you see, Romaine,' he spread his large hands in surrender, 'that's what is wrong. All wrong.'

Romy stepped forward and this time gave him no chance to escape. She hooked a finger around one of his shirt buttons.

'It's not your walking abilities that I'm interested in, Martel.'

He laughed and again it was her undoing. She let her finger slide into the opening of his shirt and touch his skin. It felt warm. She drew him closer.

'As for the war that's coming,' she said, 'I'll be running right beside you, hurling hand grenades. So we can die together.'

'I won't let you die.'

'You watch my back, I'll watch yours.'

'It's a deal.'

She undid his shirt button. 'Though I'd rather watch other parts of you right now.'

'I remember the first time you walked into my office looking for a job,' he said, surprising her. 'Four years ago. A little scrap of a thing in overalls too big for you. All blonde prickles and attitude. With a readiness to take on anyone who had the gall to deny you something just because you were a girl with a big dream. But you took a perverse delight in rubbing people up the wrong way. Except pilots. You've always respected other pilots and wanted to learn from them.' He smiled. 'Now they learn from you.'

'You remember that?'

He nodded.

'You were scary,' she told him.

'Quite right. I wanted to skin your hide for things you did in those early days. You were stubborn as a mule and determined to do things your way.' He laughed, but it was low and indulgent this time. 'I fell in love with you that first day.'

Her heart stopped. She remembered that interview. That first rainy day when Martel was the only one willing to take a chance on her, an inexperienced female pilot. But that word. Love? It frightened her more than a thunderhead racing towards her up in the skies.

'When someone loves you,' she murmured, 'they expect things of you.'

Martel drew her into his arms. 'I only expect you to be you.'

His lips pressed down on hers. It was nothing like a first kiss. Not tentative. Not greedy. Not like he wanted only to take his pleasure in her, to satisfy his own need. Romy had received a thousand kisses in the past, many from men she scarcely knew, but never one like this. This one was full of the kind of heat and passion she'd expect from a man like Martel, but more. Much more. His kiss was so full of love that it changed her.

It tore her apart. And it set her on fire. Is that what love did to you? Took you apart and put you back together in a way that you didn't recognise? It robbed her of her safety because suddenly all her walls were down, leaving her dizzy and exposed. Love made her want to pour out her soul to this man and that terrified her.

She had worked alongside Léo Martel for four years and despite his occasional grouchiness and his strictness, when it came to providing top-quality service for clients in need of air transport, he was the finest man she knew. And his commitment as a freedom fighter was unswerving. Again and again she had witnessed his courage and loyalty. Then there was that moment in the dusty street in Spain, the stolen second when he cheated death by risking his life for her. Her arms could not stay away from him and they clasped around his neck, her hands curled into his dense dark hair, burying themselves in it as if they had no intention of ever letting go. Her body melted against his. She could feel his heart, quick and strong.

'Why now?' her lips whispered against his. 'After four years, why now?'

He drew back his head to look at her and ran his lips along the curve of her forehead. 'Because I thought I'd lost you forever on that train. Those hours were . . .' No more words came. She felt his breath hot on her skin. 'Everything changed,' he said at last.

He kissed the length of her throat, his tongue furrowing the dips and curves of her collarbone, teasing a moan from her. 'But before I tear that hideous dress off you, I have a meeting to go to.'

'What?'

'You've had no sleep. Go to bed now and get some rest. I will be back from the meeting before—'

She stepped out of his arms, a deep frown on her face. 'What meeting?'

'It's with what remains of our cell – Jerome, Diane and Manu. Plus a couple of new members I have installed to replace poor François and Grégory.'

'I'll come.'

He sighed and shook his head at her. 'No.'

They both knew he was not going to win this one.

CHAPTER TWENTY-NINE

The two new members looked like killers. Romy wanted to turn and walk out. The tall one had a narrow clever face with lines of discontent and went by the name of Henri. He was a radio operator. So he said. The other one, Noam, was a skilled photographer, he claimed. He was black-haired and had grey pouches under his eyes, eyes that were so still and sharp and dark they looked like gun barrels. Yet it was Martel who had invited these two men in. He must trust them. But they set Romy's teeth on edge.

The mood in the room was tense. The gaping holes where François and Grégory should be were staring at them but no one mentioned their names. The meeting had shifted to the Pigalle district in a poky apartment above a dog-grooming salon and the stink of canines sent images of Josephine Baker's little furball dog into Romy's mind. Hot on its heels came a desire to rip out Herr Müller's tongue. But Manu had launched into a long account of how General Douville had come into his barbershop as usual, but this time with von Ribbentrop, Hitler's right-hand man, at his side.

'I could have sliced the Nazi bastard's throat open as he sat in my chair. Easy as cutting butter.'

'So why didn't you?'

It was the photographer with the gun-barrel eyes who asked. He was aiming them straight at Manu.

Manu was bald and soft and took his life in his hands reporting the chatter he heard in his barbershop each day among the government officials who had taken a shine to his place. But colour rose in his cheeks now.

'I'm not a killer,' he stated flatly, 'and never will be.'

'Shit-scared, that's why,' Noam muttered, but fell silent after a harsh look from Martel and took to picking his nails.

'The battle of Ebro River, give us news on that,' urged Diane, the milliner to a government minister's wife. 'How is it going for our boys?'

By *our boys* she meant the Spanish Republican soldiers. They all did that, thought of them as *ours*.

Martel kept it brief, his jaw set hard as if his words were chips of glass. 'General Mendez gave me details. It is a brutal battle being fought in hell down there, God help them. Each day five hundred enemy cannons are firing more than thirteen thousand rounds at our Republican troops, while two hundred of Franco's Nationalist aircraft are raining bombs down on them all day.'

Diane wailed and buried her face in her hands, her absurd hat of emerald bows tilted at a precarious angle. Romy shut down her mind. The image of flesh shredded and limbs ripped off was too much. She'd had no sleep, no food and, more importantly, no drink all day. She shouldn't have come. Martel was right.

'But our Republican troops are fighting back,' he continued. 'They are stubborn and they're brave. Modesto is leading them in an assault on the town of Gandesa with T-26 tanks, and the Fifteenth International Brigade will be launching a fierce attack alongside them.' His hands were rolled into fists at his sides. 'But it's the enemy aircraft – Hitler's Condor Legion, and the Aviazione Legionaria from Mussolini – that are doing the damage. They outnumber Republican planes by at least two to one. So, with thanks to Jerome for his financial wizardry, we start flying planes down there tomorrow.'

All eyes turned to Romy.

She nodded. 'I'm ready.'

Martel's gaze narrowed on her. 'I think not. I can find another pilot for this job.'

'Why?' Manu asked.

'I thought you said Romaine was an excellent pilot,' Diane objected.

'She is. But she has done enough. It is dangerous work, Diane, and she deserves a break.'

'I don't need a break,' Romy insisted. 'Where in Paris are you going to find another pilot you can trust to keep his mouth shut?'

'She's right,' Henri agreed, the one with the clever face. He shrugged with amusement. 'You're stuck with her.'

Romy decided that now was the time to mention Horst Baumeister. It would distract Martel from the question of who should shuttle the planes down south.

'Tomorrow evening I am dining alone with a German, one of Hitler's delegation over here to hold discussions in Paris with Daladier's Popular Front government and—'

'No,' Martel interrupted. 'It's too dangerous.'

'Of course it's dangerous,' Diane said with a warm smile for Romaine. 'But it's excellent news. What we need is—'

'No.' Martel's single word swelled to fill the room.

Henri leaned forward, a wolfish smile on his face. 'Why not? She can do it.'

'If I can find out information from Horst Baumeister on Franco's plans for troop movements and the Condor Legion in Spain, it could save hundreds of lives,' Romy pointed out. But she could see a vein in Martel's neck, taut as a bow rope.

'No.'

'She can do it, Martel,' Henri said. 'She can look after herself. She has a taste for danger.'

'You don't even know her, Henri, so don't interfere in—'

'I can see it in her,' the new member said in a soft hiss. 'If she had to, she could be a killer.'

'Shut up,' Martel snapped. 'Keep out of this.'

A killer.

Romy stood abruptly. 'I must leave now.' Without looking at Martel she picked up her bag and walked to the door.

'Romaine, please do not have dinner with the German.'

She closed the door quietly behind her.

A killer? It takes one to know one.

Romy ran down the stairs, and when she looked down at her hands, her heart leaped to her throat because they were covered in scarlet, in thick sticky strings of blood that trailed from her fingers. She blinked hard. The blood vanished. Her fingers were smooth and pink once more. Nevertheless, her father's blood was there, just under the skin, she knew it. But only she could see it.

CHAPTER THIRTY

FLORENCE

She is not here. I know it the moment I walk through the door off the street. I feel a coldness in the fabric of the house despite the July heat that bakes its stone walls and it tells me my sister is not within them. Nevertheless, I climb the five flights of stairs to check her room under the roof. I could be wrong.

But no, I am not wrong. The room is empty. Stifling, shabby, unloved and empty. The bed is unmade, which annoys me intensely. Downstairs, the concierge handed me the key to save her legs the bother of the stairs, so now I lock the door behind me while I wait for my sister. I open the window to tempt in some sluggish air and the noise of the city's incessant traffic comes at me like a slap in the face. I retreat into the room. I make the bed and smooth out the pink damask bedcover which I'm pleased to see looks clean. Well, cleanish. Only then do I sit on it.

I sit there for an hour. And then another. I am here for one reason. One reason only. To warn Romaine off the dinner with Horst Baumeister because I don't trust him. I don't know what he's up to or what he thinks he can gain by pursuing my sister, but I don't believe he has invited her to dinner just because she is an aviatrix and has a pretty face.

He scares me. I don't know why Roland can't see it. My husband is usually so sharp to sniff out trouble before it explodes in his face, that's why he's good as his job. But this time he shrugs and says they are perfect for each other. He looked at my expression and laughed. So it is all up to me to protect her.

I feel sick, the kind of sickness where your gut is on fire and the sweat on your palms betrays you. Tremors pass through me each time I tell myself that my fears are groundless, but it is not the German I fear. It is the Algerian brat. The pain in my gut starts burning its way up to my throat when I think of Karim's son and the way he looked down at his shoes to hide his hatred.

I will give him no money. I would rather throw it into the Seine and watch it sink into the black mud. Because this boy must be all too aware of the kind of money I inherited – even if Romaine refused hers – and if he thinks for one second that he can pressure me into giving some of it to him, he will never stop. He will ask and ask, demand and demand, until he sucks me dry. And every handout will be an admission guilt.

Dear God, how could Romaine be such a fool as to lavish

her money on him and his mother all these years? It is like signing her own death warrant.

And mine.

Doesn't she see it? She must stop. Right now. Between Horst Baumeister and Samir Abed, my sister is walking on a razor-edge that will cut us both to—

The door bursts open. A kick from outside ruptures the lock. The noise of it explodes into the room and I leap to my feet, but I am not someone who panics. Ask Roland. I am not someone who loses control and starts screaming as if their brains are running out of their mouth. I remain calm. I hold my nerve. I face the intruder.

'Get out!'

The stranger is tall, extremely tall, and his long limbs seem to reach into all corners of the small room. I get a flash of fair hair and a heavy cruel mouth as he comes at me. Fast. Full of menace. Intent as a wild boar on goring its victim. Before I can utter a sound he has me flat against the wall, his forearm jammed across my windpipe, his hard muscular body crushing mine.

I am helpless.

I cannot cry out. I cannot breathe. Blood is roaring in my ears. My mouth opens but nothing comes out and it dawns on me that I am about to die. My attacker's face, one cheek pockmarked like buckshot, starts to blur, his features melt into each other. I swing a feeble foot at him but connect with nothing.

Who are you?

My lips form the words but no sound emerges.

His face pushes so close to mine, our noses are almost touching and I can smell sweet cologne on him. It turns my stomach. He is no older than I am but his eyes are ancient and lifeless, pale grey eyes cut from marble. His mouth almost touches mine.

'Mademoiselle Duchamps,' he rumbles and he kisses me roughly. 'Pleased to meet you.'

He thinks I am Romaine. No, no, no. I try to shake my head but nothing responds. My brain is screaming for air and oxygen. Mist, like cobwebs, covers my eyes and I am going to be sick. The pain. The noise. The sadness. It is too much. I try to remember something but instead a blackness rolls in, dragging me under. My legs buckle. If he were not holding me jammed to the wall, I would be in a heap on the floor.

Only then does he pull back his arm. Air whoops into my starved lungs, sweet as honey, but it is agony as it forces its way through my battered throat.

I try to speak. A hoarse croak. I try again. A whisper escapes. 'I am not Romaine Duchamps.'

'You lying bitch.'

'It's true.'

'Fuck you, *putain*. I hear you like to put it about.'

He tries to force his lips on mine but I turn my head and he bites my ear instead. I feel blood drip on my neck.

'I am not Romaine Duchamps,' I whisper again.

'Blonde. Curly hair. Pretty. Lives up here.' His hard mouth curls in an ugly smile. 'You're her.'

'I am her sister.'

'Like fuck you are.'

'I am, I swear.'

'You'll do,' he says, 'just as well.'

I haul more air into my chest and the mist starts to retreat. My thoughts join up. He has an accent. Slight. But there. A German accent. Anger coils inside me, ice-cold, and I slam my forehead into his face. It catches his cheekbone and hurts me more than my attacker.

'Who sent you?' I try to shout, but my voice breaks into pieces before the words are all out.

But suddenly he seizes the front of my silk dress and tears it apart like paper. Instantly his hands are all over my breasts and his mouth is bruising my lips.

Vile. Hateful. Revolting. Blind fury tips me over the edge. I fight and I bite, I kick and struggle, I turn into a wild creature as I try to break free, but this violent stranger picks me up by the throat and throws me across the bed. I scream. But it is no more than a hoarse cough.

Fear ricochets. I lash out and my nails slice open his pocked cheek, but he laughs and pins both my wrists above my head on the bed with one hand.

'I am not Romaine Duchamps,' I spit in his face.

'No matter. You can tell her what it was like.'

I can barely breathe, his body is crushing mine. His free hand pushes into my pants, I feel them tear and I try to scream again as his fingers explore. He chuckles, a sour, hateful sound, and reaches under him to undo his belt.

That is the moment when we hear the noise. I've never heard anything like it. It sounds like the wail of a banshee from hell. I turn my head and look to the door. My sister is standing there, her face twisted with rage, her mouth wide open in a war cry that stops my attacker in his tracks for all of two seconds. But when she hurls herself at him where he lies on top of me, he bats her aside with a ferocious punch to her chest. She falls. Disappears from my sight.

'Romaine, run!' I shout to her.

But when she rises from the floor, her face has the shine of an avenging angel and each hand clutches one of the empty whisky bottles from under the bed. Without a word she slams the first one down on the back of the bastard's head. He utters a soft grunt. Nothing more. Collapses on me. The bottle had shattered and blood trickles down on me, along with jagged spikes of glass. He groans faintly.

The second bottle crashes down on him, this time square on his temple. The noise is terrible. I feel him grow immediately heavier. I see one eye slowly filling up with blood, like a red tide sweeping in, and a scarlet stream bubbles briefly from his nostril. I know he is dead.

I try to push the weight of him off me but he is too heavy – or I have lost the strength of my limbs. I realise I am shaking. My hands, my legs, my head, my lips. All shaking. A thunderstorm rages inside them. Romaine rolls him off me, on to the pink cover and wraps the inert body up in it.

With a strength I would never have credited her with, she propels him off the bed. He hits the floor with a thud that rocks the room. I stand there numb and shaking while she snatches a towel from a hook on the back of the door and sweeps the shards of glass off the bed on to the floor and brushes them up against the pink parcel that now looks more like a roll of carpet than a human being.

When it is done, she comes to me. She wraps her arms around me so tenderly, I almost die of gratitude. I lay my head on her shoulder and start to cry, shuddering sobs that feel as if they are flaying the skin off me, but I don't know how to make them stop. She strokes my head. She murmurs softly. With a gentle touch she picks out slivers of glass from my hair and off my face, leaving nicks and scratches behind and little snakes of scarlet that slide down my skin as if my body is crying.

Finally I stop. I look at my sister through my damp lashes and she has on a face I have never seen before. It is tight and hard. As though an iron door has slammed shut inside her.

I kiss her cheek. It is wet from my tears. 'Thank you, Romaine. Thank you for saving me.'

Her eyes come alive again. Her mouth pulls into an odd smile. 'It is easier the second time.'

I moan.

'Who is he?' she asks.

'I don't know. I've never seen him before.'

'Can it have been a random attack?'

We stare at each other. 'It wasn't a random attack.'

Tremors take me again as I remember his filthy fingers inside me. Romaine drapes an arm around me and steers me to the bed, where she strips off every scrap of bedding. We lie down together on the bare, stained mattress, her arms looped around me, holding me tight. We lie like that for a long time, indifferent to the roll of pink damask on the floor beside the bed, but I do not mention his German accent. Nor do I mention that he came for her.

'Well?' I ask.

My head is pounding and is thick with what feels like a hangover, though I have not touched a drop of Romaine's whisky. She is sitting on the floor in a corner drinking straight from the bottle.

'Well now,' she gives me that odd smile again, 'we are not going to the police.'

I nod.

'I've been thinking,' she says. 'We will have to drag the body downstairs in the middle of the night when everyone is—'

'No. I know someone.'

'Who will deal with this?'

'Yes.'

Her mouth falls open. There is blood on her teeth. Mine? Her own? The dead man's? I do not know.

'You know someone who will get rid of the body for us, no questions asked? Really?'

'Yes.'

She waits for more. I pick my words carefully. 'Roland works with the Intelligence Service sometimes. They have a team that clears up mess. That's their job.'

'You'll tell Roland?' She takes a swig of whisky and her eyes half close with pleasure. 'Is that wise?'

'Let me deal with all that.'

I sit slumped on the bed. My torn dress hangs off me in shreds, so I force my body back into action and inspect my sister's clothes on the hanger on a wall hook. I lift off a dreary cotton blouse and a skirt and I put them on. They are both brown and I know make me look like shit, but tonight I don't care. It is dark outside. Every bit of me hurts.

I pull her to her feet. 'Come on. We must leave now.'

She nods obediently. I head for the door, remembering to take my handbag, but she veers back to the bed and kneels down. She unlaces the strap that seals the slit in the mattress, pushes her hand in and draws out the small pouch that I found before. She doesn't look in it. Instead she pushes her hand in again, this time off to the left and pulls out a narrow box. I frown. I recognise it. I rush over, snatch it from her and flick it open. It is Papa's watch.

'Maman gave it to me,' she says quickly. 'I didn't steal it. I am going to sell it to raise money for Aya Abed's operation.'

I hold it out to her. I say nothing. I cannot speak. She bunches a light cotton dress under her arm and we leave. I pull the door shut but the lock is broken, so it is pointless. Neither of us care. There is nothing in the room worth stealing. She leads the way down the stairs and I watch her short blonde curls bob below me. Violent emotions seal my lips.

I want to ask her about the confession she wrote, the

one I tore up. But she killed a man for me today. That is enough.

'You bastard.'

I storm into Gustav Müller's office and slam the door. His is the only office with a light still on because all the other officials in the building have long since gone home. This man lives, breathes, eats his work. His office walls are lined not with books or even with the obligatory pictures of Adolf Hitler, but with rows of files. *Information is power.* That is his maxim. So he keeps the information at his fingertips, not in a dusty basement storeroom. Row after row of files. They are intimidating. I know one of them is on me.

I march over to his desk and sweep an angry fist across it, sending a framed photograph of his wife in Germany and a porcelain clock crashing to the floor.

'What the hell did you do it for?' I demand. 'Why send someone to rape my sister?'

His expression remains cool and unruffled. 'To teach her a lesson. She needed it.'

'Don't you dare do anything like that to Romaine ever again or—'

'What happened? I chose that operative because he is dedicated to his work.'

'Your dedicated operative is now a dead operative.'

'What?'

'So get rid of his body.'

'Where is he?'

'In her attic room. Send the cleaners in immediately.'

'*Mein Gott*, she is ferocious, that one.'

'Stay away from her.'

'I can't do that, *meine freundin*. She is at the heart of the Spanish Civil War support network.'

'You have no proof of that.'

'I don't need proof.'

'Müller, you are not listening to me. I'm telling you to stay away from her.'

In three brisk strides I am on the other side of his desk and yank open the top drawer. Inside lies a Mauser pistol. I snatch it up and point it at him. 'If you ever hurt her again, I will put a bullet in you.'

He laughs in my face. Almost a purr. He is pleased that he has provoked me.

I slide into bed. I lie still. I try not to wake him. Minutes tick past in the darkness and I force my eyes to shut, my limbs to remain still. But it is no good, my need for comfort is too strong. I crave it tonight. Like my sister craves her whisky. I edge across the expanse of whiteness between us and I find Roland is lying on his side, his back to me.

Are you asleep? Or pretending to be asleep?

I cannot tell, but I no longer care because I inhale the scent of his warm sleep-soaked skin and it draws me to him. I tuck my naked body around his naked body, feeling the heavy curve of his buttocks warm and solid in my lap. I run the flat of my palm over it, the way I would over a horse's rump, patting it, stroking it, caressing his powerful muscle there. When I am as close to my husband as this, I forget that his body is his, not mine.

'Chloé was asking for you.'

Roland's sleep voice is deeper, more resonant than his daytime one and I feel its vibrations pass from his chest into mine.

'I'm sorry. Was she all right?'

'Yes, of course. Where were you?'

I don't like talking to his back.

'I was with my sister.'

He sighs. I kiss the back of his neck and trail my tongue across to his ear.

'She needed help,' I say.

'Help to walk a straight line.'

'No, she wasn't drunk. Just help to sort something out.'

He doesn't ask why or how. He doesn't speak her name. I press my breasts hard against his ribs.

'Leave her to Horst,' he says in a tone that ends the discussion. 'He will look after her.'

That's what I'm afraid of.

I roll away to my own side of the bed and we lie in silence for a long time, only our breathing in tune with each other. My mind fills with the memory of a hand crushing my throat.

'Help me, Roland,' I whisper into the darkness.

Instantly my husband is beside me, is on me, is inside me, erasing all else. Ridding my body of the memory of the hands that touched me where no man but Roland has touched me. I wrap my arms and my legs around him, my hips bucking to drive him deeper into me until at last we are done, slick with sweat. The violent stranger with the marble eyes is erased from my mind. Along with all the other things erased from my mind.

CHAPTER THIRTY-ONE

By midnight Romy found her way back to the safe house on the banks of the Seine, an almost empty whisky bottle still in her hand. To her disgust she felt stone-cold sober. In the darkness, the city's lights glinted off the inky black void of the river and for all of five seconds she was tempted. A quick step. Over the edge. That's all it would take. An easy way out.

She rubbed her fist hard on her chest. A block of ice had formed there just behind her breastbone. That's what it felt like, despite the fact that her blood seemed to race hot through her veins and, with the whisky, should have melted it hours ago.

What frightened her was that she didn't know herself any more. Didn't know that she, Romaine Duchamps, could kill again. She could have stopped. After she'd walloped the rapist with the first bottle, when she'd seen his scalp split open and blood soak his hair like red paint, she could have stopped. But she didn't. She hit him again. Just to be sure.

To be sure.

To be sure of what? That he was dead? Was there a part of her that wanted to kill?

'No,' she insisted to the night breeze that ruffled the stray leaves in the gutter. 'It was to save Florence.'

I would kill for her.

'What the hell happened?'

Martel swept her into his arms the moment he opened the door to her. His face was tight with hours of worry, with hours of anger eating at him, but he took one look at her and the anger fell away.

'What have you done?'

He smelled of soap. She let the weight of her head rest on his shoulder and felt his strong hand in the middle of her back, holding her upright against him, as though he feared she might fall. But she had no intention of falling.

'Martel.' She said his name. Quick and sharp. That was enough. To tell him she wasn't broken. 'I've done something terrible.'

'What is this terrible thing you've done? You can tell me, Romaine. I won't scream in horror or run away, if that's what you think.'

'I killed a man.'

He gripped her shoulders and held her away from him at arm's length so that he could study her face in the yellow sheen of the single bare light bulb that hung in the room. Whatever he saw did not make him scream. Did not make him run. He didn't even look shocked, as if he'd always known the possibility lay within her. Instead he gave her a nod and a smile.

'If you killed a man, Romaine, then I'm sure the bastard needed killing.'

Martel fed her. Strong-smelling cheese and crusty baguette. Sweet slippery slices of peach and cantaloupe melon. He poured her a glass of red wine and watched her drink it, and when she had finished he peeled off her stinking sack of a dress and took her to bed.

Romy had expected the scars. Of course she had. She knew about the flying accident that almost stole his life, but she was not prepared for the number of them. White as silvery snail-tracks, they coiled around his hip and slunk through the dark hairs and across the muscles of his powerful chest, picking out his rib bones one by one. But the scars on his thigh were the colour of overripe plums, savage and brutal.

She lowered her head and trailed her tongue along the line of each scar. Piece by piece she licked away Martel's pain. He tasted good. Of salt and strength and something stubborn. She heard him moan. A tremor ripped through him and his hands reached for her, his eyes dark as sin with wanting her. His mouth came down hard on hers, sending jolts of pleasure crashing through her, so that her body arched against his, demanding all of him.

There were no questions. No *hows*. No *whys*. No *what nows* between them. They just needed each other. Their bodies so hungry they ached with the pain of it. Fingers caressed and cradled, lips searched out secret places, touching and teasing, until their bodies drove each other to the very brink of *la petite mort*. His hand stroked her breast with such tenderness, yet there was a wildness to him that Romy had not suspected before. Something untamed, unbroken. It tore her heart wide open.

This was the stunt pilot. Not the commercial businessman. This was the reckless Léo Martel who yearned to scorch his way across the sky again, to flip a plane through the Arc de Triomphe at dawn. Locked together, they flew high and fast, pulsing with an energy and a wholeness she had known with no other man. When they finally collapsed together, their skin was silky with sweat, limbs entwined.

Romy laid her cheek on his chest to listen to his thundering heartbeat. The sound of it and the heat of him became a part of her.

Romy woke. Had she fallen asleep? How was that possible? After sex with any man, her instinct was to run. Run as far and fast as she could. Yet here she was, curled up in the crook of Martel's arm, breathing his breath, smelling his skin, her head pillowed on the hard muscle of his shoulder, contented as a cat in the sun.

Because she couldn't bear to tear herself away from this moment, she allowed her mind to lie to her. Nothing existed outside these four walls. Nobody walked the streets of Paris except Martel and herself. There was no attic room, no empty whisky bottles under a bed, no damned-to-hell-for-eternity intruder with a German accent and hair the colour of raw steak. No snipers behind the trees to slam a bullet into their brains if they chose to stroll beside the Seine like young lovers along the cobbled alleyways of the *quais*. She'd take him rowing on the river, the way she used to as a child with her sister. And she'd laugh when he lost an oar and had to strip to his waist to dive in to . . .

'Romaine.'

She dragged herself back from the cliff edge of sleep. He was stroking her cheek, soft tender touches that loosened her focus.

'Tell me what happened.'

So she told him. Every last dirty minute of what happened in the stiflingly hot little attic. She spared him no detail. No glossing over the number of bottles under the bed or the sound of bone cracking when the second blow broke the man's skull. It felt like lancing a boil. The poison poured out. The festering ceased.

'We must remove the body immediately,' he said.

'Shouldn't you be telling me I did wrong? That I must go to the police at once?'

'Oh, Romaine, I would do exactly the same as you did without a second thought – to save the person I love.'

His gaze was fixed on her, leaving no room for doubt as to whom he meant.

She shook her head. 'My sister said she would get her

husband to deal with it. It seems that our government employs professional laundrymen to clean up their dirty messes.'

'That makes sense. I will have your room checked over nevertheless.'

'But who was the attacker? Why was he in my room?' Her pulse raced. 'Was it a random assault from a man unconnected with—?'

'No, Romy, stay calm.' It was the first time he'd ever called her Romy. He let his thumb roll gently down the pale skin of her throat and she remembered the marks of violence on Florence's throat. 'I suspect,' he said, 'that it was meant to be an attack on you. He got the wrong sister.'

He studied her with a dark, serious gaze, watching her reaction. He kissed a spot on her temple, letting his lips linger there, and she felt the warmth of his lips steady her pulse.

'But you know that, I can see.'

'Do you think he might be Cupid, the one you told us about who is trying to destroy our cells of resistance? You said there was rumour he might be German.'

'It is possible. At this stage,' he frowned with frustration, 'anything is possible.'

She didn't want this. The German in bed with them. In one quick movement she rolled herself up on top of Martel, her body stretched out along his, hip to hip, her face grinning down on him, her lips a hair's breadth from his.

'Tell me about yourself, Léo Martel. When did you start

flying? What was stunting like? Where do you get your planes from?'

His eyes smiled back at her. 'You are beautiful, Romy. Every part of you, outside and inside. Even the little scar under your chin is a perfect crescent, do you know that?'

'Don't change the subject.'

'You have no idea how lovable you are.'

She nipped the tip of his nose with her teeth. 'Stop it. Listen to me. What was your first plane?'

He kissed the hollow of her collarbone. 'A Caudron G.3 biplane.'

'Really? That old thing? They were held together by string and a prayer.'

He laughed and its vibrations stirred her.

'Tell me about your family,' she ordered. 'Are there more like you at home?'

'I'd rather talk about you.'

'Martel!'

'Call me Léo.' He said it softly, as if those words rarely saw the light of day.

She kissed his mouth, tasting the wine. 'Léo, don't hide from me.'

His eyes grew soft on hers and he started to talk. Some parts came easily. Others she had to tease out of him, pulling the threads one at a time. Unravelling him.

He grew up in Toulouse. His parents ran a printing business and pretty much left Léo and his brother Charles to bring themselves up, while they worked all hours.

'We ran wild,' he laughed, remembering. 'Got into all kinds of scrapes, but we both became obsessed with early aircraft. Especially with the brilliant aviation engineer, Louis Blériot.'

At eighteen Martel sold his father's ancient Renault 40CV, which was languishing unused in the garage, funded flying lessons for himself and his brother with the proceeds and took himself off to California to be a stunt pilot. His eyes lit up in a way Romy loved to see when he talked about the crazy thrills and spills of working on the film *Wings* with Gary Cooper. Like he had a fire inside him. And then he tumbled into pylon racing. He'd started travelling the race circuits for pilots across America. Romy shuddered. Pylon racing was a lethal way to make a living. You might as well cut your throat before you start. Under her, she could feel his heart roaring like a propeller in his chest.

'Then came 1933,' he said and the light inside him switched itself off in a hurry. 'Everything changed. The world stepped off a cliff when Hitler swept to power. As Chancellor of the Third Reich he immediately set up concentration camps for Jews and other undesirables. For me, that was it. I came home. To help protect France.'

Romy kissed his chin, her tongue prickled by his stubble. 'So that's why Hitler and his Nazis didn't dare attack France back in those days.'

He laughed. But there was no joy in it. 'My parents decamped to Detroit. My brother to England.'

She had a sudden sense of the loneliness of this man.

He picked up her hand and pressed his lips to its palm. 'So that's it. I set up an air courier service here and my brother did the same at Croydon airport in London.'

'He's the one who supplies you with the planes from England, I presume, the Tiger Moths.'

'He is. I quickly became involved with the underground resistance groups in Paris and then I hired you. And you very quickly became part of our movement.' He chuckled and snaked a hand along the curves of her naked buttocks and up over her back. 'I must have been mad.'

'You've missed something out.'

'What?'

'The accident.'

'Oh that.' He shrugged, as far as he could shrug with her lying on top of him. 'Some idiot decided to park his plane on top of me. I survived to tell the tale. Enough said. The rest you know.'

Romy rolled off him and sat on her heels on the bed, not touching him, keeping her hands locked under her knees.

'Léo, have you ever killed someone?'

Martel didn't respond. He lay without moving for a full minute, stretched out on his back, naked and exposed. Scars glinted like fish scales in the light of the overhead bulb.

Romy repeated her question. 'Have you ever killed someone?'

He rose to kneel in front of her, a powerful presence on the bed. 'Yes, I have killed.'

It caught her by surprise. 'More than one?' she asked.

'Yes.'

'Do you think about them? Do you see their faces?'

'No.'

Was it true? Or was he lying? To soothe her guilt. The way you lie to a child.

'I killed a man. Eight years ago,' she told him. 'The man was my father.' The words seemed to swell in her mouth.

Martel reached out and held her wrists, waiting in silence for her to say what she had to say.

'I don't know why I killed him. Something happened . . .' She struggled to suppress the image of the brass pyramid taking shape inside her head. 'And I had concussion, so I don't remember what happened. The memory is gone.'

She tried to remove her wrists but he held them.

'Until now,' she said. 'When I am with the Germans – Herr Müller and Horst Baumeister – it triggers flashbacks. I see things. Hear things. From that day.'

'*Merde*! So this is what you're running from.'

She nodded. She didn't mention Karim Abed or an angled metal blade that weighs forty kilograms and travels to its destination in a seventieth of a second.

'So you see, Léo, why I must have dinner with Horst Baumeister tomorrow night.'

'Yes, I see.'

But he didn't look as if he saw. He looked in pain.

'I don't for a minute think they know anything about my father, but I can't walk away from it. I have to find out the truth.'

Martel released one of her wrists. He pressed the knuckles of his hand against his forehead, trying to rearrange his thoughts by force, his mouth a hard gash across his face.

'If you go,' he said, 'I'll give you a gun.'

Romy slid him a sad smile. 'No, Léo. I think two murders are enough for anyone.'

CHAPTER THIRTY-TWO

Paris on a Saturday night is eager to impress. Like a woman showing off her new gown. Or a whore painting her nails. Her lipstick is redder, slicker, and her jewels brighter than in any other city. Paris flaunts her delights with all the assurance of a beautiful woman who knows with certainty that she is irresistible.

Romy loved Paris. Its sights and smells were a part of her, like the colour of her hair was a part of her. She walked into Le Chat Noir and exchanged a warm greeting with Émile, the rotund *patron* who had been known to pay his gambling debt to her with a feast of *tournedos à Rossini*. He was such a rotten poker player.

His restaurant was old, with black beams and ancient brickwork, checked tablecloths and candles stuck in the necks of wine bottles. Nothing fancy. Except Émile's cooking. Horst Baumeister was already there, waiting for her. He rose to his feet and kissed her hand, his smile warm and expectant.

'I'm glad you came,' he said.

'Did you think I wouldn't?'

'It was a possibility I considered.'

'But here I am.'

His eyes took her in and she wondered what he was seeing. She was wearing a dress she had bought second-hand from Louis Capel's pawnshop, the pale grey colour of Paris's zinc roofs. She had stolen a crimson rose from the Tuileries Garden and wore it pinned to her shoulder. Did Horst see someone who had made an effort? Or someone who didn't care? Or was there some other image of her in his head that she was unaware of?

They sat down at the table but the evening began awkwardly. Neither knew quite where to look or what to say. Their dancing, so intimate at Monico's, was forgotten. She needed him to trust her, so she steered him down the path that had drawn them together in the nightclub.

'I hear that Willy Messerschmitt has just been appointed chairman of the Bayerische Flugzeugwerke and renamed the company after himself.' She leaned forward and tipped her head to one side in imitation of her sister. 'He is a genius when it comes to aircraft design, don't you think?'

That's all it took. They were off and running. Over the meal they discussed in detail the importance of the Messerschmitt Bf109 to Germany's rearmament plans and the designer's innovation of merging the load-bearing parts into a single reinforced firewall. This saved weight and improved performance.

'Willy Messerschmitt himself has become quite a favourite with the Nazi party,' Horst told her and there was an unexpected sadness in his voice. At first Romy thought she was imagining it. But no. It was there. Unmistakably. But inexplicably. He cut into his tarte Tatin and when he lifted his head his rigid features had relaxed again. 'Do you know,' he asked her, 'what Messerschmitt means in German?'

'No.'

'It means knife-maker. Appropriate, don't you think, for a man who makes the finest fighter planes in the world that cut through the air like a knife?'

The wine had done its work of unlacing their tongues and Romy settled down to what she had come for.

'Horst, what is the meaning of the German words "*Ich möchte mich nicht streiten*"?'

'It means "I don't want to argue".' He waved a hand at Émile for coffee. 'Why? Who have you been arguing with?'

'Herr Müller.'

He didn't look at her. Silence fell between them. He swilled the last of the mulberry-coloured liquid and it clung to the sides of the glass. Romy had a sense that Horst was clinging to something, but she had no idea what.

'Stay away from him,' he said at last. 'Steer clear of that man if you can.'

'I thought you work with him.'

'I do.'

'So why warn me off him?'

But instead of answering he stood up. 'Come with me. I want to show you something.'

Horst Baumeister drove his sleek Mercedes saloon through the dark streets of Paris with the ease of long practice.

'How long have you lived here?' Romy asked him.

'A year.'

'Really? I didn't realise you've been here so long.'

'There's a lot you don't realise, Romaine.'

It was a hot and sultry summer evening. The streets were crowded with Saturday-night revellers and one threw a shoe at the car's windscreen. It smacked against the glass and bounced off. Horst didn't flinch.

'Some Parisians don't like German cars,' he commented. Nothing more.

'Where are we going?' Romy asked.

But he remained silent. His profile, etched by the wrought-iron street lamps, was set firm, as though something unpleasant lay ahead. Maybe she'd been unwise to climb in the car with the German but it was the only way to get answers out of him. With each turn of the wheels, her heart beat faster, Léo Martel's final words clanging in her ears. 'Be careful, Romy. Take no risks.'

But there was something about this German that she liked. Really liked. Not just his enthusiasm for aircraft – though that helped – but also his directness. As if he thought in straight lines. No convoluted twists and turns to baffle and confuse others, but straight lines that could slide you straight into hell if you didn't watch out.

'How well do you know my sister?'

He glanced across at her, surprised. 'Not well.'

'And Roland, her husband?'

'Too well.'

'What do you mean by that?'

'He is cruel.'

'What? Why do you think that?'

'I once saw him beat a man.'

He came to a junction on rue des Petits Champs and raced across, blaring his horn to force a slow-moving Citroën to give way. She looked at his face. It was angry, but not with the Citroën.

'Tell me why,' she said quietly.

'The man was Jewish.'

The building to which he took her was hidden away behind the Élysée Palace in the 8th arrondissement. An official-looking building with classical pillars and a massive arched doorway that looked as if it could withstand an army. Yet there was no plaque, no identification. Horst drew a key ring from his pocket and opened it. It was a relief to step out of the night-time shadows, but when she heard the door lock behind her the hairs on her neck rose and she thought again about the weapon she had rejected so readily when Martel offered it.

He flicked a switch. One solitary lamp illuminated a small

cathedral-like space with a high domed ceiling and marbled floor, pale and veined like an old woman's hand. Three wide corridors splayed out from it into dark unknown areas. Romy didn't know what this place was, but she had the distinct feeling it was somewhere she was not meant to be.

'Where is this?' she asked.

'It doesn't matter.' His manner had become brusque. 'It's where Müller and I work. His office is opposite mine.'

Definitely not meant to be here.

'Come with me.'

Horst set off down the central corridor, his footsteps echoing on the marble. When he realised she hadn't followed, he pulled up and glanced back over his shoulder.

'It's not a trap,' he said. 'And I have no orders to rape you.'

She inhaled sharply. Blond hair. A sticky scarlet mat of it. A bottle in her hand. This man knew.

'Lead on,' she said.

He continued down the corridor deeper into the gloom, she followed at a distance, passing closed doors on each side. Ahead of her, Horst Baumeister had come to a halt outside one of the doors. He extracted the key ring again, unlocked it and entered, leaving the door open for her. A sudden burst of electric light from the room jumped out at her and she knew this was her chance. She walked in.

An ordinary office. That's all it was. Ordinary desk and chairs and ordinary bookshelves. But the room itself was anything but ordinary. It had lovely proportions with a high-frescoed ceiling and a florid rococo frieze that twined itself around the walls. Not a room she would associate with Nazi officialdom.

'So,' she said, surveying the interior, 'this is where your plans are hatched, yours and Müller's.'

She watched him closely, half expecting him to cast off his lightweight suit and don a grey Nazi uniform, or throw up his arm in a *Heil Hitler* salute. There was something different about him here. The strong rigid lines of his Aryan features were melting, the muscles under the skin softening and she could see the boy he must once have been. She wanted to go over and take his hand. But that was a risk too far.

'Why am I here?' she asked bluntly. 'What is it you want?'

He stepped back, away from her. 'Herr Müller believes you are part of the underground movement ferrying planes illegally to the Republican forces in Spain.'

'He is mistaken.'

'And that this group of yours has agents attempting to steal information about Germany's planes on the ground in Spain. And here in Paris.'

'No.'

He folded his arms across his chest. 'Let us be straight with each other, Romaine.'

How do you tell a man he is wrong when the air in your lungs has turned solid and the tension in the room is as sharp as the paperknife that used to lie on Papa's desk? But there was something. Something. In his face. Not quite right.

Had he laid a trap for her? Was it under this fine building that the basement lay, the one Martel had warned her about?

The one where you spilled your guts to make them stop, where you'd give them your soul just to make them put down their tools. Had Horst betrayed her?

'Of course we must be straight with each other,' she dragged up a smile and approached him, putting a sway in her hips the way she'd seen Florence approach men. She rested a hand on his arm. 'We can be friends,' she said softly. 'We can be honest with each other, you and I.'

He ducked his head and kissed her lips. Brief and harsh. He pulled back his head. 'I know honest when I see it. And I know a liar. You, Romaine, are a liar. Which disappoints me. I hoped you would trust me.'

'I trust you, Horst.'

She circled an arm around his neck and drew his head down to hers. Her lips found his, warm and full of desire. She may not be able to lie with words, but she knew only too well how to lie with her body. Her hips fitted themselves to the shape of his.

'No.'

He pulled down her arm and broke free from her. 'No, Romaine. Whatever it is you want from me, this is not the way.'

He stalked over to the far side of his desk and yanked open a top drawer. Was he going for a gun? But it wasn't a Mauser he threw down on the desktop, it was a buff folder fat with documents that landed on the surface with a heavy thud. Horst left it there and without another word walked out of the room.

*

Dear God. They would kill her now. Now that she had read the file. They had reason to.

Romy was cramming facts and figures into her head as fast as she could. Laying them down in orderly rows, memorising them with the same tenacity with which she remembered the points along a flight path, the bridges and rivers and church steeples as markers along the way. Except this time it was troop numbers, grid references, dates and names. She was seated at the desk, eyes and mind focused.

She had to get out of here. Find Léo Martel. Pour into his ear the information Horst had thrown so casually within her hand's reach and use it to save lives. She heard a footstep and looked up. Horst was standing in the doorway, leaning one shoulder against it, his face veiled in the shadows from the corridor. But she could hear his breathing, fast and laboured.

Or was that hers?

He came no closer, but stood there in silence. She realised he was waiting for her to finish before he . . . What? Before he put a neat bullet in her brain, the way he had dispatched François and Gregory? Or dragged her screaming to the basement? None of this made sense. On her lap under the desk where he could not see, one hand clutched a pair of scissors like a dagger. She had found them in the bottom drawer. It wasn't much but it was all she had and she intended to make it count.

There was one final document in the folder. She picked it up. It was only one page of closely typed work, an account of various conversations. She started to read, one eye on the silent figure in the doorway, but within two seconds she had forgotten him. A pulse pounded in her ears.

This was a death sentence.

For her. And for Hitler.

Conspirators. They were crawling behind the woodwork like cockroaches. They dare not show their faces nor speak their names except in whispers.

The final document revealed a plot between a brigadier general called Hans Oster of the Military Intelligence Office, the *Abwehr,* and General Ludwig Beck, a former Chief-of-Staff of the German High Command, *Oberkommando des Heeres*.

Terror and exhilaration churned through Romy as she read the document that detailed a plot to assassinate Adolf Hitler. The paper shook in her hand.

Horst?

She glanced up, though it hurt to drag her gaze from the typed words, and she saw he had not moved. He stood still as the scaffold on which this information could put her. He must know he had sentenced her. More names jumped out at her. Goerdeler and von Moltke, others that she burned into her memory as her hand tightened on the scissors.

She put down the paper and closed the folder on the desk.

'Why me, Horst? Why now?'

This man, whom she barely knew but who was now tightly bound to her by the knowledge they shared, moved out of the shadows.

'Because, Romaine, the dark forces of evil are massing across Europe. They are marching in the bloody footsteps of Hitler, Mussolini and Franco, while just over the border in the east awaits the savage great bear of Russia and Stalin. A holocaust is coming in which we will all be sacrificed to the fire of power-crazed men, and it is the God-given duty of each one of us to play our part in battling to put out its flames before they consume mankind.'

His voice was passionate, his eyes fierce, and Romy's hand abandoned the scissors on her lap.

'Try to understand, Romaine. I was brainwashed into believing that the Führer's word was gospel. But now I see more clearly with my own mind. I have stood by while terrible acts were committed, I've seen the shops and homes of Jews smashed and ransacked, people fleeing in fear of their life. But no more. I realise now that Hitler is an evil tyrant who must be cut down before he sets the whole of Europe on fire.'

She could hear the passion in his words.

'I have been waiting for someone like you to cross my path,' he continued, moving closer to her. 'Someone to be a link between me and the French underground groups. To whom I can pass information. I gave you that last document to read because I am part of that assassination plot. To show you just how far I am trusting you.'

Romy rose from her seat. 'But can I be sure I can trust you, Horst?'

'Haven't I just proved you can by giving you those documents? I copied them all into French for you.'

'What if this is all a sham? Set up by Müller. To trick me into betraying myself and others.'

He passed a hand over his face, as if he could wipe her doubts away.

'How can I be certain, Horst?' She stood in front of him.

'Very well. I have already given into your hands the power to have me shot. Now I will give you the power to destroy not just me, but my whole family.' He took a long breath. 'My mother was a Jewess. My father was a blond blue-eyed Aryan, but she was a dark-haired Jewess. Don't look so shocked. Of course no one knows and there is no mark of Jewishness on me. But she was killed four years ago by one of Hitler's marauding bands of Jew-baiters.'

Her hand wrapped around his.

'Shall I tell you how they killed her, Romaine? They took her out into the street when she made the mistake of trying to help her father, a tailor, escape from the dangerous streets of Berlin. The evil bastards hauled my mother and her father out on to the street, poured petrol over them and burned them alive. I cannot let it go on.'

Romy felt sick. But at the same time relief slowed the blood in her veins. This man was not lying. His hatred of the evil around him was as real as the names and dates from the file, which were branded into Romy's mind.

'I'm sorry, Horst. For your mother. For your grandfather. But you must burn that folder immediately. It is too dangerous for you.'

She walked over to the metal wastepaper bin beside his

desk and tossed each page from the files into it, then picked up his desk lighter and clicked it into life. When she touched it to the papers, the flames twisted and curled as if in agony.

They sat together in a nearby bar, one of those smoky intimate dens that Paris is so good at. Horst was calmer now, two brandies to the good, while Romy nursed a whisky between her fingers. Only one whisky. That was all she allowed herself and the trail of it through her gut silenced the tremors.

She talked little. Listening to Horst murmuring stories of the good times in Germany when people used to laugh and when fear was only what he felt when his father put his Lipizzaner stallion to jump fences that would break a lesser rider's neck. She knocked back the dregs of her drink, eager to return to Martel with the information that was locked safe in her head. But first she had more questions to ask.

'Horst, what do you know of Müller's background?'

'Only that he is an ex-army man, one of Heinrich Himmler's inner circle.'

'The Gestapo leader?'

'That's him. A vile piece of work if ever there was one, but close to Hitler. His power is far-reaching.'

'Is that a warning?'

He smiled. 'To both of us.'

'Was Müller stationed in Paris eight years ago, do you know? Did he know my father?'

His reaction to her question was so swift, it was barely there. Most would have missed it. That fraction of a second's pause and a minuscule freeze of the muscles of his face. Before Romy could even think about the reason for it, it was gone and he was regarding her with a careful scrutiny.

'I honestly have no idea,' he said easily. 'I don't know what Müller was up to then, because I was working in Frankfurt at the time.'

Each of Romy's fingertips prickled, the way they do when you slip on ice. Horst was lying. She could feel her feet skidding from under her.

CHAPTER THIRTY-THREE

I am a whore.

Romy was walking with Horst to the Métro station, his arm around her waist, their bodies too close.

Whore.

When they left the bar, he had kissed her. She had not stopped him. She had not fought him off with claws raking his face. She liked this German, admired his courage. To feed information to the enemy right under Müller's hawk-like nose was a risk few would entertain. And she relished his passion for aircraft. But she did not care for his lies. Or his kisses. As they walked along the cobbled street with its arched wrought-iron street lamps and its night air smelling of the remains of someone's bonfire, his hand caressed her hip.

'What will you do with the information I've given you?' he asked, keeping his voice well below the sounds of the beer-fuelled laughter that followed them from the bar. 'Who will you take it to?'

'I know someone,' she assured him. It was enough. He didn't need more.

'There is one more thing,' he said and halted on the corner of a junction. Darkness lay like a warm blanket over the street but he had stopped in an amber pool of light from one of the street lamps and it turned his blond hair into gold. He was the kind of man who could shine, who brought an energy to his every thought and smile. He drew her closer, concern on his face, his smile tight around the edges this time.

'I want you to watch out for Roland, your brother-in-law. Be careful of him, Romaine. I mean it. He is a man who—'

The car came out of nowhere. Black as a shark, sleek and long-nosed. The roar of its engine tore apart the silence. The sound seemed to bleed into the buildings themselves, and when the impact came, Romy thought it was the noise of it that knocked her off her feet. A hot rush of blood erupted in her mouth and she could feel something like rain splatter on her face. The smell of blood hit her and swept her back to lying on a Persian rug with her hands painted scarlet. With soft sticky footsteps it chased her all the way down into the darkness.

'I saw it.'

'It didn't look like an accident to me.'

'*Merde*! The car drove right on to the pavement.'

'Is he alive?'

'Looks gone to me.'

'And her?'

The voices sounded odd. As if each word had a tiny spike in it that tapped on her eardrum, making a tinny noise. Romy tried to sit up but hands held her. The street lamps turned upside down but she blinked hard and the buildings came into focus with a halo of lights dancing around them.

'You've banged your head, mademoiselle. Don't try to move.'

She sat up. The darkness felt like tar. She turned her head, waited for her eyeballs to catch up, and found Horst. He was surrounded by people, but through their legs she could see his golden hair on the cobbles. She struggled to her feet, swaying, holding on to an arm.

'What happened?'

'A car came right at you two. I saw it, a big black Mercedes, it was. The bastard mounted the kerb, slammed into *le monsieur* and sent you flying into the wall. An ambulance is . . .'

'Horst,' she whimpered. 'Horst.'

She dropped to her knees at his side. A puppet with strings cut. His limbs lay at wrong angles. His head was twisted too far over. His jaw was slack. His eyes – those energetic blue eyes – were empty. Rinsed out. Nothing in them as they stared up at her. Grief clawed at her chest and she cradled Horst's head in her lap, stroking the blood from his cheeks. She rocked him in the dark loneliness of death.

It was starting to rain, soft warm drops that washed the blood from Horst's skin, and Romy became aware of cars and flashing lights. An ambulance. Voices, kind but firm, as they tried to detach her from him. She bent over and kissed his forehead, wrapping her arms around his inert body one last time, then she let them take him from her.

While police attention was concentrated on the victim of the assault, and asking questions about the car from those who witnessed it, Romy backed into the night's shadows against the wall, sliding out of sight, and before the gendarmes realised she was gone, she had slipped down a side street and was running with an odd lopsided stride.

Clutched in her hand was the key ring she had just stolen from Horst's jacket pocket.

Romy's hand was steady, her writing fast and precise. She kept the shaking locked tight inside. She stuck to the facts, nothing more. No mention of curious blue eyes or a kind smile or lips warm on hers, lips that were now bloodless and silent in a morgue. No mention of a key.

Four pairs of eyes followed every word she wrote. Diane and Jerome stood on one side of her, the two new members of their cell on the other, their impatience bristling. It was Noam, the dark-haired one with heavy stubble, whose large nose bent over her shoulder, giving grunts of approval.

'You did well, Romaine,' he murmured. 'Very well.'

She wished he'd go away, wished they'd all go away. Only Léo Martel left her in peace. He stood against the door, a sheet of paper hanging from his fingers, and watched her face, not the pen in her hand.

When she'd burst into the basement apartment, he had held her in his arms. He had kissed her eyelids as if he could erase whatever it was they had seen, he'd bathed her cuts and bruises and wrapped a strip torn from his shirt around a gash on her leg, while all the time she told him what had happened with Horst.

'No more, Romy.' He spoke softly but there was no softness in the knot he was tying on the bandage. 'No more of this. I can't bear it.'

She'd buried her fingers in his thick hair to show she was never going to let go, but she didn't tell him about the key to that unnamed building where she'd burned the file. He might have thrown it in the Seine.

Now Noam leaned forward and picked up the sheet of paper. 'Is it finished?'

She nodded.

He started to read aloud.

> 'The Kreisau Circle (German: Kreisauer Kreis) is the name given by the Nazi Gestapo to a group of German dissidents in opposition to the Nazi regime. It is centred on the estate of Helmuth James Graf von Moltke at Kreisau in Silesia. The main members are Moltke himself, Peter Yorck von Wartenburg and Adam von Trott zu Solz. Most are from the traditional German aristocracy, but the circle also includes two Jesuit priests, two Lutheran pastors, liberals, landowners, trade-union leaders and diplomats.
>
> 'The Kreisau Circle is in contact with other resistance groups within the Third Reich and is keen to contact

dissident groups outside Germany to exchange information. Their plan is to oust Hitler's government and establish a new one in Germany.

'Horst Baumeister, who was Jewish, was a member of this circle, and he wanted to establish contact with our cell through me. The document states explicitly that there is a plot within the upper ranks of the German army to assassinate Hitler before he marches the country into a war that will tear Europe apart.'

Jerome gave Romy a clap on the back that landed on one of her bruises. 'Fine work, *mon amie*.'

Diane kissed the top of Romy's head, too choked to speak.

Noam grinned. 'You have an address for these German dissidents?'

Romy took the paper from him and wrote down a telephone number in Germany.

'You have an excellent memory, mademoiselle.'

An excellent memory. But not excellent enough to remember who stalked her father's study the day of his death.

Martel stepped away from the door and held out his hand. 'The paper, please, Noam.'

For a moment it seemed that the new member might not comply, but with a sideways look at Romy that made her skin crawl, he handed it over. In Martel's other hand lay the sheet of paper Romy had filled earlier with the enemy's plans and defensive tactics in Spain in response to the Republican's surprise attack at the Ebro River.

It contained a list of commanders and which army divisions were being drawn for support from all over the country, a panic reaction that the Republican forces could work to disrupt. But more important was the information Romy had written down in horror – that despite his general's advice to take up a defensive position, General Franco had decided to recover the lost ground at any cost. *Any cost.* The Republican army must prepare itself for a ferocious counterattack backed by German and Italian air strikes. This was the turning point.

Martel addressed Henri, the other new recruit, a radio operator. 'Henri, you have work to do.'

'If Franco's Nationalist forces break through or split General Modesto's troops in two,' Martel continued grimly, 'the backbone of the Republican army will be broken.'

A chill settled in the room. Each one understood the importance of conveying this information to those in command in Spain. Romy rose from her chair, but Noam reached out and his long wiry fingers gripped her shoulder.

'Romaine,' he said, 'thousands of young men in Spain will thank you for this. We all thank you.'

'I don't want thanks. What I want to know is what bastard killed Horst Baumeister?'

Noam pushed her chair away, his eyes cold. 'I will deal with it,' he said.

'No,' Martel said, 'leave that to me.' He had a way of controlling any conversation with these people when he chose. He walked to the door and jerked it open. 'Thank you all for coming so late at night. You know where we stand now. Each of us has work to do.'

They said their goodbyes, each one nodding respect to Romy, a kiss from Diane. Noam was the last to leave, lingering until all but Martel had departed.

'Romaine,' Noam said, 'who is to say that the car that killed your German tonight wasn't meant for you? I have reason to believe your brother-in-law is heavily involved with the Germans and—'

'What reason?'

'Enough!' Martel said. 'Get out, Noam. She's had enough.'

Without a further word, Noam walked out. Martel locked the door and leaned his forehead against the wooden panel, pressing hard, his breathing uneven. He didn't move. Romy went to him and from behind she wrapped her arms around him, her hand resting over his heart.

'What is it, Léo?'

She rested her cheek between his shoulder blades and could feel the quakes within. It was like watching a cliff crack open.

'Léo, my love.' She kissed his back.

He turned to face her, his eyes naked.

'Léo, what is it?'

His arms encircled her. 'It's you.'

She buried her face in his neck and inhaled the scent of his skin. 'I know, my love. I know.'

CHAPTER THIRTY-FOUR

FLORENCE

I am wearing black. I hate it, but it is respectful on a Sunday. I like to be respectful, though black brings my father's funeral crashing into my mind. I fear I will be sick over Chloé's book on aviation. We are sitting side by side on the sofa reading it together and she tells me she wants to learn to fly like Tante Romy and Amelia Earhart, the American aviatrix. Gently I point out that Amelia Earhart went missing last year while trying to circumnavigate the globe.

'In a Lockheed Electra,' Chloé pipes up.

I don't want her to know such things. I put the book aside.

She frowns, her pretty face puckering, and says solemnly, 'I am needed by France. To make the country a bigger place for women.'

I stare at her. My daughter is six. Six. She may have my blue eyes but there is something in my daughter that is not in me. A sense of responsibility. It has come from my sister, I know it, and part of me admires it, but a part of me wants to tear it out of her because it will only lead to sorrow. You can never fulfil that responsibility the way you feel you should, so you are always disappointed in yourself. I've seen it in politicians, in diplomats, even in doctors and priests. The burden is too heavy. How dare Romaine lay it on my young daughter's bird-like shoulders?

'Romaine.' I snap out her name. 'What are you trying to prove?'

Chloé looks up at me with the soft amused smile that isn't mine either. 'Maman, she's not here yet.'

I glance at the clock. 'She will be soon.'

Chloé fidgets, she fiddles with her long silky plait, with the lace cuffs of her white blouse, with the buttons of her black patent-leather shoes. She is always like this before Romaine arrives, unable to contain her impatience. I try not to show that it hurts every Sunday, her eagerness to be away from me.

I dust my hand down her peach-smooth cheek. 'Tell me, *chérie*, what is it you love most about your Aunt Romaine?'

She does a slow thoughtful blink of her wide-spaced eyes and then smiles. Her smiles always dazzle me. But this one's not for me. It is for my sister.

'She shows me things that are interesting,' she says.

'Like what?'

'Like the inside of engines. And the lamination of propellers.'

I bite my tongue.

'And she teaches me things.'

'Such as?'

'The names of the stars.' She puts a finger to the side of her clear young forehead to help her think. Just as Romaine does. 'How to tie good knots.' She laughs, delighted with herself. 'And how to swim. But I am not supposed to tell you that.'

My cheeks burn.

'And Tante Romy is brave,' she adds. 'She flies.'

The doorbell rings at that moment and Chloé bounces off the sofa, racing for the door to the apartment. I remain where I am. The image of my daughter in water, held only by my sister's unstable hands, swirls through my mind like black ink.

Romaine enters the room with Chloé frisking at her side, takes one look at me and comes forward, arms outstretched. I am stunned. At the change in her. She is wearing mourning, as I am, her horrible black sack of a dress belted tight at her tiny waist, but her eyes are lit up, more golden than amber. As though something is on fire inside her. She folds me in her arms, our heads pressed together, curls entwined.

'Are you all right?' she murmurs in my ear.

'Of course.'

But she doesn't let go of me.

'Did you tell Roland what happened?'

I disentangle myself from her arms. 'No.'

'But you said—'

'The body has been removed, don't worry. But I arranged

for someone else to deal with it. A professional *cleaner.* The Intelligence Service.' I look away from her. 'I didn't want to tell Roland.'

'Oh Florence.'

I see Chloé watching us carefully, so I smile. 'Anyway, what happened to you?'

She touches the graze on the corner of her jaw. 'I was with Horst.' She shrugs.

'Oh Romaine.'

We can say no more in front of Chloé, but we give each other the look we used to give each other as children when one of us got into trouble. Part sympathy and part I'm glad it wasn't me. We haven't used that look in eight years. But I see the flame behind her eyes and I need to know what is burning in there.

Chloé slips her hand into her aunt's. 'Can we go now, please?'

'Of course, *ma petite.* Go fetch your cardigan. There's a cool breeze outside.'

The moment we are alone my sister takes hold of my wrist. 'Florence, I have heard things about Roland.'

My face freezes. I say nothing.

'Be careful, Florence. People opposed to collusion with the Nazis are getting killed in this city.' Tight lines of concern pull her mouth out of shape. 'Roland's name is being mentioned as being responsible. Please, be careful. He may be a danger. To you.'

I snatch back my wrist. Rage, hot and primal, churns

through my stomach. 'That is absurd. Vile lies. Put a stop to them immediately before . . . '

Chloé skips back into the room. She is always an observant child, and she stands uncertainly between us, wide eyes flicking from one to the other.

'Are you arguing?'

'No, my darling,' I say. 'Just discussing where you will go with Tante Romaine today. To the Tuileries, I think.'

'I have a bodyguard for us today,' Romaine announces and without another word heads quickly for the door. I accompany them and relish the feel of my child's arms around my neck as she says goodbye.

'No swimming,' I say. To Romaine.

From my balcony I watch their two golden heads emerge on to the pavement of Avenue Kléber below me. They are holding hands. I cannot rid my head of the image of my sister in her stinking little room, the jagged necks of the broken whisky bottles in her hands, breathing flames of fury over the man who would have raped me. That is an image that will not leave me.

As they move off down the road, a dark head crosses the road to join them, a big man in a black shirt and with a bright pink kite tucked under his arm. Even from here I can see that Chloé is excited. She is bouncing up and down and touching her small fingers to the kite. So this is the bodyguard. I narrow my eyes to bring him into sharper focus and I get an impression of strength and confidence, not just in the width of his shoulders or the straightness of his back. It is in the way he walks. Despite a limp, he prowls, rather than walks. Something about him does not belong in the narrow streets of Paris.

This, I am certain, is the one who has set something alight in my sister, the one who seduces my daughter with a kite the colour of her dreams. I watch her grow smaller but I do not fear for her safety because everyone knows that if they touch a single hair of her head, they will have to deal with me.

The little threesome disappears from sight and I despise myself for the tears rolling down my cheeks.

I meet Gustav Müller in the Louvre. Voluptuous women watch over our every move, their ample flesh lush and translucent and somehow so indecent that I look away. I have never been a fan of the Flemish artist Rubens who painted for Marie de' Medici these vast monumental canvases rippling with female flesh, but Müller is clearly enamoured. He cannot keep his steely eyes off the abundance of rosy nipples.

Maybe it's a Germanic thing. Breasts like creamy pumpkins and faces that belong to angels. The Hitler ideal of womanhood. I shudder. French artists are more to my taste. David and Degas are my favourites. One painted with a classical austerity that appeals to me, while the other depicted studies of women at work in ballet studios where he uncovered the bones inside the flesh. To see what holds a woman together.

'So why are we here?' Müller asks.

His manner is curt. Did I interrupt Sunday lunch with his family? Surely not. His family is far away in Berlin, scoffing sauerkraut and bratwurst no doubt. Did he have a high-class *putain* booked to entertain him this afternoon? I hope so. I smile. I like to tweak his tail occasionally.

Müller is good at his job, very good at it. Roland speaks highly of him. He has informers in his pocket at every level of French government and knows exactly what plans Daladier is hatching with Winston Churchill, the cunning scourge of the British Prime Minister Neville Chamberlain. Müller feeds information back to Berlin almost before Daladier has finished speaking, sent in encrypted form to Hitler's private office.

I may not agree with all the Führer's methods, but only Fascism is the answer for this age. He understands that. It is our only weapon against the evil sweep of Communism across Europe. Adolf Hitler is truly our Führer, our Leader, the one who is prepared to stand against it and transform his country in a way that France must copy. It is our only hope. My sister is a fool to throw her lot in with the Republicans in Spain who would have us all following in Stalin's footsteps before we can blink.

I stare at the painting in front of me. It is overpowering, not only in its enormous size but also in its fleshy triumphalism. Rubens depicted Marie de' Medici, Queen of France in 1617, as Justice itself. Breasts on full view, she is flanked by Greek and Roman gods bestowing their gifts on her.

Is Müller trying to tell me something? That France will

benefit from the gifts of Germany? Is that why he asked to meet here?

Minerva is there in her helmet, the goddess of wisdom, and I notice with a jolt that Cupid is present too with his arrow.

Cupid.

My heart slows. Is this a warning?

'I wanted to know for certain,' I say, 'that the body has been removed. Is it safe for my sister to return to her room?'

'It's safe.'

I switch my gaze back to Cupid's cherubic face. To his arrow.

'No more rapists,' I say flatly.

'No more rapists.'

He comes to stand beside me and shoulder to shoulder we study Rubens' painting. His voice is soft as a snake's.

'But she is too close. She is dangerous. Your husband should be worried.'

I look at the tip of Cupid's arrow for blood. There is none.

'Roland knows how to take care of himself,' I smile. I can smile for France when I have to.

He nods. 'I am concerned for his welfare, that's all. Roland is my friend.'

'Like Horst Baumeister was your friend.'

He shrugs one muscular shoulder. 'He was. But he forgot who he was working for.'

'Really?'

'*Ja*! Horst was all set to betray us. He was blindly enamoured of your sister and her Communist friends. He had become too much of a risk.'

'I liked Horst.'

'So did I. But sentiment is a luxury we cannot afford in this business.' He turns to face me full on, ramrod straight, eyes sharp. 'You understand?'

'I do.'

'That includes sentiment for sisters.'

I slowly swivel round so that we are standing toe to toe and give him one of my smiles, chipped out of ice. 'If you touch a hair on her head, I will kill you.'

He laughs, a loud mocking belly laugh that makes me want to smack his teeth out.

'My dear Madame Roussel, don't overestimate yourself.'

My daughter comes home full of laughter. Her shoes are scuffed and her dress is streaked with grass stains, and she is carrying the pink kite in front of her with all the pride of a sports champion displaying a trophy. She is shining. So bright I could sunbathe in her smile.

I kiss her flushed cheeks and fuss over the kite with amazement as if I have never seen such a creation before. She tells me that it came from Tante Romy's friend, Monsieur Martel, and I listen to tales of its magical feats of flying, then send her off to wash her grubby hands. But I memorise his name. The second she is out of the room, my sister and I come to each other, voices low and urgent.

'Who is this Martel fellow?' I demand. 'One of your drinking companions?'

Why did I say that?

It is the flame in her eyes. It drives me to strike out at it. I regret it immediately.

'Léo is my boss at the airfield,' she tells me.

She cannot even say his name without the flame scorching her cheeks.

'That's not all, is it?' I ask.

But she turns the subject aside. 'We must speak about Roland.'

'Why?' I ask coolly. Roland is none of her business.

'Because he is so involved with the Germans. Maybe he was equally involved eight years ago too, Florence. Maybe he was involved in Papa's death somehow.'

'Of course he wasn't. He was with me. In the garden. Remember?'

She gives me a long stare until I itch to turn away from her, but my gaze remains steadfastly on her.

'So was I. In the garden,' she says at last. 'With you and Roland. Remember?'

'Don't be absurd.'

'He knows something. I feel certain. I am remembering pieces. Another man in the room.' She flicks her face away.

'You are mistaken, Romaine, I promise you.'

I almost take hold of her to shake more words out of her, but Chloé skips into the room, waving her clean hands at us, and my sister and I back away from each other. Both smiling. Smiles that look like snarls.

*

'Roland, my sister isn't drinking.'

We are in bed now that Chloé is asleep, the warm fingers of evening sunlight stroking our naked skin on the sheet. Roland is gripping my hips with both hands and with his lips he paints kisses across my stomach. The heat of them shoots straight to my groin. He rolls his head sideways to look up at me.

'Why not?'

'Because of this Léo Martel friend of hers. She's not drinking, so she's remembering.'

'Simple. Send her a bottle of whisky. It has worked in the past.'

'It's not as easy as that this time.'

His lips are gliding up to my breast but stop abruptly. I feel his breath heavy on my skin.

'What is she remembering?' he asks.

'She doesn't really know. It's all a muddle inside her mind. But now she is thinking a German was involved. And you. She thinks you were involved, Roland.'

He lifts his head. His eyes fix on mine and his face comes close. I see the silvery specks on his chin where shotgun pellets once grazed him.

'Why me?' he asks. 'I was in the garden.'

'That's what I told her.'

'So tell her again.'

I slide my palm down the tendons of his throat. They are tense and I can feel his pulse racing.

'She was in the street when Horst Baumeister was run down last night.'

'*Mon dieu*!'

We say no more. I tap my fingers rhythmically down the sides of his ribs. He likes that. He reacts as if each fingertip administers a tiny electric shock and I feel him hard against me. I take his collarbone in my mouth and set my teeth to the bone, though I do not bite. Not yet. My tongue flashes over it. I love the taste of his skin. I have never been with any other man, only Roland, but I cannot imagine that any other man tastes as wonderful as my husband. I know what he is about to say before he says it.

'You must control her, Florence. Or I will do it.'

I bite him.

CHAPTER THIRTY-FIVE

Was the car meant for her? The one that killed Horst Baumeister. Romy had been over it a thousand times in her head, unfurling each second of that moment of violence. A deliberate act, she had no doubt of it. The black car with the long bonnet had mounted the pavement and come at them, its chrome radiator glinting like teeth in the lamplight. A Mercedes, one witness had stated. A German car.

Romy was sitting bolt upright in bed. The dreams were ferocious tonight and she didn't want to wake Léo beside her. Best to forget sleep. Instead she backed her memories into a corner from which they couldn't escape and with a needle-sharp mental ice pick proceeded to take them apart.

Papa, what had I done to make you so angry?

She chipped away, cutting right through the membranes of protective memory till sweat coated her palms and dripped down her neck. She needed a drink. So bad it was making her eyeballs ache.

She heard her father's words sound clear as a bell in her ears. 'Romaine, I will swear that you are lying. Now get out.'

But another voice broke through it. '*Nein.*'

Her heart stopped. Her mind froze. She listened again to that German voice, more carefully this time, straining to recognise it.

'*Nein.*'

A moan escaped her lips. She clapped a hand over them but too late. Léo's warm arm wrapped itself around her waist, solid and comforting. His lips brushed her skin.

'Tell me,' he murmured. 'What is it?'

She was frightened. If she told him that the shark car was meant for her, he might kill someone.

Martel left at dawn.

At the door he'd said simply, 'Stay safe.'

She'd kissed him. 'And you.'

'I have two Tiger Moths and a Miles Hawk being delivered today from my brother in England as Jerome has done such a good job of raising funds. I need to check them over.'

'Who will fly them down to Spain? I can do it.'

He ran a thumb over the graze on her jaw. 'I know you can, my love, but you have been in enough danger. Wait a while. Keep your head below the parapet. I would say stay here but I know you will go crazy cooped up, so go to the cinema. Somewhere safe. See *Marie Antoinette*.' He drew her to him and rested his forehead against hers, as if he could slide the thoughts from his head into hers when words were too flimsy. 'Stay safe. Keep away from all your old haunts.'

She kissed him to silence his words and his fears. 'Give the new aircraft my love. Tell them I'll see them soon.'

He laughed. And then he was gone and without him the gloomy basement room felt like a prison cell.

Louis Capel frequently slept in his shop in rue Lamarck. Friends would drift in with a bottle of wine or cognac under their arm and a discreet little package of pills or white powder to liven up the evening. Impromptu parties ignited most nights. Romy had been to a few of them herself in the past, waking with eyes like fireballs and in bed with someone whose name she couldn't remember, but since selling Louis the guns from Spain she had not been around.

The shutters were down; nevertheless she banged on the door. No response. She banged again, harder this time, a relentless tattoo that wasn't going to stop. When finally the door burst open it was accompanied by a stream of curses.

'It's me, *chérie*,' she said.

The cursing ceased. Louis Capel was standing in front of her wearing a dishevelled Marie Antoinette wig and a brocade gown that stank of brandy.

'Sweetheart,' he groaned, 'it's only six thirty in the fucking morning, so this had better be worth it.'

'It is, I promise you.'

With a melodramatic sigh he swept back inside the shop. His mascara had run and there were lipstick smears on his neck but he looked ridiculously happy. The interior was as usual crammed with the clothes and other items that Parisians were obliged to pawn in their hour of need and on a moth-eaten Louis Quinze chaise longue languished a beautiful young blond youth of about eighteen. He was naked and unabashed, stretching lovely limbs like a cat.

'Don't mind him,' Louis grinned. 'He likes to purr.' He drew Romy over to the counter. 'Show me what treat you have brought me.'

'You'll like it,' she said and placed on the velvet pad her father's gold watch.

Clouds had crept over the city. They had stolen the sun so that this Monday morning felt dull and ragged at the edges. Romy hurried through the Arab quarter, head down, eyes meeting no one's. She was wearing the ugly black dress and had wound a dark scarf around her blonde curls to make herself less conspicuous, but out of the corner of her eye she was aware of men looking in her direction and occasionally a sharp guttural comment came her way in a language she didn't understand.

She stood in the deeper shadows of a doorway, her back to the wall, and waited. She would have bargained her soul for a cigarette right then but kept her hands in her pockets. Louis had poured a shot glass of brandy down her throat. To celebrate, he said. She didn't ask what exactly they were celebrating.

She could smell strong Turkish coffee and it made her

stomach growl. After an hour she thought she might have missed him and contemplated knocking on the door, but counted the cobblestones along this stretch of street instead. When she got to 1,379, the door swung open. She fell into step beside the hurrying figure.

'Hello, Samir.'

He jumped as though scalded. Though only thirteen, he needed a shave.

'Are you off to work at the airfield?' she asked pleasantly.

He nodded and lengthened his stride, trying to pull away from her. She matched his pace and for a while neither spoke, until they came abreast of a small patch of wasteland that someone had forgotten to build on. Romy had more sense than to touch him but she barred his path and steered him on to the dusty patch of weeds.

'I have something for you, Samir.'

His black eyes darted to hers.

'I promised you,' she said and held out the envelope she had received from Louis. 'For your mother's operation. I didn't knock on the door in case she didn't want to talk to me.'

The solemn young man opened the envelope and looked inside. It was full of banknotes. He shut it quickly, nervous, as if it might vanish. He stood frozen in that unstable moment of time. A boy, with a man's decision to make. Romy did not press him. There was a shout from the market nearby and she glanced over to see a man wearing a fez and a huge beard juggling grapefruit and flashing gold teeth. When she looked back she found huge fat tears rolling down Samir's face, laying tracks on his swarthy skin.

'Samir,' she murmured. 'Your mother will be all right now.'

'Thank you.'

'I sold my father's watch. The gift is from him.'

He put his hands together and salaamed. 'To your father,' he said. 'He was not the one who told the lie.'

Grief and guilt twisted into a tight knot inside her. 'I'm sorry, Samir. I would change the lie if I could but it is too late. It would not bring either of our fathers back.'

His dark eyes, full of sorrow, stared at her from under thick black lashes for so long, it was as though he had got lost inside his own head. She didn't look away but her cheeks flamed scarlet.

'Mademoiselle Duchamps, I was there that day. In your father's garden. I was only five years old but I know the truth.'

Samir took Romy to a tiny café that had a grimy courtyard at the back where round metal tables sprawled but where no one else ventured at this early hour. They shared the dusty space with two tethered goats and a three-legged hound. They drank Turkish coffee so thick you could stand a spoon in it. It swirled harsh and bitter in Romy's gut until she added a slug of whisky and only then did her world stop spinning.

'You were there?'

'Yes.'

'At my father's house?'

'Yes.'

She snatched at a thought. 'I didn't see you.'

He could be lying. To threaten her.

His long face showed a flicker of anger that she would doubt him. 'But I saw you.'

'What was I wearing?'

'A lilac jumper. Your sister wore a blue cardigan.'

She nodded, unable to speak. Something was unravelling inside her and she put her face in her hands.

In a quiet but relentless voice, Samir continued to talk. 'You didn't see me because I was small and good at hiding. We lived in a shabby tenement, while you lived in a fairy palace. I used to beg Papa to take me with him when he went to garden for your father so that I could watch you all in your magical life. Exotic as zoo animals. As golden-haired as angels. You and your sister were the most beautiful creatures I'd ever seen. I used to dream about you. About speaking to you. In my own way, I loved you.'

Romy raised her head. 'Now you know better.'

'Yes. Now I know better. Under your shiny skin you were evil.'

Romy didn't flinch, though it felt like a whiplash that cut to the bone.

'I can't bring back your father, Samir.'

'I know.'

'I am sorry. From the depths of my soul, I am sorry.'

'My father was a good and honourable man. Your life in

exchange for his was not worth it. I have followed you and seen how you live.'

She expected him to lean across the grey metal surface of the table and strike her. She would not have blamed him. Instead his father's gentle smile stole across his lips but he wiped it away with the back of his hand. This young boy was not born to hate.

'Each month my mother and I waited for the day of your visit because it was the only day of the month that we ate well.'

'So tell me, Samir.' The clouds cast shadows across his face. 'Tell me what you saw that day.'

He picked up his coffee and drank it straight down. 'I was helping my father. He liked me to work hard, so I was picking up the clippings from the hedge, but when your sister came out into the garden, I ran to hide.'

She pictured him. Skinny brown legs flashing, his head full of dreams.

Did Florence see him?

'I ran round to the back of the house. That's where I knew the garden shed was.'

'My father's study was at the back.'

'Yes. I know.'

'Did you look in?'

'Yes.'

She could stop there. She need go no further. She could stand up and walk away. There was still a chance to flee from the pain that was charging towards her.

'What did you see?'

The words hung over the grubby table. His expression of sorrow was too deep for a thirteen-year-old boy.

'My father was not in that room.'

Romy nodded. 'Of course he wasn't.'

'Then why did you and your sister say you saw him go into the house?'

'We lied.'

His dark eyes burned with sudden anger and his hand curled into a fist. 'You were in the room. You, Romaine Duchamps. Standing by the desk with a dagger in your hand.'

A dagger?

It was the paperknife. She could feel the weight of it in her hand, the coolness of the metal against her skin, the fear hot in her throat.

Her father shouting, 'Are you going to kill me, your own father?'

Her angry retort, 'Yes, Papa.'

Her hands started to shake in her lap.

'Who else was in the study?'

'Your father.'

'Just the two of us?'

'No. There was someone else. A man.'

'Describe him.'

'Tall. Fair hair cut short. He was upset. I only saw him for a moment when I ran past.'

'Old or young?'

'Young. You know him.'

Her mouth was dry as bone. 'Who?'

'I saw you with him in the street when I was following you. The man who was hit by the car.'

'Horst Baumeister?'

'Don't, Mademoiselle Romaine.'

She was shaking her head, whipping it back and forth over and over, her teeth clamped so tight on her lip that blood trickled down her chin. *Horst had been there that day.* Horst had been there and yet said nothing to her. No mention. No sign. She was hurting inside, like a knife in the gut, because he could have answered all her questions but now it was too late. Too late for him. Too late for her.

She closed her eyes and a memory rushed in on her. She could see her father as clearly as if he were standing in front of her. Immaculate suit around which lingered the sweet fragrance of his favourite pipe tobacco, and a shirt so starched it looked as though it could stand up without him. A powerful man. A stern face with hard lines of discipline scored between his features, but prone to sudden unpredictable flashes of warmth. A smile, a laugh, when you least expected it. As a child she had lived for those moments. Grief writhed in her chest as she heard his voice again.

Are you going to kill me?

She prised open her eyes and focused on Samir sitting so gravely at the table. 'Why didn't you tell all this to the police?'

'I did.'

'So why did they arrest your father?'

Bitterness wound itself into his words. 'They didn't believe me. Why would they? I was a five-year-old Arab brat. A born liar, they said. They chose to take the word of two angel-faced white *mademoiselles*.' His young mouth pulled into a kind of smile. 'Who could blame them?'

'You could.'

'No. It was the voice of Roland Roussel backing up your story that settled their decision. I was cuffed and spat on as the son of a murderer.'

Romy held out a hand to the boy with no father and a sick mother. She was overwhelmed with gratitude when he took it in his.

The room was silent as the grave.

Romy couldn't stay away. She couldn't, despite what Martel had said. She had to see with her own eyes that her room in Montmartre had been *cleansed*, that no limp body with blood matted to a black crisp in its blond hair still lay sprawled on the floor, awaiting her return. It could send her to the guillotine. Sometimes she wondered if that was what she'd wanted when she'd raised the empty whisky bottles.

The room smelled of blood. Or was she imagining it? Of blood and rage. The *cleaners* had done a vicious job of work when they removed the body and had torn her room apart. The skirting boards hung loose from the walls, floorboards had been prised up and discarded, her bed stripped and her mattress sliced open so that its black horsehair filling had burst out and taken refuge in distant corners. The room had been systematically searched and her belongings bundled into a pile where usually the zinc bucket sat. She nudged it with her foot and an iron saucepan clattered to the floor, making her jump.

There was nothing that held her there. Nothing she wanted. She retrieved only one item from the bundle that was her life. It was Chloé's drawing of the Tiger Moth. She had talent that child. She had sat on the grass of the airfield and sketched the aircraft with a concentration beyond her years. She had caught its charm and the quirky profile of its pointed nose. Romy removed it from the pile.

She was wondering how on earth the *cleaners* managed all this without alerting the concierge to the noise of their destructive search. Madame Gosselin would be up here like a shot. Unless she was paid to sit her broad backside in her chair downstairs with her knitting, while the shroud was bundled out the front door. Romy stood in silence, surveying the wreck of her life, when she heard a noise. Urgent footsteps on the stairs, a rapid heavy step. She snatched up the saucepan.

The door flew open, kicked so hard it crashed into the wall and dislodged a chunk of plaster. A tall suited figure with dark hair charged into the quiet space, sending a grey mouse scuttling across the floor.

'Romaine!'

'Roland, hell you frightened me. What are you—?'

Before she could finish he was across the room, his

powerful hands seizing her shoulders and slamming her against the wall. Once. Twice. Three times, he bounced her against it. Her head cracked the crumbling plaster. She felt its dust trickle down the back of her neck and a light explode at the back of her eyes.

'Rol—'

'Where is she?'

'Where is who?'

'My wife!'

'Florence?'

'Yes, damn you, your sister.' His face filled her vision as he thrust it close to hers. 'Where is she? What have your people done with her?'

'My people? What are you talking about?'

She was still pinned to the wall, his fingers digging into her flesh. She had fought men before, men who wanted something she was unwilling to give, and she knew where to jerk her knee. But Roland?

'Let go of me, Roland,' she hissed into his face.

'Where is—?'

'Let go of me.'

Something was in her voice, something he recognised as a warning. Abruptly he released his grip on her but did not back away.

'What happened, Roland?'

'There was a telephone call last night. From a woman in tears. She asked to speak to Florence. The woman claimed she knew Horst and had information about something he was involved with that she would only give to Florence. Face to face.'

'Why not on the telephone?'

'She didn't trust it.'

'You let her go? On her own?'

His eyes narrowed with dislike. 'Don't try to put this on me. Florence is her own woman and you know it, she goes her own way.'

No, Romy didn't know it. Not with Roland. She'd always assumed her sister did what her husband said. He was that kind of man.

'You tell your people to release my wife unharmed or I will come after them and kill them. Do you understand?'

She blinked.

'Tell them, Romaine. Make them listen to you. I want her back and I'll tear Paris apart to find her if I have to. Got that message?'

Romy nodded. 'Where did she go?' she demanded. 'To meet this woman.'

'Place Pigalle. That's where I found her car. She didn't come home last night.'

'Police?'

'I've informed them. But Place Pigalle is your stamping ground, Romaine, isn't it? Her car was abandoned there. Tell your friends to let her go.' He gripped her arm painfully tight.

'If she is being treated the way you are treating me . . .' She let the words hang in the air.

His eyes widened and he released his hold on her as if she'd burned him. They stood in the shambles of the room, dust motes dancing between them.

'I'm sorry, Romaine. I . . .' he swallowed awkwardly. 'I apologise. I've been out of my mind since she's been gone.'

For the first time, Romy looked at him properly. His eyes were bloodshot, his chin unshaven, his dark hair a mess. There were lines around his eyes she had never seen before.

'Why would anyone take Florence?' she asked.

'It's obvious. To control me, to dictate my actions.'

She nodded. It made sense. 'But who?'

'Don't be dense, Romaine, Your left-wing comrades of course.'

'They would never do such a thing.'

'You are a fool if you believe that. Go ask your aeroplane friend. Ask Léo Martel where he hides defenceless women.'

Léo wouldn't touch Florence, she wanted to shout. He wouldn't. But she didn't say anything. Except in her head. To Florence. *I swear I will find you.*

Instead she rushed out of the room and took the stairs at a run.

CHAPTER THIRTY-SIX

'Léo, I have to see you.'

'I can't now, Romy, I am dealing with the new arrivals.'

She could hear noise in the background, voices demanding his time and a big gutsy de Havilland engine roar that made her hand tighten on the telephone. She was losing him. She pictured the concentration on his face.

'Léo. Five minutes. That's all. It's important.'

That got his attention. She let herself imagine a smile on his face at the prospect of seeing her. Or was he frowning, pulling those thick eyebrows of his tight together?

'At Martine's café,' he said briskly.

'Thank you, Léo.'

A pause. 'You all right?'

'No.'

A faint hiss came down the line. 'I'm on my way.'

She wanted to say I love you, but he hung up. She listened for a long moment for a click on the line but none came. She didn't know whether that was good or bad.

Romy took the Métro and found herself a pavement table in Martine's café. It was tucked away in the industrial Épinettes district and offered privacy. A watery sun was elbowing the clouds aside and Romy soaked up its warmth, but it made no kind of dent in the chill inside her. She ordered coffee. Images of Florence crowded her brain, tumbling over each other. Of her sister laid out on cold earth. Or alone and disorientated. Hands tied. In a dark basement somewhere. Blue eyes huge with fear.

'I'm coming,' she whispered.

A hand touched the back of her neck. She spun round and found Léo Martel standing tall and shadowy against the sky with a look of concern on his face. He'd sprung from nowhere. He was wearing a black shirt open at the neck, no jacket despite the cool breeze, and there was a quickness to his movements as he sat down that was unlike him. Something was not right.

'What is it?' he asked. 'What has happened?' His eyes searched hers and whatever it was he saw in them, he didn't like it, because he squeezed her hand tightly, his thumb pressed to the beat of the pulse in her wrist. 'Tell me, Romy. What? What has put you in this state?'

She was quiet. No obvious agitation and no tears or sobs. How did he see inside her so clearly?

'It's Florence.'

He raised a dark eyebrow.

'My twin sister. She's been taken.'

'Taken? By whom?'

'I have no idea. My brother-in-law believes it's you.'

He became as still as stone. Around them people greeted each other across the café, a boy with a threadbare mongrel coaxed it to perform tricks for coins, cars rattled past, everyone on the move. Except Léo Martel. His stillness was like the eye of a hurricane.

'Is that what you believe too, Romy?'

'No.'

'Are you sure?'

'Yes.'

As she said the word, she realised it wasn't just a word, it was the truth. She didn't believe Léo would do such a thing. But Noam? That was a different matter. Léo must have heard the truth in her single word because he gently lifted her hand to his lips and kissed her knuckles one by one.

'Such a small hand,' he murmured, 'to pack such a punch.'

She was not sure what he was referring to – the wine-bottle attack or the assault on her father? Her other hand touched his cheek.

'What is it, Léo?'

'I went to Diane's millinery shop this morning. She had some information for me. She was sitting behind the counter when I arrived, a bullet hole drilled into her forehead.'

Her hand closed over his mouth. 'Cupid,' she whispered. They sat in a silence of sorrow.

'I need to speak with Noam,' Romy said.

The factory was loud and dirty and stank of pig fat. It was a meat-processing plant and the years of grease had seeped into the bricks of the building, turning them black and slippery. Martel led Romy straight to the large delivery doors, through which the carcasses were wheeled each morning, and then down a passageway past giant chambers where the clank of machinery and the thwack of cleaver through bone echoed in her ears.

She followed him as he pushed open heavy double doors into a room where the cold struck her bones like a blow and their breath coiled like serpents from their mouths. In front of them, obscenely pink carcasses of pigs hung from hooks, gutted and cleaned, row after row of them, stiff and upright like an army of the dead. But it was not these that held Romy's attention, it was the man at the far end. Noam.

She made herself walk. Not run. Not throw herself at him and shake the life out of him until he told her where he had hidden her sister.

'Noam,' Martel said, 'a few minutes of your time, please.' It was a statement, not a question.

'What the hell is she doing here?' Noam indicated Romy with a flick of his head. He was wiping his hands on the long canvas apron that encased him from chin to shin. It must once have been white but now bore the lifeblood of countless slaughtered animals. 'And what brings you here, Martel? Is there news of—?'

'Diane is dead,' Martel stated flatly, cutting him off.

Noam showed no emotion but his sharp gaze swivelled to Romy and she did what she had sworn she wouldn't. She lost control. She hooked her hands into his repulsive apron and dragged him closer.

'What have you done to my sister?'

'Get your hands off me.'

He tried to break her grip but she hung on. She could smell the raw pig fat on him. 'Tell me where she is, you bastard, or I will take one of your own meat cleavers to your skull.'

'I hear you're good at that.'

'You hear right.'

'What makes you think I had anything to do with your sister?'

'Did you?'

'*Non*.'

'You're lying.'

The man's whole face tightened and the nostrils of his heavy nose flared, his breath hot in her face. 'Your sister is a traitor to France.'

Her hand shot out and slapped his face so hard, the imprint of it remained on his cheek in a fiery brand.

'Stop it!' Martel's strong arms tore them apart and he stepped between them. 'You are no better than street brats.' He turned his back on Romy and went toe to toe with

Noam. 'Did you have anything to do with Madame Florence Roussel's disappearance?'

'No, I did not.' He spat on the greasy floor and it solidified in the cold. 'But that bitch and her husband deserve the guillotine. They are handing France to Germany on a plate.'

Romy stared at him in horror. 'Is that what you think too, Léo? That my sister deserves to die?'

But he didn't reply, instead he turned to Noam. 'Do you know where her sister is?'

'No, I do not.'

Léo Martel did not stand around any longer. He took Romy by the shoulders and started to steer her back between the dead creatures towards the door, but she stopped and twisted her head to look back at the man with the dark killer eyes.

'What is it, Noam, that makes you work in a place like this?'

He spread his hands, palms up, and for the first time, Romy saw him smile, a small angry smile, consumed by some private emotion.

'Who would think of searching for a Jew among the unclean bodies of swine?'

Romy lost the afternoon, it slipped through her fingers faster than pig grease. She hunched on the floor, her head hanging over the lavatory bowl, and cursed herself. She had walked with Martel away from the hateful factory

Deserve the guillotine?

Martel bought a slice of watermelon from a market stall and fed it to Romy in the shade of a broad-leafed lime tree. He wiped the juice from her lips with his finger.

'Romy, have faith. We will find her if she is still in Paris. I will put out the word that if any of our people have her she is to be unharmed.'

Romy leaned her shoulder against him. 'Thank you, Léo.' She could still taste the poison of Noam's words in her mouth despite the sweetness of the melon. 'Do you believe him, Léo?'

'Yes, I do.'

'Why?'

'Because I know I can trust him.'

'Trust him? I would rather skewer him over a roasting pit. He is the kind of man who would smile at me as the knife slides between my ribs. So no, I don't trust the bastard.'

'His family comes from Nuremberg. His father was a jeweller, a Jewish jeweller, who was beaten to death by Hitler's bully boys in 1935. His sister was raped despite the law that forbids sex with Jews. His mother committed suicide by hanging herself from a swastika flagpole.'

'Stop it, Léo. Stop trying to make me feel sorry for him.'

Martel wrapped an arm around her shoulders and she caught a quiet sigh that slipped from his lips. 'He is my friend, Romy. So yes, I believe him. I will find out what I can for you. Trust me. Now go back to the apartment and sleep.' He ran a hand along her arm and she could feel the urgency in his fingertips. 'You need to sleep, my love.'

'What is it that Noam does for you?'

He looked at her, surprised, then smiled. 'Ask instead what I do for him.'

Fear spread abruptly, touched her spine. 'What is it you do for Noam?'

'Let me see what I can find out about your sister first. We can discuss Noam later.'

Romy kissed his lips because she wanted him to take a part of her with him, and then he was gone. He was like the shadows on a grey day, fading before you could quite grasp them. She hurried back to the dank basement apartment by the Seine, but it was just before she reached it, hurrying over the cobbles, that a thought slid into her mind as smoothly as an assassin's blade slides between ribs.

What if Léo and Noam had rehearsed that scene in the meat factory? What if they had predicted her action and had picked which words to feed her?

The thought shredded her. Her stomach cried out for the old familiar numbness. She turned into the bar on the corner with the four cats curled up in the doorway.

'Chloé.'

'Tante Romy, you're here.'

The child flew into her waiting arms the moment she entered the Avenue Kléber apartment, curls fluttering, fingers clinging stubbornly to the straps of Romy's dress. Chloé had learned the hard way that people can vanish from your life with no warning and she wasn't about to let it happen a second time. She pressed her warm cheek against Romy's and their tears mingled.

'Is Maman with you?' Chloé pleaded.

'Not yet, sweetheart, but she will be back soon.'

The child was trembling.

Romy became aware of Roland standing at the far end of the hallway, watching them.

Florence, where are you?

CHAPTER THIRTY-SEVEN

FLORENCE

I love my sister.

I realise the full truth of those words now.

That is the solitary benefit of being locked away on your own hour after hour. Your mind clears. The flotsam falls away. The strong black lines of truth stand out.

The lines are the scaffolding of life. They are made up of love. And hate.

Love of someone. Of a cause. Of justice. Of self.

Hate of someone. Of a cause. Of justice. Of self.

For years I thought I hated my sister. I was wrong. It was part of the flotsam. Once when Chloé was a tiny bundle of golden smiles and I was cradling her in my arms, smelling her skin, touching her ear with the tip of my tongue, showing her a bee buzzing on the other side of the window glass, Romaine arrived. Blind drunk. She tried to snatch the baby from me. To steal my love. But Roland was here. He threw her out.

At the time I hated her for it. But now I realise she was desperate, up to her neck in her own flotsam, drowning in it, unable to see the lines. She tried to steal my love because she had none of her own, not even self-love. Especially not self-love.

My eyes are closed. In the blackness I see my sister's pale face at the trial. A girl of seventeen with her scaffolding falling away day by day till she became someone I didn't know. I lost my sister as well as my father that day in the study.

Because of her I am here. Isolated. Alone. Fear lying heavy as a dog on my chest.

But I love my sister.

CHAPTER THIRTY-EIGHT

'Back to your old habits, I see.'

'My habits are my business, Roland.'

'Not when you're in my house.'

Did it show so much? She had washed, scrubbed her teeth and changed her clothes. She was wearing a strappy summer dress and had brushed her hair fiercely to rid it of fumes, yet still he could smell the whisky on her. Or was it in her eyes? They say alcohol robs the eyes of their soul. If that's the case, she'd lost hers years ago.

She had woken mid-afternoon, shivering. Six jackhammers were pounding the back of her eyes. She made herself presentable, left a note for Martel and raced over to the Avenue Kléber apartment to see Chloé. Maybe it had all been a mistake. Maybe Florence had returned. But no, only Chloé and Roland were at home, waiting for a key in the door.

Now she had bathed Chloé and brought her into the drawing room to say goodnight to her father. Roland was talking on the telephone but hung up immediately and drew Chloé on to his lap. She snuggled in to him and he wrapped a strong arm around her to keep her safe. Romy watched. It hurt. To see how much the child loved this man. But Romy had no right to wish it otherwise. If Chloé was happy and reassured, that's what mattered. She smiled at her sister's daughter and came over to kiss her goodbye. Amélie, Chloé's nanny, was standing quietly by the door ready to take her charge up to bed, and then the conversation with Roland would not be a pleasant one.

To Romy's surprise, when she bent to brush her lips over the tender young cheek, Roland reached out and took her hand in his. Not roughly. In a fond and friendly way. She stared at him, watchful.

'Wait a minute, Romaine.'

She waited. Suspicious. Her hand itching to escape.

'What is it, Roland?'

'I'm thinking you should stay here. With Chloé and me. Until Florence returns.'

Chloé erupted with delight and hugged her father. 'Yes, Tante Romy, say yes.'

Romy was stunned. Stay here? With the heavy scent of roses from the flowers in the hallway and the shadow of Florence over every footstep she took.

'Oh Roland, I don't think . . .'

'You must say yes, Tante Romy.' Chloé squirmed off her father's lap and wrapped her arms around Romy's waist.

By asking her in front of Chloé, Roland had trapped her.

*

Roland refilled his whisky glass. Romy's teeth ached for it. But she sipped her water in silence and felt the jackhammers reduce to one as she held his dark gaze across the room.

'I spoke to them,' she announced.

'Your friends?'

He said the word *friends* with the distaste others would reserve for scorpions.

'Yes.'

'Including your Monsieur Martel?'

'Including him. But Martel is not mine. He is his own man.'

'He is a man who is proving to be a thorn in the side of a lot of people. He should take more care.'

'Is that a warning?'

He treated her to his smooth diplomatic smile. 'A word of advice, nothing more.'

'They know nothing of my sister's disappearance.'

'Either you are lying.' His eyes narrowed to dark points. 'Or they are.'

She turned her head away from him, unwilling to look at him in case she said things in the heat of anger that would be unwise. Her hand reached for a cigarette from the silver cigarette box on the table and she was caught off guard when Roland approached with his fancy gold lighter and lit it for her. She reminded herself that he must be suffering too. His wife had been kidnapped. She could be dead.

Not dead.

Please. Don't let Florence be dead.

She exhaled sharply and looked at Roland through the smoke, seeking the signs of grief and rage that must be etched on his face, but all she could find was a man who was in total control of every muscle on his face. No sorrow. Not now. Not like in her attic room. That Roland was not this Roland.

'Why do you want me to stay here?' she asked.

'For Chloé's sake.'

'I think, Roland, that there is another reason.'

He was pacing the room with whisky in hand, but halted in front of her at that. 'And what might that be?'

'To separate me from Léo Martel.'

'And why would I want to do that?'

'Because I am your wife's sister.'

'No,' he responded with an edge to his voice. 'You've got it wrong. The only thing I'd want to separate you from is a whisky bottle.'

It was like a slap. Colour rose to her cheeks and she raised her water glass to him. '*Santé*.'

He smiled broadly. He knew he had drawn blood.

'Do you think Florence has left you?' Romy struck back.

He shook his head dismissively. 'No, of course not.' He paused, studying her face. 'Do you? Is that what you think?'

She couldn't lie. 'No, I don't. What I think is this. Because you are involved in some dangerous secret manoeuvring with Germany, intent on delivering a docile France into Hitler's greedy hands, your wife has been kidnapped. She is being held captive to pressure you to switch sides.'

Abruptly her fingers started to prod at his crisp white shirt, leaving dents in it.

'You are responsible, Roland.' Each word came with a jab. 'You. You are to blame for the fact that Florence's life is at risk. That she is probably tied up in some filthy basement, cowering in fear.' Her voice was rising but she couldn't stop it. 'You. You are to blame, Roland.'

He didn't back away. He took a long swig of his whisky, rolled it around his mouth and took his time swallowing it. He made a point of breathing its fumes in her face.

'Me, Romaine? Me? What about you? You're the one to blame for this mess.'

Roland had settled himself on the chaise longue, his hand still gripping his glass, though it was empty. His mouth was tilted in a self-satisfied twist, spoiling for a fight.

Romy decided not to give it to him. She stood motionless half a room away and kept her tone polite. 'Why do you claim I am to blame for Florence's kidnap?'

'Because it's your left-wing Communist-hugging cadres that have done this and they have been led to Florence by you, not by me.' He smacked his glass down on a side table and it gave out an audible crack. 'Tell them, Romaine, that I want my wife back.' He paused, anger burning in him. 'Or they will pay heavily.'

'I have no control over them, despite what you imagine. Don't you think I would wrench my sister from captivity if I could? They say they've had nothing to do with . . .'

'They say. They say.' He hurled his glass into the fireplace where it shattered into a thousand diamonds.

She stalked over to her brother-in-law. 'I know it's hard, Roland. For you. For Chloé. For me. And I haven't told our mother yet.'

'*Mon dieu*, keep her out of this.'

Romy walked over to the drinks cabinet, an exquisite 200-year-old piece made of figured sycamore, and avoiding the slivers of crystal that glittered on the floor, she returned with two glasses filled to the brim with whisky. She presented one to Roland. The other she placed on the table untouched.

'Roland, answer me this.'

He glanced up at her, wary. 'What?'

'Do you know the code name Cupid?'

He did not need to answer. He froze. His drink poised at his lips. His eyes grew flat and blank.

'Yes, I do.'

'Who is it?'

He laughed, a sound like pebbles in a tin can, harsh and unpleasant. 'I don't know. And if I did, I wouldn't tell you. I hear he has been creating havoc among your agents.'

'If you call a bullet in the brain *havoc*, yes, he has.'

He swilled out his mouth with whisky, his lips glistening.

'I hear he is German,' she commented.

He exhaled a rush of air. 'You are remarkably well informed.'

'I thought Horst Baumeister might be Cupid.'

'It's possible. He knew how to keep secrets.'

'But there has been another killing since his death.'

Romy saw an idea dawn in Roland's mind. 'You think it's me.'

'I did wonder, yes.'

He uttered a chuckle, low and almost soundless. 'Did you inform my sister of your suspicion?'

'No. Not exactly. But I warned her to be careful. And now she has gone. Is that a coincidence?'

His hand shot out for a grip on her, but this time she was too fast for him. She skipped backwards, staying just out of reach.

'Roland, if you touch me again I will walk out and not come back, I promise you.'

Instantly he gathered his long arms to himself, sank both hands into his trouser pockets and, with a face full of apology, said, 'I'm sorry, Romaine. Please excuse me. I am worried sick about my wife, certain that it's your friends who have taken her. You always know how to rile me. I apologise.'

Romy snatched up her shoulder bag. She was shaken but gave no sign of it. 'I am going out now but I will be back later this evening.' She turned her back on him. 'For Chloé's sake.'

'No, Romaine, don't, I . . .'

But she was out the door and running down the stairs.

The two figures walked along the river, down on the cobbled lower *quais* where the summer air was like silk on the skin. The lamplight from the bridges tumbled down into the water of the Seine and drew large brown moths with wings of velvet that flitted around their heads. It wasn't dark yet. It was that thin segment of time between daylight and night-time when the world seemed to retreat and there was only the here and now. Only Romy's hand in Martel's, the heat of his arm against hers.

They didn't hurry the words because they knew that when they were finished they must part for the evening. Their voices were soft, in time with their steps, their heads close as they mingled with the other lovers who were stealing a kiss and a caress. No different. Nothing to make them stand out. Except their eyes. Watchful. Alert. Darting to faces, picking out shadows. Quick to spot any look that lingered a moment too long.

'You don't have to go back there, Romy.'

'I do.'

'Chloé has her father and her nanny to look after her.'

'She needs me. Until her mother comes home.'

Martel murmured something too soft to hear and Romy leaned her head on his shoulder. 'Trust me, Léo.'

'It is not safe with that man.' He brushed his fingertips over the purple bruises on her arm.

'He is using me. To get to you.'

'He has nothing he can prove against me.'

'Léo, my love, if a man has a gun he doesn't need proof.'

She wrapped an arm around his strong waist and together they walked without words, just the lazy roll of the waves tilting at the riverbanks each time a boat swept past. The solitary North Star gleamed overhead but could not compete with the City of Lights as it dressed itself for a night of revelry.

'Tell me about the planes from England,' she whispered. 'Are they good?'

She felt, rather than heard, his rumble of pleasure. 'Some need work,' he acknowledged. 'Especially the Monospar.'

'You've got Jules on it?'

'*Bien sûr.*' He smiled at her.

'I can still fly, Léo.'

'I know.' He kissed the side of her head. 'When they're ready.'

'Don't shut me out of it, will you? Jerome has procured a good pot of funds for more planes. I can help deliver them to Spain, you know I can.'

'First let's deal with this.'

This.

Back at Avenue Kléber, Roland was waiting.

CHAPTER THIRTY-NINE

FLORENCE

I am hungry. I am naked.

I run my hands over my flat stomach and hear it growl. Hunger I can bear. It is a way of life for a Frenchwoman who wishes to stay slender. Hunger is an expression of self-control.

My self-control is unwavering.

But I cannot bear the hot fear in my throat. It stops me breathing. I know I must think my way around it and so in my mind I go back, step by step, misstep by misstep, until I return to the beginning. However many times I trace those steps they always lead me to the same place. To the beginning. It began in my father's study. I open the door.

I walk in. Again and again I cross that threshold but it never changes. I find her. I smell the blood. I look at Papa and nearly die of pain. I remove my cardigan. I offer her the lie and she clings to it like a life raft, as if she is drowning in the blood. I condemn us to hell.

But that is not the point.

This is the point.

I wanted Horst. I ducked out of the garden and hurried into the house because I wanted Horst Baumeister the way my sister wants her whisky. If I had not done so, things would be different now. I'm not saying that they would be better or that they would be worse, but they would be different.

For a start, Papa would be alive.

So now I lie here with fear in my throat. I can bear the hunger but I cannot bear the fear. Fear for my daughter. Eventually they will come for her.

CHAPTER FORTY

The moment Romy returned to the apartment in Avenue Kléber, gliding to the top floor in its whispering lift, Roland donned his coat.

'Going out?' she asked.

'I have things to do.'

'At this hour?'

'At any hour.'

As the door closed behind him, she breathed a sigh of relief. Without him the air in the apartment felt lighter, the rooms larger, the silence comforting. First she checked on Chloé. The child was fast asleep, her room dark with shutters closed, but by the light that slipped in from the corridor, Romy could see she was sprawled on her back, hair like a splash of moonlight on her pillow, one foot lolling over the edge of her mattress and the FROG aeroplane on her bedside table. Romy knelt on the floor beside the bed and gazed at the young face for longer than she intended, her heart tight in her chest.

Had she once been like that herself, so innocent? Had Florence? It was hard to remember.

She gently tucked the small foot under the covers, kissed the warm cheek and left the room. She removed her shoes and on silent feet she made her way to the room beyond Chloé's, the nanny's room. No light shone under the door. No sound from within. It was just after ten o'clock now, so Amélie must be asleep already. Romy turned quickly and hurried round the corner to the hallway and, more to the point, to Roland's study.

She tried the handle. Locked. That didn't surprise her. She ran to the guest room where she would be sleeping and snatched up her bag, removed her lock-pick from it and hurried back to the study. She was quick. If Roland came home and found her in there, she could end up with more than bruises on her arm.

An hour. He'd be at least an hour.

Wouldn't he?

She inserted the pick. It surprised her. The lock was an easy one. You should take more care, Roland, if you don't want others wandering in to pry into your secrets. After only three minutes of raking the pins, she felt the lock yield and the door swing open. She flicked on the light.

Her stomach lurched. Roland's study was a replica of her father's. Never before had she seen inside it and it took an effort of will to persuade her feet to enter. The same leather-bound books. The same bronze desk lamp. Same world map on the wall and even her father's mahogany desk. Roland had appropriated them all. Bile rose in her throat.

How could Florence bear it?

Without wasting time she started to search. Romy didn't know what she was searching for, but there must be something here, some letter or file that would reveal Roland to be the traitor to France that she believed him to be. Her gaze skimmed the familiar old books on the shelves but without lingering or letting herself remember. She found nothing out of the ordinary among them, nor in either of the two mahogany cabinets that she combed through with care. They contained files of routine letters from cabinet ministers and from Prime Minister Daladier himself, as well as letters and documents in German, including two sent from Martin Bormann, Hitler's powerful private secretary. They were addressed from Berchtesgaden, the Führer's mountain retreat.

Romy was tempted to pocket them, though she could not translate their contents, but reasoned that Roland would not be fool enough to leave them so readily accessible if they contained incriminating material. She shut the drawer on them.

The desk.

She approached it uneasily. Her fingers touched its surface and lifted off again instantly, a jolt going through her that rattled her teeth. She turned her hand over, memories setting her fingertips on fire. The drawers were where any secrets would be hiding, so she moved quickly behind the desk where she had seen her father stand so many times, tapping his knuckles on the polished mahogany when irritated, touching his lips when amused. She thrust the memories aside and reached for the top drawer.

Locked.

She tried the others, three each side. All locked. But none of the locks was elaborate and it was the work of no more than a minute on each one to open them.

She went through the drawers methodically, starting with the long front one, which contained a large manila envelope lying alongside a pot of black ink, a silver cigar case and a small enamelled pillbox. She flipped open the box. Inside lay a lock of silky blonde hair. The sight of it moved Romy almost to tears, though whether it was Chloé's or Florence's she couldn't tell. She removed the envelope and placed it on top of the desk. It bore no name and was unsealed.

The grandfather clock in the hall struck eleven. *Merde*! Her time was up. She dare not risk being caught. She listened for a key in the lock. No sound. Just her pulse, a drumbeat in her ears.

Hurry.

She made a rapid search of the other drawers but came up with nothing. Only routine desk contents. Stationery. A Dupont gold fountain pen. She almost smiled at the thought of what that would bring in the pawnshop. A few photographs of men in suits. It wasn't until she yanked open the bottom drawer on the right that she found the pistol. A Mauser handgun. German made. Nestled up against a silencer.

Why the gun?

But it was the silencer that terrified her. It meant he wasn't thinking of self-defence. She slammed the drawer shut on it. Moving fast now, she turned back to the manila envelope and slipped out its contents. There were six sheets of foolscap paper pinned together with a brief note. The note read: *Gustav, here are the details you wanted.* It wasn't signed, just initialled. *R.*

Gustav? It had to be Gustav Müller.

She skimmed through the sheets, and slumped down heavily in Roland's desk chair, her mouth dry, her mind spinning. In front of her lay detailed drawings and specifications of France's new single-seat fighter aircraft. The Arsenal VG-33. She was looking at top-secret information, France's answer to the Messerschmitt Bf109.

TECHNICAL SPECIFICATIONS

Engine:

860bhp 12-cylinder Hispano-Suiza liquid-cooled inline engine driving a 3.75m diameter three-blade Chauvière propeller.

Dimensions:

Length: 8.5m

Height: 3.3m

Wingspan: 10.8m

Wing Area: 13.7 sq.m.

Performance:
Max Speed: 560 kph
Max Range: 1200km
Practical Ceiling: 914m

Armament:
1 x 20mm Hispano-Suiza H5. 404 cannon.
4 x 7.5mm MAC machine guns.
Aircraft fuselage constructed from non-strategic materials – wood and canvas.

Designers:
Vernisse and Galtier.

This was to be France's mainline defence if it came to an air war with Germany and Roland was handing it to the Luftwaffe.

She could push the drawings back in their envelope and run with it to Martel and to the police. If she did, what then? There were two possible outcomes. First – Roland would be executed and Florence would hate her for it, so she would never see Chloé again. Second – she would be treated like Samir. She had no proof that the envelope was Roland's and why would the police take her word over that of a highly respected citizen? Roland and Florence would be angry with her. Either way, Romy knew she would not see Chloé again.

A strident noise broke the silence and made her jump. It

was the telephone on her father's desk. She snatched up the receiver and listened.

'Roland, is that you?' Curt and to the point. Müller's voice.

She made a sound.

'Ah, Florence, listen to me. It's late now and that blasted husband of yours still hasn't sent over those papers.'

Romy lowered her voice to sound more like her sister's. 'Which ones?'

'The Arsenal ones. You know, that new plane.'

She said nothing.

'Is Roland there?'

'No.'

Müller rumbled with annoyance. '*Scheisse*! When he comes in tell him I expect them first thing in the morning. Got that?'

He hung up.

Romy stood staring at the receiver as if it were lying to her. Her sister knew. About the Arsenal VG-33. She knew her husband, a government minister in the Ministry of Defence, was passing secret military information to the Germans. So Florence *was* a traitor.

An image of a guillotine blade slammed into her head.

Romy lay in bed fully clothed. She heard the hall clock strike one o'clock, but still Roland was not home. All she could see in the darkness inside her head were the elegant ripples of the figured grain of her father's desk. Like waves in the sand. It brought memories tumbling over each other to get to her: the Persian rug under her cheek, the panic uncoiling inside her, the stylish black brogues on her father's feet. And the blood. A scarlet veil draped over her eyes. The roaring in her ears, so loud it felt like war drums hammering inside her head.

And the knife.

Always there was the silver paperknife in Papa's throat, the edges of the wound so smooth they looked like marble lips over which red ink had been spilt.

She struggled yet again to drag together the snippets of memory from eight years ago, but they resisted and slipped from her grasp the harder she pulled. She had woken. That much she recalled. Woken in Papa's large winged swivel armchair where she liked to read his books. She could see the book now. Lying abandoned on her lap – the maroon leather volume with the title embossed in gold, *Le Rouge et le Noir* by Stendhal, about hypocrisy and desire. *The Red and the Black*. Scarlet blood. Black shoes that walked through her dreams.

Voices had woken her in the summer heat of the study, voices like bluebottle flies buzzing inside her head. She'd listened. Had heard things.

What things?

She sifted through the sounds, seeking words and found one that didn't make sense.

Zinoviev

Romy sat up abruptly in bed. Zinoviev? It meant nothing to her. It sounded Russian. But now that a crack had opened up she could sense other memories pushing and jostling to squeeze through behind it. She could feel her fear and her fury that day, so fierce her palms were sweating in that crowded room.

Crowded?

Yes. The room had been crowded.

With whom?

Samir had told her that he had seen a young Horst Baumeister there, but why? And who else? She tried to look again through the eyes of a seventeen-year-old to see which other people were present in the room.

Her father. Tall and florid. Clear as a whistle she heard him say, 'That Jewish upstart, Léon Blum, has to go. He is now leader of the Socialist Party, the SFIO, and I'm telling you he will soon be leader of this country. Be warned. He will hand France's head to Stalin on a platter and the Communists will set their yoke on us. He *must* go.'

Other voices. Loud and strident. They wove together and she couldn't find the end of the thread that would unravel them. There was a gun pointed at her. She remembered staring straight into its round blank eye, her heart caught on a pinpoint of panic as she reached for the paperknife on the desk and . . .

'Tante Romy?'

Chloé's whisper crept out of the darkness. The bedroom door was open a crack.

'Sweetheart, what is it?'

She lifted a corner of the bedcover and Chloé's small body slipped in next to hers and nestled close.

'Is Maman back yet?'

'No, *chérie,* but she will be soon.'

'Is she with Herr Dummkopf?'

'Who is Herr Dummkopf, Chloé?'

'He's a friend of Maman's.'

Dummkopf. It meant *fool* in German. *Stupid-head.*

'Does she often meet with Herr Dummkopf?'

'Sometimes.'

Romy kissed the tangle of curls against her cheek. 'Where does she meet him?'

'In a hotel.'

'Which hotel? Do you remember?'

'No.' Her small hand crept around Romy's waist. 'But I don't like him.'

'Why not, *chérie*?'

'Because when she comes back she is always excited. She forgets about me and won't play dominoes with me.'

'Excited? Why is she excited?'

She felt the child's body stiffen with annoyance. 'Because she prefers him to me.'

'No, Chloé, I know that isn't true. Maman prefers you to anyone else on earth.'

Chloé laughed. But the idea had soothed her. 'She said if she ever doesn't come back, I must go to you.'

'What?'

'She said you will know what to do?'

Oh Florence. What are you doing to your child?

CHAPTER FORTY-ONE

Romy heard Roland's key in the door at twenty-past two in the morning. She gave him half an hour to go to bed and fall asleep, and then she carried Chloé back to her own bed. On tiptoe she headed for the front door and let herself out of the apartment, her bag over her shoulder and a burst of moonlight lighting her way. As she hurried through the streets she could not shake Herr Dummkopf from her head nor the sour taste from her mouth.

Florence had been meeting a German. In a hotel.

Is that where she was now? Abandoning her husband and child for the pleasures of some hotel bed? Romy had been in enough flea-bitten hotel beds to know that those pleasures were fleeting and never worth risking your family for.

Had Roland got it all wrong?

It gave Romy a small feather of hope. She clung to it.

*

Martel was waiting for her. He had parked his car on the corner of Avenue Kléber at the Trocadéro end and must have sat there in the dark for hours. But as Romy slid into the passenger seat he leaned across and touched his lips to hers.

'You smell warm and sleepy,' he murmured.

'I'm not sleepy.'

He held out his hand palm up. 'Give me the key and go back to bed.'

She sighed. 'We talked about this. We do it together.'

'Romy, it's dangerous.'

She smiled in the darkness. 'So is loving you.'

Romy eased the key into the lock and turned it. She heard the click and opened the heavy door a crack. She half expected the screech of an alarm or the flash of a torch, but neither occurred to disturb the silence, so they slipped inside and locked the door behind them.

In her mind's eye she could still see Horst Baumeister flitting through the shadows at the entrance to the corridor and hear his soft laugh trailing behind her as she led Martel past the doors of the offices. It was Horst's key that had opened up the building behind the Élysée Palace for them. His death meant she could ask him no questions, but that was the reason she had come. To find answers. The beam of Martel's torch drilled a path through the blackness until they came to what had been Horst's office, the one where she had kissed the German and told him lies.

Opposite, he'd said. Müller's office was opposite.

She pointed to it. It bore no name. Martel tried the handle but as expected the door was locked.

'You sure you can do it?' Martel shone his torch at her bag.

'I wouldn't be here if I thought I couldn't.'

She reached into her bag and brought out her set of picks, but she caught Martel's wry smile in the pool of yellow light.

'A sign of an ill-spent youth?' he teased.

She was grateful. Tension was making her hand unsteady. She crouched in front of the door and started on the lock. First she inserted the tension wrench at the bottom of the keyhole and applied very slight pressure. Too much pressure and the driver pins would bind below the shear line. Next she eased the pick into the top of the lock, and while applying slight torque to her wrench, she began to scrub the pick back and forth in the lock.

It was a bastard. Stubborn as a mule. The pins had no intention of cooperating.

Patience. Patience.

Again and again she lifted each pin with her pick. Again and again she applied pressure with the tension wrench, feeling for that moment when the driver pins would do the decent thing and clear the shear line.

An hour passed. Romy on her knees. Martel watching her intently. He made no sound, aware of her need to listen to the pins. At one point he placed his jacket under her knees on the marble floor, at another he wiped sweat from her temples.

When finally she felt the last pin lift and the plug rotate, she withdrew her tools.

Martel uttered a muted whoop of triumph. They were in.

Gustav Müller was not a man who cared for show. He cared for order and information. His office struck Romy as basic but his amassing of information was impressive. It was no wonder he kept a bastard lock on his door.

'Romy,' Martel said. His tone was solemn. As if he stood in church. 'Look at this. It is our Holy Grail.'

One wall was stacked from floor to ceiling with brown files, shelves of them packed tight, hundreds of files, possibly thousands. Some fat, some thin. Many old and soft as netting, others new and crisp, their labels freshly typed. The room smelled of paper and ink. And of something else. It took Romy a minute to recognise it as it drifted through the gloomy room. It was fear. Raw fear. Whether it was her own or whether the files, she didn't know.

The window shutters were closed but Martel did not risk the overhead light, instead relying on the torch. Its beam guided them through the names on the files, stacked in alphabetical order.

Martel murmured them, half under his breath, half to her, as he skimmed over them. 'Arnaud, Boucher, Bousquet, Capelle, Clement, Duval . . .' His finger hovered, hesitating.

'Duchamps?' she whispered. 'Is there a Duchamps?'

He nodded, but reluctantly. It occurred to her that he feared that whatever was in it might hurt her. She peered into the grainy circle of light and reached for the file marked *Romaine Céline Duchamps*. It felt weightless in her hand.

'It's empty. Someone has removed the contents.'

'Don't look like that, Romaine. It could be that whoever it was is protecting you.'

'What?'

He shifted the torch and it highlighted his strong profile against the dark room as he turned to her with a curious expression.

'Horst Baumeister perhaps?' he said.

'Nothing happened, Léo. Between Horst and myself.' She handed him the empty file. 'Maybe it was taken to blackmail me.'

Martel suddenly grinned at her. 'It must have made good reading.'

'Not as good as yours,' she laughed and started to hunt among the M's, but she was glad that he couldn't see the blush on her cheeks in the gloom.

She found Léo's file. It was thick and heavy but she didn't look in it. Instead she handed it directly to him unopened. He glanced inside it, frowned and threw it on the floor, then went back to the names.

'Diane Motte,' he muttered and threw the milliner's file on the floor with his own. 'François Perret, Grégory Quere, Jerome Roche.' They all joined those on the floor.

'Roussel?' Romy asked.

Without a word he removed another two files. The names on them were Roland Roussel and Florence Roussel.

Roland's file was thick like Martel's, but the one on Florence felt flimsy. It was also empty.

'Something is not right, Léo.'

His eyes were hooded by the darkness. 'Why would Müller remove these files?'

'I don't know. It doesn't make sense.'

She took the torch from his hand and searched the files in the 'D' section again, while Martel stood with arms folded, staring grimly at the shelves.

'I was so sure,' Romy muttered, 'that I would find a file on him.'

'On whom?'

'On my father.'

'Why on your father?'

'Because . . . Horst was with him the day my father died.'

'Your father? You think he was in league with the Nazi party?'

Romy could not bring herself, not even now, to say yes. 'It's possible.' The taste in her mouth was sour. 'He was a government minister and had access to high-level information.'

Martel studied the files again, dancing the grainy spotlight over them, and Romy watched it track through the blackness to the top shelf under the coving of the ceiling.

'Look. Up there. Those seem older.'

He was right. The files on the top shelf were grey with age, their covers frayed. They gave Romy a fleeting whisper of hope. Behind her in the corner of the room stood a wheeled stepladder for retrieving files, so she pushed it quickly into place and scrambled up it. Martel handed her the torch and she scoured through the top shelf files. Dimly she was conscious of time flying past while she searched and of Martel removing more files from the lower shelves.

'Léo.'

Outside in the street a car was driving at high speed, engine racing. They froze. But it continued on past, leaving Romy's heart thumping. She trained the torch beam quickly on the stretch of top shelf files that began with 'D'. David. Delacroix. Deniaud. Dubois. Duchamps . . .

Duchamps.

She plucked it out. *Antoine Bernard Duchamps.* Her father. The moment it was in her hand, for some reason she didn't understand, she started to cry, a great raking sob that shuddered through her for the father she had lost.

No, not now. Not here. Not when she held in her hand the answers to so many questions.

She leaped down from the stepladder, clutching the file tight, and her feet skidded from under her so that she almost fell. She swivelled the torch beam. Strewn across the floor were hundreds of sheets of paper, climbing on top of each other in a mountain of secrets and lies. Martel was sweeping the files off the shelves at random, shaking out their contents, his breathing sharp and urgent, his movements spiked with rage.

Another noise erupted outside. Two more cars raced along the dark street, but this time they braked and stopped outside. Car doors opened. Slammed shut. Voices sounded.

'Léo, they're here.'

Somewhere there must have been a security guard on watch who had called in reinforcements. Whether they were French or German, neither Romy nor Martel had any desire to hang around long enough to find out. Martel dragged one last pile off the shelf and sent them spinning across the room. 'Then we must give the bastards something special to greet them.'

He bent down. She saw his lighter glint between his fingers. A flame leaped from it, stretching its golden tongue to one of the sheets. Hungry for more, the fire spread to another and then another, until the papers writhed and blackened, spiralling across the room. The stink of burning was suffocating as flames licked at the feet of Müller's desk.

Martel, with a bunch of files under his arm, yanked open the door and the fire sucked in the sudden rush of oxygen, letting out a roar. No uniforms were yet in sight in the corridor but Romy could hear them in the building. Shouting. Coming closer.

'Romy! Hurry.'

The shutters were closed as they stood side by side in total blackness, alert for sounds, shoulders touching. No risk of a torch. The smoke Romy had inhaled felt like the rasp of sandpaper inside her lungs and she was struggling to suppress a cough. Boots were running down the corridor, which was already filling with smoke. They had slipped across the corridor into Horst Baumeister's office using the second key on the key ring stolen from Horst's body, but it would not be safe here for long. They had to escape.

'*Feu*!'

'*Vite*!'

There were sounds of panic. Voices raised. Romy could see nothing, but Martel's hand gripped her shoulder. His fingers felt strong and calm.

'We have minutes, Romy. That's all.'

She wanted to say, I want more than that. I want a lifetime, Léo. But instead she let her body nudge against his, unable to make out his face in the blackness, and whispered, 'If anything happens to us, Léo, if they should part us . . . I want you to know I love you.'

'They won't.'

'But if they do.'

There was silence in the room. She sensed the movement of his tall figure beside her and felt the soft sweep of his hair on her skin as he leaned down and rested his forehead against hers.

'I won't let them part us, Romy, my love.'

She knew what he was saying and the relief of it caught her by surprise. They would go together whatever happened.

'The window is to our right,' she whispered.

Martel took hold of her arm and steered her across the black space until they bumped into the sill. He lifted the gun from under his jacket, raised the files to protect her face and crashed the gun down on to the windowpane. The glass exploded. Slivers of it nipped at their skin but the noise was drowned out by the shouts of panic in the corridor.

Somewhere a voice was screaming and Romy clamped a hand over her own mouth to ensure it wasn't hers.

Martel's car was parked two streets away. They ran, tucked tight against the wall. Two more shadows in a city of night-time shadows. They ducked around the glare of street lamps, moving fast away from the back of the building from which they had climbed. Aware of the knife-edge of danger they were treading.

They ran in single file, Martel hard on Romy's heels. She could hear him behind her. Knew why he was there, like an echo of herself, his broad back positioned between her and any bullet from a pursuing rifle.

There was no cry of warning. No shouts or demands. No checking of names or papers. But a hail of bullets spat out of nowhere, ripping past their ears, snatching at their clothes. Romy felt one tear at her skirt, her leg stinging. They dodged around a corner and could see the dark outline of their car waiting for them, but as they started to sprint across to it, two figures in uniform stepped out from the deep shadows of a high arched doorway into Romy's path. French Security Police. Rifles were aimed at her head.

'Halt!'

Time didn't just slow, it stopped, while she hung on to no more than a thread of life. Her heartbeat ceased. She knew she could run. A bullet in the brain would be quick. Or she could drop the file to the ground, put her hands on her head and let them drag her off to the guillotine blade.

She did neither. She stretched an arm out behind her to find Léo but his hand was already swinging up past her cheek, his grip locked around his gun, one finger squeezing the trigger. The explosion set her ears ringing and made a circle of blood burst into flower over the policeman's face. His features lost their shape and he hit the ground like a stone.

The second security officer's rifle was aimed straight at Martel's vulnerable chest and yet at the moment of pulling the trigger he seemed distracted. Even in the black night Romy saw the whites of his eyes widen and his mouth open into an oversized silent scream. There was something trickling from his mouth and his knees buckled. Romy heard the crack of his head as it hit the paving slab.

Behind him was standing Noam. He was wearing a grin so wide it threatened to split his face and in his hand lay a long carving knife. It seemed to quiver. Its blade was coated in something that looked like paint, black and glistening.

'That,' Noam said, 'is what happens to the enemies of France.'

Martel said nothing. Not even a thank you. He seized Romy's wrist and hurried to the car, his limp more pronounced. It was only when he slumped into the back seat of the car and handed the keys to Noam that it occurred to her that Léo was hurt. She slid a hand down his back and it came away wet.

CHAPTER FORTY-TWO

FLORENCE

Today Papa is in my mind.

I did not invite him in. But Papa was always a man who followed his own path with no regard for the objections of others, so if that path now leads him to my mind, in he marches without knocking. It's not that he was indifferent to the needs and desires of others – of his wife, of his family, of his colleagues – not at all. It's just that he was totally unaware of them. Oblivious.

Antoine Duchamps was a man of such internal intensity that he could see no further than his own needs and desires. He got things done.

I admire that.

Roland reminds me of him. Except that Roland is acutely aware of my *needs* and my *desires*.

Papa and Horst Baumeister did not sit well together. Like

mixing fire and water. Papa burned everything in his path, while Horst flowed around it and continued carving out his own riverbed. Yet even so, Papa saw a use for him.

'You will marry my daughter.'

That's what he ordered. Horst looked as though he'd been kicked by a mule, which, now I think about it, was a gross insult to me. But I excused him at the time because I had only just met him in the study and he probably had a pretty little *dummkopf Fräulein* back home in Berlin. But neither of us had the slightest wish to cross Papa.

Papa had plans. Great plans. We were chess pieces in his game. I was young and Horst was handsome and I believed in the Cause because Papa believed in it.

Papa was my God.

I roll on to my side now, my cheek in my hand, and I feel tears trickle over my fingertips.

Go away, Papa. Leave my mind alone. I am no longer seventeen. If I wish to change the world I can do it without you.

CHAPTER FORTY-THREE

'Hush now,' Martel murmured.

As if Romy were the one injured. She was re-dressing the wound on his back and uttering small mews of pain each time she swabbed the blood from his skin. It was almost dawn and the first grey threads of the day were finding their way into the damp basement apartment where Martel lay on his stomach on the bed.

His back was beautiful despite the patchwork of scars from the flying accident, the muscles well defined under his skin as they tensed to protect the new wound. Noam had fetched a surgeon even at that time of night and the bullet had been removed from Martel's shoulder blade. Romy had sat with him, her hand in his, crushed to a pulp as the scalpel did its work. She dosed him with brandy before and after but didn't touch a drop herself. Just the fumes of it were enough to make her gut cramp.

The surgeon left quickly, his fist bulging with franc notes, clearly nervous at being there at all. But the wound had opened up again and Romy was bathing it with antiseptic and binding it tight once more. She ducked her head and dropped a tender kiss on the finished bandage.

'Now don't you dare move, Léo Martel. Not a muscle. You hear me?'

His face was turned to the side on the pillow and she saw his full lips curl into a smile. 'Yes, Nurse Duchamps, I hear you loud and clear.'

'I will sit here all day and make damn sure you don't, you can bet your life on it.'

'Romy.'

'Am I hurting you?'

'No. Get the file on your father and bring it here.'

'No, Léo. You must rest now.' His cheek was pale and waxy even through his early morning stubble. 'I want you to sleep and—'

'Romy.' Sharp this time. 'Do as I ask. Please.'

'There's no point. I've looked. It's all in German.'

He nodded. '*Bien sûr.* Of course. But I read German.'

She laid her head on the pillow beside him, nose to nose, mouth to mouth. 'Sleep first,' she whispered. 'Read afterwards.'

His lips brushed hers. 'Bring me the file, Romy, or I will get up and fetch it myself.'

Reluctantly she fetched the file from the living room where Noam was smoking a Turkish cigarette and eating raw onion. Back in the bedroom she removed the first few pages from the file and handed them to Martel. It was awkward, reading while lying on his front, but he adjusted his position.

'I will translate it for you,' he announced. 'Then you will leave and find out whether your sister is home.'

A wind had sprung up, swirling the dust of the city on to the windscreen of the old Peugeot. Noam was driving Romy through the somnolent streets of early morning to Avenue Kléber. Only the street cleaners were about with their brooms, and an occasional flower stall. The light was silvery and soft, and it painted the roofs to look like snakeskin.

What worried Romy was that Noam did not need to ask her for her sister's address. He drove straight there. He parked a block away but Romy sat in silence looking out the side window once the engine was turned off. Noam's gaze settled on her, waiting. In no hurry.

'Thank you, Noam.'

'What for?'

'For saving Léo Martel's life.'

'I didn't do it for you.'

'I know.'

She turned and openly studied his face, his heavy features, large nose and dense black hair. 'Noam, are you Jewish?'

'Yes, I am. What's it to you?'

She shook her head. 'Nothing. But it would explain why you are anti-Nazi.'

'So would a lot of other things. You're not Jewish but you are also anti-Nazi.' He flashed her a quick angry smile. 'Unlike your sister. And her husband.'

Romy pressed her hands together in her lap. Keep still. Don't let him smell fear.

'Noam, do you know where my sister is?'

'No.'

'If you did, would you tell me?'

'Probably not.'

'Are you lying?'

A thin slippery laugh slid out between his lips. 'Wouldn't you like to know?'

Romy's hand leaped at him and seized a handful of his shirt. 'If you harm my sister in any way, I swear I will cut off your balls with your own knife and stuff them in your mouth.'

She opened the car door, climbed out and slammed it behind her. Noam leaned across and rolled down the window. He was grinning from ear to ear, his teeth large and threatening.

'I like a woman with ambition,' he said and drove off in the direction of the Arc de Triomphe.

The apartment was silent. Romy stood in the hallway, listening. The hairs rose on the back of her neck, though she couldn't work out why, except for the heavy fragrance of the white roses. She was struck by a sudden fear that the apartment was empty and she panicked. She ran to Chloé's bedroom and threw open the door but the child was asleep in her bed as normal, her limbs spread out with a contentment that steadied Romy's pulse. She kissed the warm forehead, inhaled the sweet scent of her sleep-soaked skin and left her in peace.

So what was it? This sense that something was not right. She walked on tiptoe to the door of Florence and Roland's bedroom. It was shut, but she stood there for five minutes, breathing silently, listening for any sound. She heard none. Was her sister in there? Had she returned? Romy was tempted to turn the door handle and walk straight into their bedroom but she resisted the urge. Instead she fetched pen and paper from the drawer of the hall table and retreated to her guest room with it. She sat down at the dainty chair and table and started to write.

> Antoine Bernard Duchamps. Born 5 September 1878 in Chartres. Studied physics at the Sorbonne and worked for a manufacturer of telescopes.

All this Romy knew as a child. There was a telescope in the bathroom for viewing the night sky.

> When the Great War started in 1914 he trained as a pilot officer in *L'Armée de l'Air*, the French Air Force.

'No, Léo, no, you've got it wrong. Look again,' she'd told him.

She was adamant. Her father had worked at a quiet Paris desk job throughout the war. That's what he'd told her. Why would he lie?

Léo had looked again. 'Come here, Romy.'

She'd knelt on the floor next to the bed, her head close to his. She'd considered snatching the sheet of paper from his hand and tearing it to pieces. 'It's a lie, Léo.'

'That may be true, Romy. But you should listen.'

> Antoine Duchamps was shot down in a SPAD French biplane fighter behind German lines by a Fokker Eindecker. He received medical care and was interned in a prisoner-of-war camp in Magdeburg in 1916. There he became friends with a German army officer and after the war he visited Germany regularly.

Romy had listened, her throat burning with unspoken words. Papa was a pilot? Yet he'd never said a word. No mention of flying, the sheer joy of it. Nor of the horror of being shot down. No framed photographs on the piano of Papa in uniform posing proudly next to his SPAD.

'Why?' she'd murmured. 'Why didn't he tell me? It doesn't make sense. He knew I loved fliers.'

Martel had put down the paper on the bed and taken her hand in his. 'There are a number of reasons why a man might choose to keep his war exploits secret.' His thumb had fretted at her nails, trying to rub the pain away from under them. 'Some find it too painful to talk about. Especially the plane crash. I can relate to that.' He'd given her a lopsided smile. 'It seems to me that he wanted to put it all behind him. It says here that your father never flew again, so perhaps he didn't want you to fly either. It was too dangerous.'

'He could have flown. He wasn't permanently injured.'

Martel had lightly touched her heart. 'He was injured here.'

Alone now in her room Romy sat immobile, her thoughts fighting over every word Martel had translated. The documents reported that after the war in 1918 her father had found himself employment at Breguet Aviation, but he soon transferred to a job at the Ministry for Aviation and then the Ministry of Defence. Which is where he worked for the rest of his life.

How could she not have known that? How was it possible?

He'd worked for the government, he'd said. A boring desk job. Dealing with transport. To do with railways, he had hinted. Nothing of interest.

Did Maman know? Did Florence? Probably.

She felt excluded and betrayed. She started writing again furiously. The file from Müller's office listed details of his life that no one should know. The friends he saw, the clubs he frequented, names of at least three mistresses – Marianne, Giselle and Fifi. With photographs. It listed his children – Florence and Romaine – his servants and even his dentist and doctor. Worse, far worse, it listed his trips to Germany.

So many. Why so many?

To Berlin. To the industrial Ruhr. To German aircraft factories – Junkers, Fokker, Hansa-Brandenburg, Bavarian Aircraft works – as well as visits to French aircraft factories – Avions Dewoitine, Avions Caudron, SPAD, Voisin. Again and again Gustav Müller accompanied him. But it was not his secret aircraft knowledge that wrenched all faith in her father out of her. It was his secret meetings. With Adolf Hitler. Two were listed in the file. One in Nuremberg. One in Berlin. Private one-to-one sessions with the head of the Nazi Party before Hitler took over as Führer.

But why?

A sound reached Romy from the hall. The front door closing. Someone entering the apartment. Relief swept through her and she leaped to her feet, ran out into the corridor.

'Florence!' she called.

There are times in life when a chasm opens up in front of you and you blindly step in it. It happened to Romy that day eight years ago in the study and it happened again now.

It wasn't Florence.

It was Roland.

And in that moment she became certain her sister was dead. Romy stood in the hall, drowning in the sickly scent of roses, convinced she would never see her twin sister again. There was something about her brother-in-law tonight as he threw off his coat that she hadn't seen in him before. A darkness. It belonged in another world, one where life and death were cheap. She had seen that look at poker games, it was the look of a winner. Winner takes all.

'What the hell are you doing up at this hour, Romaine?'

'I could ask you the same.'

His tie was askew, a shirt button unfastened, his cuffs hanging open. This from the man who normally went into a panic if a hair was out of place.

'What have you done with Florence, Roland?'

His eyes narrowed to weary slits. 'Don't be such a fool, Romaine.' He turned to his room and that was when she saw the lipstick on the side of his neck.

'How dare you, Roland? How dare you go with another woman when my sister is not yet cold.'

'My behaviour is not your concern.'

'It is, Roland. Because I intend to find Florence wherever you've hidden her . . .'

'Go to bed. Get out of my sight.'

'Why do you hate me so much, Roland? Is it because you had to lie for me?'

He sighed and almost against his will he shook his head. 'It is because she always loved you more than me. You don't deserve it.'

Romy stood in the hall, stunned into silence. Because she realised what he'd said. He said *loved.* Not *loves.* Past tense. Florence was dead. Yet Romy's heart didn't split in two. Instead it hung in her chest, numb and unfeeling.

He opened his bedroom door – Florence's bedroom door – and at the last minute said over his shoulder, 'The police will be coming to speak to you later in the morning.'

'Why? What can they want to ask me?'

She pictured the fire in Müller's office and the bodies of the two guards in the street, one with no face. Roland shut his bedroom door, leaving Romy with no answers. She looked down and saw blood on her skirt.

*

'You have no idea where your sister might have gone?'

'No.'

'Did she ever express a desire to leave?'

'No.'

'Mademoiselle Duchamps, I realise this is not easy for you, but I have to ask about Madame Roussel's relationship with her husband. Was there any trouble that you know of between them?'

'No, none.'

'She wasn't planning on leaving him?'

'No.'

The police officer's patience was wearing thin. He looked young and ambitious and probably wanted to be out catching robbers and murderers. Romy wanted to tell him that murderers come in all shapes and sizes.

'My sister would never abandon her daughter. Never. Something bad has happened to her.'

The officer looked at her the way you'd look at a dog that has presented you with a particularly dirty bone. He jotted something on his pad.

'Thank you, mademoiselle. Just one last thing.'

Romy arranged her face so that it didn't betray alarm. 'Yes? What's that?'

'I need to speak to Madame Roussel's mother. She may know more. May I have her address, please?'

'Is that necessary? I wouldn't want her worried without cause.'

'It's best to cover all possibilities.'

He couldn't quite suppress the smallest of smiles. It was quite obvious that he was just going through the motions, nothing more. He claimed to have turned up no witnesses to two women meeting in Place Pigalle and it was obvious he believed Florence had run off with a new lover. It happened all the time. But he didn't know Florence.

Did anyone know Florence?

'Maman?'

'Romaine, what's wrong?'

A telephone call from her daughter and immediately she assumed something was wrong. That made Romy feel bad.

'You might be getting a visit from the police, Maman.'

A faint clicking came down the line. When her mother was worried about something she tapped her fingernails against her teeth, a pecking sound that had punctuated Romy's childhood.

'Don't worry, Maman. It will just be a few questions, nothing to—'

'It's Florence, isn't it?'

Romy couldn't lie. Not this time. 'Yes, she is missing and we don't know where she is, but—'

'I told you something was wrong with your sister.'

'No, Maman, I don't think—'

'What do you know?' her mother said with a hitch in her voice.

'It seems I know very little, Maman.'

The tapping came down the line. 'What do you mean by that?'

'I mean that things happened at the house the day Papa died that you must have known about but which you have never told me.'

Only silence came back at her.

'Maman?'

'Sometimes, Romaine, it is better not to know things. You are headstrong and emotional, so sure you know what is right, just like your father. You are not to be trusted.' Oddly her voice was gentle, almost a caress. 'I love you, Romaine, but we both know that you caused trouble in the study that day. But that is an end to it. Leave it in the past. It is better for all of us that way. I don't wish to discuss it again.'

The silence returned. Romy could hear only the stunned throb of her pulse in her ear.

'Tell me, Maman, did you see the German who was there?'

'Find Florence, Romaine.'

Her mother hung up.

Romy leaned against the window of the apartment and looked down on Avenue Kléber six storeys below. Overhead the sky was ice-white, draining the colour from the world, and on the broad leafy avenue, beyond the constant rush of cars and Parisians hurrying about their business, stood a lone figure in a black suit. It was Martel. His left arm in a sling.

Léo, what are you doing here? You should be in hiding. Müller will be coming for you now.

Her instinct was to race down the stairs, across the boulevard and into his arms, but she didn't. If she did, she would have to tell him about the secret Arsenal plans and the silencer in her brother-in-law's desk drawer. She would be forced to admit that she now suspected that Roland was Cupid, not Horst Baumeister, and made a habit of putting a bullet in the brain of his enemies. Enemies like Grégory, François and Diane.

Sweat trickled down her temple. She wiped it away with the heel of her hand.

There was more.

She would tell Léo she believed her brother-in-law had killed his wife, though she didn't know why. That he had buried her and was now in the throes of an affair with another woman. Then Léo – or one of his *friends* like Noam – would kill Roland.

She couldn't allow that.

Eight years ago Roland had saved her life. He had stood up in court and lied for her. Under oath. However much she loathed the man, she couldn't let them kill him.

She would have to do it herself.

CHAPTER FORTY-FOUR

Security was tight. Gendarmes stood around in pairs looking bored. The building looked inoffensive, though its grandness was marred by the feathery black smears around three of its ground-floor windows, as if someone had left dirty handprints on the stonework and forgotten to wash them off.

Romy was wearing one of Florence's outfits, a simple summer dress in a fine ivory cotton lawn that floated when she moved. She had added a navy Chanel handbag and shoes, dusted her sister's make-up over her bruises, and chosen a single strand of pearls for the final touch. She looked so respectable, she'd be thrown out of her usual bars.

She approached the huge stone archway of the front entrance but was stopped by a gendarme before she came too close. He was armed, but young and relaxed, happy to talk to a pretty girl.

'You can't go in here, mademoiselle.'

Romy assumed Florence's authoritative manner, polite but entitled. 'Why not, officer?'

'This building is closed today.'

She looked pointedly at the black smears. '*Mon dieu*, has there been a fire?'

'I'm afraid so. Last night. Made a filthy mess.'

'Was it an accident?'

He lowered his voice. 'There's talk of arson.'

'Have they caught whoever did it?'

'Not yet.'

She smiled at him with blatant admiration. 'I'm sure you will.'

He allowed himself a smile and pushed back his cap. 'How can I help you, mademoiselle?'

'I've come to see Herr Müller.'

Instantly the young officer's stance changed. It became stiffer, his smile more guarded. 'He's not here. It was Monsieur Müller's office that was most damaged.'

'Oh, poor Herr Müller. Do you know where he is?'

He glanced around, as though about to convey privileged information. 'He's three doors further up. Until his office is repaired.'

Romy inspected the building that he indicated to her right. Not quite as grand. But just as unmarked.

'Thank you.' She gave him a genuine smile this time. 'You have been most kind.'

*

The second one was tougher. The guard placed himself solidly in her path and manoeuvred her away from the entrance with his rifle butt.

'Move on, mademoiselle.'

But Romy stood her ground. 'Will you please inform Herr Müller that Madame Roussel is here to see him?'

'Herr Müller is seeing no one today.'

'I can imagine he is not in the best of moods but tell him I have a black notebook that he will be interested in.'

The guard was reluctant to leave his post.

'He will not be pleased,' Romy added, 'if he hears that you have turned me away.'

He scuttled inside the building and Romy was left to cool her heels for a good twenty minutes, at the end of which a smart middle-aged woman who spoke impeccable French but with a German accent swept the door open and invited her inside.

'My apologies,' she said, 'for keeping you waiting, Madame Roussel. I'm afraid Herr Müller is extremely busy today after last night's disaster.'

'Of course.'

The woman in her neat black skirt and white blouse led Romy across a crowded entrance hall and up an elaborate flight of stairs to an upper floor where she came to a halt outside a pair of double doors.

'Five minutes, Madame Roussel, that is all.'

Five minutes. To save a life.

*

Müller did not look pleased when Romy walked into his new office.

'*Madame Roussel*,' he said with irony, 'you've changed the colour of your eyes.'

She stood in the centre of the room. 'But I have not changed the colour of my spots.'

His steel grey eyes regarded her with annoyance but not yet with alarm. He was seated behind a vast inlaid table as his desk and the room seemed to be filled with images of him. It must once have been a ballroom because the walls were lined with gilt-edged mirrors that threw Müller's reflection to each other, disconcerting to anyone standing in the centre of them. She suspected that was why he had chosen the room. To outnumber any visitor.

He held a fountain pen in his hand and pointed it at her. 'Get to the point.'

He did not invite her to sit down. Nevertheless, she settled herself in the chair opposite him, but decided against taking a cigarette from the ivory box open in front of her in case her hand shook.

'Say what you have to say and get out,' he ordered sharply.

The far ends of the table were stacked with files, some of them charred, she noticed. So they had managed to save a few.

'I am here to make a deal.'

For the first time he looked at her with interest. 'So, Fräulein Duchamps. Now you are ready to give me the information you withheld when we met last time in the police station. About your comrades in the Resistance.'

'No.'

He laid down his pen and folded his hands together. Romy had a sense of a man trying to hold himself together. The events of last night had pushed him to the edge.

'Explain,' he snapped.

'You corrupted my father into betraying his country and now you have corrupted my brother-in-law into doing the same. I am certain Colonel Roux at the French BCR Intelligence Bureau will be more than interested.'

'You are fantasising, mademoiselle.'

'I have proof.'

Müller did not move a muscle. He didn't blink, he didn't speak, but stared at Romy intently as if he could see right inside her head. He waited in silence for more.

'I went to see my mother and she gave me Papa's watch. A fine gold Patek Philippe.'

'So?'

She threw in a lie alongside the truth. 'And a diary.'

'A diary? Your father was never fool enough to keep a diary.'

'I pawned the watch. The diary was in code, but I am good at puzzles and deciphered it easily. He mentions you.'

One of Müller's hands crept up and rubbed a spot at his temple. Romy could see it throbbing.

'It contains details,' she expanded, 'of meetings with Hitler in Germany. It also states that he was involved in the forging of the Zinoviev letter that toppled the left-wing

British Prime Minister MacDonald and replaced him with the Conservative Stanley Baldwin.'

She pinned a smile on her face, taut as a tightrope. Müller wasn't smiling. She could see the anger behind the cold, calculating stare. She had to keep him guessing. Like sitting at a gaming table, alert to nervous tells in your adversary. Who is bluffing? Who is double-bluffing?

'He passed French military information on to you,' she risked. 'Just as Roland Roussel is doing now with the Arsenal aircraft.' She paused. 'That is treason. You and Roland could be executed.'

Müller stood, a slow push to his feet, his hands flat on the table, leaning forward. A large threatening presence in the room.

'I warn you, you murdering little *putain*, that if you don't get out of here right now and keep that drunken mouth of yours shut, you will regret it for the rest of your life. Which I promise you, will be short.'

Romy stood to face him. 'I have a black notebook from my sister's sewing basket that names names, gives secret codes, and lists the files her husband has passed over to you and your dirty-fingered department.'

She could feel his gust of breath, foul in her face.

'I will do a deal,' she stated.

'What is it you want?'

'My sister.'

She saw the tell – his shoulders relaxed, his neck rose in confidence. She'd overplayed her hand. He walked round to her side of the table.

'So. Florence has gone missing, has she?'

'You know she has.'

'No, I didn't know. That does concern me. But it will obviously be your Communist friends who are holding her, not mine.' He inserted a kind of grimace that made her skin crawl. 'You'd better ask *them*. Get her back fast.'

'That is only half the deal.'

'Don't push your luck, Mademoiselle Duchamps. What else?'

'I want a guarantee of safety for Léo Martel.'

His eyes hardened. 'Don't even bother asking. He is a marked man, I promise you. I have my men searching for him now. I believe he is guilty of burning my files last night.'

Romy was a poker player. So she didn't freeze, she didn't utter a sound or let her eyes widen with shock. But inside, something snapped. A part of her broke.

'Why Martel?' she asked. 'What makes you think he started the fire?'

'A doctor attended him. He was shot and needed medical assistance. He's a fool. Better to bleed to death than use a doctor in this city. They are all in someone's pay.'

Müller was so close she could have torn his eyes out. 'If you lay a finger on Martel, I will take all this information to the Intelligence Bureau,' she warned.

He pushed his heavy face right up to hers. 'If you do, you will be the first with a bullet in your head.' But he saw no fear in her poker eyes. Romy could see his mind hunting for a threat that would hurt. 'And your sister's daughter will be the second.'

She couldn't swallow. No words came.

He smiled thinly. 'Now go.'

'Cupid would not do that to his own child.'

She'd caught him off guard.

'Cupid?'

She nodded. 'Roland. Your assassin.'

He laughed in her face. 'You think Cupid is Roland? You are more of a fool than I took you for.'

A double bluff. Surely a double bluff.

Abruptly she became aware of danger in the room. Neither of them had moved, yet she felt as if there were a gun to her head already. It was in his eyes. In the hate. She moved quickly to the door, yet at the last moment she turned for one final play of the cards.

'You were with Horst, weren't you? That day in the study. The day my father died.'

This time she saw it quite clearly, the alarm on his face, and heard his sharp intake of breath.

'I was told you remember nothing.'

'You were told wrong,' she said. 'I remember you there. So tell me what happened.'

'I would rather cut your tongue out,' he spat at her.

Romy pulled open the door and walked away.

The basement apartment smelled of antiseptic. There was blood on the sheet. It felt dank and gloomy and abandoned. There was no trace of Martel himself, as if he'd never lain in the narrow bed with her or dripped blood on her skirt while she held him tight.

'Léo,' Romy murmured in the silence. 'Where are you?'

He'd known that Müller would come after him. Of course he did. But still he'd burned the files. How many lives had he saved by that simple courageous act? Even now when she held her hands to her face she could smell the smoke and feel his grip on her wrist. There was no going back. Was Léo already in hiding? He had stood outside the Avenue Kléber apartment this morning, his arm strapped up in a sling, but by the time she left the apartment he had gone. Had he come to say goodbye?

She sat on the bed, stretched out a hand and let her fingertips linger on the smears of dried blood on the sheet. She was touching a part of him. It was all she had.

Now Müller had threatened the life of Chloé if Romy went to the Intelligence Bureau. The bastard had known all along her weak point. Who had betrayed her to him?

Roland?

She rose quickly to her feet. She had to find Florence. The thought of her sister's bones lying somewhere under a smattering of black earth chilled the blood in her veins and she thrust it aside. She looked down at her own bare arm. Flesh and bone. The lines of it still whole. It was alive, it could move.

Surely if her sister's arm couldn't move, she would feel it. You cannot cut one twin without wounding the other at some deep level. Her arm would know. Her foot would know. Surely her heart would know, would feel the loss of its echo.

She hurried up the stairs from the basement. There was one other person who would know.

Roland.

CHAPTER FORTY-FIVE

Romy kept on the move, always on the move, because if she remained still there was no way she could stop a howl of rage escaping. She prowled the apartment in Avenue Kléber, her feet padding in silence back and forth across the tiled hall, her ears listening for the first sound of a key in the lock.

She lay in wait for Roland.

She had no notion as to when he would return home – it could be early, it could be late – but usually he liked to be back in time to kiss his daughter goodnight. Tonight he wasn't. Tonight Chloé was already tucked up in bed and the nanny had retreated to her own room to write a letter to her fiancé in Avignon.

Roland deserved to die.

Anyone who harmed her sister deserved to die. But first Romy had to find out what had happened in her father's study. All this time Roland must have known the truth but kept it from her. And if he knew, then Florence must know. They must have known that Gustav Müller was present with Horst Baumeister, but they had never mentioned it. All these years they had watched her dance at the end of a rope of misery and guilt, but had not lifted a finger to loosen the noose for her.

Is that why Roland and Müller were so closely entwined now? Not just because of their political beliefs but because of what happened in the study.

Her lungs cramped as she tried to drag air into them and found herself suffocating in the scent of roses.

And Horst? Was that why he was so interested in her? Because of the murder he'd seen her commit eight years earlier.

None of it made sense.

A key sounded in the lock. Romy calmed herself the same way she did when something went wrong in a plane, when a fuel line blocked or one of the rods snapped. She spread a white sheet in her mind, removing from view everything except what she must do to remedy the situation.

So when the door into the apartment swung open and Roland walked in, Romy was standing in the hall ready to greet him. With his gun in her hand.

'What the hell do you think you're doing?' Roland's face flushed at the sight of the gun pointed at him. 'Put that thing down.'

He moved slowly, the way you would with a rabid dog so as not to excite it. He didn't remove his coat but edged carefully around the hall towards the salon.

'Don't be a bloody fool, Romaine.' His hand was on the door handle.

'What have you done with my sister, Roland?'

'For God's sake, we've been through this already. I don't know where she is any more than you do.'

He opened the door to the salon. She thought about pulling the trigger.

'Roland, why didn't you ever tell me that Müller and Horst were the two Germans in my father's study the day he died?'

'What difference would it make? Absolutely none. So forget about it.'

'It might have made a difference to me.'

He turned away. 'Go to hell, Romaine.' He walked into the salon, removed something from the bureau drawer, though Romy could not see what it was, before he slipped it into his jacket pocket, and came back into the hall. Romy had not moved.

'Roland, tell me exactly what happened that day.'

He uttered a scornful laugh. 'I suggest you put that gun back where you found it before I return.'

He opened the front door of the apartment and left. What was she supposed to do? Shoot him in the back?

Romy gave her brother-in-law a head start and then followed him into the street. It was dark outside, the street lamps creating halos between the trees, but still early enough for the flow of traffic and pedestrians to form a barrier between her and the hurrying figure. Roland was heading for the corner, where she knew he often parked his car. She would lose him. Unless she could find a taxi. There was a taxi rank up near the Étoile and she lengthened her stride to make a run for it, but just as she was checking Roland's position, she became aware of a black Peugeot gliding to a halt at the kerb beside her.

She frowned and edged away, but the driver's window rolled down and a voice she recognised called out, 'Get in.'

It was Noam.

The rear door swung open and her heart lifted at the sight of Martel inside. She leaped into the car and grinned at him. 'Are you following me?'

'No, I offer lifts to every pretty girl in Paris.'

'I am relieved to see you. I've missed you.'

'What are you up to now?'

'Trailing Roland. There he is, just getting in his car. I believe he is having an affair. But I think he knows much more about what has happened to my sister than he's saying.'

As Roland swept into the main stream of traffic, Romy leaned towards the driver. '*Allons-y*, Noam. Let's see where he goes.'

Noam slipped into the lane behind his prey, but Romy turned back to Martel. 'How are you?' Her hand gently stroked his arm in the sling. It felt like a bear's limb in a trap, crippled and awkward. She could only guess at the frustration and anger he was feeling, but he gave no hint of it. He was as pleased to see her as she was to see him, she could tell. So she nestled against him and for the fifteen minutes that it took to drive to Place Vendôme, they sat together in happy silence with no mention of bullets or files or kidnap.

It was the Ritz Hotel.

She should have guessed that this was where Roland would hide a mistress. But the thought of it distressed Romy. She wanted to slip in behind her brother-in-law and follow him to whatever room he was heading for, but Martel stopped her.

'No, Romy. He will spot you immediately. What are you going to do? Travel up in the lift with him?'

Romy frowned. He was of course right.

'He might recognise me, but not Noam. Let Noam find the room number for you.'

Noam swivelled in the driver's seat and nodded at Romy. 'My pleasure,' he said and the tone of it sent a chill down her.

She waited impatiently in the car while Noam set off into the hotel, but he was not gone long. Before she could climb out of the car, Martel eased himself out ahead of her and held the car door for her.

'We go together,' he said.

'No, there's no need to—'

'There's every need, Romy.'

This time she didn't argue. They entered the vast foyer with its spectacular decor, its lavish marble floors, sweeping staircase and colossal marble columns. But Romy saw none of it. All she saw was her brother-in-law storming down the wide stairs with a face like thunder. He glanced neither to the right nor left, without seeing Romy and Martel beside the lift.

Romy felt uneasy. What was it? Why was he rushing back out? A row with his mistress? Martel pushed the button for the third floor and together they walked down the softly lit corridor to Room 341. Romy did not hesitate. She knocked briskly on the door.

The door swung open. A woman stood there. She was naked. 'Darling, have you come to say sorry that—' Her words froze.

It was Florence.

CHAPTER FORTY-SIX

FLORENCE

This was not meant to happen.

We are the mirror image of each other. Our mouths hang open. Our eyes blur with shock. I almost close the door in my sister's face but she is too quick for me. She leaves her man outside, pushes it open and walks in. Romaine has found me.

I snatch my silk kimono from the bed and wrap it around myself. She is wearing my dress, one of my favourites, and looks so good in it that it occurs to me for the first time to wonder whether Roland desires her when he sees her in it. More than he desires me. She stands in front of me and I cannot tell whether it is anger or confusion that robs her of speech.

'I'm sorry, Romaine,' I say. 'You left me no choice.'

She takes hold of my shoulders and starts to shake me, so hard my teeth rattle.

'What are you doing here?' She shouts it in my face. 'Why are you . . .?'

She doesn't finish. Instead she throws her arms around me and pulls me to her, squeezing me so hard that I can't breathe. She buries her face in my hair and I feel her body start to shake. My sister is crying.

'I thought you were dead,' she sobs.

Her pain cripples me, it is so fierce. I stroke her hair.

'Dead? Of course I'm not dead. You weren't supposed to think . . .'

She pulls her head back from me, though her arms still grip me tight. She stares into my face, her own tear-streaked and twisted. 'I wasn't supposed to think what?'

'That I'm dead.'

'So what was I supposed to think?'

'That I'd been kidnapped.'

'By whom?'

'Enemies of Roland.'

'You mean left-wing activists who will not stand by and watch France being handed over to Nazi Germany?'

'Something like that.'

Nothing like that. But now is not the time to argue with her.

Her eyes widen into huge moons. 'You mean you came and hid yourself away here of your own free will? To frighten me?'

'Yes.'

I do not expect the slap. Not from my sister. It is hard enough to rock my head back.

'Sit down, please, Romaine.'

To my surprise she sits in the armchair, her face like stone. I walk over to an ice bucket and pour a glass of Dom Pérignon for myself, a whisky for her – a Glenlivet, Roland's favourite. I hand it to her but she takes no more than a sip and sets it down on a side table. She has changed. I want to gather her in my arms like I do with Chloé when she is upset but instead I sit on a chair near her with my champagne and reach for a smile within myself, but I cannot find one.

'Why the hell did you do such a thing to me?' my sister demands bluntly.

I cannot blame her. 'To protect you, Romaine. And to protect Roland. You were suspecting too much and proving to be too much of a nuisance. People were getting killed. I didn't want you to be one of them. I did everything I could to keep you safe, even though you were flying planes to Spain.'

Romaine looks at me aghast. 'You know so much?'

'Of course. I am married to Roland. With my disappearance you would have to stay in the apartment with Chloé and Roland. It would separate you from your comrades and my husband could keep an eye on you for me. Roland is as besotted by me now as he was that day in the garden eight years ago, and even though he has grown powerful these days he still does what I ask.'

'He was hardly ever there.'

'Yes, I admit that part didn't work out quite right. He kept coming to me here. I couldn't make him stay away.' I do manage a smile at that. 'But I had to do it, Romaine. I had to make you understand the importance of keeping your Communist friends away from Roland. They were closing in on him.'

'They are not Communists.'

I ignore it. 'I had to get you to believe that I would be harmed if they came for my husband. I needed you to stop trusting them. For your own good, as well as Roland's.'

'So you lay around in your silk at the Ritz, drinking champagne and waiting to be bedded by your husband, while I went out of my mind with worry.'

I feel sick for her.

'I'm sorry, Romaine. I had to.' I sip a mouthful of bubbles. 'Müller was coming after you. I had to force him to stay away from you. For God's sake, Romaine, it wasn't just a coincidence that so many of your comrades were killed and you weren't.'

At that, I see a tremor go through her. She is frightened of him. 'I removed your file from his office,' I tell her, 'but he was like a dog with a bone, suspicious of you and—'

'You removed my file?'

'Yes. When Müller was distracted on the telephone.'

'And your own file?'

'Yes.' I look at her carefully. 'How do you know that? Unless . . .' My mouth goes dry. 'You,' I whisper. 'You were there.'

Romaine nods. I picture the fire that turned Müller's diligently hoarded information to ash. He would be insane with fury, lashing out at . . .

'Florence.'

There is something in her tone, something new, something that frightens me.

'What is it, Romaine?'

'Horst Baumeister and Gustav Müller were in Papa's study the day I killed him.'

The words *I killed him* come out of her mouth covered in blood, dripping strings of it on the carpet, and we blink in unison to banish the image. I want to run to her. To tell her to stop now before it is too late. But she is relentless.

She stands, comes over to me and kneels in front of me, her head no higher than Chloé's. Her hands grasp my knees, pinning us together, and I feel the heat of her palms through the silk of my kimono. I don't want to hear what she has to say.

'Did you know this, Florence? That they were there. The two Germans. Not a figment of my imagination or a dream, as you told me in Monico's.' Her grip on my knees tightens. 'Have you known this all along?'

I open my mouth to lie, but she will see the lie for what it is. So I sidestep her question with one of my own.

'What makes you think they were there?'

'Samir told me about Horst. He saw him there.'

'Samir?' My heart thumps. 'What did he see?'

'Not much.'

'And Müller?'

'I spoke with him this morning. I told him I remembered him in the room and he didn't deny it.'

The world splinters around me. I leap to my feet, dragging

Romaine with me. 'You did what?' I scream in her face. Yet I clamp a hand over her mouth to prevent her replying with the words I refuse to hear. 'You told Müller that you remembered?'

She nods. Eyes dark with anger. I know it is for me.

I release her and drop my face in my hands with a moan that I drag up from hell. 'Romaine, you have signed your own death warrant.'

We sit in the Ritz hotel bath together. I know it is odd. I know it is not what we are supposed to do, but it is strangely soothing. The shaking of our limbs stops and our heartbeats climb down enough for us to talk quietly, facing each other from opposite ends, wrapped in warm water, the way we began our life. On the side of the bath sit our drinks, untouched.

'You remembered right,' I say. 'You were asleep in Papa's reading chair. Müller and Horst had come to the house for a secret meeting and Papa summoned me from the garden to join them. He knew I supported their political aims, but also because he wanted me to marry Horst. Papa wanted a political alliance with Germany through blood ties. He was certain that Adolf Hitler would one day rule France as well as Germany.'

'Did you want to marry Horst?'

'I was interested, yes. But not after Papa's death.'

'Was he the man Chloé calls Herr Dummkopf?'

I smile. 'Yes. But nothing ever happened between us.'

Romaine sits there looking at me as expectantly as Chloé, her cropped hair twisting into tight curls in the hot steam.

I keep my account of that day short.

'You woke and heard them all discussing plans to assassinate Théodore Steeg.'

'What? *Merde*! The leader of the Radical Socialist Party?'

'The same. He was a pro-Communist traitor to our country and as Governor General of Algeria had removed power from the traditional elite. There was talk of him being made President of the Council of France and it had to be stopped. Papa was the one to stop it.'

Romaine looks at me as if I have two heads, but I hurry on. I want to get it over with.

'You made your presence known by shouting at Papa. By swearing to go to the police. If you did, Papa, Müller and Horst would have been arrested, tried and executed, so . . .' I splash some water at her as if I can splash away the images in my head. 'They were not so keen on the idea. You can't blame them.'

'I do blame them. And I blame you.'

I leave Romaine's words to float in the water.

'Anyway, Müller threatened you with a gun, but Papa said he would make sure you held your tongue. But Müller did not trust you. He came at you with the gun. To shoot you in the head.'

My throat closes. I see the study clearly. Romaine's young eyes enraged and fixed on our father. Her cry of 'Papa'. Her fear draining colour from her face.

I swallow a handful of the bathwater to wash out my mouth. 'You snatched the paperknife from the desk to defend yourself against Müller, but Papa stepped between you. He tried to defend you with the paperweight. There was a struggle between all three of you. Papa went down. Müller hit you with the paperweight.'

My words run out.

Romaine leans forward, takes my wet face between her hands and kisses my forehead. It feels like forgiveness.

'Why,' she whispers, 'have you never told me the truth before?'

'Oh my sister, to keep you safe. Müller trusted me, but if he ever thought you knew the truth and might confess all to the police, he would have been the first to pull the trigger on you. Roland was not there. He was in the garden. He has always hated you because I made him lie in court for you.'

Our eyes hold on to each other. I slam both hands down on the surface of the water, creating a tidal wave of grief that engulfs us both. 'It was an accident, Romaine, it wasn't your fault.'

There. I have given her release. She can put down her burden of guilt.

And then I say again. 'Romaine, you have signed your own death warrant.'

Romaine won't let me take her home to my apartment. Now she knows about the immediate danger from Müller, she does not trust Roland. She says he will hand her over to the

German before she even has her shoes off and when I tell her she is mistaken, she laughs and pats my cheek, the way she does to Chloé. I want to cry.

So I hand her over to her big bear of a companion with the large hands and an arm in a sling. He sweeps his good arm around her waist to show she belongs to him, not to me, and he whisks her off down Place Vendôme, driven through the darkness by an unpleasant-looking man with eyes that drill holes in me.

When I walk into the Avenue Kléber apartment, Roland is already there in the salon, whisky in hand.

'Where is she?' he asks at once. No greeting for me.

'I don't know. Who are the two men standing in the hall?'

'They want to talk to Romaine. Müller sent them over.'

I suppress the shudder that shoots up my spine. I walk over, kiss his mouth and sip his whisky. I am ice-cold inside.

'Where is she?' he asks again. 'I thought you'd bring her here.'

'So did I. She wouldn't come.'

'Where do you think she has gone?'

Does he think I will betray my sister a second time?

'To a filthy bar somewhere, I expect.'

He regards me over the rim of his glass, his eyes dark with suspicion. He can read me too easily.

'More likely to that airfield she works out of,' he comments. 'What's it called?'

He is testing me. We both know what it's called.

'DeFosse Airfield,' I say.

He downs the last of his whisky and shrugs. 'For her sake I hope that's not where she has gone tonight.'

'Why not?'

'Müller has arranged a raid on it.'

'*Mon dieu*!'

My husband smiles. He thinks he is finally rid of my sister.

CHAPTER FORTY-SEVEN

The evening air was humid and claustrophobic. It gathered in the car and tasted sour on the tongue. Her mind questioned over and over how much of what Florence had told her was true? Or was she lying to her again?

Romy was seated beside Martel on the rear seat and her hand rested on his chest, feeling the rise and fall of it as they sped through the dark streets of Paris. She worried about his shoulder wound. He should be resting it, but he dismissed any suggestion of doing so. His only concession was to wear the sling, but she knew he hated having his wings clipped. The steady rhythm of his breathing, the force within the broad expanse of his ribs, the gentleness of his hand on the thigh of her dress, calmed her.

She was on the run. In a borrowed dress and with no idea of where to flee. Müller's tentacles stretched far across France. He'd had her watched on The Blue Train and bundled off it when the mood took him. He must have a whole galaxy of corrupt French officials in his pocket, which meant she could trust no one. Maybe even now their car was being followed. She twisted round and studied the traffic behind them, watching for a pair of headlamps that hung around too long. But it was impossible. Any one of them could mean trouble.

Trouble that would take her away from Martel. That thought sent her emotions crashing into each other and she braced herself for the answer to the question she must ask.

'Where are we going?'

What she meant was where are you taking me? At what street corner are you going to drop me? He knew what she meant and he leaned forward to tap Noam on the shoulder.

'Pull over,' he ordered.

The car pulled over. Silence fell in its stuffy interior, except for the ticking of the engine, and Romy knew this was the beginning of the end. She had to leave Paris or Müller would find her. Léo couldn't leave Paris because his business was here and he was not a man who could exist except around aircraft. She knew this. She'd known she would always have to share him with his aircraft and never force him to choose. But now it had come. The path divided. Martel opened the car door.

Everything was gone. Her sister. Chloé. Her home and mother. Her job. Her flying. Her love. Müller had robbed her of them all. Even of her father. The German had been there in the study and had been the cause of the struggle that killed him. Rage choked her.

Or was she the one who had robbed herself of them all?

'Romy?'

She would not make it hard for him.

She lifted her head and found Noam was on the pavement, holding the car door open for her.

'Do you drive?' Noam asked.

'Yes.'

'Good. So climb into the driver's seat. I have other things to do.'

He vanished into the night, leaving the door hanging open.

'Well,' Martel said, 'what are you waiting for? Head for the airfield.'

The road abandoned the pavements of the city and plunged into the darker world that lay beyond the street lamps of Paris. Out here a car was more conspicuous. Its headlights carved a path through the night for all to see, but out here Romy felt freer, the air fresher in her lungs, her mind clearer. She kept a sharp eye on any headlights behind her but none seemed to linger too long or nudge up too close.

How long did she have?

Beside her in the passenger seat Martel was silent, wreathed in night thoughts, sitting very upright to ease his shoulder. Every now and again he would turn his head and stare at her wordlessly, as if imprinting her into his mind. As if saying goodbye.

When they were near the airfield, he said, 'Douse the lights.'

She flicked a switch and abruptly the darkness swallowed them. For a moment they could see nothing and no one. But that meant nothing and no one could see them.

CHAPTER FORTY-EIGHT

FLORENCE

When the front doorbell chimes through the apartment, I pay it little heed. I am expecting no one. I have retreated to my bedroom because I must lie down. Everything hurts. Inside and out.

Roland is still in the salon with his whisky bottle and, last I saw, the two men sent over by Müller are still loitering in our hall with nothing to do except outstare the portraits of my ancestors. If I were a betting person like Romaine – which I am not – my money would be on the ancestors.

With my eyes closed I see Romaine's face in the bath as I tell her the story of the struggle in the study for the gun and paperknife. Her face is alight. With pain. And with joy. The two combined like whisky and soda. Inseparable. I am thinking of that face, crippled with a desire for more, when I hear a noise. It's from the hall. And I know that noise as precisely as I know Chloé's laugh. The sound is short, sharp, like a puffed-up paper bag popping. The air snapping out of it.

It is the sound of a silencer.

I am off the bed and sweeping my hand under the mattress before another heartbeat finishes. It comes up with a Walther PPK, silencer already attached, nestled comfortably in my grip and my heart rate slows to a controlled level as I stand behind the door. Listening. Visualising.

The person I visualise is Chloé.

I open the bedroom door. A crack. The corridor is empty. The light is on. I step into it in stocking feet. I move smoothly and silently. Against the wall. Barely disturbing the air. I am good at this. This is what I do.

I reach the hall and keep my gun high as I peer around the corner. Two bodies on the tiles. Müller's men. Their blood is marring the perfection of my decor. This is not the only thing marring my hall. Outside the closed salon door a solitary gunman is standing on guard and he looks stiff and bored. We can both hear raised voices inside the salon, and as I try in vain to decipher words, a wail of pain slithers under the door. It is Roland. It is at that point, when all sound is camouflaged by the cry, that I ease back the trigger of my Walther PPK.

The gun is silenced, so the only sound it makes is a dull *pfft* that can be easily missed. The body falling to the ground will make more noise than the gun, so I run forward and catch him. He is heavy. His arms loll over me as I lower him to the floor. It is a head wound. For exactly five heartbeats – I counted them – I stand in the centre of the tiled floor and am forced to make a choice. I do not want Roland to die or to suffer the kind of pain I know they are inflicting on him. There seem to be four unfamiliar voices in our salon and if I rush in with gun blazing, the likely outcome is that we both die. I might take a couple of intruders with me, but the result will not alter. Roland and I will die.

So I choose. It sends my heart into a panic of distress. I choose Chloé. I run back up the corridor on silent feet and open the door to her room. I leave the light off. By the glow from the corridor I pick up her dressing gown from the floor and creep to the bed. I lower my face close to my daughter's, place a hand over her mouth and whisper her name in her ear. I repeat her name three times. Only then do her eyes flick open and I see panic tumble into them. I hold my hand firm.

'Hush. Say nothing. Some bad people have come into the apartment and we have to leave.' I kiss her forehead. 'Be silent.' I kiss her again. 'Understand?'

She nods. I remove my hand. She remains silent. She is her mother's daughter.

CHAPTER FORTY-NINE

An airfield at night is a lonely place. But to Romy it felt like coming home. She had missed it. Even in the dark it held no fears. The night sky was a velvet patchwork of stars and clouds, the moon rising to cast shadows where there should be none, turning a flat grassy field into a terrain of imagined potholes and pitfalls. Romy drove the car to a spot tucked up tight behind one of the hangars and switched off the engine.

In the sudden silence Martel swivelled in his seat to face her. All she could see of him was the strong black outline of his head and a thin spill of light across the pale sling on his arm. His voice was grave.

'Romy, we have decisions to make.'

'I know.' Her hand found his broad knee and stayed there. 'I can't go back. Not even for Chloé. It breaks my heart to leave her behind, but I know that Florence will always love and care for her above everything.'

'My plan is that we hole up here until dawn and make our

escape then. Your bag is in the back of the car with mine, so you'll have—'

'We?'

He paused. 'Yes. We.'

'You and me?'

'Of course, but we will need to—'

'You're coming with me? Leaving your business?'

He laughed, that big boisterous sound that always seemed to take Romy's world by the scruff of its neck and shake it into a whole different pattern.

'*Bien sûr.* There will be no business left after this anyway. But wherever we go, we go together. Surely you know that.'

She grinned at him. 'I do now.'

'So the decision to be made is where we go. We could head south to—'

'No, Léo. They're coming, the Germans. If not this year, it will be next.'

'You want to leave France?'

'No. But we may have no choice, because Müller has a network of—'

A noise cracked through the night. Ricocheted off the hangar walls. They leaped from the car, Martel cursing his shoulder, and raced to the corner. They saw two trucks. They had smashed down the barrier gate into the airfield and were roaring up to the buildings. Headlights charging ahead of them. Severing the night from the silence.

'Who are they?' Romy hissed.

A dark blue wave of men in uniform spilled out of the back

of both trucks, fanning out to encircle the main buildings that stood off to the right of the hangars. The airfield filled with shouts. With torches jabbing at the darkness. Rifles at the ready.

'Are they after us, Léo?'

Just then a tall man with silver hair emerged from the onrush of the assault force to stand at the centre, directing manoeuvres. He was in full military uniform, a German general's uniform. It was Müller. With French police under his command. It stank of corruption to Romy.

'Quick! We must get to Jules,' Martel urged.

'Jules?' He was Martel's right-hand man at the airfield. 'He's here at this hour? Why?'

They backed behind the hangar once more. Between them and the main buildings, where the officers were searching, the outlines of a row of parked aircraft were picked out by the headlights, at least twenty planes. Elegant and orderly in the chaos.

Martel was already running down the back of the hangar, out of sight in the pitch darkness of its shadow. 'Romy!'

She raced to join him, her heart thundering in her chest. As she caught up with him, she could hear his laboured breathing and feared for the jarring to his shattered shoulder blade, but he wouldn't stop. Not now. At a small door inset at the far end of the hangar, Martel pulled a key from his pocket, unlocked the door and they ducked inside.

Why? Trapped inside? It felt like madness.

'Jules!'

Martel's voice echoed in the cavernous interior. Romy couldn't see her hand in front of her face but she heard a sound. She recognised it. It was the creak of the hinge of the door to the tiny storeroom at the back of the hangar and a thin ribbon of yellow light fluttered into the darkness.

'Martel, over here.' It was Jules' voice. The wiry little engineer was usually so calm and patient, but she could hear the fear in his voice, the edge of panic.

She dodged between the planes, brushing against the new Tiger Moth from England, and entered the storeroom, Martel limping at her heels. She stopped. Her mind spinning. In front of her the table that usually stood in the centre had been pushed to one side and a trapdoor raised. Never before had she seen it. It must have been hidden under the scrap of old carpet that usually lay there. Two men with dark terrified eyes were scrambling down a ladder into a space below, barely larger than a coffin. Jules was sliding down after them, so that just his head rose above the wooden floorboards.

'It's the boy,' Jules said with anger, 'the Arab boy that cleans up here. Samir.' He spat on the floor. 'He betrayed them because they are Jews. Now close the hatch.'

Romy helped Martel lower the trapdoor and push the rug and table into place. He checked the room, then switched off the light. They were plunged into darkness.

'You hide Jews here?' Romy whispered.

'They escape from Germany and come here illegally with no papers.' They were moving quickly to the small door that would take them outside. 'I arrange a flight out for them.'

'To where?'

'To England.'

'Who flies them?'

'My brother Charles. The one I told you about who is a pilot in England.'

The noises were louder now. The police heading closer. Drawing near to the hangar. Martel opened the door a hair's breadth. Torches raked the darkness outside but not yet down this side of the hangar.

'We must hide, Léo.' She gripped his good arm. 'In one of the planes.'

'No, Romy. Trust me.'

She felt something in him so compelling that not for one second did she consider not trusting him. 'What is it?'

'Müller has used the excuse of finding German Jews to come after you and me using the sledgehammer of the French police. He will have them search every plane on the airfield. Don't underestimate that man.'

Romy felt sick in her stomach. 'We could get in your car and try to drive through the perimeter fence.'

He kissed her forehead. 'We would be mown down before we got anywhere near it.'

'So we go out together.'

'Romy, there is one plane already fuelled and ready to fly.'

'Léo, we can't reach the aeroplanes out there. As you said, the police are all over them, searching each one. We would be shot before we even jumped up on the wing.'

She didn't say it. But he knew what she was thinking.

That he was slow and clumsy at manoeuvring himself into a cockpit. With a broken shoulder blade, even worse.

An explosion ripped through the night, tearing it apart and sending chills through Romy. But hidden in the doorway, she held Martel, binding them together.

'A hand grenade,' Martel muttered. 'In one of the other hangars. Come, we must run. To the plane.'

'Which plane?'

'The Percival Gull. It's parked on its own, fifty metres from here.' He spoke quickly. 'The Gull is ready to go. My brother was flying in here tonight in another Moth but was going to fly back to England in our Gull because it has two passenger seats. For the Jews. But he won't be coming in tonight, not now. Not with all this mayhem going on.'

The moon slipped free of the clouds and silhouetted the Percival Gull in the distance. It made Romy's heart gallop. Hope spread its fingers.

'They will see us,' she whispered.

'Not if you're quick.'

She gripped the edge of his sling. As if it were a piece of him. 'Not if *we're* quick.'

'You go for the cockpit. I'll swing the prop.'

'One-handed?'

'Yes, I can do it.'

She believed him.

He wrapped his muscular palm around her chin and held it tight. 'I can't climb into the cockpit fast enough, Romy. We both know that. You have to go without me.'

'No.'

'Yes.'

'No, we go together.'

Tears were rolling down her cheeks. He kissed them. His eyes were hooded as he let go of her.

'Be quick,' he said.

The police search had reached the row of planes parked nearby.

'We go together,' she said. 'Or not at all. But what we need is a distraction.'

Romy chose the Dragon Rapide. It was constructed of wood and fabric. It would go up like a torch. She chose it because the fuselage was big enough to put on a good show that would set the night on fire for quite some time.

She stole around the corner of the hangar and willed the moon to dive behind a cloud but it lingered. The sight of the police crawling like rats over everything made her want to turn and run, but she waited. Her heart at her throat. And just when she knew she could wait no longer, the moon sidled into a black cloud that switched off its light.

The darkness would be brief.

Suddenly she was running. Ducking under wings, dodging behind an undercarriage, slipping out of the path of a torch beam heading her way.

She crouched under the Dragon Rapide. Two quick breaths. Forcing herself to swallow. She stood up and emptied the petrol can in her hand over the wing and tail fin of the plane, whispered an apology to it, and touched Martel's lighter to the canvas. It roared up in flames so high that they knocked her back and singed her eyebrows.

Shouts and screams echoed around her. Boots raced in her direction. Cries for buckets of water. Müller's stern voice swearing vengeance. A raging, roaring furnace that leaped to neighbouring planes and set the night sky on fire.

But Romy was not there to watch the chaos. She hurtled across the grass away from the inferno, jinking in the direction of the Percival Gull where Martel was standing ready to swing the two-bladed propeller. She had almost reached it when a two-headed shadow fell across her path and she came to an abrupt halt.

The explosion of a fuel tank rattled her eardrums and sent a ball of fire glowing above them. The shadow vanished. In its place stood Florence. Chloé lay in her arms.

'Take her.'

'Florence, what are you doing here?'

'I came over the fence.'

'You could have been killed. Shot at any moment.'

'I came to find you.'

Chloé clung to her mother in the darkness, her blue eyes huge and terrified by the monstrous noise and explosions. Another tank caught fire. White heat streaked through the air.

'For God's sake, Florence, go home.'

'I can't. Not with Chloé.'

'Why not?'

Martel's shout reached her above the noise. 'Romy, hurry!'

'You're escaping,' Florence stated.

Romy didn't deny it.

'Take Chloé. Please, Romy.'

'Don't be absurd.'

But in a sudden flare from the fires Romy saw her sister's face clearly. It was bone white. Her lips moved but no sound came out.

'They are coming for me,' Florence said finally in a voice cracking at the edges. 'They have Roland already.' She stepped forward and thrust the child into her sister's arms. Chloé started to cry silently when Florence turned away.

Horror swept into Romy's chest. She reached out, seized her sister's hand and held on to it. 'Florence, don't. This is crazy. Come with us. We can put you and Chloé in the second passenger seat.' She tried to pull her sister forward. 'Quickly, before—'

'No.' Florence snatched her hand away. 'I have to go back for Roland.'

'Don't, Florence. Come with us.'

Romy clasped Chloé tight as if by doing so she could keep Florence at her side. For a minute she thought she had succeeded because her sister stepped forward, her arms outstretched. She wrapped them around Romy and Chloé, kissed first one, then the other, and then retreated.

'No, Maman,' Chloé cried, her young body shaking.

'Why?' Romy shouted after her. 'Why go back for Roland?'

Already half merged with the darkness, as though the sister Romy knew was fading into something that Romy could never reach, Florence turned to face her.

'Because I love him.'

'I thought you married him to get him to lie for me.'

A smile touched Florence's lips. 'Oh, Romy, I love you, my sister. But I love Roland more than my life.'

Darkness descended on the spot where she had stood.

Romy helped Chloé on to the wing. Bundled her into the cockpit. The hinged cockpit cover was tilted back and the child slid into the rear passenger seat, nerves jumping each time a flare of flame shot into the sky.

'I'll keep you safe, Chloé,' Romy promised.

Her fingers hurried to fasten the safety harness and wrap a blanket around the small shivering child. Chloé's teeth clamped together. She didn't utter a sound. Quickly Romy took the pilot's seat, heart thumping as she watched Martel spin the blade.

'Contact!'

The Cirrus Major engine roared into life. It would be their lifeblood tonight. But the sound of it cut through the crack and hiss of the flames and suddenly heads turned their way. Away from the hangar and still in shadow, there was a moment's doubt among the searchers and in that moment Martel leaped for the wing. He hauled himself up with one hand, threw himself into the cockpit's empty seat.

That was when the first rifle shot rang out. Romy

abandoned the pre-flight checks and let the years of flying knowledge in her hands take over. The Percival Gull started to rumble across the airfield. Bullets whistled around the cockpit, and Romy felt a handful of them smack into the fuselage. She pushed the plane harder, faster, racing down the runway, and prayed that nothing vital had been hit. The Gull was larger and heavier than the Tiger Moth but had a faster rate of climb. When it finally dragged itself off the ground, she could feel its power as it rose into the air. It came alive.

Below her the fires still raged. Müller marched, while Paris slept.

CHAPTER FIFTY

FLORENCE

Blood thumps through my veins. Maman has asked for roses. I am in the garden kissing with Roland behind the yew hedge and his fingers are like firebrands on my breasts. I pass the roses to Maman through the kitchen window and Papa summons me to his study.

I know why.

He wants me to marry the German, Horst Baumeister. He wants a bridge between them and us. I am to be that bridge. I understand. Really. I understand.

When I see Horst my body wants him, he is so beautiful. Tall, well-muscled, skin that I want to caress. Hair almost white, it is so blond. Eyes that are bluer than a summer's sky at first, but I know if I peel away their surface, each layer will reveal a darker and darker pool. I stand in my father's study and cannot take my gaze off this German.

Words grow hot in the room. My father and Herr Müller argue over the best plan to assassinate Théodore Steeg, the leader of the Radical Socialist Party. I only half listen. If Papa says it is right to remove this man, then I believe him. Death of an individual is not important. It is the end result that matters. Communism must be stopped. By whatever means. We all agree on that.

And then you go and destroy everything, Romaine. You end our world.

Suddenly you are here in the room with us and I can feel your rage at Papa hot on my face. In your anger you are so pure, you shine with light, but Romaine you are so wrong. I want you to stop. Stop. Right now. But you will not. You instruct Papa on the immorality of his plan and you swear you will go to the police unless he abandons his treacherous plotting with the Germans. You are righteous in your rage.

Righteous. And foolish.

My heart dies when Müller draws out his gun and aims it at your chest.

Papa, stop him! I step closer to you.

You will not lie down, even now. You snatch up the paperknife. A knife against a gun. You threaten Herr Müller and he laughs at you, mocks you, raising the muzzle of the gun until it points straight at your face. Your precious face. Papa moves between you and Müller, and your knife is almost at his throat.

'Are you going to kill me, your own father?'

And all this time Horst stands to one side, his face like stone, watching but doing nothing to restrain his German master. And in that second I learn to hate him. I know I cannot marry him. Not even for Papa.

The air trembles. Or is it me? The four of us come together in a violent quivering clash. I seize the brass paperweight from the desk and swing it at Müller, but it goes wrong, all wrong. You leap for his gun and the brass pyramid slams into your head instead. At the same moment I snatch the paperknife from your hand.

But your hand goes limp. You are crumpling to the floor. Why don't you try to hold on to the knife, Romaine? Why don't you resist? Your eyes roll up in your head and you let the knife fly from your hand. It is all over so fast, before my next heartbeat, as my hand clutching the silver blade accelerates before I can halt it. If you had resisted, Romaine, it would not have shot through the air so fast, right into the mottled flesh of my father's throat. Before he hits the floor, I know he is dead. I stare in terror. Blood swims across his shirt front.

'Scheisse!' *Müller shouts.*

He moves over to your limp form and puts the gun to your temple.

'No!' I scream. I throw myself on my knees beside you.

He grimaces. 'She will have me arrested for accessory to murder and for stealing military secrets. Go away, Florence.'

My throat is jammed. I have to force the words out. 'No, Herr Müller, no. Romaine will say nothing. She knows that if she does, I will be tried for murder and guillotined. She won't say a word, I promise.'

I am shaking, my heart is torn to shreds, everything in me is coming apart. But I look up into Müller's cold grey eyes and I steal a scrap of his calmness for myself.

'You can trust us,' I say. 'Both of us. To stay silent.'

For the first time Horst speaks. 'I believe her, Herr Müller.'

Too little. Too late.

Müller nods at me and my relief is so strong I am almost sick. 'I trust you, Florence. You understand that what we are doing and planning is for the good of France, as well as Germany. But your sister . . .' Slowly he shakes his head. 'I can never trust her. She will always be a danger to me.'

'No.' I stand up. God knows how. My legs are not connected to my body. All the pain seems to have sunk down into them. And then I say them, the words that will change your life, Romaine. 'There is no need to kill her, Herr Müller. I will tell her that she stabbed my father just before she lost consciousness and that she can't go to the police without incriminating herself. She won't want to face the guillotine, I swear to you.'

He smiles.

I force my lips to smile back at him.

'I like you, Florence, you are clever.'

He puts away his gun. 'What about the police?'

'I will deal with them.'

Horst Baumeister is staring at me the way you stare at a snake.

'Aufwiedersehen, Fräulein,' *Müller says and walks out.*

Horst lingers for two seconds. 'Your sister will have a terrible mountain to climb.'

Then he too is gone. I am alone. With the smell of blood. And my betrayal. I walk slowly over to my father and kneel down beside him. No tears. No outpouring of the grief in my chest. But I hold his hand in mine.

I enter the apartment on Avenue Kléber, Cupid returning for one last execution. The hall smells of blood. Not of roses.

I am quiet. On silent feet I walk past the bodies of Müller's two men and step over the guard on the floor outside the salon door. The one I shot before I left.

I open the door to the salon and find what I expect. Three men. And Roland. And the smell of blood. The three men are startled and guns fly into their hands. They fail to shoot me on the spot because I am a woman, that is the only reason. If I were a man, I would be dead by now.

'I have come to say goodbye to my husband,' I announce.

Only then do I look at Roland. A blackness swoops down at the back of my eyes and I have to blink twice to clear it. He is tied to a chair. He still has all his fingers, that is the best I can say. His face is blackened and swollen. His teeth are smashed, his nose is broken, half of one ear is cut off. Blood weeps down from his forehead. But when his bloodshot eyes see me, they shine. They shine with love and pride, the way they did the day I married him.

He knew I would come.

In the two seconds I have before my husband's torturer reacts – the one with the killer's eyes who was driving my sister away in a car earlier tonight – I stoop and kiss Roland's ragged mouth. The men are swearing at me but I do not hear them. I inhale my husband's breath deep inside me.

'Goodbye, my love,' I whisper against his lips. I taste his blood.

My gun is in my hand before the men can move a muscle, my bullet slams into Roland's brain. His head slumps down on his chest. It is then that the men's hands come at me, but each flicker of time has stretched, so I see them as slow and clumsy. I am too fast for them. The gun is in my mouth. My finger squeezes the trigger.

Darkness reaches up for me and I fall at the feet of my husband.

Goodbye, my love.

CHAPTER FIFTY-ONE

The darkness opened up as Romy soared through the night sky. She felt the joy of it burn away the fear that had gripped her on the ground. The clouds had moved away to the east, unveiling the stars, pin-sharp in the vast sweep of the black canopy. The wind was light and from the south-west, aiding her speed, and the bright moonlight turned her wings to solid silver. She was cruising at 200 kph, her course set for England.

With Chloé in the plane. As well as Léo Martel. She could scarcely believe it. As her hands adjusted the controls and guided the plane in the direction of Croydon Airport, she was overwhelmed by a rush of gratitude to her sister. They both loved Chloé with a fierce protective love and yet Florence had given Romy the chance to start her new life with this beautiful child at her side, to watch her grow and blossom into a fine young woman.

'Thank you, Florence,' she whispered into the night.

Behind her, Martel had been soothing Chloé and finally she had fallen into a fretful sleep. He was good with the child, sensitive to her, the way he was to planes. He reached forward and rested his hand on the back of Romy's neck. She was cold without her flying suit but at least it was a closed cockpit and she had a blanket around her. His touch was warm. It melted a part of her.

'Romy,' she could hear the creases of pain in his voice, 'I know you want Chloé in your life, but she belongs to Florence. She is her daughter. It is only natural that one day your sister will want her back.' His tone was tender. 'I don't want you to get hurt.'

They had to raise their voices against the growl of the engine.

'She is not Florence's daughter. She is mine.'

'For the moment,' he said. 'She is yours, but only for the moment.'

But Romy wanted the truth between them. It was time to lay it out for him to see. She wanted this man she loved to know her, to understand who she was. No barriers in place between them. To her surprise, the words came easily as though they'd been waiting a long time to be spoken aloud.

'Chloé is my daughter, Léo. Not Florence's. I gave birth to her when I was only nineteen. Florence couldn't have children, so when Chloé was born, so small and defenceless, I gave her to Florence. She has looked after her with all the love and devotion I could wish for my child. I am so proud of both of them.' Tears pricked her eyes but she shook them away. 'Chloé's father was a poker-playing drunk just passing through Paris, a one-night stop on his way home to Australia. He doesn't even know Chloé exists. Oh Léo, I was in no fit state to raise a child. A drunk. A gambler. A wh—'

'Enough,' he said gently. 'Chloé is a lucky child to have for a mother the Romy I know and love.'

She could hear the smile in his voice. The thought of Chloé coming along with Romy seemed to please him. She opened her mouth to say thank you. But that was when she felt a blinding pain. It cut deep into her head and a cry spilled from her.

'Romy? Are you all right? What's wrong?'

She nodded. She couldn't speak. Images started to unroll in her head, images of Florence and herself as children swimming like fish in the Seine, of the time when Florence had laughed with delight when Romy had leaped off the garage roof on to a mattress to prove she could fly. Of Florence holding Chloé the day she was born, tears of happiness rolling down her cheeks. Of Florence in the bath with her yesterday, smacking her hands on the water and swearing the stabbing of her father was an accident, not Romy's fault.

Of Florence kissing her goodbye.

Sadness swept through her as she felt a hole gouged out within her. She had wondered before if she would know if ever her twin sister's heart ceased to beat. Now she knew. The answer was yes.

Florence's heart had just ceased.

An infinite sense of loss seeped through her. It was like

losing a part of herself. But she had Chloé. Their daughter. And Chloé was part of Florence as much as she was of Romy. Always she would see her sister in her blue-eyed child.

She glanced down through the canopy at the silver sheen that the moonlight had painted on the water below. Her new life was drawing closer. It made her heart beat faster. Yes, they were crossing the English Channel but she and Martel would not give up the fight for France. With Britain standing firm at France's side, there would be no war with Germany. As she adjusted her bearings, she felt hope spring to life. She glanced over her shoulder, back in the direction of France, lying unseen in the darkness.

'Florence,' she murmured, 'I promise we will return.'

Ahead of her the stars shone bright.

Acknowledgements

A huge thank you to my wonderful publisher Jo Dickinson for her insight and her quiet patience, and to all the brilliant team at Simon & Schuster, especially Suzanne, Sara-Jade, Laura, Emma, Hayley, Gemma, Gill, Dom, Joe and Rich. They are superb. And SJ's parties are legend!

My thanks as always to my stonkingly fabulous agent, Teresa Chris, whose loyalty and support make my job so much easier and more enjoyable.

I also want to express my gratitude to Nigel Reid for sharing his knowledge of all things aeronautical in this book. He brought Tiger Moths to life for me. Any errors are definitely mine, not his.

Thanks to the talented Ben Chhoa for introducing me to the thrills of poker and high flushes.

Warm thanks to the lovely Marian Churchward, not only for her keyboard skills but for her heartfelt enthusiasm for the whole business of book writing. It all helps.

Thanks also to my friends at Brixham Writers for listening to my woes and for offering encouragement along with tea and biscuits to tempt the muse back to my shoulder.

Finally my thanks to Norman for always being there for me with ideas and advice and for cracking the whip on the odd occasion when I was hiding under my duvet.

Kate Furnivall

The Liberation

Italy, 1945.
A country in turmoil.
A woman with one chance to save herself.

Caterina Lombardi is desperate – her father is dead, her mother has disappeared and her brother is being drawn towards danger. One morning, among the ruins of the bombed Naples streets, Caterina is forced to go to extreme lengths to protect her own life and in doing so forges a future in which she must clear her father's name.

An Allied Army officer accuses her father of treason and Caterina discovers a plot against her family. Who can she trust and who is the real enemy now? And will the secrets of the past be her downfall?

This epic novel is an unforgettably powerful story of love, loss and the long shadow of war.

'A thrilling roller-coaster of a read, seductive, mysterious and edgy. I LOVED it'
Dinah Jefferies, author of *The Tea Planter's Wife*

Paperback ISBN 978-1-4711-5555-0
eBook ISBN 978-1-4711-5557-4